To Dan,

An the bus

[signature]

SKY HIGH

BY

EDWARD JOHNS

ACKNOWLEDGEMENTS

This book is dedicated to all those who have suffered at the hands of greed.

Also in the Harry Travers series:

Genesis

1

What was the true meaning of life? What was this existence all about anyway? He wasn't a religious man, he believed in God, of that there was no doubt, but what was all this really about? Was he being set some kind of test? Was his resolve being challenged? He was angry, he knew that, damned angry, killer angry: happiness had been his for a fleeting moment and he was livid that it should be wrenched away in the most painful way imaginable: a pain that wracked his soul for every waking moment. Why him? And why when he had promised to give up everything for her should he lose her; life wasn't fair, but if life was easy then we'd all be good at it, but we're not and he wasn't.

Harry chastised himself for being weak and that last statement proved it: he was weak and pathetic, and he needed to grow a pair and suck it up. God was testing him.

He was due to return to flying duties tomorrow and was unsure, confused even as to how he should behave or react to any polite enquiries into his well- being or hearing someone other than him mention her by name. Suck it up, was all he said and moved on to another topic, any topic that took his mind off Sheila Wallace.

The daily chores were completed in a solemn silence and Harry readied himself for a walk once they were complete, a walk to nowhere in particular, just a walk to get out of the house and out into civilisation.

The air was crisp and he filled his lungs and thought of Sheila; the pain was unbearable, but at times, in fleeting moments, it was becoming manageable; a constant ache always just below the surface waiting patiently to explode forth and rip his guts out, but he was becoming adept at diverting the pain and concentrating on work, attaining new skills, anything. A good friend recommended golf as a pastime to alleviate his soul: it was a game, he added, that would cause him more chagrin than women would ever do. Want to forget anything, take up golf.

His walk took him towards the local golf course. This would indeed be a long walk. It was welcoming. It started to rain. It was good for his soul.

The road that bisected part of the course and led to the clubhouse, driving range and practice area was welcoming to a man searching for something to help alleviate pain. He would enjoy it here, that was instantly apparent to him; the ambience, the club's layout appealed and would make practice a pleasure; if what his work colleague had said about this game was true then the endless hours of practice fitted that part of his personality demanding perfection.

The walk home always seemed to take half the time, but he fell through his front door blissfully fatigued and ready for an early tea and a warm bed. Harry would fill in the membership forms in the morning.

* * *

Harry was uncomfortable, apprehensive, nervous and angry; he couldn't help but be angry with himself for being nervous, as he stepped into the crew-room for the first time since Sheila's death. The crew-room was quiet: the only crew there were his on this bright, sunny afternoon preparing all the pre-flight paperwork for the flight to Corfu. One of the crew acknowledged his arrival then he watched as her head dropped out of sight to inform the others.

He would print off his paperwork and get that first awkward conversation out of the way; break the ice, got to break the ice and move on.

'Afternoon Harry.'

Sarah Calder was a thirty-year-old slim, attractive, blue-eyed blonde and former dancer who a couple of years ago decided she needed a change of career and took up flying; it appealed to her adventurous spirit to fly big jets, the bigger the better in her eyes. JaguAir recently announced they were going to acquire two Airbus A330's and begin a long-haul summer program. Sarah was setting her sights on gaining enough experience to fly the A330.

'Afternoon Sarah.'

'How are you today?'

Here was that first question. He paused before answering. Did Sarah know? He took the gamble she didn't: 'I'm fine. How are you?'

'Building hours.'

'Good.'

The first aim of any new first officer was to amass that magical 500 hours on type; this made you marketable in case at the end of the summer you or the company decided your career prospects lay elsewhere.

The paperwork was expeditiously printed, stapled, examined before the fuel was ordered. Harry glanced over at the crew; he knew he had to make an appearance as anything else would be construed as a sign of weakness and extreme bad manners.

'Fuck Willis!' he whispered. He needed to get angry, getting angry helped in embarrassing and awkward situations: it allowed him to exude a confidence only found in those situations when one believes and feels they are on the side of the righteous.

The entire crew watched him approach. Harry was livid inside.

'Good morning,' he said politely.

They all replied in kind.

Harry passed on all relevant information before he realised some of the crew had tears in their eyes. He stopped mid-sentence and smiled. Tears began to well.

'I won't deny it's been hard, but let's not be sad,' he said, looking at each crew member in turn.

The cabin manger, Claire Thompson, stood and kissed him on the cheek: 'She was a friend to all of us.'

It was not what he wanted to hear: the tears welled up with a vengeance and he was forced to drop his head and wipe one away.

'Let's have a good day out,' he managed to get out. His voice was holding firm.

Harry returned to where Sarah was readying herself for the long, laborious walk out to gate 23.

The long, laborious walk to gate 23 was soon behind them and it wasn't long before boarding commenced once all the security checks were completed.

The forecast was for a fine day right across Europe and this helped set a relaxed mood in the flight deck; his last flight to Corfu had been spent dodging weather. It was the first thing Harry checked before leaving the house. With life not exactly playing ball right now, another stressful approach into Corfu was not what the doctor ordered.

It was the day Harry prayed it would be: they experienced no delays; nobody asked any awkward questions; the entire crew were respectful and courteous; and the passengers on both sectors were well behaved.

Baslow Drive was quiet by the time Harry got home; on any normal day he would kick his front-door shut with his trailing leg and bound up the stairs for the inevitable sharpener before retiring for the night, but today he simply leant his weight against it and listened for the latch to click shut. There would be no message on his answering machine, no cheeky, sexy giggle, no promise of any surprise. His heart was heavy. There will be no sharpener, he was exhausted.

* * *

One of the main signs of fatigue is that a good night's sleep does little or nothing to relieve the tiredness, and Harry woke up feeling just as exhausted. He made coffee. It didn't help. His favourite breakfast failed to have the desired effect. What was needed was another case, a case to get the juices flowing and the blood pumping. Harry was on a late standby starting at 14:00 local; he had the morning to begin a search for that all-important case.

It was a pleasant enough walk: he was listening to the birds singing when he happened to turn a corner to be confronted with a couple in the middle of a heated argument, which surprisingly made him chuckle; he admired many a car, classic and modern out for a drive on this bright, sunny September day and duly arrived at his local newsagents as cheerful as he had been in many a day. Harry made a beeline for the local paper; there would be no cards posted on notice boards today, he was going to study all the local news and pick the hardest case for himself, even if it was a case currently under investigation by the local constabulary.

There were two that caught his attention, but one in particular that really caused the hairs on the back of his neck to rise: a man, a father of three, was missing, and had been for at least a week. The wife was understandably upset, and the police were publicly asking for any sightings or information on the man's possible whereabouts. His name was Joshua Underwood.

Harry bought a paper, milk, eggs, and enjoyed the walk home immensely.

His next dilemma was how to get the attention of the wife without alerting the police to his intentions. It was obvious, he thought while navigating his way through traffic. It was so simple it was brilliant.

After breakfast Harry searched through the telephone directory and made a note of all people named Underwood, then rang each one in turn proclaiming to be a friend of Joshua. The second number turned up a brother. All he had to do now was to stake out his home, wait for the wife to show up and follow her. It was that simple. From her picture in the local paper it would not be difficult to recognise her. The brother even told him what day, and time, his sister-in-law was going to visit.

* * *

The brother's house was a fine four-bedroom detached house in Bramhall. Harry parked up and waited. Waiting was going to be a pastime he would embrace. For over an hour he waited, but eventually his patience was rewarded; a blue four-door Ford appeared out of Hartington Road and headed North up Bramhall Lane South. Harry followed at a respectable distance.

Exactly 20 minutes later by his Porsche's clock, Harry parked up thirty yards down the road from a similar looking detached house in Woodley. The family had money; that was good, he might get paid.

Now he had the address he would return tomorrow after a morning flight to Reus.

* * *

The lady's front-door was ivory white. The bell was the push button type: a white button on a black body. Harry pressed it once, long and hard. An attractive, late forties brunette answered the door with a polite enquiry. Harry introduced himself and explained the reason for standing outside her front-door. He produced his driver's licence as identification. There was a pause while his introduction sank in, and there was a second when he nearly backed out, but she finally accepted who he was, why he was standing outside her front-door and invited him in.

'It never occurred to me to use a private detective, Mister Travers. I'm about to make coffee, would you like one?'

Harry answered in the positive. He followed the lady into the back of the house and the kitchen. It was a clean house; Harry could see she kept herself busy cleaning. It was a logical time-wasting tactic in order to maintain a grip on your sanity. Harry took a seat at the kitchen table.

'Nobody really does.'

'Can you help?'

She was about to cry.

'I'll find him for you,' Harry replied confidently.

She didn't cry.

'What can you do that the police cannot or haven't?'

Harry paused: it was a deliberate tactic to make her believe he was choosing his words carefully.

'I can operate within and outside the law, they cannot.'

Mrs Underwood nodded and made coffee.

'How do you take it?'

He liked it white with no sugar. She handed him his mug, handle first.

The drink was hot, and at just the right temperature. She sat opposite him.

'Tell me about your husband; I know you've been over this with the police, so please humour me.'

She ran through everything there was to know about the man. Harry got more information than he bargained on.

'Did he empty your accounts?' he asked.

'No!'

'Did he have an account of his own?'

'No!'

Mr Underwood was a plumber by trade and the next question was a logical one: 'Does your husband do cash-in-hand work?'

This time it was Mrs Underwood's turn to pause.

'No need to answer that one,' he said.

'What are you insinuating?'

'On my way here I had two schools of thought: you and your husband were on an insurance fiddle, I apologise if you find that offensive-'

'The police are ahead of you on that front!'

'Secondly, he's done a runner. Why?'

Mrs Underwood stared into her coffee.

'No accounts have been emptied: he's a self-employed plumber; he can start up again anywhere he pleases, so the perfect solution to beginning this new life would be to bank all the cash-in-hand work and disappear.'

Mrs Underwood continued to stare into her coffee. 'I can see why people do not hire private detectives. You're just like the police.'

'Mrs Underwood, I am not trying to hurt you or make this situation worse, I simply want to bring you closure.'

'And get paid!' She looked up from her coffee.

'That would be a bonus, yes.'

'He did his fair share, we'll leave it at that, okay?'

'Okay.'

She returned to her coffee.

'You have your doubts?'

She nodded but failed to look up.

'You didn't tell the police?'

Mrs Underwood locked her eyes on his; there was anger, frustration, humiliation in them and all in equal measure.

'Don't answer that one.'

'I have standards, Mister Travers.'

'I'll find him. I need to look at his van, where he worked from home, what his hobbies were outside work, things like that.'

The anger in her eyes abated: 'When?'

'When we've finished our coffee,' he replied between sips of the still hot drink.

Mrs Underwood showed Harry everything that he requested; she never complained or objected in any way. After an hour or so of gathering information, and getting a feeling of how this man lived, Harry had a plan formulating in his head, but was mindful not to reveal anything until the time was right, even if the lady was impatient to know how he was going to achieve his boast. He promised to be in touch by the end of the week.

Harry sank into the driver's seat of the 924 and gunned her into life. He had all the information he needed on Underwood's last thirty jobs. Now it was time for a lot of legwork; this disappearance would be well down on the list of police priorities and the answer was hidden in that thirty.

* * *

Harry saw off two further day flights to Spain, one to Malaga, the second to Ibiza. On the third day after his meeting with Mrs Underwood he set off for the first address on his list. It threw up nothing, as did the next eight: all of the customers were happy with the quality of the man's work; his general demeanour; his manners were impeccable; and all would willingly recommend using him again. Travers was frustrated. He stopped for lunch at a local cafe.

Harry sipped his extra hot latte with caramel and studied the next ten names; after these, if he came up blank, he would call it a day and recharge the batteries. His order arrived: it was a cheese and ham panini.

It was a wasted afternoon; none of the next ten produced any leads worth following.

A surprisingly upbeat Harry arrived home and gratefully fell into his sofa to watch the evening's entertainment guaranteed to allow him to switch off. He checked his mobile for messages. There were none and none arrived the whole night.

Morning proved no different, but there were still eleven more customers to track down. By 09:30 Harry was out of the house; if these eleven proved fruitless he didn't want the day to be totally wasted.

The first four proved fruitless, but the fifth introduced him to a rough looking forty-something male, living in a smart semi-detached house in Bird Hall Lane on the way to Cheadle. From the smell of him he had been on the drink since sunrise.

'What do you want?' The rough looking man said aggressively.

'I represent the local council and we are just asking households at random if they have any issues with local tradesman; in particular we are searching for those individuals whose standard of work, and behaviour, was not up to that required or expected. Have you recently employed any local tradesmen?'

The man stared back blankly.

'Any at all, say, in the last three months?'

The man still didn't answer. He was a dead end. Travers was about to say his farewell when the man finally replied.

'One!'

'Just the one?'

'Like I said, one!'

'May I ask who this person is?

'Off the record?'

'If that is what you wish: we have a strict confidentiality code. Your name will not be mentioned, but he or she will be investigated.'

'His name is Underwood,' the man said smiling. He was getting his revenge. 'He's a plumber!'

'Thank you.' Harry made a note of the name in a pad he was carrying. 'I won't bother you any further.'

Harry made the bottom of the path before the man asked the obvious question: his name. 'Shaw, Andrew Shaw.'

Any more questions may prove embarrassing and he was through the gate and up the road in double quick time.

'Bingo!' Harry had his man: all it will take now is to stake out this property, wait for her to turn up or him to leave, tail either until they produced Mr Underwood. He toyed with the idea of calling Mrs Underwood but abandoned that course of action. Only a living, breathing Mr Underwood will do.

* * *

From the initial conversation with Mrs Underwood to placing a folded piece of white paper with her husband's new address in her hands took ten days. Mrs Underwood was understandably upset at having any fears confirmed. Harry didn't take payment for his ten days' work but left his number lest she should need his services again. It just didn't seem right to take the lady's money. He drove home in a sombre mood.

His house for once was warm and inviting; he tried in vain over the last week or so to push any memories of her to the back of his mind, even to the point of creating new memories for various parts of the house. But there were still days when it was hard to survive from one minute to the next and it was a break just to go to work.

Work on this day was a day flight to Dalaman; he enjoyed this particular duty, as it allowed him to spend an hour or so in the sun during turnaround: feeling the warm sun on his back rejuvenated his soul and recharged his batteries for the next day when the minutes dragged on and he fought back the tears. Dalaman did not disappoint.

The next day was torture: he was on a morning standby and didn't get called, which caused Harry to clock watch incessantly; and in a darker, more troubled moment he took the decision to personally valet the Porsche. Under the passenger seat he discovered a tube of her lipstick. Harry sat in the passenger seat and sobbed. The pain was unbearable, and he feared that any resolve to overcome his loss would fall way short of the mark.

Harry went for a drive. Drives in the 924 were just the fillip required to get back on track. An hour later he pulled into his drive with an appetite.

For once he chose to cook. It was nothing more complex than spaghetti bolognese.

* * *

The secret to true happiness, some wise man once said, is to make your hobby your job, and the job came to his rescue: two enjoyable early morning flights to Palma de Mallorca and Ibiza were the precursor to a confusing message left on his answer phone.

The owner of the soft, velvety voice had been given his number by the less than happy Mrs Underwood.

His initial inclination was to delete the message and have a large scotch. It was another missing husband case and he now had three days off. But he didn't. Right at the last he pulled the finger away from the delete button and replayed the message and made a note of the woman's number.

* * *

He returned the call first thing the following morning, wrote down the lady's address and promptly at eleven o'clock stood outside a fine four-bedroom house on Biddulph Road, Congleton.

The house had been the subject of a couple of extensions, which had been built in keeping with the original red brick design and enhanced the buildings overall appearance. Harry was impressed. To the left sat a double garage. Harry always had a yearning to look inside locked garages; he was searching for that one containing the rare classic car gathering dust. He rang the bell.

A slim, well dressed, dark-haired lady in her early forties answered the double glazed, white front door. Harry clocked the Mortice Dead Locks.

'Mister Travers, I presume?'

'Mrs Bennett?'

'Thank you for coming so promptly.'

She invited him in.

Harry studied the interior. It was tastefully decorated. This was a well-loved house inside and out.

He followed her at a respectable distance into the kitchen. It was all open-plan and Harry chose the chair nearest to him and took a seat at an expensive looking oak table.

'Tell me about your husband, Mrs Bennett.'

'He drinks too much!'

Tea was offered and he accepted.

'Maybe he's sleeping off another bender somewhere.'

'I've looked in all his old haunts, but nobody has seen or heard from him.'

She finished making the tea.

'Have you contacted the police? I know I should have asked you over the phone, but have you?'

'No!'

'Any reason why not?'

Harry accepted his tea with his right hand. She sat opposite him.

'I have my reasons.'

'Okay.'

'You know my husband, Mister Travers. It is one of the reasons why I wish to hire your services.'

'Bennett.'

She smiled at him.

'He definitely drank too much,' he said slowly. 'I wouldn't want the police delving into my personal affairs either, if I could help it.'

'He said you played well.'

Both sipped their tea.

Harry spoke first: 'He didn't strike me as a novice.'

'I checked all the casinos, including Nero's, and he hasn't shown his face in any of them.'

Their tea caused a natural break in the conversation.

'Does he owe money?'

'Not that I know of, but that doesn't mean anything now does it?' Mrs Bennett took a large gulp of tea before continuing. 'And before you ask, no he does not have any lady friends. He may have his vices, but women are not one of them.'

Harry was happy not to have to ask the awkward question. But it would not stop him making all the relevant enquiries.

'I can see you do not believe me, Mister Travers.'

'I am not in a position to disbelieve you, Mrs Bennett.'

'What's that supposed to mean?' she replied angrily.

'You are hiring me to find your missing husband, and it would be amiss of me not to look thoroughly into his nocturnal activities.'

Harry cared not whether his last statement upset the lady: it was a part of their contract, and he needed her to understand.

There was reluctance in accepting this part of the deal but nod she did after a minute or two.

'I will be discreet, Mrs Bennett.'

She held her teacup in her right hand with the saucer in the left. The right hand began to shake. Harry leant forward and placed his left hand over her right. She stopped shaking.

'When it's convenient Mrs Bennett,' Harry said with the greatest of respect, 'I'll need as much information as you can provide me with.'

'I have it right here.'

Mrs Bennett produced a brown envelope from behind her seat and handed it to Harry. Harry didn't open it.

'When can you start?'

'Today,' he replied confidently.

'You have been very polite and professional in not mentioning money, Mister Travers, but it is an area I would like cleared up between us before you start.'

'I charge a hundred a day plus expenses.' Harry had no idea if this was exorbitant or just the norm. It didn't seem to matter, as Mrs Bennett accepted his fees without question.

Half an hour later, armed with all the information Mrs Bennett was willing to provide, Harry fired up the Porsche and headed for a familiar haunt.

2

Nero's stood cold and silent beckoning him forward to enter armed only with the memories of broken dreams, and the promise of more pain and suffering, but only through pain and suffering, he promised himself, can there be true salvation. He gave it no more thought, lest he talk himself out of it. He entered.

The foyer hadn't changed, not that it would, and he hated every step, hated navigating every inch of the thick red carpet leading him to those tables, those croupiers and that man. Willis would study the CCTV footage and know of his arrival before he exchanged the crisp pound notes burning a hole in his pocket for chips.

The croupier froze on seeing Travers take a seat. Of all the tables to sit at, this man has sat at mine, he thought, the very man who has caused my life to be made a misery after that poker game, a poker game I had refused to deal at, but none the less did, and has subsequently dragged me down into a hell I wish to forget.

The management Travers was to discover, now minus the odious Mister Moore, had been complimented by the equally detestable looking Mister Raquette: Raquette was born of a Scottish mother and a French father, who abandoned his mother when he was only three, and the scars ran deep. He never let anyone get close, kept his guard high and hid his true feelings behind a mask of pure hate. Raquette grew to be an imposing six-foot three instrument of torture for whoever paid his wages. He became so adept, so proficient at whatever task was asked of him that his promotion to management was inevitable. Travers would soon have the pleasure of his company.

'Mister Travers,' the croupier said politely.

'Good afternoon,' Travers replied coldly.

'It's good to have you back.'

Sure, it is, thought Harry, you are just loving me being here.

Harry exchanged some of his previous winnings for chips. He stacked them in neat piles while valiantly attempting to get his mind, body and soul in the right order. Harry won his first six hands.

The croupier looked off to his right and Harry naturally followed his eye-line. He gripped the side of the blackjack table with a vice like grip; it was the only way not to kill Willis there and then.

'Mister Travers,' Willis said, never taking his eyes off the man daring to enter his casino.

'Mister Willis.'

A tall, broad shouldered, dark-haired man appeared behind Willis. The whole atmosphere turned sinister the split second he spoke.

'Is this him?' The man asked.

'This is him!'

'I'm Raquette, Mister Travers.'

Travers knew there and then that he and this stranger were on a collision course that would only end one way. 'I did wonder who would fill the vacancy.'

His chip count was impressive considering his mind was elsewhere for ninety percent of the time, but this haul still failed to leave any kind of mark on the evening's entertainment until now.

'You haven't lost your touch, Mister Travers,' the mean looking one opened with once the other players had left the table, leaving just three of them plus the croupier. Raquette went to his left, Willis to his right.

'You never lose it!'

'An old friend of mine once said that,' Willis added.

'Did he now!' replied Travers.

'You might remember him,' Raquette said, placing his elbows on the table and leaning forward.

Travers cared nothing for the man or his feelings.

The dealer dealt the cards. Travers never looked at his. He just bet. The other two watched him closely.

The croupier waited for some kind of response from Willis and Raquette, but nothing was forthcoming from either. Should he finish the deal? Travers was the only one to bet and he hadn't even looked at any cards. He cleared his throat. This snapped the two men back into the moment.

'Finish the hand,' Raquette said gruffly.

Willis nodded in agreement.

The croupier finished the hand by turning over his cards and making twenty-one.

'Feeling lucky?' asked Raquette sarcastically.

Travers never paid the man any attention. He simply flicked over his cards. He made twenty. Chuckling to himself he stood, collected his chips, turned and left without saying a single word.

He could feel their eyes burning into the back of his head, but it strangely invigorated him, positively bringing a spring to his step. He may have not spotted Bennett but causing Willis and his new friend sleepless nights made the whole evening worthwhile.

The crisp evening air cleared his head and brought on a hunger long since forgotten. There was a fast food joint on the way home that served the most delicious home-made burgers that deserved a detour, and a detour he would take.

* * *

Travers opened his laptop and surfed all the casinos in the Manchester area, after that he needed to have a quiet chat with Steve; a few of his locals were known to frequent less salubrious establishments from time to time. He was going to pamper to his darker side. He wrote down the names and addresses of all the casinos to be visited tomorrow.

The following day any enthusiasm he mustered, when he began his search for Bennett, evaporated the moment he vacated his warm bed for the obligatory coffee, but he was saved by crewing offering a day off payment if he would work a night flight to Rhodes, Greece. It would be his salvation from any boredom today.

* * *

Familiarity, they say, breeds contempt, but only in the weak-minded and weak-spirited, and Harry was neither of those. He strode into the crew-room displaying an outward confidence that everything in his world was rosy.

Nobody in the crew-room paid him any mind, and he was grateful for that. Harry wasted no time preparing all the pre-flight paperwork and cross-checking its validity; he was on autopilot and rattled through this all-important part of the pre-flight process in double quick time.

'Captain Travers?'

The voice belonged to one of a number of cadets the company had employed that summer. A few were kept on and here was one of them: his name was Ian Hudson; he was fresh faced; twenty-two years old; and as keen as mustard to fly big jets. Harry had seen the type before. I'm going to nickname you "Dijon", he said to himself then laughed at his own little joke.

'What's the joke?' Hudson asked.

'Nothing,' Harry replied, and shook the lad's hand.

'Harry Travers. Just call me Harry, everybody else does.'

'I've never been to Rhodes before, Harry.'

'You want to take it out?'

Hudson thought on this for a second before accepting the invitation.

'How much fuel do you want?'

Again, Hudson thought for a second after examining all the paperwork. The fuel figure he came back with was a little less than Harry would have liked, so he added an extra 500 kilos to it. For mum and the kids was his excuse.

Harry rang the fuel company and ordered their fuel.

The cabin crew appeared, and they all left together for the tortuous walk through the shopping maze that was now Manchester International Airport.

Harry kept himself on autopilot; it was the only feasible way he could see for him to stay sane: just don't think about it and let it pass you by. He remembered a quote from Sir Winston Churchill: "If you're going through hell, keep going." The signs for gate twenty-nine kept his mind focused.

The flight deck was warm and inviting, a far cry from the early morning flights, and both men set about their duties with a quiet efficiency. An engineer appeared right on cue, armed with a fuel receipt, and the technical log was completed. Boarding went without a hitch, and the doors were closed and armed a full fifteen minutes before their scheduled departure time. Ian gave his departure brief prior to the Before Start Checks being completed and the departure clearance was obtained. After a small delay they gained push back clearance and the tug pushed them onto the taxiway to face West.

All departures this evening, were off the easterly runway 05 Left and Ian taxied at the designated speed to the holding point Alpha One for 05 Left.

Ten minutes later they were airborne and following the Instrument Departure on their flight plan.

Harry prayed for a quiet flight and his wish was granted: the weather this night was fine and clear and just the tonic; the surface wind at Rhodes was calm on runway 24; no passengers caused any trouble on either sector; and the whole duty was a pleasure. The flight was so relaxing for Harry that he ran through all the next steps in his search for Bennett. Returning to Nero's was more to remind Willis he was still around and to galvanise any latent animosity. He saw Raquette as just an annoyance.

There were number of other casinos he needed to investigate, only to see if Bennett was still plying his trade, after that Harry needed to frequent some of those less than salubrious establishments. The thought of these put a smile on his face: how would he explain getting caught frequenting one of these?

Harry pulled into his drive at 05:30 and wasted no time getting his tired old body to bed; his next duty was a late standby finishing in the early hours with a night flight to Gran Canaria to end his block of four days.

* * *

His mobile started to vibrate; it was his alarm warning him his standby duty had begun. He turned off the alarm. He would wait an hour before leaving: if there was any possibility of him being called off standby then the first hour was the most critical.

The Porsche fired up first time. Harry made a few phone calls at breakfast and had a number of addresses to investigate.

He eventually pulled up outside a nondescript looking semi-detached house on the outskirts of South-East Manchester. Harry double-checked the address. This was going to be one of those jobs that absorbed large amounts of time. His phone burst into life. Lucky for him it was nothing other than an insurance company trying to sell him house insurance. He pulled away and searched for a quiet parking spot. It was getting late and if business was going to be brisk then he needed to be ready.

The houses all looked the same once you stood outside each one and studied them in closer detail. How would the neighbours know? How would anybody know? His immediate problem was how to remain inconspicuous: if he walked up and down the street every fifteen minutes sooner or later somebody would either suspect him of being an undercover policeman or a future client.

Harry noticed one house three doors behind him that bore all the resemblance of owners being away on holiday.

The drive held a solitary car facing the garage. From behind it he could get a clear view of the semi and all its comings and goings through a gap in the fence. It wasn't the most glamorous of stakeouts, but it would have to do.

Harry sat down out of sight of the road; the tarmac on the driveway was cold and his butt quickly went numb, but it was comfortable enough for a prolonged stakeout. Why was he putting himself through all this shit, for an overweight alcoholic gambler with a possible penchant for loose women?

He felt guilty for thinking ill of the man but snapped out of it when a suspicious looking character skulked out of the semi before flicking up the hood on his hoodie. Fat lot of good that'll do you, thought Harry. I still clocked your ugly mug.

A second customer vacated the house; he seemed almost proud of his achievement, he stood upright, scoured the street for any onlookers, as if he was itching to stare down any nosey neighbours daring to challenge his right to an existence on his terms. Harry watched him closely: there was something uncomfortable about him; the way he carried himself unsettled Harry. This man could be Raquette's brother.

Harry sat there behind that car for nearly two hours freezing his butt off. There was no sign of Bennett. He left not the least disappointed.

* * *

Tea was a simple concoction of chips, fried egg, sausage and bacon. It was best not to count the calories. He ticked the semi off the list;

it amused him to think of God fearing, law-abiding citizens bucking the system behind closed doors. Who really was taking the advantage here?

Harry turned off the TV and hit the sack.

The flight to Gran Canaria passed without incident. He now had four days off to investigate.

* * *

The list now consisted of four addresses, all situated on the outskirts on Manchester. Harry chose the one furthest away to the North; he would get that one out of the way then work his way clockwise towards home, finally ending up in the South-West.

The drive grated on his nerves: he was impatient and bad tempered; he vented his spleen at the handling skills of various motorists who drove with their brains clearly parked in neutral with a thumb stuck firmly up their arses.

The first two threw up nothing of any note. It was a boring start to a potentially boring day. The third was no less productive and he parked up outside the fourth with all the enthusiasm of someone needing root canal work.

He opened a pack of extra strong mints, a recent addiction to add to all the others, and froze. There he was again, the arrogant man from the first brothel, still carrying himself like he didn't give a damn whether anybody saw him or not. The man looked straight at Harry. Harry stared straight back, unblinking. The man got into a black BMW and pulled sharply away.

So, he had his little pleasures, so what, thought Harry, once the BMW turned left at the end of the road. We've all got to have a release in this world, a way of handling the pressures modern life places on all of us from the day way we first draw breath to the last. No one has the right to judge.

Two hours later, Harry had seen enough to know Bennett was not going to frequent this establishment on this day.

The M56 was busy. More roadworks exacerbated the already heavy throng of traffic. Harry was about to let rip when a familiar face caught his attention. The man was right on his tail. Harry laughed.

'Fuck you, and your BMW!'

Harry revved the Porsche. He couldn't outrun the BMW, but if he could get off the motorway, he might stand a chance. But why run? Harry exited for the airport. The BMW followed.

'Fucking amateur,' Harry said, then remembered the man's arrogant air. 'So, you think you can follow me and not worry about any comeback. I know where you go when the lights go out. I know your little secret.'

The exit for the airport was quiet and Harry opened up the Porsche. The BMW fell back then closed to two car lengths. The lead up to the airport came to a halt at a set of traffic lights. Harry slowed even though the lights were green. Thirty yards shy of the lights they changed to red. Harry floored the accelerator pedal and crossed the lights on red. A motorist blew his horn, but he ignored it and continued to accelerate on towards Heald Green. On Ringway Road West he pushed hard; he needed to make the B5166 turn-off then double back and try and get the jump on him. Harry took the B5166 exit and floored the accelerator. The 924 obeyed its owner's command and Harry turned left into Ringway Road in good time. He swung the Porsche through one hundred and eighty degrees, parked up and waited. The BMW didn't materialise. Harry waited fifteen minutes.

Harry stepped out of his car and scanned the dual carriage way in both directions; the safest course of action would be to head North towards Simonsway, turn right onto Finney Lane towards Heald Green, checking for the BMW, and head home.

Baslow Drive was quiet, his house warm and inviting. Harry laughed when he remembered a double-glazing joke. Melancholy soon followed, but he shook it off, refusing to be dragged down into his own personal pit of despair.

That final address on his list was suddenly an address of real importance and the BMW driver was someone he really wanted to become acquainted with. Harry had an early night; tomorrow was going to be a long day.

* * *

The house looked no different but was different. He knew its deepest, darkest secret, hidden away in this seemingly respectable part of town. Harry parked up on the right, fifty yards before the house facing East. And there he waited, and waited, and waited. People came and went, but not him. This was a time requiring great patience and perseverance and he sat back, chewed on a sandwich he had prepared earlier, and waited.

A knock on the driver's window woke Harry up and he squinted at the vision staring back at him from the street. It was an elderly man with a stoop out walking his dog.

He knocked on the window a second time. Harry lowered the window.

'Is this a 924?' asked the man clearly on the wrong side of seventy.

'It sure is!'

'It's a beauty! I've always loved this car. Is it a two litre?'

'Yes, the standard two-litre.' Harry took greater notice of the man: his long brown coat was expensive; his black golf-style hat was new; he wore a stylish, modern watch; and he spoke with a public-school accent.

'Love the blue: a car always looks better in blue I think.'

'I bought it based on the colour.'

Harry kept one eye on the house. The man's dog jumped up at him, momentarily putting its paws on the driver's door. Harry ignored it and tried not to let it annoy him.

The dog jumped again, but this time the old man reprimanded the animal and it knew not to argue with its owner.

'Do you ever take people for a drive in her?'

'If you like.'

This would give him more than enough reason to keep an eye on the house, plus a perfectly valid reason to be parked up in the street.

'Do you live locally?'

'Over there.'

The man pointed to the house two doors up from the brothel. Did he have any idea what was transpiring right under his nose? Harry needed to find out.

'What are you doing tomorrow?'

'Nothing, nothing at all. In fact, I'm free all day.'

The elderly gentleman was almost overcome with the offer of a drive in one of his favourite cars.

'I'll come by around eleven, how's that?'

'That'll be great.'

The dog was eager to be on its way, and for once the owner gave in to his trusted companion's request.

3

Harry was good as his word and arrived promptly at eleven. The curtains from the left front window flickered. He knew his every move was being watched closely; it was a natural reaction to any stranger, especially a stranger bearing a gift.

The old man met him as he approached his front door.

'I'm glad you came. I forgot to ask your name.'

'Travers, Harry Travers.'

'Well, how do you do, Mister Travers,' the old man said, extending a warm handshake.

Harry took the warm handshake. The man's hands felt bony to touch.

'My name is Cantlay, Joseph Cantlay.'

'Good morning, Mister Cantlay. Where would you like to go?'

'Oh, I don't mind.'

Harry figured the house two doors down wouldn't have much activity this time of day, and a long pleasurable drive with a nosey neighbour would prove ideal.

'Let's just hit the road, see how the M6 looks, and take it from there. Sound good?'

The old boy was more than overly enthusiastic with the idea.

'Who's looking after your dog?'

'Jasper is with my next-door neighbour.'

'Let's hit the road then.'

Harry wanted, needed, the old boy to open proceedings regarding his street, and sooner or later knew the question would be put to him. He didn't have to wait long.

'So, what brings you to our part of town?'

'I'm looking to move into the area and a good friend recommended your street.'

'You won't find a better one!'

'What are the neighbours like?'

The old boy paused, only for a second, Harry realised, but he did pause.

'Not of the perfect kind then?' Harry said, fishing.

Again, Mister Cantlay paused.

'I've got a few of them myself.'

'Not like these you haven't, but that being said it is still a lovely place to live.'

Harry took the M56 West, heading for the M6 motorway. He was planning to head North towards Preston and blow away any cobwebs; the horses were not going to be spared.

'They pretend to be respectable,' Cantlay added.

'Yeah, they all do, don't they?'

'The other people in the street don't know, they don't realise the kind of individuals they have living right next door to them.'

'There's nowt as queer as folk,' Harry replied. He kept his eyes on the road.

Harry took the exit for the M6 North. Mister Cantlay offered nothing further. He didn't need to.

'Thank you for the ride,' Cantlay added after a few minutes.

'My pleasure.'

Once on the M6 Harry put his right foot hard down.

* * *

Cantlay's street was exactly the way it was when they left. Not a single car had moved or arrived. Harry dropped the old boy off, took the man's phone number, made an excuse not to come in for coffee, and promised to be in touch the next time he was free. Out of the corner of his eye Harry saw movement from that house. A stranger vacated. Cantlay's eyes saw the same.

'Enjoy the rest of the day,' Harry said before pulling away.

The stranger was not the man he was waiting on. Harry was bitterly disappointed. At the end of the road he turned right and pulled in by the side of the road.

The stranger appeared shortly after driving a Red Mazda 3. He also turned right. Harry followed at a discreet distance; he had no idea why he took the notion to follow this complete stranger, it just felt like the perfectly logical thing to do. The Red Mazda headed South-South West and took the A56 towards Sale. A left turn onto the B5397 Dane Road then a right onto Clarendon Crescent brought them both to Worthington Park. The Mazda pulled in and parked in Broad Road, but the stranger never left his car. Harry parked up nearby and waited.

His sixth sense was about to earn its keep.

Harry opened the glove compartment and removed his Swiss army knife and placed it in his left pocket. The sagacity of his move was confirmed when the Black BMW parked directly behind the Mazda.

This day just got interesting, very interesting, thought a smiling Harry Travers.

The arrogant man vacated the BMW and boarded the Mazda. Harry could see them talk. If he needed another skill to learn then here was one: lip-reading. How hard could it be to learn lip-reading?

The two men were having a heated conversation. The Mazda driver was pleading his case, but the other was deaf to his earnest appeals.

The BMW driver pulled a slip of paper from inside his jacket pocket. The Mazda driver reluctantly took it but refused to read it. Instead he handed over an envelope.

Harry realised the true nature of the scene being played out before him: the BMW man is a pimp.

The pimp went back to the BMW. There was a good chance he would recognise the 924, but if he was preoccupied with his confab with the man in the Red Mazda then maybe, just maybe, he would be less than attentive. The BMW did a one-eighty degree turn and headed south down Clarendon Road.

Harry gave it a few seconds then went in pursuit. The Red Mazda driver never paid him any attention. He knew their meeting place; that was enough of a bonus for now.

He had taken the necessary precautions after Wilmslow and hid the guns away from the house. Enough time had elapsed now for him to begin to move them and the SW1911 and its two friends would find a new home in the 924 and Baslow Drive. Any person who was willing to endanger themselves by following a complete stranger should be carrying the required hardware. The Black BMW driver would be.

Harry kept two cars lengths back. They were now heading North on the A6144 towards Manchester. His phone burst into life. It was Crewing.

'Hello.'

'Harry, it is Lucy in Crewing.'

'Hi Lucy, what can I do for you?'

'Would you be able to operate a Dalaman tomorrow for a day off payment?'

'Sure.'

'You're a star!'

'Just send me the details, and I'll confirm the changes on my roster. I can't really talk right now.'

'Thanks Harry.'

'No problem, bye.'

'Bye.'

Harry was always amenable to helping out with extra fights when the occasion called for it, plus it would give him time to re-evaluate this case and organise retrieving the guns.

It was heading towards the M60 when he finished the call. Harry took a moment to relax and enjoy the day; he was growing to love his new-found vocation. The Black BMW didn't stay on the M60 for long and took the turn off for the A56, which lead them onto the A5145 and the East of Stretford. Harry nearly moved here a few years back; there were some nice properties in this part of town. The BMW turned left into Norwood Road and stopped. Harry kept on and turned left to take Kenwood Road. He knew these roads were all linked and two-thirds down Kenwood Road, a left on Longford Avenue connected him with Norwood.

The Black BMW was parked in the drive of a very smart looking semi-detached house. Harry didn't stop.

* * *

The check-in time for the Dalaman flight was 06:30. Harry was up and out of bed and full of the joys of spring. His new case was helping and aiding his tortured soul: Sheila would be a part of his life forever, he was glad she was, but life must go on and time, the experts told him, is the greatest healer and what better way to spend your time than a pleasant flight on this early October day down to Dalaman.

Harry breezed into the crew-room and headed straight for one of the many new terminals conveniently positioned for arriving and departing crews.

'This is new,' Harry said to a member of Cabin Crew, who was new to him.

He was politely informed that the investment in computer terminals was to cater for a new long-haul program due to start this winter. Harry was aggrieved for all of a second; he had too much going on to feel hard done by for not being considered as a long-haul candidate.

'Morning Harry,' said a familiar voice.

'Morning Curtis,' Harry replied, 'how's tricks?'

'Still broke, blissfully broke.'

'Glad to hear it.'

'Is Tony Belisse still on this flight?'

'I haven't seen the check-in sheet. Why do you ask?'

Curtis paused before answering. Nobody was in earshot.

'He's just back from long term sick.'

'Is it a secret? You clearly aren't comfortable discussing it.'

'He got beaten up,' Curtis whispered.

'Let me guess.'

'Yep!'

'How bad?'

'Hospitalized!'

'Where?'

'Coco's.'

'Anybody else hurt?'

'No!'

Harry looked over to where Tony was sitting; if he hadn't been given the intel, he would have been none the wiser, but Harry paid the man's face a closer inspection. Feint scars were visible even from this range.

'What does Galley FM say?'

'Three, maybe four jumped him, as he left.'

'The first, most obvious, question is why did he leave the club alone at that time of night?'

'He was on his way to meet to a friend.'

'Obviously!'

Both men printed off the necessary paperwork and set to work.

Harry was calmer now, in an odd, strange kind of way: his personal loss brought with it an acceptance that whatever pain and suffering life was going to throw at him, he could and would except the burden and carry on regardless. You are weak when what you love and hold dear is threatened, he thought, as he navigated the Duty-Free shopping at Manchester Airport. This momentary inconvenience bothered him no more.

The crew were ahead of him, and he studied the back of Tony Belisse closely. The man walked with a slight limp: he favoured his right leg.

The jet was parked on stand 25 and their passengers had already begun to mass by the gate. The female agent let them onto the air-bridge. She informed Harry that he had picked up a departure slot twenty minutes after his scheduled departure time. He wasn't too fussed, as they could still push on time if no passengers were late.

Curtis was flying the outbound leg, so on this crisp autumn morning the external inspection was his responsibility. As he was leaving the flight deck, Tony appeared.

'Hi Tony.'

'Hi.'

'Do we have the pleasure of your company up the front today?'

'Today is your lucky day,' Tony replied smiling.

Harry noticed a cracked tooth. He tried not to stare at the feint scars.

'Drink?'

'Coffee, decaf, please. Curtis what do you want?'

'Full fat coffee for me, thanks.'

Harry left. Tony made the drinks.

By the time he arrived back all the security checks had been completed, they were catered, and the Cabin Manager Linda Montrose, recently promoted, was ready to board.

Harry sipped his coffee and thought of Sheila; how he yearned for her to place a soft, caressing hand on his shoulder and tell him everything would be alright. It was at times like these that she haunted his soul and he felt that stabbing pain rip right through him, but it was a pain he embraced for it forged a continuing connection.

The agent brought the load-sheet and both he and Curtis completed their performance calculations before cross-checking them. The engineer appeared soon after and handed him the aircraft Technical Log to sign off. The pain was still there, but the job made it bearable.

The pain became a dull ache and the ache was still there when Harry fell back through his front door.

* * *

Harry reported back to Mrs Bennett with disappointing news; she was not unhappy in any way, she simple asked Harry about the bill for his time to date, which was his cue to ask if she wished him to continue, which she did. Mrs Bennett was going to claim on the insurance; if you pay your premiums, Harry thought, as the ache returned.

He had to get out of the house and was in the Porsche and down the road in ten minutes. His first stop was Norwood Road, but it was quiet; second was Clarendon Crescent, Harry waited for nearly an hour until he became bored. His remaining options were either to return home with the ache or pamper to any lingering belligerence and head for Nero's. Belligerence won the day.

* * *

Harry smiled at the newly installed CCTV cameras following his every move; he kidded himself that Willis and his new-found buddy were expecting his return. Harry couldn't have cared less; the ache was feeding a pugnacious spirit ideally suited to its present environment.

The blackjack table hadn't changed; the dealer was male and by his knowing smile recognized Harry. Two other players paid him no mind. Harry took the same seat as his last visit and produced five hundred pounds in used notes. The dealer slickly replaced them with chips. How quickly could he lose the five hundred? There was a second five in his pocket, which equated to ten hands to guarantee a confrontation.

Harry played with reckless abandon; the more hands he played the more his anger and indignation rose to scupper any semblance of self-control. The croupier began to display traits of a dealer wishing he was anywhere but on this table.

'Something wrong?' Harry asked.

'Nothing, sir,' was the less than convincing reply.

The croupier had stopped dealing, but significantly had not looked off to one-side. Harry kept his eye-line straight ahead.

'Can't play without cards!'

The man dealt slowly, with a deliberateness that meant Harry would not have to wait much longer.

The two men to his left looked left. Harry followed suit, and there stood Willis.

'Good afternoon, Mister Travers,' Willis said most cordially.

'Good afternoon,' Harry replied.

'I didn't think we'd have the pleasure of your company for a while.'

'It was a quiet day, and I needed cheering up!'

'I bet you did.'

Harry gripped the table with his right hand; there are too many witnesses here, he thought.

'Would you like a drink?' Willis asked.

'Splendid idea.'

'You can leave your chips on the table. I'll have them brought over.'

Willis turned sharply and headed for a set of stairs leading to the restaurant and bar. Not foolish enough to go to his office, Harry conjectured before it dawned on him that this was the sensible thing to do: everybody in the vicinity heard the invitation and only a fool would consider retribution with the inevitable numerous testimonies invariably stacking up against him.

Harry followed at a respectable distance.

The bar was busy and any patrons enjoying their liquid refreshment paid both men no attention. Willis ordered two beers.

Harry leant against the bar facing Willis.

'I know the truth, Mister Travers.'

'Do you now!'

'We are not stupid men, even if certain members of our exclusive club tend to behave that way.'

'Your exclusive club?'

'We are always looking for new members, Mister Travers.'

Harry smiled.

'This amuses you?'

'If only you knew the pain, the suffering, the agony you have caused me and continue to cause me.'

'Mister Travers-'

'Call me Harry.'

'Harry, I can only apologise for those members.'

The barman placed two bottled beers in easy reach of both men.

Harry took a large mouthful of beer.

'So, what do you want?'

'I, we, have been led to believe you are a reliable Private Investigator.'

Harry drank more beer. He hadn't advertised, so how did he know?

'What do you need me to do?'

'It's a delicate matter.'

'Who for?'

'For me Harry,' Willis said softly.

Harry could see that whatever was causing Willis concern was behind the heavy bags under his eyes. For a second Harry felt sorry for the man. Willis ran his left hand through his hair. He wore no wedding ring.

'Is the delicate matter for an Eve or a Steve?'

'Does it make any difference?'

'None whatsoever!'

'Good!'

Willis took his first mouthful of beer.

'His name is David,' Willis said wiping the excess beer from his lips.

'David,' Harry repeated.

Willis put his bottled beer on the bar. Harry knew it was coming long before Willis said it.

'This is confidential, Mister Travers; I know I am stating the obvious, but it calms my soul to know that it has been discussed.'

'I understand.' Harry finished off the remainder of his beer.

Willis put his left hand inside his jacket, pulled out a business card and handed it to him. 'My personal number is on the back with David's address. I totally understand if you do not want to help.'

'Why me?'

'You would be the last person anybody would suspect.'

'I suppose.'

'I had you followed; it wasn't hard to find out about your little side-line.'

'I should be more careful.'

The ache began to return, and Harry felt an overwhelming urge to run for the exit. Instead he wrote his mobile number on a napkin and handed it to Willis. 'Time to go,' he said. 'I'll call you tomorrow and you can give me all the information I need.'

Willis nodded. 'I'll have your chips cashed.'

The Porsche fired up first time allowing Harry time to compose himself and suppress the tears welling up inside. He wanted home, needed to be in his surroundings, surroundings that eased the pain and numbed the ache. He selected reverse and backed out of his parking bay; every muscle in his body began to complain at once, so bad was the ache, that he doubted whether he had the fortitude to make it home, but home was the antidote and he better get there as quick and as safe as possible. Harry wiped a tear from his eyes, focused, and began the painful drive to the antidote.

Harry had his emotions in check and sufficiently composed when he entered his house and saw he had a voicemail on his mobile phone. He made coffee before listening to the message.

The message was long and drawn out; the male voice didn't introduce itself until the end as a Mister List. Mrs Bennett had given him the number. He played back the message and made a note of the man's number. Mister List believed he was being followed; he had no idea why or by whom. Harry was intrigued. He would definitely take this case. And just like that there were three to solve.

4

Harry got a text from Willis the following morning: David would be free to meet with him around 2pm, if he was available. He was, and the meet was made at the Coffee shop in Terminal 1 in Manchester Airport: if Willis was up to any tricks a busy terminal would act as his wingman.

* * *

David sat alone at a table designed for two. Harry made eye contact with the man and sat opposite him to size up the cause of Willis' heartache. He could have been seated next to Tony Belisse, the similarities were glaringly obvious.

'When did it happen?' Harry said before introductions were over.

'You must be Harry?'

'I am!'

'I was informed you were of the abrupt type.'

'And what else were you told?'

'You're good at cards,' David added abruptly.

'Just lucky!'

'Lucky at cards, unlucky in love!'

David's quick riposte struck every nerve in Harry, and he must have seen the reaction his comment had for he looked away and pretended to study the menu on the wall behind a display of cakes, and two women taking orders and making coffee.

'What would you like?' asked Harry.

'Large skinny latte, please,' replied David, relaxing a little.

Harry went to buy the coffees.

A few minutes later Harry returned with two large extra hot coffees in take-away cups. Harry sat back opposite.

'What can I do for you David?'

David paused and took two sips of his coffee. Harry answered for him. 'How bad was the beating?'

'Bad!'

'Hospital?'

'Overnight.'

Wow!'

'You want revenge?' Harry asked, taking the first sip of a decaf Latte with caramel syrup.

No, they're tormenting me. I was walking home from work-'

'So, they know where you work?'

'Exactly, and they wait for me every night, tormenting and taunting me.'

'Why doesn't Willis deal with them himself?'

'I'm his secret,' David said without any hint of anger.

'He's afraid people will use you against him?'

David nodded.

'He must really love you?'

David nodded again.

'Okay,' Harry said becoming serious for a moment. 'What do you want me to do?'

'Warn them off. Can you do that?'

'That's not really my thing.'

David looked down at his coffee. 'I didn't quite mean that to come out the way it sounded. Although, it could only come out meaning one thing. What I meant was, could you dig up something that I could use to warn them off.'

Harry drank more of his coffee. The thought of digging up dirt on more unsavoury individuals who thought they were untouchable appealed to him. 'Sure, I can do that.' Harry looked David straight in the eye. 'When are you working next?'

'Friday.'

Harry had two standby days starting Friday then was working the next three.

'Friday, I'll follow you home. You won't see me, so don't look for me.'

David nodded a third time.

Harry finished his coffee and took a notepad and pen from inside his coat pocket. 'What's your number?' David called it out.

'I'll be in touch regarding details, I don't want to do it here.'

He would have sworn he saw a tear in his eye. 'Don't worry we'll get them off your back.'

David smiled: 'Thank you.'

Harry didn't dwell. He made his farewell and left.

The day was cool with a wind off the North and he pulled up the collar on his coat just in time to witness Tony Belisse exit the courtesy bus from the staff car park. Harry made a beeline for him and called out his name. Tony stopped dead in his tracks. The look on his face spelt fear until he realised it was Harry.

'Oh, hi Harry.'

'Hi Tony, you got a minute?'

'Sure.'

Harry examined Tony's face in greater detail, and this only confirmed the beating the man had taken. 'Tony, I need to ask you a very personal question.'

'How personal?' He answered.

Harry took a deep breath: 'It's regarding your,' he paused, 'your stay in hospital.'

Tony looked Harry straight in the eye. He admired him for that. 'What do you want to know?'

'Describe them to me.'

'I've already informed the police.'

'I need to know,' Harry said removing the pad and pen.

'Why? If you don't mind me asking.'

'I can't tell you right now, but you need to trust me when I say that the information would help a friend of mine.'

Tony studied Harry closely to gauge his sincerity.

Harry thought for a moment he was going to deny his request, but the next second furnished him with all the information he required.

'I'll need your mobile number,' Harry added after Tony had finished. Tony gave it to him.

'I'll be in touch. Take care of yourself.'

Tony smiled; it was an odd smile, a mixture of gratitude for taking an interest mingled with a plea not to embarrass me for sharing such personal information. Harry smiled back, more to reassure the man than anything else.

Again, Harry didn't dwell and boarded the courtesy bus back to the staff car park.

His evening Jujitsu class was at 18:00 and he ate a light tea; another class in the masterful, traditional Japanese art awaited and he was patiently working his way towards the red belt; Harry was advised from the get-go to anticipate at least a couple of months of hard work before being ready to upgrade to the next belt. He didn't mind, he was more than happy to wait, watch and learn from those much better than him.

Harry was in a vengeful frame of mind when the class finally started: the two conversations with Tony and David angered his soul and tore at the very fabric of decency that was the bedrock for what he held as a prerequisite for virtue, manners and morality.

If life was easy, we'd all be good at it, but we're not and therein lay the secret to true happiness for Harry and he was fond of quoting a line from Tennyson's poem 'Ulysses' - 'To strive, to seek, to find, and not to yield'. We must all find our way in this world and his duty, as he saw it, was to aid these two on that path, minus the hindrances. To refer to the problem as "hindrances" would help detach him personally from what was inevitable.

Harry had to free-fight a much higher belt at the end of the lesson; the young lad, who was only twenty-three, beat him with ease once he'd figured out Harry's style, but Harry had learnt another move and countermove. He left the class calm, relaxed and with a ravenous hunger. An early night was called for; after his next standby day there were three early flights awaiting him to mainland Spain and the Balearic Islands.

* * *

The check-in time for Reus, the capital of Baix Camp in the province of Tarragona in Catalonia, Spain was at 05:00.

For such an early hour the crew-room was a hive of activity and Harry was grateful for the anonymity this afforded him.

Simon Weston would be his first officer for today and tomorrow with Curtis for the third flight. Simon had only recently transferred in from London Gatwick. Harry printed off the paperwork.

'Captain Travers?'

Harry turned to see a fresh-faced lad in his middle twenties with blonde hair, the obligatory blue eyes and an engaging smile. He stood an inch or two shorter than Harry but carried himself well. Played rugby this lad has, he thought.

'That's me!'

The lad shook Harry's hand. It was a firm handshake. He introduced himself.

'The printer's doing its job,' Harry said pulling out the first few sheets which contained the outbound flight-plan.

'Any preference?' he asked.

'Can I take it out?' Weston replied tentatively.

'Fill your boots!' Harry handed him the first few sheets.

On this busy morning there were three crews readying themselves to depart and Harry took a moment to study each set of cabin crew. He toyed with the idea of going over to each in turn and introducing himself, but that meant leaving himself open to any embarrassing questions over Sheila, and he was unwilling to place himself in such an awkward and potentially emotional situation.

Simon announced the fuel figure he wanted to take; Harry agreed, and he ordered it along with passing on the trip information for their load-sheet. Now for that walk.

The middle of the three crews Harry had been studying earlier came past and the cabin manager introduced herself and informed both men the jet was parked on stand 25.

Harry handed over the white envelope containing their flight paperwork to Simon: 'All yours.'

It was time for that walk and both men followed the crew of six girls out of the crew-room and towards security.

He was determined not to let anything or anybody place any stress on the day; Harry wanted a quiet flight to ponder his three cases, even though he had yet to talk directly to the gentleman who believed he was being followed. David was working a normal day shift and if they got back on time then he would have more than enough time to shower, change and get into position to observe David leaving work.

The flight went smooth enough; they had problems with boarding in Reus due to it being right at the end of the summer season, the winter programme began next week, and passengers arriving late at the gate. It meant they pushed back fifteen minutes late. Most of it they managed to claw back, and Harry arrived on stand 26 only five minutes behind schedule.

Within the hour Harry was closing his front door, putting the kettle on before running the shower. An hour after that he was gunning the Porsche back into life and heading off for his rendezvous with Spikes' Hair Salon: David was one of the head stylists at the upmarket salon on Bridge Street, Central Manchester.

Harry parked the car within an easy walk of the salon, found a nice spot to monitor the street then went in search of a coffee.

The time was 16:30 and Harry savoured the taste of the decaf coffee with caramel syrup.

At 17:00 precisely David left the salon. Harry waited a few seconds before following to see if he had company. This was new territory and he felt invigorated, this was just the fillip his soul required. Nobody else followed the man.

David periodically checked to see if he was indeed being followed, but Harry stayed out of sight. There were courses one could take to perfect the art of tailing people, but if he was going to book one, he'd need to go legit and register himself as a Private Investigator.

Harry kept his distance, as the two men headed north up Deansgate towards Harvey Nichols. At the junction with Saint Mary's Gate, David turned left making a beeline for Argos. Harry waited patiently outside studying every person leaving and entering. Nobody stood out. Twenty minutes later David exited, hailed a cab and left for home. Harry took his time returning to his car. There was no rush, he had two phone calls to make once back home.

* * *

Mister List was a nervous sounding man who immediately put Harry in the picture regarding his situation: he was convinced he was being followed and suspected it was his wife's new boyfriend. Harry asked the obvious.

'What makes you think it's your wife, Mister List?'

'She has a history of this kind of behaviour.'

'She has had gentlemen friends before?'

'Yes,' List replied after a few seconds.

Harry had his suspicion and ran with it: 'You were the boyfriend once?'

The phone went dead.

'Well fuck you, Mister List!'

Harry made the second call. During his latest Jujitsu class, the young lad who had taught him that new move, mentioned he was learning Karate to help compliment the traditional style of Jujitsu: in his opinion it was best way to become the complete fighter. Harry searched all the local schools offering training in varying styles of self-defence and he settled on the Korean martial art Tang Soo Do. Harry spoke to a man named Ken. Ken's class was on a Thursday and it fitted in nicely with his Jujitsu class on a Tuesday.

The phone rang the split second his call ended with Ken.

'Hello, Mister List,' Harry said without waiting for the caller to speak.

'Hello, Harry. Sorry about before, you touched a nerve.'

'I figured,' Harry replied, and went to make a coffee.

'And what were you expected to do as the boyfriend?'

'We joked about it, or so I thought,' List replied. He didn't try and hide any concern and Harry respected that.

'You want me to follow you or her? It would be easier to follow her, identify any new boyfriend and then tail him.'

'Whatever you think is best.'

Harry took a sip of coffee.

'Do you require any money in advance?' List added.

'No, I don't. Payment is due when my services are no longer required by you, Mister List.'

'Thank you.'

'I'll need all the info on your wife's itinerary plus a contact number,' Travers said after taking too large a mouthful of coffee, 'and you are not to call me again, I'll call you. Delete this number off your phone and under no circumstances do you text me!'

'Okay,' replied List. Harry wanted, needed List to understand this was no game with him and the tone of the man's voice informed him he did not.

List rattled off all the required information. Harry made careful notes and the conversation ended with Harry again reiterating that he would call him.

As soon as the call was over, he dialled Mrs Bennett. The confab was short and extremely sweet: the upshot was she still wanted him to continue to search for her missing husband. So adamant was she that Harry never had a chance to counsel her against it due to the rising cost of his expenses.

* * *

It was Simon's turn to beat Harry to the crew-room for the second of the early morning Spanish flights to Palma de Mallorca. The printer was spewing out sheet after sheet of pre-flight paperwork when Harry dumped his flight bag by the terminal Simon was using.

'I'll buy the coffee,' Harry said studying the outbound plog. 'Which way do you want to take it?'

'Not fussed,' Weston replied, 'I've one more Palma on my next roster!'

'I haven't looked at mine!'

Harry went to a spare terminal and printed off his latest roster.

'I'll take it out then,' he said on his return.

Harry was hoping not to be too delayed, as he ordered the fuel: Palma de Mallorca flights during the summer season were renowned for being delayed due to Air Traffic slots; if you missed your original slot it wasn't uncommon to pick up an hour or so delay while your Operations Department tried to re-negotiate another departure slot for you. He would follow David again today then pamper to his curiosity and see what the Black BMW was up to. It was time to give the delightful Mister Cantlay another run in the Porsche.

The outbound sector was uneventful bar encountering light to moderate turbulence, as they left London Airspace and were handed over to Brest Control in Northern France. The weather in the Balearics was perfect for an end of season flight: light winds from the West, clear skies and a temperature in the mid-twenties.

After landing Harry taxied slowly along the South, Link and North taxiways, once he'd vacated runway 24 Left. Their designated stand was stand 8 on the north side of the airport.

Once on stand their turnaround was slick, and with a slot only ten minutes after their standard departure time they pushed back on time. The flight home was equally uneventful bar encountering the turbulence from the opposite direction.

* * *

Harry parked his Porsche in the same spot as last time and waited patiently for David to quit work. He wore a dark hoodie with a black baseball cap. It was a cool afternoon, so nobody paid him any mind.

He examined each passing citizen going about their business with increased scrutiny; some were obviously not the threatening kind, others clearly looked the part, but weren't the type. That was the conundrum facing him: who were the kind of people likely to carry out a homophobic attack? And more importantly what did they look like? Harry moved to a different spot. He needed a coffee to help keep his wits about him.

Fifteen minutes later David exited the Salon and checked his mobile phone for messages. One had to be Willis, thought Harry. David stood rooted to the spot for five minutes, as he read, studied and then replied to a number of messages. Finally, he turned left and headed for Deansgate.

Harry gave him a thirty-yard head-start and followed from the opposite side of the street; he was anticipating a change of route and it came pretty damn quick: David turned right instead of left. Harry knew the tram stops and railway station were a right turn down Deansgate.

David kept up a steady pace, never once looking over his shoulder or at his phone. Harry on the other hand was constantly looking up and down the road for anyone tailing David. There was no one looking even remotely suspicious in that department.

His client crossed over Great Bridgewater Street navigating his way to the Deansgate Castlefield Tram Stop, or so Harry thought. There was a second when he pictured David taking a left into the Hilton Manchester Deansgate, but he kept going taking the left into Trafford Street then a right took David over the Rochdale Canal and onwards towards Deansgate Railway Station.

Harry dropped further back; if David knew he was being followed he never showed it.

The road to the station was strangely deserted given the time of day and Harry had an overwhelming feeling of foreboding. He inwardly braced himself for the attack and quickened his pace.

The split second the decision was made three youths appeared surrounding David. The leading assailant, without any provocation, hit David hard with a sharp left hook. Harry broke into a sprint. The nearest youth spotted Harry and confronted him. In times past he had been too quick to make the first move, but his ju-jitsu training had the added benefit of calming any future tendencies to be the aggressor.

The man wasted not a second in his violent intent and swung hard and fast at Harry. Harry parried the blows until the opportunity presented itself to counterattack. Grabbing the man's left hand with his, he placed pressure on the wrist, twisted it, disabling the attack in full swing. He took a step to his right before placing his right hand on his attacker's left shoulder, pushing it down and forcing his head to waist level. A swift knee to the stomach winded him badly. A sharp right elbow down on the shoulder joint finished the man off.

David was pleading for the two others to stop beating on him. Harry approached the two men. One of them saw his friend on the floor and backed off.

'Suggest you fuck off!' snarled Harry.

The leading assailant was not for fucking off and attacked Harry after hitting David one more time. Harry took a backward step and blocked two stinging blows before retaliating with a swift one-two to the nose and jaw. The man was only stunned for a second and attacked again.

Harry had been taught that a hard kick to the knee is more effective than a kick to the solar plexus, and the youth felt the full force of Travers' blow to the kneecap. The scream was ear piercing and he only just managed to stay on his feet. Harry gave him a sharp blow to the jaw with the palm of his left hand; a blow of this kind eliminated any risk of damaging his hand. The man fell back against a wall and fell to the floor.

'Go catch your train!' Harry said to David.

'You go the other way,' he said to the second youth who had backed off.

David left to catch his train.

Harry approached the youth on the floor, once the other had left, and who had now taken to using the foulest of language. He took a second to check on the first one who had attacked him: he was nowhere to be seen.

'Looks like your friends have abandoned you!' Harry said smiling.

A middle-aged woman walked past, stopped then stared at the prostrate youth.

'Finally got your comeuppance I see!' she said before heading for the station.

Harry slowly narrowed the gap between the two of them. The lad looked up at him; for the first time Harry saw the hate in lad's eyes: the utter contempt in his heart for anybody who failed to yield to his will and beliefs. Harry stood on an ankle. The youth let a muffled scream.

'Give me your wallet!' Harry said with menace. Harry was left waiting for any kind of response.

'Give me your wallet, or I'll break it!' Harry put all his weight on the ankle.

The wallet duly came his way. Harry emptied it of everything but kept the driver's licence, spilling the contents over the walkway to the station. Harry took out the licence and threw the wallet over his right shoulder. He read out the name and address off the licence.

'Adrian?' asked Harry.

Adrian didn't reply.

'Adrian, from this,' Harry began, waving the licence at him, 'I will find you, and hurt you, if you ever cross the path of my friend again, do you understand?'

Adrian stayed mute.

'Do you want to keep your ankle?'

'I understand,' he finally said.

'Good, now fuck off!'

5

There was an overwhelming feeling of déjà vu for Harry as he watched, with no small amount of respect and gratitude, Curtis print off the pre-flight paperwork.

'How's the Porsche?' he asked, dumping his crew bag on the floor.

'Beautiful! How's the 924?'

Getting old disgracefully! But that is down to the owner not my baby.'

Curtis collated the paperwork before stapling sections together. 'We'll be getting the packs e-mailed to us soon, which should save time checking everything over.'

Harry could tell Curtis was itching to ask the obvious.

'I'm okay before you ask.'

'Glad to hear it. Mind if I fly outbound.'

'All yours my friend and I'll buy the coffee, as I've become accustomed to pampering to that particular addiction on the way to the gate.'

'You've become Americanized,' added Curtis.

'I am cosmopolitan in my thinking and cosmopolitan in my attitude.'

Curtis placed the paperwork in the flight envelope.

'Do you know the stand?' Harry asked Curtis, as the crew approached. Before he could answer the Cabin Manager, Rebecca Lawler, appeared with the rest of the crew and answered for him. More déjà vu thought Harry. It was stand 31 this morning.

Fifteen minutes later with a hot decaf latte in his hand, sweetened invariably with caramel syrup, Harry entered the air-bridge on stand 31 leading down to the jet. Curtis was only two steps behind.

This was the last Ibiza of the season and from next week their winter season kicked in with a large part of the programme flying to the Canary Islands with weekend flights to Palma de Mallorca and Tunisia. Come November the ski flights began, December brought the Christmas charters to Rovaniemi and Kittila in Finland.

Harry was thankful this Ibiza would be mainly families and those people planning to spend the winter in the Balearics; his last two Ibiza trips back in August had been troublesome: on the first two lads had been refused passage for being drunk, so drunk in fact they could barely walk down the air-bridge to the aircraft; and the second Harry was forced to make a PA due to certain groups on board raising hell and blatantly disregarding anything the cabin manager had to say.

The aircraft doors were shut ten minutes early and they pushed five minutes early. It was a good start to what would be a thoroughly enjoyable day: he had great company; the crew were great; the weather was fine; the turnaround in Ibiza was slick; there was no slot for the return sector; and they had no delay when they arrived back in Manchester.

Travers' day only took a downturn when he parked up outside Mister Cantlay's drive. The road was empty. There was no Black BMW to be seen.

Harry rang Cantlay's doorbell twice. Not a sound came from within. Harry rang again and waited. He was about to leave when he heard someone approach the front door. A breathless Mister Cantlay answered: 'Sorry, I was down the bottom of the garden.'

'My apologies, I called round to see if you wanted another drive in the 924?'

'I'd love to, but Jasper isn't well,' Cantlay replied.

'Hope it isn't anything serious,' Harry added with genuine concern.

'We'll have to wait and see. Would you like some tea?'

'That would be great,' Harry said accepting the offer to enter the man's house.

The house was well decorated. Harry was impressed.

'Make your way to the back, Harry. We'll have tea in the conservatory.'

The rear of the house mirrored the front. Harry took a seat in the conservatory looking out over a manicured lawn. Asleep in a custom-made bed, on the putting green smooth grass, was Jasper. Mister Cantlay made tea.

'You have green fingers, Mister Cantlay,' Harry said admiring the array of brightly coloured flowers. 'I'm ashamed to say I do not know any of the flowers in your garden bar the roses,' Harry added, as Cantlay placed tea and biscuits on a table in front of him. He sat opposite.

The two men sipped hot tea. Neither said a word.

'Been quiet here then,' Harry began.

'On the contrary,' Cantlay replied.

'Now you've got my attention, what's been holding your interest?'

'Oh, you wouldn't know them or him.'

Let me be the judge of that, thought Harry.

'Has he, they, been keeping you up at night?'

Cantlay paused before replying: 'Three doors up, there lives a woman, a respectable woman she would have you believe, who lives well without ever having done a day's work in her life. She has plenty of company, if you know what I mean, and from one man in particular.'

'I think I get it.' Harry got it alright, but he desperately wanted to hear about him.

Cantlay said nothing more.

'What about him?' Harry took the lead once it was obvious his host was not going to expound further.

'He is one of her regular friends, he arrives daily around eleven in the morning, stays until two in the afternoon then returns at ten in the evening.'

'Daily, he arrives daily, does he?'

Cantlay nodded between sips of tea.

'You've had a run-in with him?'

Cantlay nodded again: 'That obvious.'

'Must have been serious?'

'What gives you that idea?' Cantlay said quizzically.

'Call it a sixth sense; I can always tell.'

'The gentlemen in question,' Cantlay began, clearly determined to maintain a semblance of dignity, 'is an oaf, a bully and a more pernicious, insidious individual you will not meet!'

'Do you have a name?'

'Haffenden,' Cantlay replied, losing that dignity for all of a second.

Travers wanted another run-in with Mister Haffenden and his Black BMW.

'He is the reason Jasper is not the dog he once was!' Cantlay said staring into his tea. The love the man had for his dog was in those eyes fixed, unblinking on the hot brew.

'Poison?' Harry asked, risking the man's wrath for asking such a delicate question.

'Can be no other way,' Cantlay replied still staring into his mug.

'Thankfully not fatal,' Harry said eyeing Jasper through the conservatory windows. The dog still hadn't moved since he'd arrived. Harry began to think the poisoning might still be a success.

'It was a close-run thing, but the vet is confident that Jasper will make a full recovery.'

Harry tucked into the biscuits and finished off his tea. 'How?'

'Jasper has a sweet tooth, and I saw Haffenden feed Jasper what I believe was a biscuit. He has a bad habit of going walkabout whenever he felt the need and it is too much of a coincidence for Jasper to fall ill later that afternoon, so soon after swallowing Haffenden's treat.'

'What did you tell the vet? I know it wasn't what you just told me.'

'Are you a detective or something?' Cantlay asked.

'I do the odd bit of investigating,' Harry replied before adding, 'and you and I have the same opinion of Mister Haffenden.'

'Were you following him that day we met?'

'I cannot say,' Harry replied, smiling.

Cantlay knew not to ask any more awkward questions.

'Tell me everything you know of the man,' Harry asked politely, 'and I'll make the tea.'

While Harry made them both a fresh mug of tea, with directions from his host on where to find all the ingredients, he heard all about the man with the Black BMW.

* * *

Harry rushed up the first flight of stairs, into the TV room and opened a drawer on a small writing table that backed onto the left-hand wall. He pulled out a pad and pen and made notes from what the old man had told him. Once Harry had finished and was content the notes were accurate without any omissions, he sat back in a sofa and read them over.

'Well, hello Mister Haffenden,' he said quietly, 'I think you and I ought to become better acquainted.'

Harry had two days off in which to cross the man's path and make his presence felt, but the three previous early starts were beginning to take their toll, so he ate a simple concoction of cheese, tomato and bread and hit the sack.

* * *

With the 924 parked in the street opposite Cantlay's, Harry approached the house that held so much attention for him and marched right up to the front door and rang the bell. A stunning brunette with an hour-glass figure and brown eyes, which just begged you to jump right in and drown in ecstasy, opened the door.

'Good morning,' she said seductively.

'Good morning,' Harry said back.

'Can I help you?'

'You were recommended to me by a colleague, who spoke very highly of your service, or services.'

The brunette said nothing for a second or two, as if there was a third person listening in on the conversation. Out of the corner of his eye Harry spotted a small CCTV camera; there was the third person who she was waiting for a decision from. How they relayed their message to her Harry wasn't a hundred percent sure, but it was in his favour and she pulled the door fully open to allow him to enter.

The hallway of the detached house was tastefully decorated, not to his taste, but pleasant none the same. Harry was asked to take a seat from one of the four comfortable looking armchairs off to his right. He took the second. The brunette walked to the far end of the tastefully decorated hallway and disappeared behind a white door.

Harry studied the flowery wallpaper in greater detail; he knew they were monitoring his every move, he couldn't see any other cameras, but to search for them would alert whoever was on the other end as to his motives. The wallpaper was definitely not to his taste. The brunette returned.

'Follow me please, Mister...?' Her voice trailed off.

'Further, Mister Neil Further,' Harry said, wondering if they'd ever get his little joke.

'Well, Mister Further, please follow me.'

The brunette led Harry through the white door into a large reception room with more comfortable looking armchairs surrounding a table. A bar sat in the back-right corner. Three of the armchairs were occupied by middle-aged men all drinking alcoholic beverages.

'Please take a seat,' said the brunette before leaving with a swiftness that put him on his guard.

Harry took a seat and sank into the armchair. There was a very real danger here of relaxing and enjoying oneself. The three middle-aged men all watched Harry closely, clearly trying to place him somewhere in a past life. He'd never seen them before, so worried not a jot.

The brunette returned along with a stunning dark-haired girl with beautiful brown eyes in a figure-hugging black dress and heels; she had the obligatory hour-glass figure and could carry it off with aplomb.

'Mister Further,' she said in soft, velvety voice.

'That's me,' Harry replied unable to break his gaze away from her beautiful brown eyes.

'Which colleague was it who spoke highly of our services?'

The brunette whispered something in her ear and left to entertain one of the three middle-aged men.

'A Mister Bennett,' Harry said searching for a reaction. He may only have had a second to register any, but it was there like a flickering flame hanging on for dear life in dying embers.

'I can't say the name means anything to me, but then again a lot of lonely people pass through our doors.'

If she was after a reaction, she had wasted the "lonely" line on the wrong client. 'Well, he was most impressed with you, which is why I am here.' Harry smiled afterwards, relishing this polite confrontation.

'Excellent, Mister Further, do you have any preference?'

'I am a lover of all things,' Harry stated.

'Then follow me.'

Harry rose out of the armchair and followed at a respectable distance towards a flight of stairs hidden behind a curtain.

At the top of the stairs Harry was led off to the left and the second door on the right along a dimly lit hallway. The girl took a step to one side and waved Harry inside. Harry slowly turned the door handle to reveal a brightly lit room in complete contrast to the hallway. He entered confidently with the dark-haired beauty close behind him.

'Tea, Mister Further?' she asked moving swiftly towards a kettle and two white mugs sitting on a table in the far left-hand corner of the room.

'White no sugar, please.'

From a drawer below the kettle she produced teabags and milk and within minutes Harry was furnished with a piping hot mug of tea.

'One of my colleagues will be with you shortly,' the dark-haired beauty said as she left, shutting the door behind her.

The room smelt fresh and the bed linen on the king-size bed was new. Harry drank his tea. He liked his tea hot and was not one to let it stand and cool down. The taste was alien to his palate, but nonetheless enjoyable.

Harry, being a particularly nosey investigator and not being too bothered that he was being monitored in the bedroom, began to open the topmost drawers in a vanity unit. They contained nothing but make-up products from various manufacturers.

He tried the bed, it was comfy. On one side of the bed there stood a bedside cabinet, and on the cabinet placed at an agreeable angle for whoever took that side of the bed was a silver cigarette case. Harry had not seen one so stylish for years and not being a smoker examined it in great detail. It was indeed solid silver and very well made. He flicked it open and froze. Written in scruffy handwriting, on a small white piece of paper, by someone obviously in a hurry, was an ominous message: Get out while you can. Harry slowly closed the lid and remained calm: they were watching his every move. Supposing they knew of the message, they must do, he thought. Remain calm at all times and leave, he told himself, and fall back on all those years of flying training instilled in you to maintain resilience and create options. The sound of the bedroom door opening caused him to put down the mug and get to his feet. His legs were heavy, and he initially struggled to maintain his balance.

A leggy, blue-eyed blonde, dressed in sexy red lingerie, entered purposefully and kicked the door shut with a sharp looking six-inch stiletto heel.

'Mister Further, I presume,' she said closing the gap between them in a flash.

'You presume right,' Harry just managed to get out before she thrust her tongue down his throat.

Harry pushed her off: 'Steady on!'

'I thought this is what you wanted,' she said kissing him again.

Harry pushed her off a second time and took a sizeable step back. His felt woozy. The leggy blonde closed the gap between them instantly.

Travers' lack of awareness for the potential dangers associated with his present circumstance had now backed him into a corner, but the leggy blonde with her insistence on reducing the space between them played into his hands.

'Let's take this a little slower shall we,' Harry whispered and kissed her tenderly on the cheek. They had drugged the tea and like a complete idiot he had walked straight into a trap. Harry needed to generate time to think to help create those options.

The blonde visibly cooled and even took a half-step back.

'You like small talk?' she said, smiling.

'It's nice to set the mood,' Harry replied. It was a stalling tactic that she probably saw straight through. Harry crossed his hands in front of him in a subtle combat stance, guarding himself against any strike. He controlled his breathing and could feel himself beginning to relax. How much time he had available to him was impossible to know; Harry could only guess as to the level of toxicity of the drug in the tea.

'What would you like to talk about?' she asked, still maintaining the gap between them.

'I'm new to all this,' Harry said, trying hard to sound the novice.

It seemed to do the trick. The leggy blonde began to talk about a recent holiday she had taken to Florida. As soon as she had finished the door opened and the dark-haired beauty entered the room followed by a redhead of equal stature.

'Has he talked yet?' It was the redhead who spoke first.

Harry gave serious consideration to a pre-emptive strike; they may be gorgeous looking women, but they exuded menace out of every pore.

'And what exactly am I supposed to have spoken about?' Harry took a step to his left and stood sideways on to protect himself. So far, he was managing to maintain some semblance of control.

The redhead answered: 'Bennett discussed us with you. Well, did he?'

'He recommended you, yes, although I am beginning to question why.'

'When did Bennett talk to you?' the redhead added.

Harry knew there and then that Bennett was dead. 'A week or so ago, I can't exactly remember.'

'That was very kind of him,' the redhead said sarcastically.

The three women positioned themselves in a way in order to block any escape move Harry might be contemplating.

'Mister Bennett was a screamer!' the blonde said exuding that menace.

'That's more your area of expertise than mine,' Harry replied. He was calculating which one of the beauties would get the pre-emptive strike before he attempted to disable the other two.

Any further deliberation was cut short by the dark-haired beauty launching her lithe frame against him. She had fine, manicured nails ideally suited for slicing a man's face open to the bone.

Harry blocked the attempted blow to his left cheek with both hands and exerted maximum pressure on the wrist joint before rotating it upwards and applying downward pressure on her shoulder joint with his left elbow. A sharp right knee to her rib cage winded her badly: a knee to the face ran the risk of crippling his own knee and leaving him at the mercy of the other two.

The redhead was next to react, but not how Harry expected: she ran straight for the door and called for assistance. Harry never wasted a second: he closed the gap between them and threw a straight right into the redhead's face, bloodying her nose. Chivalry be damned, he had a long way to go to get to safety.

Harry pushed her against the right-hand wall and made a beeline for the door, only for it to be blocked by Haffenden. The look on the man's face spelt death. Harry head-butted him and pushed him back into the hallway, but Haffenden knew a martial art and attempted to throw Harry over his shoulder. Harry managed to use a wall to stay upright, but three sharp, painful knees to the ribs followed by kicks to the lower part of his right leg nearly did him in. The man was a kickboxer.

Harry needed to remain calm and breathe, difficult as that was, after the brutal strikes to his ribs and drinking the tea, but the kickboxer needed to get closer to him in order to make these strikes effective. Haffenden closed the gap and Harry feinted to double over with pain, but instead positioned his hips under Haffenden's, lifted him up and threw him to the ground with a double leg take down. Four sharp punches to Haffenden's face broke his nose and chipped a front tooth. Harry tottered, but didn't fall over. He staggered for the stairs, bouncing off the walls. At the top of the stairs the dark-haired beauty caught up with him and pushed him down them.

Harry hit the bottom with a bone-crunching thud. By some miracle he was still intact. He got to his feet and tried to focus; he was confused and began to feel the sensation of being unable to control his actions. He could make out the comfy armchairs and knew the hallway leading to his salvation was off to the left. Suddenly a heavy blow to his head sent him reeling towards the chairs. Harry put out his hands to break any fall, but his body functions were seriously compromised, and he missed them all and fell headfirst into the carpet. He rolled over onto his back and kicked out. It saved his life. The blonde was going for his eyes with a stiletto heel. The kick sent her over an armchair and onto the floor.

Harry somehow managed to get to his feet and turned right towards the door; the floor was covered in spiders and he felt like screaming, but any rational thought was yelling at him that he was hallucinating and to ignore the arachnids and head for the door. Harry forced his legs to move and closed in on the door handle. It would not move. He tried it again. It didn't move a second time. Looking back the way he came he saw Haffenden and the blonde bear down on him. Harry yanked the door handle down and the door opened. He fell out into the driveway and bounced off the Black BMW and onto the ground. The gravel driveway hampered his getting up, but he did it and swayed and lurched for the road. Harry made it without looking back and fell headlong into the road, gashing his forehead above his left eye. The blood blinded him. Haffenden and the blonde did not immediately follow. He got to his feet, but knew his time was up and collapsed thirty yards short of the 924, now completely at their mercy.

It was down to the blonde beauty to finish him off; she had put a coat on and strode over to where Travers was desperately trying to reach out on all fours for his car, but his sensory motor skills were badly impaired by the toxins invading his system. She got to within three paces of her prey when a friendly voice froze her to the spot.

'Harry?'

Harry looked over his right shoulder. Cantlay's face filled his field of vision.

'Harry, what's happened to you?'

Cantlay looked at the blonde with utter contempt: 'I'll take it from here.'

She backed off without a word.

Cantlay picked Harry up, as best he could, and guided him over to his house.

Harry collapsed onto a sofa in Cantlay's front room; his head was spinning wildly and he attempted to speak, but even Harry could only make out one word in three, as the other two were just a jumble of slurs and half-words that were totally indistinct from any known language.

Cantlay appeared beside him with a bowl of warm water and began to clean the wound over his left eye. The fresh blood mixing with the dried now covered half his face.

'What the hell happened in there?' the old man asked.

'Poisoned,' Harry slurred.

'Poisoned, how?'

'Cup of tea,' Harry said trying to feel the extent of the damage over his eye. Cantlay stopped him.

'A cup of tea,' Cantlay repeated.

Cantlay's dog poked his head around the corner, didn't like what he saw and disappeared.

'How much did you drink?'

'Most of it, why wouldn't I, I saw her make it front of me,' Harry said while attempting to right himself after sliding off to his left. Cantlay gave him a helping hand.

'Datura Stramonium,' Cantlay began, 'or jimsonweed as the Americans call it, or devil's snare, devil's trumpet, take your pick, but you are displaying all the symptoms.'

'In a mug of tea?'

'It is one of the preferred methods of ingesting it. Datura Stramonium is a powerful hallucinogen and deliriant and fatally toxic in high amounts.'

Harry tried hard to digest this information, but it was proving difficult.

'You are a very lucky man, but I need to get you to hospital to confirm the toxins in your system.'

'No,' Harry said with as much conviction as he could muster.

'You need the proper medical attention,' pleaded Cantlay.

Harry did not need any of this to be in the public domain: 'I'll take my chances.'

Cantlay could see Harry was not going to budge: 'If you insist, it's your funeral.'

If I get through this it'll be somebody else's, Harry thought through hallucinogenic visions; he was ignoring them as best he could, albeit with a fear that was almost tangible.

'Twenty-four to forty-eight hours should flush it out of your system, but it can take a lot longer than that.' Cantlay pronounced every word slowly and precisely for Harry. He was grateful for that: it helped him focus on his voice and not the visions plus alleviated any feelings of confusion.

6

Harry woke with a cranium splitting headache. It was 08:00. He was happy for small mercies: the visions had stopped and any lingering doubts as to where he was evaporated with the sight of Cantlay's dog. Cantlay appeared soon after with a mug of tea in each hand and a packet of bourbon cream biscuits under his right arm.

'This tea is quite safe,' he said with a smile.

Harry thought of Haffenden: 'They'll know where I am.'

'Good luck to them,' the old man said sitting down beside him. 'Biscuit?'

'Don't mind if I do.' At least Harry hadn't lost his appetite.

'Any time they want to pay me a visit, I'll be more than willing to oblige them.'

Harry admired the man's spirit.

'How are you feeling?' Cantlay asked, showing genuine concern.

'Like I've been run over. Did they pay you a visit?

'They wouldn't dare shit on their own doorstep; if they're going to cause me any trouble it will be when things quieten down and I'm away from here.'

Harry smiled.

'You're going to be side-lined for a wee while,' the old man said between sips of tea, 'they turned you over pretty bad.'

There was an admiration in his voice that Harry found comforting. He needed to call work, but away from here: the last thing he desired was anybody to know his true business.

'Yeah, they saw me coming, or I didn't see them,' Harry said while rubbing the top of his eye. 'Either way I grossly underestimated them.' Cantlay had done a sterling job and closed the wound with steri-strips; they should hopefully negate the need to visit the local A&E. He was trying to think of a valid excuse for the injury, but sometimes the most outrageous excuses are the ones that are most believable. He settled on tripping on his hallway carpet and head-butting a table.

Harry tried to get to his feet but failed miserably the first-time round. Cantlay offered his hand. Harry politely refused. The second attempt was successful, and he was happy to discover that his head was better, clearer than first anticipated. He walked a few steps.

'Your body is banged up,' the old man said watching Harry intently. 'If you want this kept on the QT, which I have to add I don't blame you, I know a lady who runs a dog rehabilitation clinic; she has a pool the animals use for post-operational care and rehab. If I ask her nicely, she'll let us use it and you can get back on your feet a lot quicker, if you'll pardon the pun, without alerting anybody.'

'Thank you,' Harry replied, thankful that once again he had stumbled on to yet another valuable ally.

His ribs and leg on his right side hurt like hell, and his stride length mirrored the pain shooting up his leg and side.

'I'll call her now.' Cantlay left to make the call.

Harry collapsed back in the sofa and listened carefully to the conversation in the next room.

'I'm going to make your day,' he said when Cantlay returned.

'Oh, yeah,' the old man replied, curious to finds out how.

Harry put his hand in his jean pocket, removed the keys to the Porsche and tossed them over to Cantlay: 'You drive.'

Cantlay beamed back a smile: 'Do I have to spare the ponies?'

'No,' Harry said, easing himself out of the chair. 'Let's go!'

Cantlay led the way out to the car, unlocked it and helped Harry inside before checking on Jasper and locking his front door.

Harry felt invigorated being back in the familiar surroundings of his Porsche 924.

Cantlay drove at a sedate pace for the first few miles.

'Are we driving Miss Daisy today?' Harry joked on seeing the speedometer never get over forty.

'Just respecting them ponies, Mister Travers.'

Harry checked to see if they were being followed. The road was clear.

'I've been keeping an eye on our tail, Harry.'

'Thank you.'

'You never said what it is you actually do for a living.'

'I find people, even when they don't want to be found.' Harry chose his words with caution.

'Who are you looking for? Or can't you say?'

'Client confidentiality, you understand.'

'Had to ask,' Cantlay added, as Harry gave him directions to Baslow Drive, Heald Green.

Once parked in the drive, Cantlay phoned for a taxi after Harry refused help to his front door; having a stranger in his home was a clear invasion into the space he regarded as sacrosanct to her memory. Nobody would be allowed to frequent that space bar him and her.

Harry offered to pay for the taxi, but Cantlay flatly refused. He waited by the 924 until the taxi arrived and left then limped his way to the kitchen and medication.

* * *

Harry was frustrated that any stiffness in his leg and ribs had not begun to abate after a few hours' sleep following the obligatory painkillers. He had made the call to Crewing, informing them of his unfortunate slip getting out of the shower and head-butting the side of the hand-basin. The idea had come to him the split second he'd dialled the number. The upshot was he had a week off to recuperate. Harry would have to fill out a self-certification form and send it to the company. He limped to the kitchen and made coffee.

It was dark outside when he woke up. Being a Thursday, it was day one of some golf tournament in America and he sat back with another hot mug of coffee and a packet of chocolate biscuits.

Whoever was leading was being interviewed: he had struck the ball well; putted well, which was welcomed as he'd been struggling with the 'flat stick' for a while; and his course management was what his coaching team would have expected. Harry was pleased for him but turned the TV off and went to bed.

* * *

Morning brought some welcome news. His body was on the mend; the famed Harry Travers powers of recovery were still there.

Breakfast was Ibuprofen along with scrambled egg and bacon and washed down with three large mugs of coffee.

He was dreading the next part of his day. Harry dialled Mrs Bennett's number.

'Hello,' said a familiar voice.

'It's Harry Travers, Mrs Bennett.'

'Hello, Mister Travers,' she said cheerfully.

How was he going to say this, it was the first time Harry had ever been in a position to inform somebody they had lost a loved one.

'I need to see you, Mrs Bennett.'

Her voice changed when she realised the seriousness with which Harry was taking the conversation: 'I'm in all day.'

'I'll be round in an hour.' He hung up.

* * *

Harry paid the taxi driver and limped to her front door. She must have seen him arrive for the door was open before he made the front step.

'My God, Harry,' she cried on seeing his face. 'Come in, come in, and sit down.'

Harry made the armchair nearest the window in the front-room off to the left. His leg was giving him grief, but it was manageable. Mrs Bennett appeared after a few minutes with tea and biscuits.

'Milk? Sugar?'

'Just milk please, Mrs Bennett.'

'He's dead, isn't he?' she said without looking at him.

'I believe so,' he replied as sombrely as possible.

'You believe so?'

'Mrs Bennett, the individuals responsible for this,' he added pointing to his face, 'did it because I knew your husband. What he was involved in or who he owed money to, I don't know, but I believe they've killed your husband.'

'Can you prove it?'

'Sadly, not at this moment, Mrs Bennett, but I will find the necessary evidence.'

She handed him his tea. 'Biscuit?'

Harry helped himself to two chocolate chip cookies.

'What do I owe you, Harry?' Mrs Bennett asked after taking a bite out of a custard cream.

'I'll draw up a bill,' he said.

She nodded and the two of them drank their tea in silence.

* * *

Harry painstakingly worked his way up his stairs to the first floor and slumped down in front of his TV. He needed to replace the old steri-strips with the new ones he'd bought on the way back from Mrs

Bennett's. She had paid him a thousand pounds for his trouble, he had tried to refuse the money until a proper bill could be drawn up, but she flatly refused and insisted on paying him there and then. The eye could wait, he was exhausted. Once again, the movie channel came to his rescue: Harry loved westerns and was a huge John Wayne fan and here to take his mind of his eye, his leg, his ribs and the exhaustion was a John Wayne, John Ford classic: The Searchers.

By the time John Wayne's character had successfully saved Natalie Wood's and taken her home he was ready to clean the wound over his eye and replace the strips.

'Now that's what a call a shiner,' Harry exclaimed, while studying the damage to his face, 'one to be proud of Harry my boy!'

It did kind of explain why Mrs Bennett was keen to pay up and not quibble over his bill, but if he was willing to accept such payment then Harry Travers was going to have to go legit and register himself as a Private Investigator. He suddenly felt very tired.

* * *

It was dark outside by the time Harry returned to the here and now, but he felt invigorated enough after the much-needed rest to go for a walk and stretch his leg; it didn't seem too bad and Harry was impatient to deal with Haffenden and his band of Harpies. He prayed this was a sign he was on the mend.

Having wrapped up warm Harry picked the post by the front door and deposited it on the bottom stair for when he returned. He would walk the couple of miles to the high street and use the exercise to stock up on supplies.

An hour and a half later he picked up the post and made for the kitchen; he was hungry, another sign he was on the mend, and re-stocked the fridge with milk and eggs, and the cupboards with bread and biscuits. Harry gave himself a convincing argument that his sugar levels were low and there now was a dire need for milk chocolate biscuits. The post ended up on the kitchen table.

'Interesting,' Harry said picking up a white envelope. It was from across the pond.

'Knew this was coming,' he added, slicing the envelope open with a knife. It was a letter explaining when the inquiry was scheduled into the shooting of the lawyer Jeffries and Harry's presence, and evidence, was required. It brought a smile to his face when he thought of meeting up again with Tommy and Uncle Jack: 'I wonder who you've pissed off now, Uncle?'

Thankfully, the inquiry fell in one of his periods of winter leave, so there was no need for anybody to know he was out of the country. He'd call Marvin Schular in the morning and get him to convey to the authorities his attendance on that day.

* * *

Harry phoned Schular the following morning and left all the finer details to him. He could not afford to waste any more time on recuperation, or any leads could go cold, and as it had been over 48 hours since his poisoning he was beginning to feel more like his old self, albeit with a few bruises.

Harry fired up the Porsche and backed it out of his drive; there was no need for a satnav to find this destination. He drove at a sedate pace and parked up at the far end of Cantlay's street, and there he sat for a full half-hour before negotiating his exit from the car.

The first few steps worked the stiffness out of his leg, and he stretched his right side while praying Haffenden would vacate the house when it finally came into view. Somebody up above must have been listening for sure enough the split second he espied the house Haffenden exited and boarded his Black BMW. Harry ran back to his car as fast as his body would allow him.

'I'll get you now, you bastard!'

The Porsche was fired up and on the move in less than a minute and closed to within three car lengths of the BMW before Haffenden turned right at the end of the street.

'Back off, Harry,' he said quietly.

He dropped back until the Black BMW was out of sight; there was no need to hurry to reach the park.

Haffenden was delightfully predictable, only this time a Green Mazda met his Black BMW. Harry witnessed the whole scene while fighting the urge to confront Mister Haffenden and send him on his way to a better place.

The man became very agitated with the driver of the Green Mazda. Harry laughed. A few times during the heated confab Haffenden looked in his general direction, but as he was not expecting to see Harry, or his car, that's if he remembered what Harry drove, nothing registered.

Now Travers never confessed to be an expert lip-reader, but even he could make out the name Neil Further from Haffenden's lips. Harry smiled every time he saw Haffenden's chipped tooth.

'So that's your game?' Harry said, relishing the thought of doing battle with the Green Mazda. Haffenden was not the kind of person to get his hands dirty when he could get someone to do his dirty work for him.

Haffenden vacated the Green Mazda, walked smartly back to his BMW and left.

The Green Mazda now had Harry's full attention; the driver was in his late twenties, broad shouldered with closely cropped brown hair and dark brown eyes. Even from this distance, and the man seated, Harry knew he stood well over six foot.

The Green Mazda pulled out into the road and headed his way. Harry slid down into his seat. He needn't have worried for the man never looked at him.

Harry followed at a discreet distance: 'Now where are you going?' Harry conjectured. 'You don't know where I live, and if you did Haffenden has friends in some very high places, so how are you going to find out about me? There is only one way.'

Harry stopped following the Mazda and put the 924's superior handling skills to the test.

* * *

The house was quiet, thankfully, with no sign of the Green Mazda. Harry had parked out of sight and his leg and ribs didn't hurt as much. Don't you just love adrenaline, he thought.

He tried not to look too conspicuous and walked up the road until he faced the house that he fell out of a few days previous. He did an about turn and walked back to Cantlay's.

The Green Mazda appeared ahead of him. Harry turned sharply into the drive of Cantlay's neighbour and marched up to the garage door as if it was the most natural thing in the world to do. The driver of the Green Mazda never paid him any mind: why would you alert your presence to a neighbour working outside his house by looking straight at him and giving that person the perfect opportunity to make a mental picture of your facial features.

The man parked up across the street and approached Cantlay's front-door. Harry stayed behind a large bush bordering the drive leading to the garage. The man stopped short of the door and looked around.

'If you want to look guilty then that will do it!' Harry whispered. 'Fucking amateur,' he added.

The man took the path to the right leading to the rear-garden.

Cantlay will be in his garden totally oblivious to the danger, and with his dog still recovering, won't be in much of a position to defend himself.

Harry marched round to Cantlay's, once the man was out of sight, and peered through the patterned glass front-door. He was nowhere to be seen. Harry checked both front rooms. The dog was asleep in the first.

This is really going to end badly, he thought, and continued around to the rear-garden. His leg began to complain.

'Not now, please,' he said in frustration.

Harry heard voices, one of them familiar, as he came to the wooden gate marking the entrance into the garden.

Neither of them realised they had a captive audience.

Harry took stock, watching the confrontation; Cantlay was not for answering the man's questions and his body language was defiant for an elderly gentleman facing a younger one.

Harry stepped back and continued to monitor Cantlay through a tall bush in a clay pot. He couldn't rush the man. That would be foolhardy: Cantlay would signal his arrival long before Harry could get within 10 yards of them. Harry might have to let Cantlay deal with the stranger. No, stupid idea, Harry would rather charge the younger man and take his chances than let Cantlay take a beating meant for him.

The man grabbed Cantlay by the throat and pushed him to the ground then knelt on his chest before threatening the old man with a pair of garden shears. Harry was off the split second the shears tickled the old man's throat.

The man pushed down hard with his right knee until it slid inexorably up towards Cantlay's neck. The old man began to make sickening gurgling sounds as pressure was brought to bear on his throat. Cantlay tried to push him off, but to no avail.

'Where can I find this Neil Further?' the man snarled.

'Right behind you,' Harry said the split second before his left foot impacted on the younger man's jawbone. A stomach-churning crack followed the impact. Harry knew straight off his jaw was broken.

The younger man fell off Cantlay, dropped the shears, and rolled to his right before jumping to his feet and taking up a boxing stance. He was unsteady on his feet and spoke through gritted teeth: 'That was your first fucking mistake!'

'I shan't ask about the second,' Harry replied scornfully.

The man sprung upon him, but Harry had seen this all before and brushed him aside like swatting a fly. The man swivelled and attacked a second time, swinging haymaker punches with both hands. Harry stepped inside a wild right-hander, grabbed the man's arm with his left, wrapped his right around the left shoulder and threw him to the ground from over his right hip. Three sharp punches to the nose finished off a very short fight.

Harry pulled Cantlay to his feet before grabbing the shears.

'Now, he's mine,' Cantlay growled. 'Give me the shears!'

'You need to remain calm, Mister Cantlay.'

'Fuck calm! I want that prick's balls on a plate!'

Harry put the shears behind his back.

The man tried to stand but was making a right meal of it. Harry was not fooled and smiled. Cantlay went on manfully trying to convince Harry to hand over the shears. Harry gave in and handed them over, still smiling.

'Get it over with,' Harry said to the younger man.

Cantlay stared at his broken-jawed, bloody-nosed aggressor awaiting a response.

'Whether you're carrying on or not,' Harry said slowly, 'I'll give you a fighting chance.'

The young man's speed was impressive, and he lunged at Harry now armed with a small knife he had produced from behind his back.

Harry stepped back and swung his left foot in an outside to in kick at chest height. It hurt his right leg but hit the blade square on and sent the knife cartwheeling across the grass into a flowerbed. The man stopped dead in his tracks.

'Think you better leave,' Harry said.

Before the man could reply Cantlay added his weight to proceedings: 'Or you'll be wearing these!'

Cantlay waved the shears at him.

The man was not for listening and rugby tackled Harry sending them both crashing to the ground.

Cantlay attempted to hit the man over the head but held back lest he should hit Harry.

The younger man began to take control on the ground and slammed three brutally hard punches into Travers' sore ribs.

The situation became critical very quickly. Cantlay stood undecided whether to attack the stranger. Harry knew another blow to his ribs could finish him off. Why had he been stupid enough to get himself into this position?

The man telegraphed another punch to the ribs and Harry accepted the pain guaranteed to rip through his side. He attempted to gouge both the man's eyes out with his thumbs, as the punch hit home. The man let out a scream. Harry lifted the man on top of him.

'Now fucking hit him!' he shouted.

Cantlay brought the shears hard down on the man's head nearly concussing him. Harry pushed him off.

Chivalry has for a long time been forgotten – Harry got to his feet and kicked the man twice squarely in the ribs: 'Take that back to Haffenden!'

'You have no idea what you've done, or who you're dealing with,' the man gasped.

'You're not the first prick to threaten with that line!' Harry replied. Another kick soon followed.

'So, don't forget the message,' Cantlay added, placing the end of the shears on the man's throat.

'I don't need to know your name,' Harry said trying hard to hide the rising discomfort in his side. 'I can find you anytime I wish.'

The man slowly got to his feet and staggered out of the garden with Travers in close attendance. Harry saw the tell-tale twitch of the head to the right – the man was checking to see if they would follow him off the property and onto the public highway.

'Tell Haffenden I will be looking forward to our next little chat,' Harry said softly, 'and next time he'll need something stronger than jimsonweed.'

'The younger man looked at Travers, and Harry knew he knew about the poisoning. He wanted to punch the man's lights out there and then, but that would run the risk of losing control of his emotions, and he was loath to do that.

At the road the man turned right, away from that house. Harry turned left and went to stand outside it. And there he stood until he saw a curtain flicker.

Cantlay was in his kitchen making a cup of tea when Harry re-appeared.

'How are you doing?' Harry asked, watching the man closely.

'Fine, I'm fine,' Cantlay replied, not looking at him.

'Then I'll be going then.'

Harry waited a few seconds to see if Cantlay was going to offer a reply, but when he didn't, and instead started to prepare himself lunch, he left.

Harry made the kitchen door before Cantlay spoke: 'Thank you.'

Harry turned to face him. 'Whether you like it or not, Mister Cantlay,' Harry said smiling, 'we're now in this together.'

He never waited for Cantlay to answer and left closing the front door quietly behind him.

* * *

Peter Sasal, Travers' Pilot Manager, called his personal mobile to enquire after his well-being; Harry painted a picture of an unfortunate accident while stepping out of the bath; he had to chuckle when Peter informed him that Harry was the third pilot this year to slip in the bath. The only downside was he would need a doctor's sick-line to cover the days following the initial seven: Harry couldn't work until his black-eye healed. After promising to email a copy of the sick-line Harry hung up and called Mister List.

List was home and agreed to meet at a Costa coffee shop in Manchester City Centre at 2pm that afternoon. A change is as good as a rest, contemplated Harry. List was being followed by his wife's supposedly new beau. What kind of life insurance did the man have? Had he upset anybody in a past life? This may have nothing to do with his wife. Had List witnessed something that he was unaware of? Was there a work colleague wanting him out of the way? All these questions bounced around in his head while he drank a coffee and prepared to have a shower. Harry would take his time driving into town and maybe get a little retail therapy in, and talking of therapy he needed to get some shooting practice in. It had been a while since he last fired a gun. Mister Moore could testify to that if he was still around.

* * *

When Travers and List met at Costa, Harry remarked quietly to himself that he looked as though he had been served with the mother of all tax bills. List stared at Harry's eye, but said nothing.

'Things not good then?' Harry asked before offering to buy the coffees.

'You could say that!' replied List.

Harry bought a large latte with caramel for himself and List a large Americano. Taking a seat at one of the tables triggered List to begin talking.

'I've spoken to her new boyfriend.'

'What's his name?' Harry was intrigued to find out as to why List would want to exchange words with the very individual, he suspected of wanting to do him harm. The last thing that would do is give the man the opportunity.

'Ken.'

'Ken who?' Harry said, frowning.

'Ken Mollett.'

'Ken Mollett,' Harry repeated, 'why on earth did you get into a conversation with Ken Mollett?'

'I didn't,' List said taking two large gulps of Americano, 'he began talking to me.'

'And you know he's the boyfriend? Your wife has told you?'

'No, not exactly; Mollett is a work colleague of hers, she has only mentioned him in conversation, and this guy didn't come right out and say.......' List's voice trailed off.

'He told you nothing, didn't he?' butted in Harry. 'You only realised that once your heartbeat got back below eighty.'

'You're good at this, aren't you?'

'It's why you're hiring me.'

List stared into his coffee.

'This has nothing to do with your wife-'

'You don't know that!'

Harry took a moment to choose his words carefully, and drank his latte: 'If your wife is involved in any way with this Mollett, and that's if this guy is Mollett and, or, the boyfriend, then he would have taken the utmost delight in telling you, but he didn't. What he did was let you know that he can find you whenever he wants. Now that begs the question, as to why he needs to find you.'

List said nothing.

'You don't know why then?'

List shook his head

'You upset anybody at work?'

List shook his head.

'Owe anybody any money?'

'Mister Travers, I have run over and over in my head every possible scenario,' List replied after letting out a deep breath.

'That's not entirely true is it?'

List stopped shaking his head.

'You only suspected your wife, and I believe, I honestly believe, your wife had nothing to do with this. This is something from your past, somebody you've upset who holds a grudge against you.'

'But I've upset or angered no one. You can ask my wife, she will tell you I'm the most affable man she's ever met, which is one of the reasons I doubted her: it annoys the hell out of her that I don't lose my temper, and why am I not like her friends' husbands.'

'I detect a reason for that,' Harry said looking List straight in the eye.

'Her first husband was a bit free with his fists!'

A raised eyebrow was the only response Harry would allow to such a statement.

List drank the rest of his Americano and the two men sat in silence for a few minutes.

'This goes back further than you think, Mister List,' Harry said once he had finished off the last of his latte.

'How far?'

'Give me all the details you have on the ex, although I'll add that it's too obvious to be him; he would take the greatest of pleasure informing you-'

'Yeah, I don't think it's him,' List admitted.

'Somebody from your past has spent a long-time planning this, and this is just the beginning; he may not be the one to deal out the final retribution, he's here to set the scene, lay the groundwork so to speak.'

Harry stopped when he saw the colour wash out of List's face.

'Look at the positives Mister List-'

'Which are what exactly?'

'You know they're coming; they want you to suffer, they wish you to suffer how they've suffered for all this time, so think, and think hard, cover everything and go back decades if need be.'

List nodded.

'And don't fret, I fully appreciate that is easy for me to say, but I mean it.'

'It's hard not to show it,' List said looking away.

'If you want to flush this person out then you need to show that whatever this is does not bother you; if they see that you're going about your life as if nothing has changed, and nothing better change, Mister List, then they'll show their hand well before time.'

Travers' words hit home, and List perked up.

'This person knows your routine, probably better than you know it yourself!'

'That thought has occurred to me.' The anger in List's voice was evident. 'They'll know you now!'

'Good! It will save me the time searching for them.'

Harry looked at his watch.

'Yes, I need to go too,' List said, rising out of his seat and offering his hand.

Harry stood and the two men shook hands, promising to keep in touch if there were any further developments.

List handed Harry a business card and left the coffee shop first while Harry hung back to gauge people's reactions. There was nothing strange or untoward with anybody in the coffee shop.

Once in the street Harry looked left and then right before watching List disappear into a crowd of shoppers. Travers waited a few seconds before following.

The shoppers were many this fine sunny day in October and Harry was happy that his leg was not causing him any bother. It didn't take long for him to catch up with List and witness him rendezvous with his wife and disappear into a toy shop.

Harry turned to make his way back to the Porsche when somebody caught his eye: it was Tony Belisse, and he was visibly limping. Harry thought the worst and tailed him.

Belisse hobbled into a discount store and bought essentials before heading for a small cafe and lunch. Harry waited across the street from inside a fast food joint and polished off a large quarter pounder with cheese, a diet coke and two normal cheeseburgers.

Tony ordered a bacon and cheese pannini and two large coffees.

Forty-five minutes later Harry was back on his tail. The limping Belisse was a doddle to follow.

Harry studied the body language of all passers-by, anticipating an imminent attack on his work colleague. All was well.

Tony stopped off at a bus stop where a small queue had already formed. Harry hid himself three passengers back, out of sight. Fifteen minutes later the bus arrived.

Travers leaned forward to hear Tony's final destination, as the queue shuffled into the bus. Once he knew what stop Tony was taking, he backed out of the queue and ran as fast as his leg would allow him to where he'd parked the 924.

Harry took the most expeditious route to Tony's stop; the roads were clear, and Harry enjoyed the drive, relishing what may or may not be waiting for him. He arrived a full fifteen minutes before the bus and parked up fifty yards further up the road.

Belisse was the only passenger to vacate the bus at this stop. Harry stayed in his car, and from where he was parked could watch Tony limp up the road for a good two hundred yards.

Suddenly Tony stumbled and fell over. Harry got out of the car but kept the driver's door open. Tony struggled to get to his feet. Had he just stumbled due to his limp? Harry was unsure and his growing concern transmitted itself into him taking three strides up the road once he'd swung the driver's door shut. Tony looked left into a doorway and a fist appeared, striking him firmly in the face.

Travers was off, but he still closed the gap on Tony in seconds even with a dodgy leg. A familiar face met his: it was the young lad, Adrian, from the railway station.

'You fucking asshole!' Harry shouted, the venom in his voice surprised even him.

Belisse was as shocked to see Harry, as much as Adrian was.

Harry speared a hard, straight right at the man's nose, but he ducked, and Harry missed. Travers now found himself defending a combination of punches. He took all of them on the arms. The lad looked off to his right.

Tony got to his feet but was in no condition to help.

Harry stepped back, took a stride to his right and blocked the attack he knew was coming from his blind-spot on the left. The impact on his left arm stung. His attacker was clearly a boxer, his nose gave that away.

Harry watched the man take a boxer's stance; Travers was remarkably and surprisingly calm: he didn't know if it was apathy, or experience, but whatever it was his mindset was for counterattacking. The man began with a straight left jab. Harry leaned to his left and watched the punch slip harmlessly by. Frustrated, the man next threw a straight left jab followed by a right cross. Harry leaned left and ducked out of the way. Never did he retaliate.

'Have you quite finished?' Harry said.

'Fuck you!' the lad sneered.

'Is this the guy?' the man asked, attempting a third time to land one on Harry.

'If you're referring to the episode at the station, yes I am,' Harry replied, again dodging all the punches sent his way before striking the lad with an open hand to the chin.

The man, incensed by Travers' attack, swung wildly.

Harry found the whole experience slightly comical: the young lad just stood almost dumbfounded that Harry had the temerity to strike him with his boxer friend present; and the boxer friend had lost complete control of himself leaving Harry all the time in the world to read exactly where the punches were going and dodge them easily.

Harry got bored very quickly and kicked the Boxer on the inside of his right knee before smashing the palm of his left hand into the man's nose. Blood oozed down onto the Boxer's chin. It was a technique he'd witnessed being used years ago and so naturally adopted it.

The fight ended quickly.

'I'll kill you for this!' snarled the Boxer.

Harry ignored the threat.

'We'll get you for this!' Adrian added.

Harry ignored the second threat.

'You okay?' he asked Tony.

'I'm fine. Can we go?' Tony replied. His body language backed up the tone of his voice.

Harry felt like leaving these two with a parting gift but rejected the idea.

'Let's go,' Harry said calmly.

'We'll find you and your boyfriend,' the Boxer said without looking at Harry, 'and then you'll wish you'd fucked off when you had the chance.'

Harry hit the man on the side of the head with a hard left. He hurt his hand, but the Boxer ended up on his knees. Harry took the man's wallet from his back pocket, threw out all the credit cards, but again kept the driver's licence.

'From this I'll find you and all your associates.' Harry waved the driver's licence in the man's face. The young lad remained quiet.

'Then they'll be two less gays in the world to worry about,' the man replied.

Harry was about to retaliate, but Tony pulled him back: 'I want to leave.'

The two men walked back to the 924.

'You hurt your hand.'

Harry looked down at his left hand on hearing Tony air his concern. It had begun to swell.

'I've had worse!'

Harry looked back at the two men. They had left.

'Does it always happen like this?' Harry asked.

Belisse didn't want to answer at first and Harry feared he would have to ask him again.

'No, they don't seem to follow any pattern.'

'They?'

'There have been five.'

They boarded the 924.

'Where to?'

'I'll give directions,' Tony answered softly.

Harry pulled away and followed directions when given.

It didn't take long to reach their destination.

Tony got out of the Porsche and reached his front door before Harry managed to extricate himself from the car.

Belisse entered his house and shut the door. Harry stood staring at his work colleague's front door. He felt sorry for him and didn't hang around to see if he'd re-appear.

On the way home he called Crewing to advise them he was ready to return to work; it would prove difficult to explain any absence now that Tony had seen him during his so-called convalescence.

7

It was a Friday and a day flight to Tenerife South when Harry eventually returned to work. He looked for Tony. He was not working today.

Harry studied each of the separate briefing booths and tried to guess which crew was his today. In took all of a minute for him to give up and go and print off the flight paperwork from the nearest terminal. He was in the process of stapling the relevant sheets together when a fifty-year old man in uniform approached him: 'Are you Captain Travers?' the man said in soft Dublin accent.

Harry nodded: 'Sure am.'

'I am John, John O'Connor.' John held out his hand and the two men shook hands.

Harry clocked John look at the last remnants of his shiner and the cut over his eye. He realised straight off the man was new to the company. He just had that look about him. You could always tell the new first officers, by their body language and crisp new uniform.

'New to the company?' Harry asked.

'Career change,' John replied. 'Used to be in banking-'

'But always had a desire to fly.' Harry had met similar pilots like John who just got fed up with their previous career and decided to follow their dreams and fly big jets.

'That's it!' John said with the broadest grin you ever did see.

'Excellent!' Harry took an instant liking to Mister O'Connor.

'Any preference?' Harry did the polite thing and gave the man the option of which leg to fly.

'Can I take it out?'

'It's all yours. How much fuel do you want?'

Harry was getting used to flying the inbound sector and slid the paperwork across the briefing table. John took his time studying the flight-plan, en-route and destination weather, notams: notices to aircrew which detail all the relevant information regarding the arrival, destination and en-route airfields, before arriving at a fuel figure he was comfortable with. Harry agreed with him and ordered the fuel. No sooner had the phone hit the cradle than Ricky Ager, a Senior Cabin Manager, appeared to inform Harry and John they were parked on stand 22 and he and the crew would see them out there.

'We'll be right behind you,' Harry said handing the flight envelope with all the paperwork to John.

The eight crew members walked out to stand 22 as a group with Harry spending most of the time thinking about Cantlay. He would pay the man a visit on the way home.

Although the Tenerife flight was full, the boarding went without a hitch and Harry was grateful to be able to push off stand on time and get airborne with a healthy flight time outbound, taking into account the upper winds at their cruising flight level of thirty-five thousand feet: it was always best to have the headwind on the outbound leg, have a quick turnaround and then make the most of the tailwind on the inbound sector; it always meant you got back home ahead of schedule.

The flight time to Tenerife was a shade under four hours and twenty minutes, and three hours into the flight Ricky requested entry into the flight deck.

Ricky's expression made Harry's heart sink: an elderly lady who has history of angina was not feeling well and the crew had felt the need to put the lady on oxygen.

The routing down to the Canaries from Manchester, and most of the UK airports, invariably took them down the Tango Routes; these were airways that formed part of the North Atlantic High Level Airspace (NAT HLA) and any airline wishing to fly these routes must have them within the geographic area of the company AOC (Air Operators Certificate). The additional requirement is to remain within one hour's single engine flying time, 400nm for an A320, of a suitable alternate airfield thus allowing aircraft who are not ETOPS (Extended Twin Operations) to utilise them.

Ricky left to check on the lady.

Harry checked the nearest suitable airport in case a medical diversion was necessary. It was Porto Santo in the Madeira Islands and the weather was good for an approach and landing onto runway 36.

So much for a quiet first flight, Harry thought, while mentally preparing himself for hearing the news that a diversion would be required.

Ricky requested entry back into the flight deck.

'We've had to put her on a second oxygen bottle, Harry,' Ricky said, 'but she seems to be stable.'

'We'll call MedLink on the SAT phone,' Harry replied, selecting the SAT phone option on the A320's Audio Control Panel.

Satellite Communication (SATCOM) was a new addition to the Airbus fleet and it allowed the flight deck to have two-way communication and exchange of information between them and a ground network. The system provides pilots with both voice and data channels.

Ricky handed over the MedLink Pilot Patch Checklist, a form designed to allow the Cabin Crew to obtain all relevant medical details needed when talking to MedLink Telemedicine.

MedLink Telemedicine, based in Phoenix, Arizona provide an invaluable service to the crew, as they can be contacted on the ground or in the air at any time and from anywhere in the world by either phone or radio patch. It allows the crew to talk directly to a medical professional who will advise them on an individual basis and will arrange for paramedics to meet the aircraft on landing, if required.

Harry handed over radio control to John, so he could talk to MedLink on the SAT phone. Ricky returned to the lady. He studied the form while waiting the few seconds for the phone connection to be made. The lady had a long history of heart problems, and her last medication had been taken before they got airborne, but not since; this reminded Harry of the last time he nearly had to divert due to a medical emergency when an elderly gentleman who also suffered from angina had left his own medication, GTN (Glyceryl Tri-Nitrate), in his checked-in luggage. Luckily for him they carried Nitrolingual spray, and this along with oxygen helped relieve his angina attack until they could get him on the ground. It begged the question as to why the lady had not taken hers when she began to feel unwell.

MedLink answered his call.

The upshot was that they would arrange for an ambulance to meet the aircraft on stand in Tenerife.

Harry called back to the cabin. A junior cabin crew member answered, and he inquired after the elderly passenger before passing on all the information regarding the arrangements being made for their arrival in Tenerife.

Tenerife's main airport is situated on the southern part of the island and was under construction in the late seventies at the time when one of the worst aviation disasters in history occurred when two Boeing 747s collided in fog at Tenerife's Northern airport in 1977. The runway at Tenerife South runs from East to West with the arrival taking you around Mount Thaide with the associated problems from turbulence and possible wind-shear if the winds at 2,000 feet blow from the wrong direction when compared to the surface wind. Luckily, today was a relatively calm day for Tenerife South with 07 the runway in use and a surface wind of 180 degrees at 8 knots.

It was busy for a Friday and their arrival routing meant they were following an Airbus A321 and a Boeing 737. On instruction from Air Traffic Control they were told to slow down earlier than normal to guarantee a safe separation from the aircraft ahead – the lead aircraft was asked to maintain high speed for as long as possible.

From previous experience Harry knew that ATC would get the departing traffic away in-between the arrivals. It all worked out perfectly and Harry and John were cleared to land on passing a thousand feet. Harry advised John to keep the autopilot in – it was always good practice to keep the automatics engaged until cleared to land in case there were any problems with the departing aircraft still on the runway.

After landing John exited the runway via one of the high-speed exits and they were cleared to change frequency over to the ground controller. The lady controller instructed them to follow the marshaller and informed them of their stand. They had been allocated an air-bridge today and less than ten minutes later with the engines shut down, and the air-bridge attached, the paramedics boarded the aircraft to care for their elderly passenger. Prior to parking on stand Harry had made a brief PA to the other passengers to remain in their seats to allow the paramedics to board and make their way down the cabin.

With the elderly lady being cared for, the passengers disembarked, thanking the crew as they left. John and Harry immediately prepared the jet for the return journey; even with a sick passenger to care for they still had to try and maintain On-Time Performance for the airline.

Their dispatcher arrived promptly, took all the trip information for the load-sheet, informed them there was no departure slot and duly left.

John left for his exterior pre-flight inspection and to dial up the required fuel figure on the fuel panel for their return home. Harry programmed the FMGC with the inbound route. Sheila invaded his thoughts, but he pushed her to the back of his mind and concentrated on the job; he was becoming more adept in avoiding the searing pain with each passing day: he had kept himself busy with his 'other job' to prevent any quiet moments torturing his troubled soul. He still loved her with a passion and longed to be able to hear her sweet voice one more time if nothing else. How he wished he could be like the many couples they flew down to the Canaries at this time of year who were retired or nearing retirement; he ached to be able to grow old with Sheila and take a well-earned winter break in Tenerife, but that was one dream that had been cruelly ripped from him. Harry blocked Sheila and any anger and resentment out until he got home. Then and only then would he shed tears; he would fall asleep with the memory of her ripping his insides to shreds.

* * *

His insides felt like they were torn to shreds way before he made home. It had begun the split second he had shut down both engines on stand. John had sensed that all was not well with Harry and politely enquired as to his well-being. Harry lied.

At least his home was warm and inviting, he thought, and went to make coffee. Harry had drastically reduced his alcohol intake: under his present circumstances it was best to eradicate it all together. Alcohol did not numb the pain, it only added to the melancholy that inevitably overwhelmed him whenever he thought of her.

He turned on the TV. It did nothing to lighten the mood: on BBC they were broadcasting one of their new cookery programmes and today's contestant was preparing an Italian dish. Harry was sorely tempted to go for a drive, but he was exhausted and thankfully fell asleep before the dish was served.

Harry slept well and woke in the early hours. He dumped his shirt at the bottom of his bed then carefully folded his work trousers over the end of the bed in readiness for the Larnaca flight later that day.

* * *

Any lingering pain was dissipated by a call from Willis; he was ringing not only to thank him, but to request the pleasure of his company for lunch. Harry felt like refusing but convinced himself to go for no other reason than it kept the man close, and you know what they say about friends and enemies. The date was set for tomorrow afternoon at a cafe called Sweet Trees, near the city centre, once Harry returned from this night flight to Larnaca.

Harry left his house for the short drive to the airport, and longer bus drive to the crew-room, with a strange sensation slowly enveloping him: he was glad to hear from Willis, he even missed the man. Harry wasn't sure why he felt this way; eventually concluding it could only be that Willis represented one of the last connections he had with Sheila.

For a night Laranaca the flight didn't drag on and Harry was excited to discover exactly what it was that caused Willis to phone him.

* * *

Sweet Trees was not hard to find, and Harry chose a table next to the window so he could watch all the comings and goings; he was becoming a right nosey parker. Willis arrived precisely five minutes after him. The man was polite, apologised profusely for being late and asked whether Harry had ordered. Harry replied that he was still in the process of studying the excellent fare on offer.

Willis sat, but did not study the menu. You come here regularly, thought Harry. Smart, very smart, choose somewhere you are known, that way if there is any trouble, they will vouch for you as a loyal customer and easily remember you should anybody ask.

'Bet you were surprised to hear from me?' Willis asked with the feint hint of a smile.

'I sure was,' Harry answered, eagerly anticipating what this man was going to say next, but desperately not wanting to give away his true feelings.

'I shan't ask about your eye.'

'It's just a scratch.'

'You may not want to hear what I'm about to tell you!'

'Oh, yeah!'

'Raquette,' Willis said slowly, over pronouncing every syllable. 'Mister Raquette has developed and intense dislike for you!'

'Good friend of Mister Moore, was he?' Harry said, watching Willis' reaction very closely.

'He most certainly appears to be,' Willis replied. 'Shall we order?'

'Sure. I am now very hungry, very hungry indeed,' Harry said rising out of his seat.

Willis pulled back his chair and followed Harry to the counter at the rear of the cafe where you ordered the food.

The female cashier smiled at Willis: 'You're usual?' she said.

'You know me too well,' Willis said jocularly.

Harry placed his order for lasagne with a side salad. Both men ordered coffee.

Back at the table Willis began to expound further: 'It would be amiss of me not to warn you about Raquette's plans, considering all you did for me, which I thank you for. I knew he was friendly with Moore, but even I failed to appreciate how friendly.'

Harry sat down. Willis followed suit.

'What do you know of this Raquette?' Harry asked. He needed to build a mental model of the man.

'He has a reputation of being a bit of a sadist with those he takes a disliking to. Moore had similar tastes.'

The waitress brought over the coffees. Both men thanked her.

'How much time have I got?'

'I'm not sure.'

'Take a guess.'

'He's away on business right now, business that has nothing to do with me, but when he returns, I'll let you know. That's all I can do I'm afraid.'

'You didn't have to do this.'

'I do, you know I do.'

Harry sipped his coffee. It was just the right temperature.

'Okay, I want to know Raquette's itinerary when he returns,' Harry said after a second sip of coffee.

Willis nodded.

The waitress returned with their food. Both men thanked her again.

Harry was ravenous: the thought of crossing swords with Raquette filled him with unending joy and made him tingle with delight. The adrenaline was already beginning to surge through his veins. Due to his injuries Harry had missed a couple of marital art classes. He wouldn't miss another.

The two men ate lunch together, as if it was a regular occurrence, with the topic of conversation ranging from England's chances in the next soccer World Cup, to Brexit, to which holiday destination would prove to be the most popular next summer. Harry throughout was respectful enough not to mention David unless Willis himself brought him up, which he didn't. Times were definitely a changing for Harry: here was a man that only a short time ago he envisaged sending into the next world, if he should ever come looking for him, with a few choice words, but who Harry had now spent a very enjoyable lunchtime with.

* * *

Harry was on two days off following his rest day after the night Larnaca; he spent the first day catching up on some sleep. He would need it with a Tang Soo Do class planned for that night.

Travers approached the class with renewed vigour, throwing every ounce of energy into the class knowing that there was an end goal awaiting his efforts in learning this new skill: Tang Soo Do was more physical than Jujitsu with what seemed to Harry, on first reflection, a vast array of kicks to master, but the kicks were one of the joys of this particular art and Harry ached the next morning like he had never ached before. A hot bath was in order.

The second day off Harry went to see Cantlay. He found the man working in his rear garden, trimming the edges of the grass. Where else would he be.

'Good morning, Mister Cantlay,' Harry said admiring the man's work.

'Good morning, Harry.'

'How's things?' Travers knew it was always best to cut to the chase.

'Quiet,' the old man replied.

'Good!'

'Saw Haffenden this morning.'

'And?'

'And I was polite and wished him a very good morning.'

'I bet he enjoyed that,' Harry said picturing Haffenden's reaction.

'I'm sure he did.'

Cantlay finished off the last of the grass before inviting Harry in for coffee.

'We'll have it on the patio, I'll bring it out,' the old man said pointing to some garden furniture. 'Make yourself comfortable.'

Harry sat down and again admired the man's garden; green-fingered he was not, but it did not prevent him from admiring the work of others.

Five minutes later Cantlay returned with a tray containing two coffees and biscuits.

'Got to make the most of this Indian summer,' he said joyfully.

'It's very pleasant,' Harry replied taking his coffee.

'That it is.' Cantlay sat down and helped himself to three biscuits.

Sweet tooth, thought Harry. He was just about to ask after the dog when Jasper duly appeared. Cantlay gave him a biscuit.

'He's feeling better then?' Harry enquired.

'A lot better, thanks.'

Harry could sense the old man was going to add something further but checked himself.

'Why do I get the impression......,' Harry deliberately stopped mid-sentence.

Cantaly took a mouthful of coffee, finished off a biscuit and looked Harry squarely in the eyes: 'I want to lull the man into a false sense of security, I want him to believe he has my number, that somehow he has scared me into keeping my counsel. And then....,' It was Cantlay's turn to stop mid-sentence. 'And then I will deal with him. You know what they say about revenge, Harry.'

'It's a dish best served cold,' Harry replied.

'Exactly. What do you have in store?'

Harry shrugged his shoulders.

'Come now.'

'When the time comes, you'll be the first to know,' Harry said, choosing a chocolate biscuit.

Both men knew the conversation had naturally run its course and sat back to enjoy the day.

'I'm still not entirely sure what it is you actually do for a living, Mister Travers or is it Further?' Cantlay asked while picking up the two empty mugs.

'It's best to be on a need to know basis.'

'More coffee?'

Harry nodded: 'That would be most acceptable.'

Cantlay went to make coffee.

'You find people you say, Mister Travers?' Cantlay said on his return and handing Harry his coffee.

Before Harry could answer Cantlay went on: 'Yes, best we leave it on a need to know basis, for I get the feeling that to know too much about your business would be bad for one's health.'

'Only for some,' Harry replied.

'Would a Mister Haffenden be on that list by any chance?'

Harry smiled: 'Before we leave the subject of Haffenden, I need you to do me a favour.'

'Name it!'

'I need to know all his comings and goings.'

'Oh, that's easy, I've been doing that for months.'

Harry was shocked but knew he shouldn't be. 'Have you got any pictures?'

'No, I make notes.'

'Can I read them?'

'After coffee; if there's one thing I hate it is cold coffee.'

The two men retired to Cantlay's front room with Jasper in close attendance. The old man went straight to an old-fashioned writing desk that you very rarely see these days and removed some papers and handed them to Harry.

Travers was initially interested in only one customer, and more to satisfy his own curiosity than anything else plus to prove himself right. He found Bennett on the third page of customers.

'You found something?' asked Cantlay eager to see if his note taking had borne fruit.

'I found one person I was looking for.'

'Who?' Cantlay said suddenly excited.

Travers had to prevent himself from laughing such was the man's enthusiasm to discover the mystery customer described in his notes.

'A missing wayward husband presumed dead!'

Cantlay's enthusiasm evaporated in an instant.

'These are the kind of people we're dealing with,' Harry said solemnly, 'so you better keep the whereabouts of these papers a secret.'

'You're the only other person that knows about them, all that is except my neighbour.'

'Would that be the neighbour who looks after Jasper?'

'That's the one,' Cantlay said going to his front window and looking down the street towards his neighbour's house. 'He's reliable,' he added looking back at Harry.

Harry read through the descriptions of the remaining customers. The two Mazda drivers were there. Harry wondered when was the last time Cantlay had read his notes for he failed to recognise the man.

'Bearing in mind what we just discussed, can I have copies?' Harry asked handing back the man's papers.

Cantlay promised to have them ready for him the next time they met.

Harry had an early check-in the next day to Lanzarote and politely made his farewell promising to call within a few days.

The nights were drawing in and it would soon be time to turn the clocks back. Harry drove slowly home.

8

The green fees at the local Golf Club were more than reasonable in Travers' opinion, once he took into account the facilities available to him. Harry appreciated he was the kind of guy who suffered from the addictive personality and if there was ever a sport designed for his kind of personality then golf was it.

His first attempts to master the game of golf were nothing short of comical with Harry using an old set of clubs a friend had once given him, and the ball deciding it was going to go anywhere other than the direction Harry wished it go. But the addictive personality kicked in with a vengeance forcing Harry to hit balls until his hands bled. He looked down at his blood red hands. Harry was content: to him this was a sign that the correct amount of effort was being applied to the job at hand; he may not master the game of golf, but he would play it to a high standard even if it cost all the skin off his hands. Harry believed you always got out what you put in and here was a pastime he could apply that philosophy to.

Following a flight to Lanzarote there was another trip to the Canary Islands and this time Fuerteventura, the second largest of the Islands sitting 100km off the north coast of Africa, and the main alternate airport for Lanzarote.

Both flights went without a hitch with them departing ahead of schedule and returning early.

Harry was grateful for the early return for he was eager to hit more balls on the driving range; he had read a book by the legendary Ben Hogan called Five Lessons: The Modern Fundamentals of Golf. Hogan is one of the greatest golfers ever to play the game and there is no one who knew more about the golf swing than Hogan, hence Travers' eagerness to read his book.

A large bucket of balls didn't draw any blood, but there was a definite improvement in the timing of his swing and ball striking:

Harry was beginning to hit the ball straight and long, the only downside was it was only one ball out of three. He would practice again tomorrow before his jujitsu class.

On the way home Harry called List to touch base and get any updates. List was clearly agitated when he answered the phone.

'Did you get a good look at them?' Harry said before List could add anything further.

'Are you psychic or something?' List said quickly before adding in an even faster voice that a second man had been following him, a man he had never seen before.

'Why did you not tell me sooner?' Harry was angry that he should be hearing this now.

'It only happened yesterday, and I wanted to see if they would appear again today. And it's definitely not the ex.'

Harry's anger abated on hearing List's excuse.

'Today's been a quiet day.' The relief in List's voice was almost tangible.

Harry was on standby tomorrow followed by two days off.

'Mister List, do you leave the house promptly at nine every morning?'

'Yes, I do.'

'Tomorrow you will be late.'

'Okay.'

'Do you take the same route to work every morning?'

'Yes, I do.' List said again.

'Tomorrow take a longer route. I will call you later and you will tell me what route you are going to take and what car you will be driving.'

'Okay,' List said slowly.

'I will be waiting half-way along that route, I won't tell you where, but I will be waiting for you and watching. If you don't hear from me then I have them.'

'Thank you.'

'We'll get them!'

Harry didn't feel the need to say anymore.

* * *

Travers rang as promised and List gave him the route he intended to take to work in Stockport plus the make, model and registration of the car he was going to drive. It was his wife's Ford Fiesta, and it came as no surprise to find that the man was a second-hand car dealer. List would leave his house exactly twenty minutes late.

* * *

Harry parked up early on Ladybridge Road in Cheadle Hume in order to get the most advantageous spot to witness List's arrival and departure, and sure enough he drove past him exactly twenty minutes after his anticipated ETA for that part of the route. Harry pulled out into the traffic four cars back from List. By now Harry couldn't have cared less if they recognised his 924. He loved every second of this game of cat and mouse.

One of the four cars turned left onto Councillor Lane leaving the others to maintain station following the rest of the work traffic to Stockport.

Maybe List sold this person a dodgy motor, he thought, picturing an irate customer swearing oath after oath alongside promises of heinous retribution.

Flippancy was not what was required here, he realised, and so began to pay closer attention to the three cars between him and List and those immediately behind. His phone rang. He let it ring out before checking the number. It wasn't Crewing or List. He'd ring it later and find out who the owner of the number was.

The train of cars headed straight on into Bird Hall Road and towards the A560 via Edgeley Road, which would take them into Stockport.

The M60 was almost nose to tail at this time of the morning, but they only had to go a short way before they exited onto the A626 to Heaton Chapel. One of the cars stayed on the motorway, two followed List. None of the cars behind Harry followed him. List then turned right at the first roundabout onto Reddish Road then left into Greg Street. One car followed List: it was a Green Audi. Harry hung back, checking he still wasn't being followed. List pulled up outside his car dealers and spoke to one of his salespeople from inside his car. The Audi pulled in fifty yards up on the left. Harry parked up on the right, before the car dealers. From his vantage point he could cover both List and the Audi.

List finished giving instructions and parked the Ford. The Audi hadn't moved. Harry remembered he had a camera with a lens in his glove compartment, which he had bought on a whim a couple of weeks ago for occasions such as these.

Harry focused the camera on the back of the Audi; the driver was looking off to his left, so Harry had the driver in profile. He took a picture. The driver took out a pair of binoculars. Harry took another picture and watched the man closely.

The man got out a file and studied it.

'What have you got yourself involved in, Mister List?'

The man leafed through the file.

'You're not police, so who are you?'

Harry turned his attention back to List. He was checking all the cars on his lot, one by one. They were immaculate to look at and only a few years old. Travers sat back, put the camera on his lap and kept his line of sight on the back of the Audi. It was a nice car, not as good as his old 924, but a nice car none the less. Harry was biased and he knew it. Audi made good cars, popular cars the world over. Harry put the camera back on the Audi driver: 'Got you!'

He needed a quiet chat with Mister List and waited a further fifteen minutes to see if there would be any developments, and when there was not, he left after leaving a message on List's mobile phone that he would call him later.

* * *

Twenty-four hours later Travers parked up over the road from List's used car dealership, and once again remarked how professional and conscientious the man was. Harry checked for the Audi then went to see his client.

'Mister List, please,' Harry said to the salesperson List had spoken with yesterday.

List heard Harry and came out into the showroom. 'It's okay,' he called out, as the salesperson turned towards his office, 'he has an appointment.'

List led Harry into his office. It was bright, airy and fresh smelling thanks to those long-lasting air-fresheners that plug into the wall.

'Please.' List gestured to Harry to take a seat.

Harry sat in an extremely comfortable leather backed chair. List slumped down in a similar looking chair behind a large modern looking desk.

'Put me out of my misery, Harry.'

'Like I said, it's not your wife.'

'Who is it then?'

'Where do you get your cars from?'

'Auctions normally,' List said leaning forward on his desk.

'You buy any from the general public?'

'Some.'

'Who services them?'

'I have a local garage I use. They are very reliable. What are you trying to say, Harry?'

'You're a drugs mule, Mister List and didn't know it, but they think, whoever they are, that you're trying to rip them off.'

'A drugs mule,' List said, trying hard to comprehend what Harry had just told him. 'You don't know who these people are?'

'Not yet!'

'And you're sure that this is what it's all about?'

'Pretty damn sure: Mister List I believe one or more of your cars is carrying something belonging to these people, the problem for you is that they don't know which one, but obviously think you do.'

'Drugs are the most logical,' List said now leaning back in his chair.

'Can you trace every car on your lot?'

List nodded.

'Let's pray that you still have the car in question.'

The colour drained out of List's face.

'You have to prepare yourself!'

Again, List nodded.

'They drive a green Audi, keep an eye out for it, but don't do anything stupid. I'll be here tomorrow morning ahead of you and then leave them to me and we'll start putting some names to their faces.'

'Thank you.' List went to a drawer in his desk.

Bit early for a drink, Harry thought, but he couldn't blame the guy.

List produced an envelope and slid it across the desk towards him: 'Hope that covers it.'

Travers hadn't given payment for his services any thought. 'Wait until this is all resolved-'

'I don't like owing money!'

'Fair enough,' Harry said pocketing the envelope.

'You don't want to check it?'

'I trust you Mister List, and anyway I know where to find you,' he added, laughing.

It broke the tension in the room.

'I'll be in touch.' Harry rose out of his chair. 'Not one to tell people their business but check out those cars and look for anything out of the ordinary, or cars bought way too cheaply.'

'That's my today job then,' List replied standing and walking round the side of his desk.

The two men walked to the office door. List opened it and politely allowed Harry to leave first before giving his secretary instructions to gather all information on sales going back at least six months. From the look on her face she was expecting a quiet day.

Back at his Porsche Harry checked the street both ways for the green Audi then any car looking remotely suspicious with the driver still inside. There were none.

He was about to unlock the 924 when at the last minute he decided to walk the length of Greg Street. It took twenty minutes to arrive back at the blue Porsche with nothing untoward found and this part of the street still how he left it. Harry was desperate to get his hands on Cantlay's paperwork. The Porsche fired up first time and Harry left List to sell more cars.

* * *

He stood on the opposite side of the road to Cantlay's house and ran his eye over the entire front section of the property; something had been bothering him and on the way over he decided to put whatever it was to bed, plus it would aggravate Haffenden, or his associates, to see him standing in the street.

After about ten minutes of study and calming any rising indignation towards Haffenden, which was going to have to wait for another day, Travers crossed the road to knock on Cantlay's door. Three steps shy of the door the studying paid dividends: Cantlay didn't own a car, or if he did it was parked safely in the garage situated on the right side of the house, as you looked at it from across the street: there were no tyre tracks, oil spills, or any markings on his drive to signify that the man owned any vehicle.

Harry rang the bell twice. Jasper barked. You're feeling better he said to himself.

Cantlay answered with Jasper hiding behind his right leg, ready to pounce on his master's command.

'I've been expecting you,' he said cheerfully.

Harry was glad to see the old man in good spirits.

The old man led him into the kitchen and there sitting in a neat pile on the kitchen table sat the papers Harry was so eager to get his hands on.

'I have copied them all and put them in order for you.'

Harry picked up the topmost sheet and ran his eyes over the first few customers to catch Cantlay's eye. Harry was impressed at the very thoroughness of his descriptions. He thought of Mrs Bennett and whether it would serve any purpose to pass on this new information regarding her husband. Harry quickly dismissed the idea.

'I rarely saw the same man twice,' Cantlay said with his back to him while he made tea, 'women, yes, men, no!'

'No?'

'No, yet they always seemed to have a steady stream of male clientele and it frustrated me at the time that I could never find out how they advertised their services.'

'The thought has occurred to me.' Travers now had another piece of the jigsaw that made up his mental picture of the odious Mister Haffenden, and his harpies.

Cantlay put a hot mug of tea in front of him: 'I know I forgot to ask. I hope tea is okay?'

'Tea is fine.'

Jasper hovered around Travers' ankles, but never in a position in which to strike. Harry ignored the dog.

'How long have you watched the house?' he asked.

'Over a year!'

'And nobody took any notice other than you?'

'Not as far as I know; none of my neighbours have ever levelled a complaint against them to me.'

Harry sipped his tea.

'Contacting the police straight off would have been a waste of time, as they had not openly committed any crime. I could have lodged a complaint, but what advantage could I have gained? They need proof and my detailing all those who came and went was going to be that proof once the time came.'

'You don't drive, Mister Cantlay?' Harry asked changing tack.

The question did not faze the old man: 'Not anymore: epileptic,' he replied between sips of tea.

'Sorry to hear that.'

Harry could see in his eyes an acceptance that such questions were going to be part and parcel of any friendship between the two.

'You got any names for these customers?' Harry posed the question not expecting anything positive in return. He was not disappointed when the reply was in the negative.

'One of them did come to an unfortunate end in a bodged carjacking, but I can't remember his name.'

'How do you know he was one of their customers?'

'He looked familiar from the photograph in the newspaper, but by then my enthusiasm was beginning to wane, and so I never followed it up.'

'How long ago was this?'

'About a month ago.'

Harry was secretly overjoyed to have some much-needed homework.

Thirty minutes later Harry sat in the 924 with the engine running watching that house in his driver's side mirror. There was no movement. He grew bored and pulled away. A quick check of his mirrors confirmed he was not being followed.

Harry needed to get online and subscribe to those websites offering backdated newspapers; he was eager to make the connection between Cantlay's notes and this victim of a carjacking.

Harry was in heaven; he loved the donkey work, the slow and methodical search through page after page of news reports. Cantlay reckoned it was a month ago, but Harry began his search back eight weeks. It took him over an hour before he discovered the first reference to a carjacking in a local paper. Harry made a note of the date: it was exactly a month from today's date. He checked other papers printed on that day and two days after. Harry finally found a more detailed report in the Manchester Evening News: a middle-aged man by the name of Brian Hawkins was killed during what the police believe was an attempted carjacking gone wrong on a quiet country lane. There were no witnesses. The case was ongoing.

'Convenient,' Harry said softly.

There was a picture of the poor unfortunate Mister Hawkins; Harry compared the photograph to all the notes taken by Cantlay. Hawkins was on the third page.

Why Hawkins? What had he done to them? The man had not put up any sign of a struggle, according to the report. Had they drugged him first? But surely that would have shown up on the autopsy report. There was no mention of it in the newspaper. He needed to speak to Hawkins' widow, but only after a thorough search through the archives.

Harry searched for rest of the day but found nothing new. He would start early the next day and continue his search and every available day after that.

The week evaporated before his very eyes; the loss of time does indeed bring on the greatest loss of all, and this alone drove Harry forward at a relentless pace at times to fill every minute, hour, day with something worthwhile, but personal achievements and goals fail to excite the onlooker unless they themselves have a vested interest in the outcome. Cantlay would understand, he would appreciate the effort.

It was a Tuesday when Travers returned to see the old man. His heart sank when he saw the ambulance parked outside his house with a group of ten or so people witnessing proceedings. He didn't stop. As he passed that house there was a flickering of the curtains, but he could have imagined it. He was prejudiced and knew it.

The ambulance took an age to move away. From his parking spot Harry could not see Cantlay being loaded into the back; it had to be him for the old man never materialised.

Travers' anger expressed itself through white knuckles gripping the steering wheel; the sinking feeling he felt on first seeing the ambulance increased further when he finally caught a glimpse of the stretcher.

The ambulance pulled away. Harry followed.

Travers parked the Porsche in one of the hospital's pay by the hour car parks; he was here to watch over a friend, but the car park was nearly full with family members, relatives and friends paying their respects to those having need for one of Britain's greatest institutions. It was cheapening itself by this blatant use of emotional blackmail – parking should be free.

Harry strode over to the main building where the ambulance transporting the old man was still parked. The rear doors were open. The ambulance was empty.

He entered the hospital and immediately sought out the information desk; there was a thirty-something bearded man reading some papers seated behind a glass partition. Harry waited patiently for the man to look up. He didn't. Harry politely coughed. Still the man kept on reading. Harry thumped the glass. The man nearly fell out of his chair.

'When you can spare the time,' Harry snarled.

'That kind of behaviour is not tolerated in this hospital,' the man replied, clearly flustered.

'And blatantly ignoring me is?'

The man did not answer.

Harry pushed his face up close to the glass: 'Point me in the direction, please, to where I need to wait in order to see my uncle: he was the one who arrived just now in the ambulance.'

Out of the corner of his eye Harry witnessed a group of four people, two men and two women, enter the hospital agitated and distressed to the point of shouting at each other. Harry took a step back. The four approached the information desk and addressed the man behind the glass partition. They enquired after Cantlay. Harry slipped away out of sight and mind.

Outside the air was cool with a promise of colder weather to come. When it comes for my time to go, he thought, I want to die on a hot sunny day with God's omnipotent beauty there for all to see.

One of the four, a middle-aged woman with dark hair, brown eyes, scruffily dressed in jeans, sneakers and a brown jumper, that had seen better days, appeared beside him. She smiled, displaying receding gums that were the tell-tale signs of a smoker. She lit a cigarette.

Travers watched her take a long first drag on the cigarette.

'It's not easy is it?' Harry said as an opener.

'Sorry?' answered the lady, quite unsure why this stranger should want to talk to her.

'Waiting to hear on sick loved ones.'

'Sick loved ones,' she repeated then laughed loudly.

Harry was incensed but hid it. It occurred to him that she had nothing to do with Cantlay, so he came right out with it. 'Are you related to Mister Cantlay?'

The lady nearly dropped her cigarette. That'll be a yes then, thought Harry.

'And you are?' she asked taking another long drag.

'A friend. And you are?'

'Leaving,' she said turning on her heels, leaving Harry with her cigarette smoke hanging in the air.

He kept looking straight ahead; there was no point following her. Where was she going to go?

The cigarette smoke faded, and Harry turned to make his way back to the hospital. A large, balding, overweight man was blocking his path.

'So, are you a friend or a nephew?' the balding man said.

There was something in the way the man posed the question that sowed a seed of doubt. 'Nephew,' lied Harry, 'and who are you?'

'Family friend,' the man said nervously, shifting his weight from one foot to the other.

'I'm sure my uncle will be pleased to see you when he wakes up.' Harry took two strides towards the hospital, stopped, and gesticulated for the man to walk with him: 'After you.'

The man reluctantly, tentatively, took one step then stopped. 'I need a cigarette.'

'Sure. I'll see you inside.'

Harry walked briskly towards the hospital. He swore he could almost hear the man's fingers over his mobile phone warning the other members of his party of his imminent arrival.

The other three were, by their body language and facial expressions, on the defensive by being on the offensive.

'So, you're the nephew,' said the second male. He was only slightly smaller than his friend, but with more hair, of the mousey coloured variety.

'And who are you?' Harry asked closing the gap between the two of them.

There was that doubt again, as to their authenticity, but Harry didn't push it and went and sat down.

An hour or so later the man behind the glass spoke directly to Harry: 'Your uncle will be taken to the ward, soon.' He gave Harry detailed instructions on how to find it. Great, he thought, they will know exactly where to go, too.

The old man was heavily sedated when he finally reached him, not that he expected any form of confab.

Harry sat there for half-an-hour, primarily to see if any of the four would dare to turn up. Who are they? Had Haffenden sent them to finish the job off? They were bloody incompetent if they were here to finish a hit! Cantlay may have genuinely had a heart attack with no outside interference, but Harry knew that was a load of crap.

A female nurse came in and checked on Cantlay. Harry asked for an update. She filled him in as best she could. He knew it was time to leave, and so discreetly made his exit.

Harry took his time walking back to the Porsche. He was being watched and monitored by four imbeciles and he found the whole episode hilarious; he didn't care what they reported back to Haffenden. Just don't go drinking the tea.

'Tea!' Harry stopped dead in his tracks.

All was quiet when Harry pulled out of the car park. He wasn't comfortable leaving the old man, in case he should wake during the night and find he was alone. The man never wore a wedding ring; Harry didn't put much emphasis on that, but maybe there was more to it, maybe there was an estrangement, an ongoing family rift. Harry was on standby tomorrow from midday.

Fingers crossed he wouldn't be called, but worst-case scenario Harry could make the early visiting times. A red Vauxhall pulled up within half a car length of his rear bumper, but it was three young lads showing off. They soon overtook him, beeping their horn and giving him the finger. Harry laughed and waved them on.

* * *

Cantlay was sitting up in bed when Travers entered the ward. The old man smiled weakly, but he was happy to see a friendly face.

'You're looking better.'

'Feel better. Weak, but better.'

'What happened?' Harry asked in a hushed tone.

'The devil's snare affects different people different ways. I knew I would have the heart attack minutes before it struck and was able to call an ambulance and unlock my front-door.'

Harry was impressed.

'I came to see you last night, along with a group of four rather suspect individuals-'

'They weren't allowed to see me, were they?'

'Don't know. I lied: I said you were my uncle.'

'Good!'

'Care to enlighten me?' Harry was already making plans for them and wanted their names.

He sat down on the only chair anywhere remotely near Cantlay's bed and handed over his gift of the obligatory assortment of fruit.

'No flowers?' Cantlay said with tongue firmly in cheek.

'Have a guess; you got a fifty-fifty chance of getting it right.'

Harry made himself comfortable in the chair and thought of his uncle and the enquiry only a few weeks away. He was pleased to be going to Tennessee again, but it was a complete waste of judicial time to him: the lawyer was guilty on all charges and this enquiry was just an exercise in how to waste the tax-payers money, but, as any judge would surely tell him – the law is the law.

'They're my ex-partner's kids, at least the two boys are,' Cantlay said breaking his train of thought. 'She died just over a year ago.'

'Sorry to hear that.'

'She was a lovely, lovely lady,' Cantlay added, 'but her sons are a couple of assholes!'

'Their partners don't seem much better!'

'Don't speak to me of them!'

Harry was in no hurry to.

'They've been after my money, and waiting for me to die,' Cantlay continued. 'I don't have any children of my own.'

'They weren't too happy to meet your nephew.'

'I bet.' Cantlay laughed, but by the grimace on his face afterwards he shouldn't have.

A nurse arrived to check on the old man.

'Food here's great,' Cantlay said admiring the angel caring for his every need.

'Got you appetite back then?'

'Thank God for jimsonweed.'

The angel gently chastised him, but secretly loved the attention and the appreciation; there is no more selfish being on earth than a sick one, Harry was once told by a medical professional, they do nothing but want, want, want twenty-four seven. Now it is wrong of anybody to tar everybody with the same brush, and here before him was proof that not everybody lacked that essential consideration for their fellow human being.

The angel left with a spring in her step with the old man's eyes still admiring her curves.

'On a serious note, what happened?'

Cantlay stopped smiling: 'Tea!'

'I thought so. Made by your own fair hand was it?'

'As always: no self-respecting tea lover would accept anything else in the comfort of his own home.'

'You're in hospital!'

'Some fucking prick broke into my home and mixed jimsonweed into my tea leaves.'

'Anybody who spends as much time in their garden as you-'

'My garden and Jasper are my children!'

'You'll need CCTV.'

'Would you?'

'I'll ring around.'

'Thank you.'

Harry could see the old man was getting tired, and not one who liked to outstay their welcome left him to rest up.

9

All was quiet for a few days and Travers took a break from searching through press reports to try and fine tune his golf game by getting a couple of rounds in; by his own admission he was crap with two scores of 96 and 93, but was still satisfied though because he'd managed to break 100. Harry had the bug and booked more tee-times.

Running parallel to the golf was his classes in self-defence; these he paid particular attention to, practicing hard when he could and taking up running to improve his overall fitness; being an ex-rugby player Harry loved running, he felt at ease jogging the streets, especially in the rain: running in the rain he felt as if the streets belonged to him and gave him much needed inner peace; Harry would run over and over in his head each of the cases, where he stood with them and what his next course of action should be.

Back at the house after a late-night run, he rang List and left a message. Tomorrow he was on another Tenerife and Tony Belisse was one of the crew.

* * *

Harry sought out Tony the split second he entered the crew-room. He found him on the first time of asking and nodded to the man. Tony smiled back an acknowledgment.

Well, at least he's not deliberately ignoring me; this pleased Harry for the thought had been nagging away that Tony would just blank him as if the whole episode was just a bad dream.

Sarah Calder was the first officer today and she appeared the split-second Harry began to print off the paperwork.

'Morning Harry.'

'Morning Sarah.'

'My turn to buy the coffees.'

'I will never argue with anybody who starts their day with an opening statement like that. You can take it out.'

'Thank you.'

Fifteen minutes later the two of them stood in a short queue waiting to place their order for coffee.

'I was talking with Tony the other day,' Sarah began, but was interrupted from saying anything further by placing their order.

'Oh, yeah,' Harry answered slowly. Was his secret out?

He was left waiting a few excruciating minutes before he received the answer he was looking for: Sarah and Tony went to the same gym and their topic of conversation was nothing more than the shortage of cabin crew due to those taking maternity leave.

Harry breathed an inward sigh of relief, but then began to question whether he needed to: Tony was a very private person and you didn't need to be Einstein to figure that one out.

They reached their gate to be met by the agent who immediately asked Harry if it was okay to board; Harry informed the young lad that once fuelling was complete and he'd checked with the cabin manager that they'd finished catering and all security checks were complete then yes: JaguAir policy was not to board passengers while the jet was being fuelled.

The cabin manager today was guy named Ricky who was a true cockney, as he was born within the sound of the Bow Bells, and although he had moved North to Manchester many years ago had not lost his accent.

Once refuelling was complete the first passengers made their way down the air-bridge and boarding began. All went smoothly and less than thirty minutes later Ricky appeared behind them and confirmed the passenger figure and the number of wheelchair passengers needing assistance. Two minutes after that the agent appeared repeated the same figures and departed with a copy of the load-sheet. Ricky was given the go ahead to close and arm the passenger doors and Harry made his PA to the passengers, passing on the relevant details of the flight such as flight-times, the weather en-route and at Tenerife.

Manchester was busy today and they had to wait to push back and start engines once all their checks were completed, but once they had clearance to push everything went without a hitch.

Their routing today, due to strong southerly winds, took them on a South to South-westerly track down towards the South of England, across the English Channel, through France, Northern Spain and Portugal before heading more South-westerly towards the Canary Islands.

Weather en-route was good, although during her PA in the cruise Sarah advised the passengers to keep their seatbelts fastened at all times for their own comfort and safety. The weather for Tenerife was to be breezy from the East. It is one of the main reasons, Harry was once told, that windsurfers enjoy the Canary Islands. It is invariably windy.

Over France and Spain there was not a cloud in the sky and the panoramic beauty of the two countries along with the mountainous border was truly breath-taking. Harry appreciated how lucky he was to be doing this job and it hit home hard when flying on days like today. It is too easy to get blasé.

There was plenty of traffic working its way down to the Canaries and the Portuguese controller asked them to speed up to Mach .79 to maintain separation on the aircraft behind and in front.

Just as Harry was thinking about List, and whether or not the man had discovered anything untoward regarding the cars on his lot, there was a request to enter the flight deck. A quick check of the flight deck video system revealed Tony Belisse. Harry unlocked the door.

Tony looked straight at Sarah and continued a conversation that the two of them had clearly begun while at the gym. Harry never looked at Tony or Sarah and spent the time studying his latest roster, which covered a period of six weeks. He was back in the simulator in a little under two months.

The conversation reached its logical conclusion and Tony enquired if either of them required a hot drink. Harry ordered a coffee, Sarah a tea. Sarah left with Tony for a comfort break. Tony returned before Sarah. He handed Harry his coffee over his left shoulder so if there was a spillage it would not fall on the centre console and damage the electrics. He carefully placed Sarah's in the cup-holder moulded into the DV (Direct Vision) window.

'I never properly thanked you.'

Harry turned to look at Tony; he still bore the scars.

'No need,' he replied.

'I should have, it was very rude of me.'

'There is no need to say anything, but I do want to know if they return.'

Tony nodded.

'No, I'm serious.'

Tony nodded again: 'Okay.'

'I've got to ask. Have they?'

'No, not yet, but I haven't been going out much. I've kind of kept myself to myself. Well, more so than usual.'

'Go out!'

Tony looked straight ahead out of the cockpit window. The skies were clear, and the breath-taking views had not diminished. Harry could sense he was using Southern Portugal to bolster his flagging spirit.

'Okay,' he finally said. Harry could tell he wanted to be back in the cabin: the other crew members would be asking questions soon as to why he was spending all this time in the flight deck, plus Sarah's return was imminent.

Right on cue Sarah requested entry.

Harry was polite and courteous and didn't push it any further.

Even after a slick turnaround and a less than four-hour fight time home, it still meant that Harry fell through his front door ready for his bed.

He checked his mobile phone messages. Harry hadn't bothered before driving home, he was that tired. List's reply was there. He played it but was not really listening and only really picked up half the words. Harry got the gist: List discovered three cars on his lot where the paperwork was not complete. Tomorrow's duty was a standby from 10:00 to 16:00 local, and he was happy for small mercies. Following that there were three days off.

* * *

The call was short, sharp and to the point: there were three cars for which he found paperwork from private buyers he could not trace, or whose contact details were out of date.

'If you didn't buy them-'

'My partner,' List snapped, the disappointment in his voice almost tangible,

'Have you spoken to him?'

'No!'

'Then don't. Best he doesn't know.'

'He's away on an extended holiday.'

'That's convenient.'

'Isn't it just!'

List had come to accept the same conclusion as Harry, which would make any uncomfortable decisions in the future easier to swallow.

'When is he due back?'

'Next week,' List rasped.

'Have they been back?'

'If they have then I haven't seen them.'

'If you're sure which three cars are suspect,' Harry went on, 'then take each one home in turn, I'll follow, and we'll see what transpires. I've come to the conclusion they don't know which car contains what they want, so this will force their hand and reveal themselves.'

'I can write-off the car.'

'Good. Then all we do is wait, keep watch and follow if they take one. I'll require one of your cars, they'll recognise my 924 in an instant.'

'We'll start tomorrow. One's a Mercedes and I want rid of it!'

* * *

Harry was early and parked his 924 in Birkdale Road, off Greg Street, then cut through Baryl Road heading South onto Colwyn Crescent to meet up with Greg Street. He kept walking until he came to the junction with Reddish Road. And there he waited.

It was dark by the time List exited his premises in a smart 4-door red Mercedes-Benz C-Class.

'He must have some right nice cars on his lot to want to be rid of this one,' Harry joked to himself.

List pulled away. Harry waited a few minutes to check for tails. There were none. He would drive to List's and wait. The man had taken Travers' advice and parked a second car down the road from his house for use as their tail.

The next day Harry waited at the junction, only this time he parked closer to Reddish Road in Bangor Street. List appeared driving an Audi A6, again there were no followers.

The third day Harry was confident they'd get their man, but when List pulled away in a Vauxhall Insignia and nobody appeared behind him his confidence took a beating.

The drive to List's did nothing to lighten the mood.

Harry pulled up on the left before turning left into the road containing List's residence. His gut feeling was screaming at him to play this with caution. Harry got out of the car, walked briskly to the last house on the left and peered around the wall that marked the house's boundary, and searched the street. A silver Audi was parked opposite List's house.

Harry watched the Audi for several minutes. It was proving difficult to tell whether the driver was still in or not. He checked for the Insignia. It was nowhere to be seen.

'Bugger!'

He walked up the road on the opposite side to List's house. The Audi was empty.

'Double bugger!'

Harry stopped by the silver Audi, had a look inside, as if there was going to be anything in there to help him, and walked on. His phone sprang into life. It was List.

'The car's gone!'

'I know,' answered List. From his voice he was clearly driving. 'I watched them steal it.'

'Do you have eyes on the car?'

'Sure do. I'll text the address once we've parked.'

List hung up before Harry could reply. He walked briskly back to his car.

Harry tried hard to be patient; he was angry and frustrated with List for going it alone. Would he have done the same? After half an hour with no reply Harry drove home to wait for the text.

An hour and twenty minutes later Harry got a text with an address in Oldham. He didn't reply.

Harry drove back to List's and waited. No more texts came his way. Now, he was angry.

It was nearly midnight before Harry arrived at Egerton Street, Oldham in the 924. He found List's car without too much effort. It was empty. That was no great surprise. In the gutter under the driver's door was List's mobile phone.

'Clever,' Harry said pocketing the phone.

Travers drove home.

Harry was not being cruel or heartless or threatening not to give a damn about his client, in fact it was the exact opposite. It was only a matter of time before they discovered his identity and felt pressured to guarantee his silence.

He parked the 924 right outside his house, not even bothering to stick it in the drive. The loaner was parked up the street. Once inside he left the light on in his front-room and kitchen and threw his jacket over the back of a chair in the kitchen. From previous experience Harry unlocked the backdoor: any confrontation would be solely on his terms. It made him think of her. The gut-wrenching pain had been subdued these past few days with all this extra work, but now it returned with a vengeance, but his pain, the very pain tormenting his beleaguered soul, turned to burning indignation and slowly metamorphosed into a warm, deep eternal love; Sheila was protecting him, coming to his aid when most needed, watching over him, counselling against rash judgements. This was their space, her space, and no outsider would be allowed to sully that memory. Harry descended the stairs to the ground floor. Three steps from the bottom his backdoor opened. Furtively he ascended the stairs back to the first floor. On the first floor there was a small store cupboard where Harry kept junk biding its time before a trip to the local tip. There was just sufficient room for him to hide inside in the little time there was available to him.

Harry held his breath, listening intently to gauge how many there were. He guessed only the one. The next conundrum was how long to wait.

All was quiet, too quiet for his liking, and Harry was not carrying any protection; disposing of this body would be a pleasure and an education.

He cracked open the door an inch. Harry braced himself against an attack from behind the door. None came. Sooner rather than later this intruder will exhaust all obvious possibilities and back Harry into a corner. The guns were not kept in the house; they were safely buried on a friend's property, not that he could use one anyway. No, this was going to be a proper acid test of his self-defence skills and commitment to his client: did he have the "minerals" to see this through? Well, now was the time to find out. Harry ventured out onto the first floor. He paused, held his breath and listened. They were doing the same. The game was on.

Harry inched towards the door leading into his front-room and the kitchen. He paused a second time and scoured that part of the front-room he could see. All seemed as it should be. Harry bent his ear towards the second floor. They were giving nothing away. There was nothing for it, Harry needed to clear this floor and corner the intruder up on the second floor. It was time to gamble.

Three full, silent strides put Harry into his front-room; a large stride to his right hugged the wall and protected his rear. He had to regulate his breathing: it was going to give him away. Harry hugged the wall until the kitchen came into view. He moved away from the wall to get a better look. The inside of his kitchen didn't get chance to register. A striking brunette in a plain white t-shirt, jeans and knee-high black boots cart-wheeled out of the kitchen and kicked him hard in the solar plexus. Harry hit the far wall with a thud. The whiplash caused his head to rebound off the wall and meet a sharp, straight right-hand. It blooded his nose.

Harry feigned a far worse concussion and began a slide down the wall. The striking brunette fatally paused. Harry lunged forward, catching her off balance, lifted her off the floor and slammed her headfirst into the carpet, but she was not about let one strike finish her off and wrapped her legs around his neck and gripped tight. Harry struggled to breathe as she attempted to choke him to death. Travers hit her hard in the stomach; it did not loosen her grip.

He was surprisingly calm and held onto what breath was in his lungs. Harry lifted the girl off the floor, walked over to the door frame marking the entry into the front-room, swung her fully round to his left then back to the right. The brunette could see what was coming and lifted her left arm up in a vain attempt to protect herself. Harry smashed her head against the door frame. The brunette's arm took some of the impact. Harry did it again. The girl's head took the full impact and her grip on his neck began to weaken. A third blow and she released her legs. Harry took several deep breaths, but in that time the brunette was back on her feet, producing a six-inch blade from her black boots. She swiped the blade at his throat. Harry grabbed a copy of Blessed: George Best's autobiography, which he'd been meaning to start reading for some time and blocked the attacks. Harry hit her in the jaw with a knife hand; it didn't have the desired effect and she lunged at his heart. He placed the book over his chest and the knife embedded itself in the front cover.

'Sorry George,' he heard himself say.

Harry grabbed her right wrist with his left-hand, dropped the book, placed his right thumb on the back of the hand, wrapped the other four fingers over the top until they could take hold of the knuckle of the little finger and twisted hard. The brunette attempted to break free, but Harry held firm with his left before moving up to the shoulder joint and pushing down, bending her over. He didn't pause to take stock of his superior position. He kneed her straight in the stomach and followed it up with a stinging right to the temple. The girl fell to her knees.

Travers released his grip and took a step back after picking up the book, still containing the knife, in his right-hand.

'So, who are you, and who sent you?'

The brunette offered no reply.

'You want me to hit you again?'

She still offered no reply.

Harry was disappointed, but not a little surprised by the reaction, or lack of it. 'Haffenden sent you, didn't he?'

The girl looked up at him.

'Well, that answers that question!'

'You are dead and don't realise it. You think this is the end of it, this is just the beginning Travers, just the beginning!'

'The drugs didn't work, so now I get the personal touch!'

He looked into her beautiful brown eyes and saw pure hate, a perniciousness lurking, menacingly just below the surface waiting for any excuse to explode forth on whatever poor unexpected victim appeared on her radar.

In a previous life his heart would have sank at a sight of such animosity, but not now: 'Move and I'll-'

'And you'll what?'

Harry took a deep breath. Here was a conundrum which sadly required steely nerve and determination, coupled with abandoning hard-fought values for those of a more primal nature.

Without hesitation he hit her hard on the right side of her face with the fiercest left hook he could muster. She went out like a light. He put the book and knife in the oven.

Procrastination is the thief of time, to quote Charles Dickens, and Harry had only a little time to play with. He picked up the brunette and carried her to the ground floor before laying her down by the front door. He checked to see if she was genuinely out cold. Her breathing was slow and rhythmical. Harry was loath to leave her, but the car keys were upstairs in his jacket pocket.

He took two stairs at a time and was back on the ground floor inside a minute and badly winded a second later. Harry fell back against the hallway wall. A thunderous blow to the side of his head rendered him nearly unconscious.

'Idiot,' he said, as he slid down the side of the hallway wall. He could still make out the brunette unconscious on the floor, and that of a male voice, as the second blow put him down. The man walked calmly over to the brunette placed a cord around her neck, strangled her, and went to leave by the front door.

Travers summoned every ounce of strength to get to the girl; his overwhelming desire now was for her safety, but his legs failed miserably to respond to any demands to move and he crawled on all fours to the brunette. The man laughed, but never spoke. His job was done, and he quietly closed the front door as he left.

Harry felt for a pulse: 'Shit!'

Time was short, Travers gave himself five minutes.

He fell headfirst against the wall with his first attempt to pick up the brunette; the second was slightly more successful; the third achieved the success he craved.

Harry staggered to the backdoor, pulled open the door and fell into his rear-garden. He thought he could already hear the sirens. The night air cleared his head, bringing into sharp focus the dead girl now in his arms. Taking the Porsche was a no-brainer: they would pull him over within a mile. Harry picked up the brunette, threw her over the fence leading into next-door's garden, followed her within a second and dumped her body into his neighbour's recycling bin. Any lingering pain was forced to the back of his mind: Harry needed to tidy the house before the police arrived.

On first reflection his front-room looked normal, only if you paid particular attention to certain details within the decor could you tell there had been a recent altercation. Harry left it as it was and washed his face in the kitchen.

Three sharp knocks on his front door followed by a long ring of his doorbell signalled the beginning of Travers' greatest ever performance.

'Yes?' Harry said, pretending to have just been woken up.

A male voice informed him it was the police and requested he open the door.

Harry unlocked the front door.

Two police officers, one male, one female, gave Harry the once-over.

'Are you Mister Harry Travers?' said the male officer.

'I am.'

'May we come in,' the officer continued.

'Why?'

'We've had a report of domestic violence at this address!' added the female officer.

So that's your excuse for being here, thought Harry, in order to console my battered wife or partner.

'I live alone,' Harry replied filling the doorway.

'Can we come in?' the male officer asked again.

'I can't stop you.'

No, you cannot,' replied the female officer.

Harry stood to one side and waved them in.

He hoped his willingness to co-operate would sow the first seeds of doubt. The two officers followed Harry up to the first floor.

'You said you live alone,' the female officer said, while maintaining a steady gap between her and Harry.

'I do.'

Harry led them into the front-room. 'Do you mind if I sit down? I've had a long night.'

He didn't wait for a reply and slumped down on the sofa. The doorway where he slammed the brunette was unmarked; he was lucky no blood was spilt. It was a mistake by her killer to strangle her; if he had to do it all over again then slitting her throat would have sealed his fate: there would be no getting away from the forensic evidence in this room and a bloodied hallway downstairs.

Harry looked over at the oven. I hope they're not the cooking type, he thought.

The male officer stayed with him while the female officer searched his premises. Harry had not had time to investigate upstairs and prayed neither had the brunette.

The female officer returned with a resigned look on her face. Harry knew he was safe. The officer shook her head at her male colleague then set about searching the first and ground floors.

Harry felt smug, not with the officers, they were after all only doing their job and had every right to enter his house if they thought an offence had been committed that should result in an arrest. It was the unknown male Harry was thinking of.

'Something funny?' the male officer said seeing Harry smile.

'I was just thinking about the person who made the call,' Harry said, holding onto the smile.

'What about them?'

'I'm sure they're sitting at home, wherever that is, toasting my imminent incarceration.'

The female officer stood in the doorway to the front-room after she returned from the ground floor. 'You must have upset them pretty good!'

'I must have.'

'We will be making further inquiries as part of an ongoing investigation.'

'You have your job to do.'

'You said you live alone,' the female officer said again, 'but when was the last time you had company or guests?'

She was taking notes.

'Best you hear it from me,' Harry began, 'and you can ask the neighbours who will corroborate this, but the last female company who crossed my threshold was killed in a road traffic accident.'

'When was this?' asked the male officer. The female officer continued to take notes.

'Months back; she was rundown by a taxi after we were both assaulted by three men in a black car.'

Neither officer said a word.

'You have yet to make any arrests!'

'I can't comment on that,' answered the female officer.

'Ongoing investigation, I think is the expression,' Harry added.

'Something like that,' the female officer said, as she scribbled notes.

'You're not going to be asking me to accompany you down the station then?'

'I don't think that will be necessary,' replied the male officer, 'but we may need to talk to you again at a later date.'

'I understand.'

Harry stood and walked the two officers to the front door. Talking about Sheila and that night was breaking his heart.

'Thank you for your time, Mister Travers,' the female officer said.

'No problem,' he answered quietly.

He looked at her and she could see the tears welling up.

'She must have been special,' she added.

'She was.'

'We'll be in touch,' the male officer said before striding off to their patrol car. The female officer was reluctant to leave and studied Harry for a second or two; if she thought he was play-acting she was way wide of the mark.

Eventually she followed her colleague: 'Goodnight, Mister Travers.'

'Goodnight.'

Harry waited for them to leave before shutting the door. Once the door was closed, he hurried to the first floor and peered through the curtains. His eyes were still moist, and he struggled to focus on the street. His heart was aching. and he desperately wanted it to stop. Harry chastised himself for being weak then the split second later began to cry.

Ten minutes passed before Harry made his way to his neighbours recycling bin. Luckily for him they were out. Within ten minutes the brunette was back in his house wrapped in plastic sheet by the backdoor.

Harry turned all the lights out and sat on the bottom stair and waited. He checked his watch: it read 02:00.

* * *

Travers' watch read 04:00 when he reversed out of his drive. All had been quiet since the police officers departed.

He drove at a sedate pace enjoying the calming influence the 924 gave him.

Cantlay's property looked quiet; the old man had been discharged into the care of a female cousin. Harry cut the car's lights, pulled into Cantlay's drive and shut down the engine.

He held his breath and listened for engine noise. His heartbeat was racing. All remained quiet. The adrenaline rush heightened his senses to near biblical proportions.

Travers vacated the Porsche, lifted up the hood on his hoodie, opened the passenger door and carefully, and respectfully, lifted the brunette out of the Porsche and carried her to the door of that house, but not before checking for CCTV. He laid her down as softly as any human being could do to another. Harry did not wait or ponder on his actions. He was gone from the scene in seconds.

Once back at the Porsche Harry again paused and bent his ear to pick up the slightest engine noise. His heartbeat returned to normal.

Before Harry returned home, he gave Cantlay's house the once over.

* * *

It was a little past five in the afternoon when Harry called on the old man in Macclesfield after a morning flight to Malaga. Cantlay was pleased to see Harry and even more pleased when he heard his house was untouched. The cousin enquired after tea or coffee. The answer was tea.

'How's things with you?' asked Cantlay.

'Okay.'

'Don't kid a kidder!'

Harry paused.

'Someone you're looking for didn't want to be found, eh?'

'Something like that,' Harry said respectfully.

Cantlay knew it was best not to continue with this line of questioning.

'Have you seen Haffenden?' the old man said quickly and quietly. His cousin entered carrying a tray of tea and biscuits.

'You two catching up?' she said cheerfully.

Harry noticed there were two cups on the tray. The cousin placed the tray on a table within easy reach of them both.

'I'll leave you two to it.'

She closed the door softly behind her. Harry took a seat opposite the old man.

'In answer to that last question, I think so.'

'You think!'

'I can't be a hundred percent sure.'

Cantlay took a sip of tea. 'What exactly do you know about Haffenden?'

'Nothing, that helps.'

'What do you want to know?'

'Tell me everything!'

'Well, he likes to drug his victims first. I can personally vouch for that,' Cantlay said, laughing.

Harry laughed with him. 'What else you got?'

Cantlay pulled a file from beneath him and tossed it over.

Harry studied it in silence.

'It's all there,' Cantlay finally said after ten minutes of silence.

'You've been busy!'

'I knew him before he became the man he is, but in his arrogance Haffenden didn't remember me.'

'Wow!

'At first I was a little put out-'

'But not now!'

'No, now I'm just chilling the dish.'

Harry laughed again.

'What's your suggestion?'

'He likes his money, and he likes his women,' Cantlay answered in a deep tone, 'but the women especially.'

'I've seen his type and the way he treats them when they're no longer useful to him,' Harry said, flicking through the file a second time. He took a deep breath and sat back in his chair. 'Maybe he finally figured out who you were.'

'Maybe, but it was only going to be a matter of time......'

'Then you get poisoned,' Harry interjected.

'Yeah, after that you get poisoned,' Cantlay joked.

Harry looked back at the file.

'What's in here that Haffenden doesn't want to be made public?'

Cantlay drank some tea. 'That's for you to find out.'

Harry went back to page one.

'Take it with you. I don't want to see it again.'

'What you got planned?'

'Nothing; I'm going to sit here, recuperate, and then go on a nice, long holiday.'

'Don't kid a kidder.'

Cantlay smiled.

'I work alone,' Harry added, 'and there are times when it suits and times when it decidedly works against you. What I'm trying to say, very badly, is call me when your recuperation is over, and don't holiday alone.'

Cantlay agreed and the two men changed subject, drank more tea and did their best to eat his cousin out of biscuits.

Harry got back to the Porsche. It was going to rain: you could smell it. Harry loved days like these. He would go for a run tonight and clear his head: as well as Haffenden he still needed to find List, and he knew it would not take long for Haffenden to show his hand.

The street was full of parked cars. There was not a space to be found anywhere. Travers unlocked the 924 and deliberately dropped the car keys. There were two cars that were not parked in the street when he arrived. Both contained drivers. The car to his right was a white Ford, the one to his left a blue Vauxhall. They could both be for him, or neither could be waiting for his departure, but the brunette had two final jobs to do: one was to help Harry find List, it was too much of a coincidence for Haffenden and one of his girls to attack him on that night, and Harry didn't believe in coincidences; and secondly Haffenden needed his hand forced.

Travers righted himself and boarded the Porsche. He guessed the Ford and wanted to get a jump on them.

Harry pulled out into the road and accelerated hard.

Monotony can be the bane of most existences, but Travers' had become anything but tedious and repetitive, his life had become a series of never-ending car-chases, fights, flights and making enemies.

At the end of Blakelow Road Harry turned left onto Buxton Road towards Macclesfield. The Ford was the one to follow.

The road was clear, and he wasted no time pushing the Porsche past eighty. If Travers stuck to the A537 he could head West towards Henbury and pick up the A34 to the airport. Harry wasn't for heading home first off, he had some digging to do.

The Ford kept at a steady three car lengths back.

Henbury came and went. Harry wasn't concerned with the Ford: they knew where he lived, where to find him, but now they knew how he played their little game. The Ford would soon be a distant memory.

Halfway to Alderley Edge Harry took a quick detour to the right along a country lane. House prices were out of his league in this part of the country with most properties set back from the road, but this suited his purpose. The Ford stayed out of sight, but Travers knew where they were.

* * *

Harry walked slowly back to the 924 after his little detour with a brown leather bag in his right hand. In his left was the white Ford's little surprise. Why drive a car that could easily be seen on country lanes? Drive anything but a white car.

The Ford was empty, and Harry kept out of sight behind a hedgerow, waiting for their return.

A lean, athletic, gym rat casually walked over to the Ford and climbed aboard. Harry could see the man was a novice. He smiled, that was him only a short time ago. The man pulled out his mobile and dialled out. The sense of déjà vu was overwhelming.

Harry approached from behind, keeping out of his mirrors. The man spoke in an excitable voice, definitely a novice. Harry was angry, indignant even; how dare they send out a novice to keep tabs on him, possibly take him out if the occasion arose, and to add insult to injury he drove a white car.

Travers stood and walked around the driver's side and tapped on the window with the butt of the Smith and Wesson. The man's face drained of colour.

Impatiently he waited. The man just stared back at him.

'Either you lower the window or-'

The window was lowered.

'Your boss,' Harry said pointing to the phone.

The man nodded.

The Smith and Wesson's barrel never left the man's face. 'Hand me the phone.'

The man, after hearing an instruction from his boss, handed it over.

'Where's List?' Harry said straight off.

The voice denied knowing a List.

'How about I cap this son of a bitch in the head, leave ample evidence leading back to you and then fuck off!'

The man wet himself. His boss said nothing.

Travers took a gamble: he had never heard the man's voice before, but instinct kicked in: 'Haffenden, you've tried once, no, twice, to rub me out, so now it's my turn, either you hand over List or-'

'I don't know who this List is!' Haffenden snapped back.

'Then you better fucking find him then!'

The man fidgeted constantly, and it was beginning to grate on Travers' nerves.

A car on the road to Alderley Edge caused him to stand between the gun and the driver of the Ford. It took the man's left hand out of his line of sight, but a novice is a novice and if Travers had learnt anything in this line of work, there is little time or room for manoeuvre. He kept the barrel pointed straight at the man's temple.

Silence reigned.

The man didn't look at Harry or the barrel of the Smith and Wesson, but Harry knew what was coming long before the man thought of it.

'Your man has a death wish!'

Haffenden didn't reply; he was clearly waiting to hear what his man's intentions were.

The man looked at the barrel of the Smith and Wesson.

'Well, you feeling lucky, punk?' Harry couldn't help himself and laughed.

The man didn't appreciate his sense of humour.

'You are making life very difficult for yourself Mister Further, or Travers, was is it?'

Harry pictured Haffenden laughing.

Haffenden had told him what he wanted to know: 'I want List!'

'I'm sure you do.'

'You didn't find it then?'

Haffenden again didn't reply.

'Expecting me to lead you to it, or lead your client to it,' Harry added.

'We seem to have found ourselves in similar situations, Mister Travers.'

'I'm not interested in whatever it is your client has mislaid-'

Haffenden burst out laughing.

'Glad you find it funny!'

'Mislaid,' Haffenden said still chuckling away. 'You want your client back? We'll be in touch, and then the onus will be on you to deliver. Now kindly hand the phone back.'

Travers had no choice but to go with the flow. He tossed the mobile phone onto the man's lap, folded his arms to keep the gun out of sight, and backed off. The white Ford was on its way within seconds.

Baslow Drive, when he arrived, was a hive of activity: an elderly neighbour, who lived opposite, had left the chip-pan on and set fire to the house. Harry was cautious entering his: the fire, and the commotion it caused, would be the perfect cover to break-in. He slowly cleared each floor in turn.

'You wouldn't want a quiet life, now would you?' Harry said slumping down in the sofa with a mug of coffee.

A quiet life now would be the death of him: this existence was becoming his life blood, what he got out of bed for every morning, what drove his every action and thought.

10

The crew-room was once again a hive of activity; this was becoming the norm for his flights, but it did have one major advantage: Harry could enter quietly without fuss and get on with his duties at his own pace. A familiar voice interrupted that pace: 'You lucky man, you've got the pleasure of my company today!'

'How's the big boy's toy?'

'Doing its owner proud,' Curtis said grinning. 'What happened to your eye?'

'Slipped in the bathroom.'

'Ouch!'

The winter schedule was in full swing now with the majority of Travers' flights to the Canary Islands. Today was Lanzarote, the northernmost and easternmost of the autonomous islands and reputedly named after the Genoese navigator Lancelotto Malocello, whose name in Latin is pronounced Lanzarotus Marocelus.

The weather was forecast to be good with surface winds on the island from the Northeast.

Due to the engine failure procedure on take-off from the northerly runway requiring an early right turn away from the high ground the company dictated that the take-off should be performed by captains only, so Curtis flew the outbound leg from Manchester.

'So, how did you get the mark over your eye?' Curtis asked after an hour into the flight.

'Slipped in the bath.'

'Course you did.'

'I slipped in the bath, which-'

'Harry, everyone uses that "slipped in the bath excuse" when they want to hide the truth, hide what really happened.'

Should he tell the truth, or a version of the truth? He could easily tell a half-truth then embellish it with complete fabrications, and if anybody should ever enquire at a later date as to its authenticity he would simply concentrate on its truthful aspects and swear blind it was all true.

'I was free-fighting in a martial art lesson and got kicked in the face.'

'Seriously?'

'Yes, seriously!'

Well he did get in a fight, so there was the half-truth.

'Did you win?'

'Of course!'

Another lie: mendacity like nicotine is addictive.

'How's the love-life?' Harry asked, wanting to change the subject.

'Abysmal, how's yours?'

'Abysmal.'

Well, that didn't work as well as expected: he was still answering questions about himself.

'You know there's a certain someone onboard who has a serious soft spot for old Harry Travers.'

'Who?'

'Harry, you figure it out!'

He was a detective, of sorts, and here was a less than stressful case he could crack.

Harry smiled for all of a minute. The image of Sheila put paid to that, but for the first time he questioned how long he was going to mourn her loss; maybe these would be the first tentative steps towards that acceptance of life after Sheila, the first tentative steps towards normality. The smile returned with a vengeance: what was normality? Normality was being shot at, poisoned, stabbed and framed for murder.

'What's funny? Thinking of your secret admirer?'

'Wouldn't you like to know!'

It was Curtis' turn to exercise the facial muscles.

'Right,' Harry said with conviction, 'who is it?'

'Fuck off!'

'No, I'm serious.' Harry was determined to get a lead. 'Who is it?'

Curtis remained mute. He just looked at Travers with a blank expression.

The buzzer from the back cabin interrupted proceedings. Harry answered after handing over responsibility for the radios to Curtis.

It was the cabin manager Rebecca Standhope calling from the forward cabin asking if either one of them desired a drink.

Harry ordered a coffee, Curtis a tea.

After she'd rung off, he searched for any clue in Curtis' facial expression. There was none. It wasn't Rebecca.

A couple of minutes later another request came to enter the flight deck, and after checking the flight deck display of the Cockpit Door Surveillance System, Harry let the crew member enter.

Georgia Allen appeared carrying the two drinks in the obligatory configuration: one on top of the other.

She gave Curtis his drink first from over his right shoulder.

'There's that preferential treatment,' Harry joked.

Curtis smiled.

Harry received his from over his left shoulder.

Georgia was keen to get back to the passengers, but before she left Harry asked after them. They were all good was the reply.

After Georgia had departed, Harry realised Curtis was still smiling.

'No fucking way!'

'I'm not saying a word.' Curtis held onto the smile.

'You don't need to. She can't be more than twenty-two!'

'Twenty-three. I asked for you.'

'You asked for me?'

'I knew you'd want me to know.'

This was the quickest case Harry had solved, but how was he going to use this new-found information? When he left the house this morning his thoughts were occupied with List and Haffenden plus there was his imminent trip across the pond, but now there was Georgia Allen.

Georgia, on first reflection, was the complete opposite when he compared her to Sheila: she was dark-haired where Sheila was blonde; her eyes were green; her hair was short; and she seemed the quiet type. But Georgia Allen was a beauty and maybe, just maybe, she was perfect and everything he needed. He felt guilty and any smile evaporated.

Curtis read the situation perfectly: 'I can't pretend to know how you feel Harry, but surely there must come a time, if not now, where you've got to start living again, start dating again'

'I feel guilty just thinking about it.'

'I can appreciate that, but where's the harm?'

After a few minutes silence during which time he ran over and over in his head every conceivable excuse not to date again Harry answered: 'Got to get busy living, so I'll give her a reason to say no.'

'She's a good-looking girl.'

Harry wasn't going to argue with him on that point.

The only topic for discussion for the remainder of the outbound sector was left for the arrival into Arrecife Airport. Both men had been there many times and were comfortable with the arrival.

The weather over the Canaries was clear skies with forecast northerly surface winds. Harry was grateful for that: on a previous flight to this part of the world the surface wind swung round to the south in Lanzarote, and coupled with less than perfect weather conditions, caused most arrivals to divert to Fuerteventura, Las Palmas and Tenerife, as the weather was below limits for a landing on the southerly runway. The deteriorating visibility on the other islands, due to the southerly wind blowing in off Africa, caused the diversions to eventually get to a point where no more could be accommodated and the airspace over the Canaries was shut to any further traffic causing them to divert to North Africa.

Today was a stress-free day and their arrival into Lanzarote was totally uneventful.

A quick turnaround meant they pushed back off stand after exactly 55 minutes.

The inbound sector followed the outbound in respect to its eventfulness. Georgia never came into the flight deck and Harry made a conscious decision not to think about her. Four hours later Harry taxied the jet onto stand and readied himself to deal with Haffenden. The longer it took him to recover List from whoever had abducted him the more violent would have to be the repercussion.

Once both engines were shut down and the Parking Checklist was run Harry turned on his mobile phone. There were three messages. He didn't listen to them.

Harry wasn't always the most patient of people, but today he accepted that his second job would have to wait until he was in the comfort of his own surroundings, and that was going to take patience given the time it took to get to the staff car park followed by the drive home.

* * *

The kettle was on the split-second Travers entered his kitchen and the messages were played the split-second after he took that first sip of hot coffee.

It was an unknown male voice requesting his presence at a time to be decided by another phone call. It was the same message repeated three times. Travers was bitterly disappointed: he wanted, needed to lock horns with these undesirables.

He was getting really concerned about List. Calling his wife was out of the question: one he was still a suspect, of sorts; and two she might not know what he was up to and be blissfully unaware of his present predicament. More patience was called for. Thankfully, he was on standby for the next three days and was confident that he wouldn't get called, giving him three days to crack some heads. He thought of Georgia.

* * *

Harry gave himself a week, a week to get the List case put to bed. He checked all the local papers for any news on police raids breaking up drug rings. There were none. Then he searched again through known missing persons and cross-referenced them with Cantlay's description of clientele arriving and leaving that house. He ended up with three; they probably had nothing to do with List, but definitely with Haffenden, and Haffenden was involved with List. Harry needed to talk to the three families of the missing persons before he received another phone call.

The day went by without a call from Crewing and him being able to talk to two sets of relatives; Harry didn't lie, he just bent the truth by saying he was working for the family of a missing father whose case bore more than a passing resemblance to their loved ones. Travers learnt nothing new. His phone rang.

'Surprise me!' he said sarcastically.

'We want a car! Surprised enough?'

'I don't steal cars!'

'You will this one, or they'll find your client face down in a puddle,' the voice said with no small amount of malice.

'Where is it?' Harry knew very well where it was.

'List's place.'

'What car?'

'A silver Audi A8.'

That was a nice car, and to a petrol-head it was a fine car to have to steal. The voice read out the registration.

'We want it tomorrow at 8pm, the keys are on the driver's front wheel. We will call you with an address.'

'Why don't you steal it?'

The voice hung up.

Harry needed to work fast and take the car tonight, but where to hide it. The police would have a day to find it. The person who bought the car to List's clearly is not in a position to collect the Audi, so Travers was going to have to become a car thief. The thought excited him.

* * *

List's second-hand car dealership was quieter than a graveyard on Halloween night. Harry knew he was being watched, that was a no-brainer, which in itself was a blessing: any call to the police they would automatically know was not from him, and whatever it was they were desperate to get their hands on meant it wasn't from them either.

Harry approached the gate dressed all in black: there was no need to give someone an easy collar. He pulled out a small zipped up pouch, opened it, and removed his lock-picker's tool kit. The first padlock on the main gate was unlocked and off in seconds, the second at ground level in a little under a minute. The gate complained bitterly at being asked to operate at such an ungodly hour, but Harry needed it fully open and ran the gauntlet, praying no neighbourhood watch would be out this cold, crisp night.

The Audi fired up first time. Now was the moment of truth; a gate opening out of hours was one thing but followed in quick succession by a 4.2 V8 FSI engine springing into life was another thing all together. Harry was out of the yard and closing the gate within seconds. He toyed with the idea of leaving the gate open but abandoned it: if any neighbourhood watch should drive past then he needed them to see a closed gate. Only a true car thief would get out of the car and check the locks on a cold night.

He made the end of the road without being stopped. His heart was pounding out of his chest, but he was in control. The Porsche was parked a few streets up and well away from the scene of the crime.

Harry pulled onto the motorway and headed in a Westerly direction. He was still not a hundred percent sure where to park the car, and he was still being watched and no doubt followed.

He checked his mirrors at regular intervals, and it didn't take long for them to show themselves. Another novice, he thought, and he started to laugh, partly out of relief for not being apprehended and partly for finding himself in a familiar situation which revealed the answer to him: there were disused garages behind a row of shops in Outwood Road; one or two of them were in a dreadful condition, but empty, and ideal to hide a car. First though he had to lose the tail. With all these horses under the bonnet it shouldn't prove too difficult. Harry floored the accelerator.

The Audi was a seriously impressive car. The 430 HP V8 made light work of the car behind.

Harry took the A34 exit off the motorway and killed his lights. He was driving purely on autopilot. They would expect him to head for home and be waiting, but if you're going to fight a battle, fight it on your terms and on your ground. He turned right onto the A560 towards Gatley then left onto Church Road; this would lead him into Heald Green via Styal Road. He still kept his lights off. Traffic was light, not that he expected it to be heavy at this time of night.

Travers took a left into Finney Lane and Heald Green High Street. A left into Outwood Road meant he could enter from the North end. He made it without being seen and turned behind the row of shops minutes later. The third garage had no padlock. Fight your battles on your ground and on your terms. The Audi was a perfect fit. His mobile rang.

'Your man lost?'

'Don't play games with us, Mister Travers,' Haffenden said angrily.

'Where's List?'

'Where's the car?'

'You get the car when I get List!'

'Don't push me!'

'Then don't fuck with my clients!'

Haffenden took a second to absorb Travers' less than sympathetic response.

'Let's be professional about this, Mister Travers.'

Travers bit his tongue.

'You tell us where to make the exchange,' Haffenden went on, 'and we'll be accommodating.'

'Accommodating,' Harry repeated.

He looked at the number on his mobile's screen; it had to be a burner phone and the next number would be different. Here was an opportunity for a small, but significant, victory: make him keep the phone, it will knock him out of his stride for a short time and make the man concede ground. 'I'll call this number.' Harry hung up before Haffenden could reply then turned off his mobile in case they were trying to trace him via its position. Tomorrow he would get a burner and knock him off balance a second time.

Harry was careful to make sure he was not followed as he walked the well-trodden path to his front-door. At Baslow Drive he stopped and scoured each car in turn; he was getting better at this and quickly ascertained that none of the cars in view contained people, so they must be watching from a distance. The loaner was still parked where he left it. The walk home from the garage took fifteen minutes at best and to appear now would alert even a novice that the car was parked only a short distance away. Harry waited half an hour before navigating his way to his front door.

The house was warm, and cosy and it had the effect of making him sleepy. He tried to concentrate and remain alert, but it was a struggle. He made the kitchen before his eyes burned with tiredness and his head began to throb. The first floor was clear, and Harry trudged up the next flight of stairs to bed. God help anybody who had the temerity to cause any delay between him and his bed. He was asleep the split second his head hit the pillow.

* * *

Who wants a quiet life? That was the underlying message in Travers' dream, a dream guaranteed not to make for a refreshing night's sleep.

What was the meaning of it all? Was the big man upstairs trying to tell him something? He had always consciously, and would always consciously protect the innocent, those who were unable, for whatever reason, to protect themselves or their family. So why have a dream about a quiet life that was not wanted, requested, or sought? Harry was angry, but being angry with God gets you nowhere, fast. Maybe it was to show him the life that he could have if he packed it all in this instant, or at least until he got List back safely to his family. Harry made coffee, scrambled egg and bacon with lashings of tomato ketchup and contemplated being angry with God. It was futile and he knew it.

Breakfast hit the spot and fuelled him for his mini shopping spree.

He dressed casually in jeans, sneakers, a blue jumper and a dark leather jacket; if there was to be a fight along the way he wanted to be ready to move quickly without hindrance. Thirty minutes later Harry was the proud owner of a burner phone. At a nearby payphone he rang Haffenden. Any tail would relay his movements this morning, but he cared not a jot. He would soon disappear from their sight and collect the Porsche.

Haffenden was less than amused at having to wait for Travers to call. It brought a smile to his face. Harry arranged for the swap to take place somewhere public. He chose the Trafford Centre, today at 4pm.

* * *

The Trafford Centre was its usual self: busy. Harry parked near the cinema entrance and waited. He sent a text with his position and requested the registration of the car they were driving. No reply was forthcoming.

The Audi was parked between a BMW and a Mercedes, which was quite apt: keep all the German cars together.

Travers vacated the Audi and sauntered over to a spot where he could keep an eye on proceedings without being detected; an idiot he was not, even though he had been prone to doing idiotic things, like approaching his uncle's house in broad daylight.

A dark blue Mercedes crawled past the Audi. Harry watched it closely, but it never returned. Five minutes later a silver Skoda did the same thing, passing by from left to right. It reappeared soon after from the opposite direction. Neither of the two men inside were Haffenden. Harry scoured the car park, all the while trying to stay out of sight. He found neither Haffenden nor List.

The Skoda parked directly behind the Audi and a tall, slim, dark-haired man got out. He used a key to enter the car.

Travers left his hiding place and approached the Audi in a wide arc from the left-hand side. By the time Harry made the Audi the driver of the Skoda had no time to warn his colleague. The tall, dark-haired man exited the car carrying a small package. Harry hit him once across the jaw with a knife-edge strike. The tall man hit the deck, collapsing like a pack of cards. Harry kicked him hard in the solar plexus and relieved him of the package.

The driver of the Skoda left the engine running and didn't even close the driver's door. He managed to get three steps around the front of the Skoda before Harry threw a right hook, which he anticipated being blocked then caught him square on the jaw with a left-footed roundhouse kick. The driver collapsed even faster than the tall man, who was still on the floor.

That was far too easy, Harry realised far too late as he stepped back from the Skoda and bounced off the bonnet of a large black car. He finally came to a rest twenty feet from the point of impact.

Travers was hurt, and hurt bad, but he tried manfully to hide it. The black car hadn't moved since the collision and annoyingly nobody came to his assistance. Outside interference would have given him valuable thinking time and breathing space.

He finally got to his feet but could not hide the limp from his left side. It was all he could do to put weight on the leg. It was now he saw Haffenden's smiling countenance in the driver's seat of the black BMW. There was minor damage to the front of the car.

The tall man was on his feet and bearing down on him. In the short time at his disposal Harry tried out the leg. It was bearable, but his right side was fine. There was only one course of action open to him: he tucked the package into his belt and put all the weight on his right leg but kept up the pretence he was a sitting duck.

The tall, slim man threw a wild right haymaker. Harry jumped back but couldn't help but stumble due to his left leg. He just managed to keep upright before a second haymaker from the man's left clipped him on the top of the head. Harry felt a sharp, stinging pain rip through his left side. He bit his lip, put all his weight on his right leg and flicked a roundhouse kick with his left at the man's head. The top of the left foot impacted on the man's temple.

It stopped him in his tracks. Keeping his weight on his right-side Harry shot out a side kick to the man's ribs; he mistimed it, but it still hit the spot and winded him. The man dropped to a knee.

Harry hopped on the spot, keeping his left leg off the ground and studied the driver then Haffenden. Haffenden had a face like thunder. Harry laughed while still hopping. He beckoned the man to try and run him over a second time. Haffenden floored the accelerator pedal on the BMW, and there was a second when Harry thought he'd pushed his luck beyond all reasonable measure.

The car flashed past his left side: Haffenden had banked on Harry pushing off on his right leg and steered the car accordingly. The pain ripping through Travers' lefts side was temporary; the adrenaline helped null any discomfort arising from his launch to the right.

Harry ended up in-between two Fords. He heard Haffenden's aggressive application of the brakes and got to his feet in time to receive a body-check from the Skoda driver. He was back on the floor between the two Fords.

Travers kicked out at the man's nearest standing leg and he stumbled forward; with his body weight now bringing the man towards him, Harry kicked upwards into the man's chest and he flew off to the left, bouncing against one of the Fords. A loud voice immediately followed swearing oath after oath.

The owner of the Ford took the Skoda driver by the collar and dragged him off his car and punched him hard in the face. The driver's nose broke instantly.

Harry was desperate to get to his feet: the owner of the Ford was a big man and he was at a distinct disadvantage physically with this man.

The Ford driver turned on Harry and went for him until the tall, slim man arrived from his right and clocked the Ford driver with a perfect straight right. He collapsed like a house of cards in a strong wind. So much for size, thought Harry, but didn't dwell on the man's glass jaw. His problem was back with the tall, slim guy and Haffenden.

Haffenden appeared from behind the left of the two Fords. 'We've underestimated you, Mister Travers.'

'Thank you,' Harry replied, keeping an eye on each one.

'List is in the Trafford Centre. He will be allowed to leave when we're seen holding the package and driving away.'

'And I have your word on that!'

'You do.'

There comes a time when you have to trust someone, and that time for Harry was now: his leg hurt like hell and he would struggle to keep them off, but they also needed to get the hell out of here before the police arrived.

Harry tossed the package over to Haffenden.

Less than a minute later they were gone.

Harry limped over to the Trafford Centre after a few words of warning to the man with the glass jaw.

List met him by the nearest entrance: 'We'll get you to hospital!'

'No!'

List knew it was a crap idea: 'Yeah, you're right, but Harry you need medical attention.'

'Nothing's broken I just need rest.'

Harry pulled out the burner phone and handed it to List: 'Know any cab firms?'

List rang out and fifteen minutes later a Silver Skoda appeared from a local taxi firm. List gave his address.

The taxi driver asked after Harry but was informed by List that his friend fell down the escalator. The taxi driver advised suing the Trafford Centre.

Travers was in too much discomfort to worry about being tailed by Haffenden's men or whether they'd be waiting for him at

Baslow Drive; he'd deal with that if and when the time came. He closed his eyes and dozed.

He was woken by List's wife opening the rear passenger door; she was clearly relieved, angry and concerned in equal measure. List had some serious explaining to do.

He was led into the house by the wife after List paid the driver from emergency funds kept in the house.

As soon as the door closed, she got the full story from her husband: one of his salesmen, a guy named Harrison, had got himself caught up with some less than salubrious characters over some unpaid bills. Harry thought of gambling and Sheila's brother. To help pay the outstanding debts Harrison was to steal a car in which had been planted certain documents. He had no idea what or who these documents relate to, but they're obviously of an extremely sensitive nature. Well, Harrison disappeared; he's been gone weeks now. At first, he'd thought he'd just had enough of selling cars and didn't pursue it, but now it all makes perfect sense.

Harry and List's wife got all of this before they made the back of the house and the kitchen.

Harry sat at the kitchen table. The wife went to find the first aid kit. List went on talking.

Now that Harrison had done a bunk, and vanished into thin air, they suspected that he was involved, for Harrison had the foresight to move the package to another car, which is why they didn't know straight off which car it was and took to following him.

'Harrison's dead,' Harry said rubbing his side. 'How would they know which car to steal.'

The wife returned with the first aid kit.

'You need to go to hospital,' she said examining Travers' left side.

Harry undid his belt and pulled his trousers off his left hip while lifting his shirt. The bruising was bad. He had a cut over his left hip.

'My wife used to be a nurse,' List added.

'No doctors,' Harry said quietly, but forcibly.

'You'll need some sort of physiotherapy. What happened by the way?' List's wife asked.

'He got run-over,' answered List.

'Run-over!'

'It could be worse-.' Harry didn't get chance to finish.

'How?' said the wife, sarcastically.

'It could have been a Skoda!'

The wife did what she could with the limited resources at her disposal.

'Can any of your friends help?' List asked of his wife.

'I wouldn't put them on the spot, it's not fair.'

'I'll be fine,' interposed Harry. 'I just need time.'

'There is a way we could get you some help, it's a bit unorthodox, but it might help.'

'You've got my attention,' Harry said wincing, as he adjusted his position in the seat.

'There's a lady I know who runs a therapy clinic for dogs. She has a pool the dogs use for therapeutic and assisted swimming: it helps aid their recovery.'

'You're the second person who wants me to walk around a dog pool!'

'It will aid your recovery and keep you out of hospital.'

'Will she not ask questions?' butted in List.

'No!' his wife answered abruptly.

'You can be sure of that?'

'Her brother needs help,' she replied looking straight at Harry.

'What kind of trouble?' Harry found himself intrigued.

'You can ask her yourself,' she replied, dressing Travers' wound.

List went to a drawer and pulled out an open pack of ibuprofen and handed it to his wife: 'I knew you'd ask me.'

She took the pack and handed two to Harry. 'You forgot the water!'

'Can't remember everything,' List said smiling at Harry while pouring him a glass of water.

'You're both remarkably cheerful,' Harry said before swallowing two tablets with water.

'I'm alive,' List said.

'He's alive,' the wife said straight after.

* * *

Harry prayed his standby duties would stay standby duties. His prayers were answered. He now had two weeks' leave and a trip across the pond for the enquiry into Jeffries' death. Two weeks leave would give him ample time to recover. Harry pulled a small card from his jeans pocket: it was a business card for the dog rehabilitation clinic. He made the call. He was eager to hear what kind of trouble her brother was in.

A lady with a soft voice answered the phone. Harry introduced himself. Before he could finish the lady admitted she knew who he was and why he was ringing.

'How bad is your leg?' she said.

'It's not my leg-'

'What is it then?'

'It's the whole left side from the ribs downwards.'

'Ouch!'

'Yeah, that and other four-letter words were uttered.'

The lady laughed. 'When do you want to come over?'

'Today or tomorrow, is that okay?'

'I have a free slot tomorrow at eleven, will that suit?'

'Eleven is perfect.'

The lady gave Harry detailed instructions on how to find her and then rang off wishing him a nice day.

* * *

The lady's address was a detached house on Giantswood Lane on the way to Congleton. It was impressive.

Harry parked the 924 in her drive. Luckily for him nobody had touched the Porsche while he was away dealing with Haffenden and the taxi fare wasn't as dear as he anticipated. He still had the loaner as a back-up.

She met him at the front door: she was an attractive lady with shoulder length dark-hair, brown eyes, that seemed to interrogate his every move, slim build and standing a little over five feet three inches. Harry needed to be on his guard; for the first time since Sheila he had met a lady that definitely flicked his switch.

'Hello, my name is Jane Bellings.' She held out her hand for Harry to take, which he did eagerly.

'Harry Travers,' Harry replied, and gently squeezed her hand.

She stepped aside and waived him in.

The hallway was bright and airy and smelt of freshly cut flowers. Another gardener thought Harry. The door closed behind him and he was unnerved for all of a second.

'I watched you vacate your car and studied your limp, Mister Travers. You definitely favour the right leg.'

'Yep!'

'Car accident, I was told.'

'Run-over!' Harry turned to face her: he wanted to see Jane's reaction.

'How painful is it?'

'I can't go to hospital,' Harry said still gauging her reaction.

'I heard.'

It didn't matter to this lady one bit if Harry was in trouble; clearly Mrs List had asked for a favour and Jane Bellings was going to give it.

'Follow me into the back,' she said walking past Harry towards the kitchen.

'Absolutely!' he replied, hoping it would get a suitable response. It didn't.

The kitchen contained a vase of freshly cut flowers. The smell was intoxicating.

Jane led him through the kitchen and towards a set of French windows. Harry could see the garage off to the right. The French windows were not locked and swung outwards into the rear garden. Jane held them open for him and he naturally gravitated towards the garage. It was the logical place to run her type of business. He stopped short of the side door leading into the garage.

Jane produced a key from her jeans pocket and unlocked the garage. She entered first. Strange, he thought: the French windows into the house were unlocked, but the garage was not. Did she have something to hide? Surely there wasn't much worth stealing. Who would steal a rehabilitation pool full of water?

She put on the light and Harry saw for the first time the pool the dogs used for their therapeutic and assisted swimming programs. It was no different really from a small swimming pool, only this one had a ramp for the dogs to walk up before jumping into the water to get the muscles working, stretching and building strength and confidence without putting too much strain on the dogs' body.

'Did you bring a swimming costume?'

Harry had forgot, he was only going to get a feel for the place and didn't expect to literally jump straight in.

'No, I forgot.'

'No problem, I've got some spare.'

It was only now that Harry noticed no wedding ring; so much for being the great detective.

Harry couldn't quite picture himself in budgie smugglers.

Jane produced a pair of swimming trunks from a drawer that were happily for him not budgie smugglers. 'Try these for size. You can change in the house, there's a changing room next to the kitchen.'

Harry took the trunks. 'So, all I do is walk or shuffle on my knees around the pool?'

'You can float on your back and work the leg muscles if that suits; it all helps with the recovery!'

'Okay.'

Harry felt a complete idiot wearing a stranger's pair of swimming trunks along with the thought of shuffling around a canine's therapy pool, but was the alternative?

Over the next half-an-hour Harry exercised his badly bruised left side using the therapy pool. He tried to focus on the benefits of such a treatment, but each time he thought he was getting anywhere, all he could think of was how much he'd love to see Jane Bellings in a swimsuit and what he'd love to do to her in one. It was strange for him to entertain such thoughts for he never felt anything like the guilt he would have expected. It was a sign that a corner had been turned.

'Can I book another appointment?' Harry asked while drying himself off.

'You enjoyed it then?'

'Immensely: I can see how the dogs must love it!'

'Once they've had a session you can see in their little faces how much enjoyment they get out of it, and of course it aids their recovery.'

'That should be your catchphrase: it aids their recovery.

'It's not a bad one, is it?'

'It's aiding mine. You are aiding mine,' Harry added putting down the towel.

'Good.'

'Now, what kind of trouble is your brother in?'

Jane Bellings' smile evaporated in an instant.

'Don't worry, everything we say is confidential. Your brother will not hear of this.' Harry was in serious shit mode.

'Stealing cars and joyriding!'

'That figures.'

'My brother is only nineteen and thinks he's bulletproof, thinks nothing or nobody will get him and he's smarter than everybody else-'

'Let me get changed, Jane, and you tell me all about it over a coffee. How's that sound?'

It sounded good.

The coffee was hot, and the strength Harry liked. He sat at the kitchen table without invitation. Jane didn't seem to mind.

'A friend says you're a private investigator, of sorts,' Jane said sitting in the chair to Harry's left. She didn't sit opposite. His heartbeat went up by twenty beats a minute; Harry tried surreptitiously to slow it down with controlled breathing, but it was a fruitless task and he gave up very quickly.

'His name is Mark, like I said nineteen: that age where everything seems acceptable, even breaking the law; he recently got involved with what I can only describe as a gang that goes around stealing cars and going for joyrides.'

'He's not been caught yet?'

'Not yet! But that's only a matter of time.'

'Do you know if the cars are stolen to order?'

'No, I'm afraid I don't.'

'Stolen to order indicates they're working for somebody, who themselves would have a boss.'

Harry sipped hot coffee. Jane did the same. It gave the conversation a natural break.

'We'll set him up!'

'What?'

'We'll set him up. He can steal a car. Mister List will loan us one, one he doesn't mind getting a wee bit of damage, and we'll catch him in the act and scare the shit out of him. What do you think?'

'Yeah, sure, if you think it'll work.'

'If it doesn't you've got a career criminal for a brother,' Harry said going back to the coffee.

'How much do you want?'

'Nothing!'

'Nothing?'

Harry went for it: 'You'll have dinner with me.'

Jane blushed: 'Dinner?'

'With me, those are my terms.'

There was a second when Harry thought he'd spectacularly crashed and burned.

'Okay,' she said holding a half-smile, a half-smile that Harry thought, hoped, would erupt into a full-blown cheesy grin.

Harry fought off a cheesy grin of his own.

He knew not to outstay his welcome and so finished off his drink, stood and held out a hand. He felt a fool but didn't know why. He had only asked her to dinner.

She shook his hand.

'I'll call you when the trap's been set,' he said holding onto her hand longer than necessary.

She kissed him on the cheek. He wanted more. He knew the guilt would come and overwhelm him, but in the moment, he yearned for more. She sensed it and looked straight at him.

'Thank you,' she said softly, 'and I'm partial to Italian.'

'Great, I love Italian.'

'But I can't recommend anywhere though.'

'Leave it with me.' The guilt arrived in all its glory and his smile vanished.

Harry gently pulled away his hand and started for the front-door. He needed to be gone, he needed the comfort of his 924; funny how something as simple as driving a car lifted the spirit.

The Porsche started right on cue. He waved to Jane who stood in the doorway watching his short walk to the 924. He pulled away and let out a long, slow breath. Now to deal with the guilt and fight any melancholy daring to ruin the rest of his day.

Jane Bellings was the first woman who had aroused anything within him since Sheila's death and Harry counted the number of days since he'd lost her. There needed to be more. He would take his time setting up Mark. Any guilt quickly subsided. Anyway, he reminded himself, he had the trip to America to arrange and that would naturally delay any plans.

* * *

Harry used Delta Airlines again out of Heathrow for his next trip across the pond to Atlanta. He emailed Tommy with all his travel plans; it had been months since they last conversed, but you wouldn't have known by the tone of the correspondence. Harry was eager to see his friend again.

The days leading up to his departure were quiet and Harry was grateful for that: he failed to realise how fatigued he was becoming. It was all in own fault. This trip was just what the doctor would have ordered.

Harry called List as he stood in line waiting to board. It was a follow up call to an earlier one just to confirm all arrangements would be in place for Jane's brother when he returned; Travers was not shy coming forward with his globetrotting exploits, solving crimes around the world. List would tell his wife who would tell

Jane. He looked skyward briefly and thought of Sheila, praying she would understand. He missed her terribly, but life, he was now telling himself, had to go on. Harry fought off any arguments that he was using life as a lame excuse to chase Jane Bellings. He repeated over and over until the guilt subsided that life is our greatest of gifts and every second must be treasured, as if it's your last.

The image of Sheila flying through the air after impacting the taxi filled his thoughts. The smile that followed the tears was for the revenge he took. For that he felt no guilt.

He wiped away the tears and placed the duty-free bag containing the obligatory bottle of Jack Daniels on the floor. His emotions were in turmoil: one second apologising for even considering Jane Bellings and daring to forget Sheila; the next urging him to live life to the full and arguing that living a fulfilling life was not to be misinterpreted as forsaking a woman he deeply loved.

Harry boarded for Atlanta.

11

There would be no hire car to Athens on his arrival in Atlanta: Tommy was insistent he was going to collect him in person.

Once Harry passed through Immigration, he collected his luggage and made his way to where Tommy told him he was parked up.

'You splashed out!' Harry said on eyeing the gleaming metallic gold Chevrolet Colorado.

'She's a 5.3 litre, V8.' Tommy couldn't hide the smile only hinting at the joy driving this truck was giving him.

Harry climbed aboard. It was the kind of truck he could envisage driving one day. The Colorado's General Motors 5.3L V8 kicked out 300hp at 5200 rpm with 320 lb-ft of torque at 4000 rpm; the Direct Fuel Injection and Variable Valve Timing optimized power and efficiency. Tommy gunned the Colorado into life. Harry was hooked.

He lowered the passenger's side window and took three deep breaths and let the moment take him to that place where only the soul knows it can find peace: Harry loved America.

'You certainly know how to build trucks,' he said after ten minutes of blissful tranquillity.

'She's a beauty, alright.'

'So, tell me about Uncle Jack. I'm afraid I've been a bit busy to keep up to date with recent developments.'

'It's not looking good, Harry. It's not looking good.'

'I only have what my lawyer told me, which is to be here, as requested.'

'They're going to charge him with murder.'

'What!'

'They say that he could have disarmed Jeffries and didn't need to kill him,' Tommy said never taking his eyes off the road, 'and they've got a point.'

'I suppose,' Harry replied quietly, so quietly in fact that Tommy barely heard him over the road noise.

'This is a preliminary hearing, yes?' Harry asked.

'That's right. It's really to see if there is a case to answer and if there's sufficient evidence for them to prosecute him.'

'Why has it taken so long?'

'Gathering evidence; I've been grilled over the affair!'

Harry took three more deep breaths; he needed to get back to that place where the soul needs peace. 'But why have they not contacted me? I was there for fuck's sake!'

'But if he's admitted to it, they're not going to need any statement off you, are they? If he's admitted to picking up a gun, from a known hiding place around the house, and shot Jeffries stone dead he's going to get charged, regardless of the fact that he was held hostage, presumed dead and withheld medication that would probably have killed him anyway!'

'They charge him with murder, looking for a manslaughter charge, and get a conviction. And of course, there were no extenuating circumstances,' Harry said, quietly seething.

Both men sat in silence for a few minutes each with worry for a friend and relative etched across their features.

'Hungry?' Tommy asked.

'Famished, you thirsty?'

'Throat's as dry as a desert.'

'What will be, will be,' Harry said as a way for both of them to reluctantly accept the way things were. 'I'm sure Uncle Jack will give them hell!'

'You better believe it!'

The two friends moved the topic of conversation onto their respective adventures since Harry's last visit. It took huge chunks out of the drive-time to Tommy's place and each was grateful when it came into sight. Harry was itching to put a dent in the bottle of Jack Daniels, as much as Tommy was. Since Sheila's passing his sobriety was one topic he was not going to share with Tommy. Tonight, he was going to get wasted.

* * *

The feeling of déjà-vu was overwhelming: Harry woke up to find himself half on, half off, the sofa, staring at the ceiling. Tommy's snoring could be heard through the wall and a closed bedroom door. Harry rolled onto the floor.

'Fuck!'

He'd been here before alright.

His head swung from left to right and back to the left; he was out of drinking practice. His abstinence had seriously lowered his resistance to alcohol. This was not a bad thing in his line of work.

Harry finally made the kitchen, gave serious thought to throwing up in the kitchen sink, but decided to make a strong coffee instead. Tommy was still snoring.

The kitchen was ergonomically friendly. Harry was impressed at the ease at which he found all the necessary ingredients to make coffee.

'Come on!' he said impatiently. The coffee percolator was taking its own sweet time.

Tommy stopped snoring.

'You read my mind.' The hoarse voice of his American host mirrored his own.

'Don't know about you, but I'm getting too old for this shit!'

Tommy laughed.

'I forget: milk, cream, sugar?'

'Milk, two sugars,' Tommy replied, leaning on the kitchen worktop with his head in his hands.

'That bad?'

'That bad!'

Harry made two coffees. If there is one nation that can be said to be connoisseurs of coffee, it is the Americans. Harry did his best to live up to expectations.

'Breakfast?' Tommy managed to get out between sips of coffee and dropping his head in his hands.

'Ham and eggs will do just fine,' Harry said laughing.

'What's so funny?'

'I feel like shit!'

'Ham and eggs, it is then.'

Harry nodded and then dropped his head into his hands.

'A pain shared is a pain halved,' Tommy added seeing Harry adopting a similar posture.

'It's a problem halved is a problem shared.'

'Pain seems more apt right now!'

The two men attempted to stand up; Harry managed to remain an upright for all of a minute before seeking the aid of the sofa; Tommy ended up with his head back in his hands.

* * *

Jack Hennessey was due to have his hearing at the General Sessions Court in Athens, Tennessee on the Thursday, which gave the two of them a couple of days to kill. Harry wanted to see his uncle, but he wasn't keen to see anybody else at this time.

'He's going to see himself as the victim twice over,' Harry said as they left Tommy's residence.

'Wouldn't anybody?'

'The Boyd clan are still keeping themselves scarce then?'

'Nobody can find them; it's like they've just vanished off the face of the earth!'

'The trouble is the authorities need us to supply the evidence to convict them, which in turn convicts us!'

'Exactly!'

Tommy pulled up outside his Uncle Jack's house, which was still the way he remembered.

Harry got out first and headed straight for the house; he heard Tommy shut the driver's door and knew he was but two or three paces behind him.

Uncle Jack opened his front door and stepped out onto the front porch to greet them.

'You took your time!' the old man shouted.

'You losing your hearing?' responded Harry.

'No, I just wanted the neighbours to know you're late!'

'Love you too uncle,' Harry added stopping one pace short of the porch.

Tommy appeared by his side right on cue: 'I'm with him, Jack,' he added, slinging a thumb in Harry's direction.

'You two can fuck off!'

'And how shall we fuck off oh great one?' Harry tried to keep a straight face but failed miserably.

'You can go off people you know,' Uncle Jack said turning on his heels and heading back inside.

Harry and Tommy followed. Tommy shut the door.

Travers began to accept that all future conversations, regardless of whoever they were with, would end up taking place in the kitchen.

'Coffee please,' Harry shouted out.

Tommy wasn't for being left out: 'Make that two!'

Uncle Jack failed to reply, but when they finally caught up, he was fulfilling his coffee making duties.

'Nervous,' Harry asked. He was watching his uncle closely.

'No, should I be?

'No one would blame you.'

'The bastards are out to get me, no matter what I do, and when you eventually accept that everything becomes plain sailing: decision making is easy.'

'Isn't that a bit defeatist?' Tommy said taking a clean mug from a row of them standing serenely on the kitchen counter.

Uncle Jack liked the minimalistic design and the entire house reflected that taste.

Both men refused to take a seat and leant with their backs against the kitchen worktop.

'When your time is up, your time is up!'

'Oh, come on!' It was Harry's turn to air his displeasure.

'What do you want me to do? I shot the bastard and I shouldn't.'

'What were you to do?'

'When the charge was read out at my initial arraignment I pleaded not guilty because I honestly believe that I am not guilty of murdering Jeffries, but Harry I could have made him drop the gun, I could have, but I was so incensed I shot him dead instead.'

Uncle Jack made coffee.

'What's your lawyer say?' Harry asked once his uncle had placed a hot mug of coffee in front of him.

'To expect the worse, and don't get my hopes up; this is going to trial, as they cannot be seen to let somebody off with blatantly killing another human being even though the stupid fucker deserved it. The rule of law applies!'

Harry sipped his coffee. 'I'm not going to ask what bail was set.'

'Good!'

Tommy said nothing. Uncle Jack handed him a mug.

'Wow,' Harry said solemnly between sips, 'wasn't expecting this: thought all the way over here it was just going to be a formality and we would be in court no more than ten to fifteen minutes then go down the pub for a drink.'

'There's no jury involved son, just a solitary judge and I'm told they can take minutes, or up to two hours. I have not waived my right to a jury, which is another reason this will go all the way.'

Tommy added his weight to the conversation: 'The judge must find that there is sufficient evidence to provide probable cause to believe that a crime has been committed.'

'And there has, and I did it,' Uncle Jack said drinking his hot brew, 'and I don't give a shit if it goes to trial, I want my day in court. Like I said before, decision making has been made easy.'

'They don't want to hear from me then?' Harry asked, not sure whether he should feel aggrieved or not for being here.

'No, you don't need to be here as far as I can see.'

He would have come regardless; there was no way Harry could let his uncle go through this alone.

'You both want to stay the night? I got a fridge full of beer.'

That was a no-brainer.

* * *

The court was half-full when Harry entered alone. Tommy was off talking to some guy he hadn't seen for years. His uncle appeared shortly after with his lawyer. She was an attractive, slim woman with short blonde hair whose body language oozed confidence. Uncle Jack was comfortable in her presence.

The judge entered and everybody stood. The whole affair was very formal and conducted in a matter of fact kind of way one expects of law courts.

Harry was fascinated by the whole affair: preliminary hearings were like minitrials where the prosecution presented its case, called witnesses, for the defence to cross-examine, and introduced evidence. It was obvious very early on that Uncle Jack's lawyer could or did not object to certain evidence being presented, even if that evidence could not be presented at a subsequent trial.

The hearing lasted exactly one hour and twenty minutes by Harry's watch, and he was placing his money on the judge concluding there was probable cause to believe a crime was committed by the defendant and a trial date would be scheduled.

'This is a complete waste of time,' Harry whispered sarcastically.

He paid close attention to the back of his uncle's head, making a mental note of any nervous twitches when he leaned over to discuss anything with his lawyer and whenever the focus was switched to the prosecution lawyer.

The judge was patient, listening to all the arguments for and against his uncle and the need to go to trial. Harry had no legal expertise, but even he knew that this case was going to trial, and this was reflected in his uncle's physical discomfort: he leaned forward when evidence was set out against him then sat back when his own lawyer cross-examined; these movements were punctuated with seemingly disinterested examinations of the court itself and its occupants. He even looked bored on occasions. How could you be bored when your life and liberty were at stake?

Harry wondered what the sentence was for manslaughter in the state of Tennessee. Only now did he study those in the courtroom, especially those showing any interest in his uncle's inevitable journey to trial. One individual caught his eye. By his very appearance he knew who he was reporting back to. Should he follow? He would need a hire car, but that was out of the question. Another hire car returned with extensive damage would probably bring him up in front of this judge.

Self-chastisement is a necessity in this line of work and Travers took a second to give himself a severe talking to: not everybody was guilty, even if they looked and played the part to Academy Award nomination standard, and until the particular individual, or individuals, committed a crime he should leave them well alone. Travers sat back suitably rebuked.

The court proceedings reached the unavoidable truth and the judge announced that Jack Hennessey would stand trial for the murder of Anton Jeffries, based on the evidence presented in his court. Harry let out a sigh. 'What a surprise.' A quick look over his shoulder at Tommy sitting a row further back slammed home the realistic possibility of his uncle spending the rest of his life behind bars: Tommy was on the verge of crying.

Harry studied Sheriff Poulsen who had seated himself on the opposite side of the courtroom and a row in front of him. The man never made any eye contact.

Travers was angry: why had he not been called to give evidence? If anybody should have it should have been him. It could only have been his uncle not wishing him to be on the stand. Why? But the prosecution hadn't called him either. He could surely undermine their case and put that element of doubt in the judge's mind.

This would now go to a formal arraignment where Jack Hennessey would plead not guilty. Harry might struggle to get the time off. He left the courtroom. Tommy stayed put.

The hallway was cool when compared to the courtroom and Harry took a seat. Was Jack Hennessey the kind of man to feel guilty with his life in its autumn years? Was he trying to balance the books with the almighty and try and make amends for his past indiscretions? Uncle Jack was the kind of person to have plenty of skeletons in closets scattered here and there.

Uncle Jack exited the court, with his lawyer by his side, carrying the broadest of grins. It was that funny was it? Maybe he was trying to ameliorate his standing with the Lord.

Well, that's me fucked, thought Harry. There were five names on his list, five souls dispatched to the next world with a smile and a cheery wave. Only Harry couldn't have given a damn one way or the other what new experiences they navigated to the next world

'That went well,' Jack Hennessey said cheerfully.

'You think,' answered Harry.

'Depends on your point of view,' the old man added, smiling.

'Uncle, my point of view is this should never have gone to trial. This is a travesty!'

'Son, rule of law applies. I killed the son of a bitch and have to answer for it.'

Tommy was noticeable by his lack of input. Harry had not seen him leave the court, but now they shared the briefest of looks.

'Who's hungry?' Hennessey asked.

'I have a little time,' the lawyer said, looking straight at Harry; she had a husky 40 cigarette-a-day voice that Harry loved, but he loved a woman he would never be able to love, touch, or hear laugh again, and it hurt.

'Vanessa McVeigh,' the lawyer said, holding out her hand.

They shook hands. It was all very formal.

'McVeigh,' Harry said, 'is that Irish?'

'It is, but sadly I have yet to set a foot in Ireland. It's on my bucket list.'

'Anybody got a preference?' butted in his uncle, not that it stopped anything developing.

'Steak,' Tommy said crisply, taking a sizeable step towards Miss McVeigh.

Harry backed off and looked up and down the corridor for the guy from the courtroom. He found him at the far end staring straight back at him.

The man lifted his right hand, turned it into the shape of a gun and pretended to shoot Harry.

Travers smiled a devilish smile and refused to blink. The man shook his head. Harry winked at him.

'Anything wrong?' Tommy said quietly and followed his line of sight.

'Do you know him?' Harry asked.

'No, but I'll find out.'

The man was not for locking horns with both men and left.

'I can take an educated guess.'

'You don't need to be Einstein,' Tommy whispered.

'It makes life interesting, very interesting.'

Tommy's smile was one to be cherished: 'Don't know about you Harry, but I'm in need of a little sport.'

'Nancy's got a score to settle.'

'Nancy Boyd wouldn't dare show her face around here for fear of Littlehorn chasing after her.'

'Surely the police can find them?'

Tommy took a deep breath; this was clearly a topic keeping him awake at night: 'The police have more important things to do than chase after suspects in a murder, and I use that term respectfully, when the prime suspect has already admitted to the crime.'

'Budgets don't stretch that far, eh?'

'Nope!'

The last part of the conversation was said quietly, and out of earshot of Harry's uncle.

'Let's get a bite to eat,' Harry said.

Tommy agreed.

* * *

Jack Hennessey's choice of eatery was a steakhouse in the middle of town offering the best steak in Tennessee, which was a boast-and a-half.

'There is nothing like a good steak,' he told them all, 'after a hard day in court.'

Vanessa laughed.

Harry was eager to find out when the court date would be set.

'They'll be another hearing,' Vanessa said.

'Do you need me here for that?' Harry knew the answer to the question but wanted to hear it from Vanessa.

'No, you don't have to.'

'I'll be here for the trial, just let me know the dates as soon as you can.'

'He would appreciate that; he won't tell you but know he'd very much like you with him.'

Clearly Vanessa McVeigh had sussed out Jack Hennessey.

Uncle Jack during this short confab had been talking to their waitress and she led them to a table. He was right about one thing: court proceedings made you ravenous.

Vanessa sat next to Harry with Jack and Tommy opposite.

The waitress took their drinks order and handed out menus.

Steak, Harry wanted steak and right there in front of him was a picture of a delicious T-bone steak just crying out to be ordered. Harry ordered his with pepper sauce.

If this was all there was to see at the present time regarding Uncle Jack's case then Harry was taking a few days' R&R before heading home early to check up on Jane Bellings' brother; find out whether Tony had been the recipient of any further visits; and send a broadside across Haffenden's bow with the help of his less than friendly neighbour.

Harry would call Delta later and change his ticket onto an earlier flight.

It was a glorious two days' fun filled with copious amounts of alcohol, sun and great mirth coupled with some much-needed shooting practice. Harry had not lost his touch: the spread was still as large as his hand. The date for the trial was still to be set, but he took a gamble and booked some dates off as leave.

When the day came to leave, he called List while Tommy drove him to the airport. His phone was engaged. Jane Bellings' was also engaged. Harry contemplated ringing Tony but decided against it.

Tommy was not one for long drawn out goodbyes and the two friends parted company with a handshake and a hug.

* * *

Travers dumped his bags on the kitchen floor and read the post he'd collected off his doormat – it was all junk mail and bills, nothing but rubbish.

His mobile phone burst into life. It was List.

'How are things?' Harry said, starting a conversation deliberately with a question.

'Good: everything's been quiet, that salesperson and my partner have not returned, or surfaced anywhere.'

'Excellent. I need to return your car, or do you want to use that for the sting?'

'Just return it. I've got a newer one just waiting for you to come and pick up,' List replied joyfully. 'By the way Harry, what do you reckon was in that package stored in the car?'

'It wasn't drugs. Probably a ledger of some sort containing incriminating evidence on a number of high-ranking people, that's my guess.'

'That would explain a lot.'

List had Harry's attention: 'Like what exactly?'

List paused.

There was a second when Harry believed his former client wasn't going to answer. He thought about repeating the question but paused himself.

'There were two or three visitors while I was incarcerated - they were clearly of great importance for they were shown great reverence.'

'Interesting!'

'I tried to remember their faces and took to drawing mental sketches. I became pretty good at it.'

'Can you draw those sketches?'

'You think you might know them?'

'No, but I know a man that might.' Harry was trying hard to hide his excitement.

* * *

List was busy drawing when he entered his office, and by the reams of paper littering his desk had been at it for quite a while.

Any joy?' Harry asked, studying one of List's efforts. He placed the loaner's keys on the desk next to another set.

'Look like anybody you might know?'

There was a feint familiarity about one of them, but not something you would write home about.

'No, nothing concrete,' he said with an air of disappointment.

'Here, try this one.'

List slid a drawing across his desk.

Harry picked it up and a chill descended the length of his spine: before leaving the house, he had read over the reports given him by Cantlay and here was a sketch matching one of the descriptions Cantlay made. He called him 'PM', as he only arrived in the afternoon and was gone by 5pm.

'Can I take this?'

'Sure, any use to you?'

'Oh, yes.'

List was eager to learn more.

'I need to talk to a man first.'

'Anybody I know?'

'No, but I'll be in touch once I've spoken to them. What else you got?'

List supplied Harry with three more sketches; neither had the same impact as the one in his hand.

'I'll be in touch,' he said before picking up the new set of car keys and executing an about turn.

List never replied.

* * *

The drive to Cantlay's, after he'd dropped the new car off, was nothing short of reckless: Harry fell only a fraction short of thrashing the 4 cylinder, 125hp VW engine, but she held up fine and delivered him right on cue to Cantlay's in double quick time.

Cantlay opened is front door when Harry was three steps short of it: 'Knew you'd be back.'

'I've got something to show you.'

Harry walked past him and headed straight for the kitchen. Cantlay followed closely behind.

He pulled out the sketch, given to him by List, and handed it to the old man. The adrenaline surged through his veins. He loved that buzz.

'Recognise him?'

Cantlay gave the drawing the once over: 'Always arrived in the afternoon.'

'You called him 'PM'!'

'Left at 5pm, and no later!'

'Anything else you can remember?'

'He always wore that superior air, liked he owned the place, which he probably did.'

'Another client has said that 'PM' was high ranking.'

'I shan't ask who this client is.'

'I'd never tell you, but you have a right to know where the sketch came from.'

'We need to know where Haffenden stands in relation to 'PM'.'

'Can't think straight with a throat as dry as mine,' Harry said cheekily.

'You only have to ask, Harry.'

'Can I have a mug of your superior coffee please, Mister Cantlay.'

Harry followed up his request with a cheesy grin.

Cantlay made coffee.

'How often did this guy frequent the establishment?' Harry said getting serious. 'It wasn't mentioned in your notes.'

'Regularly,' the old man said instantly, relishing how the investigation had suddenly kick-started again.

'He's our man!'

'You think? Why?'

'Because Haffenden would have to defer to him on anything of importance, that's if my other client is correct.'

'And there's no reason why your client would lie?'

'No.'

'Come let's sit!'

Cantlay led the way to the kitchen table. They sat opposite each other.

'How are you feeling? Are you up for resuming your previous career?' Harry asked.

'I'm feeling just fine, and you try and stop me – I owe that man!'

'Are you doubly sure it was him?'

'There can be no other, Harry – he either carried it out, or paid someone to do it for him, but either way he's behind it!'

'Okay.'

'And he's going down!'

'Wow!'

'Shocked you, did I?'

'A little; I kind of figured you'd get there eventually.'

'There's plenty of fight in this old dog yet!'

'I can see that.'

'I'll start tomorrow,' Cantlay said, eagerly, 'it won't be long before he shows his face again and then we can get an idea of his itinerary and if he still has the same pattern to his behaviour.'

'You should be the investigator,' Harry added, jocularly, 'with an attitude like that.'

'Let's get him!'

'It will bring him out into the open, especially if we can bring pressure to bear on him from above. He'll be more likely to take chances.'

Harry finished his coffee and was eager to be on his way to see Jane Bellings.

Cantlay promised to keep in touch and let him know immediately if anything should transpire.

Sitting back in his 924 he rang her mobile number but got the answer machine. Harry left a short message before heading home.

Due to his early arrival back from Tennessee it meant that Harry had a week to burn. He hadn't played golf for a while and his self-defence training needed bringing up to scratch.

* * *

Harry's first 18 holes back were a complete disaster: it felt like he had taken a huge step back and learnt nothing. Golf is a game requiring constant attention to achieve any desired standard; this was going to be a hard lesson learned.

He booked a tee-time for the following afternoon and planned to hit at least a hundred balls at the range before venturing out in an attempt to break 90: 90 was Harry's next target; in one of the many golf magazines he'd read people had made scratch between 18-36 months, but they played every day. Harry played every fortnight if he was lucky. Not good enough.

* * *

Travers stood while a four-ball teed off; their standard was well ahead of his, so he was content that the chances of catching them up and playing through were slim.

Harry went out in 46. He was happy with that. The back nine was negotiated in 47, a total of 93. Harry was very happy with that: here in only his 4th full round of golf he had nearly achieved his goal of breaking 90.

During the drive home he would analyse the round and highlight those areas where shots could be saved. Ultimately it always came down to the short game.

That evening Harry went to his Tang Soo Do class and got beaten up by a seventeen-year-old in the free-fighting section of the lesson, but he was good and three belts higher. It was educational.

The following morning his back was sore. He chose to go and practice his short game. His mobile rang. It was Jane Bellings. Harry was excited to talk to her.

It was nothing less, or more, than her wishing to know when Harry and List were intending to put their plan into action.

'Day after tomorrow,' he said, knowing that nothing concrete had been agreed.

'Day after tomorrow,' he repeated when she didn't offer any reply.

'I'm worried for him!' she finally said.

'It'll work just fine, Jane.'

'He won't be alone. That will cause a problem.'

'You just leave that to us,' he said calmly, hoping the tone of his voice would help relax her.

She accepted his faith in the plan and audibly relaxed.

Jane Bellings hung up and Harry called List to confirm the day and time for the sting. Next, he called Tony Bellise, and this time got through: 'How's things?'

All had been blissfully quiet, and the man thanked him profusely.

'Don't mention it.'

'Could you help a friend of mine?'

He knew where this was going but was powerless to refuse: he had helped Tony and Willis' friend and to deny this person his help would not go down favourably and potentially seriously damage his reputation.

'Sure.'

'I'll get him to call you, his name is Gary.'

'I'll wait his call.'

Travers had been told only recently that the name Gary was under threat of becoming extinct among boys' names, and yet here was his first Gary.

Better get fit, he thought, as this was going to end up with yet another run-in with that undesirable element in our society. Travers relished the thought.

The death of the brunette had been another acid-test passed: he had remained calm and focused in the face of genuine danger, and continued to do so; the police now had him on their radar and it would only be a matter of time before they followed it up with a second visit. It was another reason to stay single: any enquiries about him would back-up his statement of living alone.

* * *

Two days later Harry met up with List and the two men parked an expensive looking Ford in a road Mark was known to frequent regularly in attempt to entice him to acquire it by any foul means available.

And there they waited for nearly two hours parked opposite the Ford in a dark green Skoda. Nobody paid the car any attention at all, and Mark never materialised. Arrangements were made to resume the next evening.

Harry had four days to trap the brother before he was on his roster. The next two evenings proved fruitless. On the third Mark announced his arrival by appearing alone, drunk and staggering up the road while attempting to eat what looked like a kebab. The Ford received three hard kicks to the offside rear and front doors. List was for slapping the lad there and then.

'Patience,' Harry said softy.

'That's one of my fucking cars!'

'And the little shit will pay every penny of the repair.'

Mark walked on by but came to an abrupt halt as soon as it struck home, in his inebriated state, that the car might be unlocked.

In what would have taken a sober man five to six strides to return to the Ford, Mark ended up taking double that before he was able to get his paws on the driver's door handle. He nearly fell backwards over a small wall, as he pulled the door open.

'He's not?' List said.

'He is!'

'The boy's an idiot!'

'I can't argue with you there.'

Mark hung onto the door for dear life and hauled himself upright.

'I'm getting out.'

Harry grabbed List's right arm: 'Just give him a few more minutes.'

'I know Jane wants him to be taught a lesson, so why don't I go over there and beat it into him?'

It was a fair plan, and worth due consideration.

Mark finally got into the Ford and there was a second when the two men thought the lad had fallen asleep, but he eventually started to move again. It took nearly five minutes for him to realise the Ford was a push button start, but still in his drunken state he made an attempt to access the ignition wires needed to start the car. He slammed the steering wheel when it finally sunk in it was hopeless.

'Now we got to go!' Harry said with urgency. It was clear that Mark was going to take out his frustration and anger on the Ford.

List was out of their car and across the road in super quick time and Harry struggled to close the gap on his former client before he got hold of the lad and beat him senseless.

Mark couldn't quite believe what was happening when List pulled open the driver's door and let rip with a volley of oaths any sailor would have been proud of.

Harry just stood back and enjoyed the show.

'You can fuck off!' Mark shouted back and fell out of the car onto the road. List took a step back. It took Mark three attempts to get to his feet.

Finally, he made it: 'You can fuck off!' he said again.

List hit him with a straight right, knocking the lad unconscious.

'Oh, great,' Harry said with just a hint of anger. He raced over to where Mark ended up.

The lad was indeed unconscious. Harry rolled him into the recovery position.

List helped him make the lad comfortable.

'That was a tad over the top.'

'This is my car, and you only have it on loan!'

'How am I going to explain this?'

'You'll figure it out, you're Harry Travers.'

Harry had to laugh at that last statement.

Mark began to regain consciousness.

'Help me get him into the Skoda.'

Once Mark was stretched out on the back seat of their car. List went to the Ford. 'I'll see you tomorrow. Say hi to Jane for me.'

Harry climbed into the Skoda, fired it up and drove at a steady pace to Jane's trying to think of an excuse as to why her brother got knocked out in the street.

The drive took twenty minutes at the speed Harry was driving, but he pulled up outside her house and she ran out to meet him.

'Oh, great,' he muttered.

She took one look at Mark and exploded: 'What the fuck happened? You weren't supposed to beat him up!'

'I didn't-'

'You promised me your plan would work.'

Mark slurred something incomprehensible to his sister.

'You're drunk!'

'And?'

Harry needed to placate the irate Ms Bellings before any of the neighbours got wind of what was going on; he hated nosey people and nosey neighbours with a vengeance.

Jane had the rear passenger door open and her brother's head cradled in her lap in one smooth movement.

You lucky bastard, thought Harry.

'What happened?'

'He tried to vandalise the car.'

'And you didn't think to stop him!'

'List did!'

'Don't get funny.'

Harry raised his hands in a surrender pose: 'It was his car.'

'Then you should have thought of that when drawing up your brilliant master plan.'

Harry knew why he lived alone without any outside interference. That being said he'd take all the grief under the sun to have her back just for one day.

'I'll carry him in.'

'I'll do it,' she said, angrily.

Harry lost it for all of a second: 'Your brother steals cars from hard-working, law-abiding people, and probably thinks he's the business to be so unlawful. Well I don't. Your brother's a fucking 'tea-leaf'. Now I will get him in the house then I'll fuck off!'

Jane Bellings fell silent.

Harry leaned inside the car, took Mark by the shoulders and carefully guided him out of the car. Jane still said nothing.

Mark staggered down the small path that led to his sister's front door. He leant on Harry's shoulder, making the most of the support.

Jane stayed exactly one step behind them.

Harry kept his counsel, opened the front door and navigated his way towards her front-room where the younger brother collapsed onto the sofa. Harry left before Jane could say anything. It would have been a complete waste of her time and she knew it.

Harry was gone and up the road before he muttered anything and then it was only a quiet oath against making any kind of plan like that again.

With his master plan now a complete disaster, he was determined to have a quiet, relaxing time before returning to work. His constitution was crying out for it.

* * *

His first day back was another trip to Tenerife, which was blissfully uneventful; his second was a flight to Lanzarote, it wasn't the longest of days, but everything was beginning to catch up with him; day three was a standby day followed by a trip to Enfidha, Tunisia on day four.

Harry was glad to have days off – he had only got back from leave, but he needed them. He rang Tony to get the contact details of his friend, as Gary still had not called him. Tony answered on the second ring. Harry wrote down the number and rang Gary straight away. A soft voiced man answered on the fourth ring.

'Am I talking to Gary?'

'Who's this?'

The man answered a question with a question.

'Am I talking to Gary?' Harry said again.

There was silence that lasted several seconds.

'I am.'

'My name is Harry-'

Harry didn't have time to finish.

'Tony recommended you: he says you are the man who can help with my little problem.'

'Tell me all about it,' Harry said once Gary had finished.

Gary went into a well-rehearsed speech.

Harry geared himself for the inevitable.

Gary was yet another having trouble from certain undesirable individuals. They couldn't be the same group because Tony would have told him. Harry resigned himself for another confrontation then reminded his troubled soul that he loved confrontation, especially confrontation of this kind.

Gary finished his well-rehearsed speech.

Harry requested Gary's itinerary over the next few days. He informed his new client of his fees; he hadn't charged Tony, but this was a recommendation and he believed Tony would not have informed him of how much his services had cost.

Gary accepted the rates without a second's hesitation.

At least he'd get paid, but he would have to earn it – whoever these people were, he could not see them being very accommodating.

The conversation ended with Harry passing over his mobile number and a promise to furnish him with that itinerary. He went down the driving range and hit a hundred balls. His swing was starting to take shape and the consistency he sought appeared; Harry still made the same mistakes, just not on such a regular basis, but the quality of strike was there.

That evening Harry ate curry and enjoyed it: for once he did not think of her.

* * *

He woke up to a missed call from Gary. He rang back. Harry wrote down Gary's planned movements for the coming week; he had two days off to discreetly follow him on his way home from work. This would afford Harry the opportunity to get his own day set and put essential chores behind him.

His new client worked for a rival airline, so Harry was at ease when he parked in the staff car park at Manchester Airport and waited. Gary was on the early morning flight to Palma de Mallorca. He lived in Stockport and took the M56 and M60 home. Harry's heart sank: he knew that route well.

Thirty minutes later Harry followed Gary off the M60 and headed down towards the roundabout and the exit for the A626 to South Stockport. Gary drove a sliver Nissan Micra and he found it easy to follow at a discreet distance.

Gary exited left into Graham Road, turned right at the end onto Ludlow Road then followed it until it became Bideford Road. The lad pulled up outside a tidy looking house and smartly entered through a bright green front door.

Harry waited. He wasn't expecting anything untoward to happen, but he needed to get a feel for Gary's way of life and routine. Harry sat in the 924 for over an hour. Gary never reappeared.

He gunned the 924 into life and headed home in readiness to return first thing tomorrow morning.

* * *

Harry luckily found the exact same parking space that he occupied the previous afternoon. Gary's Micra was still parked outside.

Thirty minutes later Gary appeared in a freshly pressed uniform for his flight to Dalaman and jumped into the Micra. The return tail to the airport was a piece of cake. He noticed no suspicious vehicles and followed Gary into the car park to guarantee his safety. There was no activity at all. Not that he truly expected anything to happen.

Gary vacated his car, locked it and boarded one of the courtesy buses. Never at any time did he attempt to locate Harry. He would return later when the Dalaman was due in. Next stop though was shopping and a quick 9 holes.

* * *

With a larder full of groceries, and the front 9 played in 40 strokes, Harry parked the 924 a full row behind Gary. From the outset Travers knew nothing was going to happen; he couldn't put his finger on it, but it, whatever it was, filled him with growing confidence that today was going to be a quiet day.

Gary finally arrived at his Micra and was out of the car park and up the road in double-quick time. Even Harry was impressed with the speed at which the man was out of the car park.

Harry fell back two car lengths.

All was quiet and Harry immediately became bored and began to wonder what all the fuss was about. Just live and let live, that was his motto; life is hard enough at the best of times without these people making it even harder.

Gary took the same route via the M56 and M60 back home. The roads were busy leaving Travers working extremely hard to keep track of all the cars. It was proving nigh on impossible. Finally, he narrowed it down to two.

At Roscoe's Roundabout Harry dropped back to allow the two cars on his radar to get ahead of him. The drivers were in their twenties; about the same age as the lad he had the run-in with a couple of weeks ago. Both cars followed the Micra. Harry mentally prepared himself for the coming confrontation.

All four cars navigated their way along the A626, but only Gary took the left into Graham Road. Harry followed the other two for a couple of miles before doubling back. The Micra was parked as before and all was quiet.

His new client was now on days off; Harry text to double check Gary's plans over the next few days. The reply he got was from Jane Bellings. It took him a second to realise it was just a coincidence that she should reply at that exact moment.

Gary replied: he was going to the gym in the morning then meeting a friend for lunch.

Harry replied to Jane's text: she was upset at her reaction towards him once she had spoken to her brother and discovered the truth.

He informed her not to worry. Any interest in a relationship had evaporated that night.

After acknowledging Gary's message, he drove sedately home.

* * *

In preparation for a hard days' investigation, Travers ate a hearty breakfast of scrambled egg on toast with a mug of coffee. He needed to be ready for any eventuality, and if it involved a stay in hospital, as melodramatic as that sounded, he would also need fresh, clean underwear.

As a precaution against boredom he put his golf clubs in the rear of the 924. He would get some practice in if the day unfolded the way he hoped it would.

Gary, being the thoughtful client, waited patiently in his Micra with the engine running. As soon as Harry appeared, he reversed out of his drive and left for the gym.

For all the preparation Harry was tired this morning and knew his constitution would be crying out for a powernap – he couldn't see whoever was making Gary's life hell attacking him in the gym. That would solve the case for him but prevent him from being paid. On that front Harry needed to give List a nudge in the right direction to settle his bill. A charity he was not.

* * *

Gary parked outside one of those posh gyms that are in vogue and charge membership rates to reflect that.

Harry parked two rows directly behind the Micra, reclined his seat and took a powernap.

He woke with a start and immediately checked the time off his mobile phone: he had been asleep for just over thirty minutes. A quick examination of the cars in the car park containing their owners revealed, to his bitter disappointment, a dark blue Audi parked off to his left on the end of the row in front of him. The driver was male, in his thirties, dark-haired, with a least three days' stubble. The man never took his eyes off the entrance to the gym.

He's waiting for his partner, thought Harry, but it was wishful thinking and he knew it.

Harry studied the man intently for many minutes, and not once did he look his way, he was more interested in sending messages. If he was waiting for his partner, then they better be worried.

Two good-looking ladies in their twenties exited the gym talking continuously. By their dress they were on their way to work after a workout. The man paid them no attention.

'What's your game?' Harry said. He raised his seat to a height that allowed him to still make out the man without bringing attention to himself.

Two guys now vacated the gym and again the man ignored them.

'If I watch you,' Harry started, 'and look to my right when you get excited, I bet it's my client. Now what's your problem, other than the obvious?'

Harry rubbed his chin; he hadn't shaved this morning.

'What's so important about members of the gay community?'

The man became alert and adjusted his seat in readiness to start the Audi.

Harry knew. He didn't need to look.

The man gunned the Audi into life.

The sound of the Micra's engine soon followed; it was easy to recognise the sound of each car's engine when you needed to.

Harry delayed starting the 924 until both cars had left the car park. Why rush.

The traffic was heavy at this time of day and it was simple to follow both men.

Harry pulled up at a set of traffic lights protecting a major junction. He could see Gary tune the Micra's radio. The Audi driver studied his every move.

'What is it with these people?' Harry was exasperated along with angry: it annoyed him that people should get so worked up over someone else's life choices – get a life, that's all people want to do: get a life and enjoy it.

The lights turned green and they all turned left onto the A34 heading South back towards the M60.

Gary joined the flow of traffic on the motorway heading in the easterly direction; the Audi mirrored his every move from only one car length behind.

'You're crap at this!' Harry exclaimed. 'Definitely crap.'

Harry held back – experience in these matters paid dividends.

The exit to Roscoe's Roundabout and home for Gary came and went. He was in the dark now when it came to Gary's private life and he preferred that way – if jobs took themselves into the realms of what went on behind closed doors then so be it, but apart from that Harry couldn't care less what his clients got up to. A lawyer he was not.

Gary finally indicated left and took the exit to a large roundabout then the first exit off that to a smaller one. At the smaller roundabout Gary headed for Bredbury via the third exit.

This road was the A560 and when it connected with the B6104 Gary turned left. The Audi dropped back for the first time, but never turned. Throughout it all the Audi driver never once checked his mirrors. Harry naturally followed suit. At least his client would have some breathing space.

Harry checked his rear-view mirror as a matter of course. The road was clear.

The Audi kept to the speed limit. He had to know Gary's final destination.

Harry now had a new dilemma: should he double-back and catch the Micra, but that meant possibly alerting the Audi to his presence, or just go with the flow and see what transpires – if the Audi had an accomplice then he needed to alert Gary. He sent a text.

The Audi was two lengths in front and adhering to all the laws of the road. Harry checked and re-checked his mirrors. All was good.

Gary replied with an address in Bredbury. Harry pulled in by the side of the road and witnessed the Audi disappear into the flow of traffic. A quick google of the address confirmed what he suspected: the address was behind him. Harry smiled: it was a smile that only hinted at the pleasure and the adrenaline rush that now awaited him. He was the target.

12

The Audi crawled back down the A560. He found Harry's 924 parked on his left, facing North. The driver pulled in on the opposite side of the road forty yards further on. The driver kept the engine running and never took his eyes off the 924.

The road was quiet for this time of the day bar a steady stream of traffic mainly heading North.

The man sat and waited patiently. Harry was nowhere to be seen. He shut down the Audi and dialled out.

Haffenden was trying to get the jump on him, Harry thought while studying the stranger from behind a large hedge. He was not surprised. The man wanted revenge for the brunette.

The phone conversation went on for many minutes. Harry text his client to make sure all was well and not to be too concerned with his absence.

The reply put him at ease: he was with a friend.

Harry turned his attention back to the Audi driver. What to do with you? Lead the man up a quiet road and dispose of him, or wait and follow him back to Haffenden? That would allow him the opportunity of removing both these thorns in one go. But he knew how to get to Haffenden, so why choose the latter. If he was leading then he could dictate proceedings: you were at an advantage if you knew there was a tail, plus Harry couldn't stay here all day.

There was a Newsagents over on the other side of the road. The man didn't see him enter the shop. Harry bought a newspaper and mints then returned to the Porsche. Out of the corner of his eye he could see the Audi driver leaning half out of the driver's side window.

'Fucking amateur,' snarled Harry. He kept his line of sight on the 924.

Harry swung the classic Porsche through a one-eighty degree turn and accelerated hard up the road towards the M60.

The Audi pulled away and closed the gap on the 1982 classic instantly.

Harry would struggle to break-away; he needed to utilise the classic's main strengths.

He made his way to the motorway and headed West to the Airport.

Harry was not for heading home, instead he tried to plan a route where the 924's superior handling could be brought to bear.

The M60 connected to the M56. Harry contemplated heading straight on to Liverpool. The satnav was in the glove compartment. There was peace of mind right there. He accelerated to 80mph and made a point of not moving or twitching his head; he had the upper hand, for now, but the time was approaching when the Audi and Haffenden would realise the game was up.

The Audi closed to one car length.

Travers had spent the best part of 6 years restoring the Porsche: it was on his bucket list to restore a classic car, but the car was also purchased as a learning tool for basic motor mechanics; Harry quickly came to love the car and after eventually solving and curing the car's problems he decided to keep her as his daily run-around. Such was Harry's knowledge of the car, and where to find all the spare parts required, that he began to drive her with supreme confidence, knowing that any mechanical gremlins or body work issues he could deal with.

Haffenden knew where to find Harry and how to get to him: he had proved that with the dead girl. Here was the man's retaliation.

Poor blue Audi driver, thought Harry, you're going the same way as the unfortunate girl. He felt no guilt, or sorrow, or remonstrated against himself for the calculated, premeditated act of aggression – the Audi driver was going to get Haffenden's comeuppance, or at least a taste of things to come.

The afternoon traffic was heavy, and he was now hungry of all things. He made a beeline for Jack's Bar. The Audi followed him like a little lost kitten.

'Fucking amateur,' Harry said again.

Before the M56 Motorway he turned left onto the A34 and pushed the accelerator pedal to the floor.

Once on the road heading South to Heald Green, Harry changed his mind and made tracks to a quiet cul-de-sac he knew off Schools Hill Road.

Harry kept his speed at 80mph; he only slowed on the approach to the exit leading to a large roundabout spanning the A34. He had the advantage of leading and ignored any traffic already on the roundabout and entered at speed. The Audi wasn't as adventurous and was held up by traffic having to make allowances for the Porsche.

The blasts of horns were wasted on Harry: he cared not a jot for his reckless driving; their lives were not in peril, their existence put in jeopardy by one odious individual.

Harry swung left off the roundabout and hit the noisy pedal hard. The Audi had more torque at lower speeds; its acceleration left the 924 standing, but his handling was better and again he needed to make that count. Now on Schools Hill Road he would follow that by taking the third left into the cul-de-sac called The Downs.

In his rear-view mirror the Audi closed rapidly, too rapidly, to a car length. He had played right into Harry's hands: Harry braked hard, almost coming to a standstill, but still maintained his course on the lead up to The Downs. The front of the Audi twitched under braking then violently began to fish-tail as the driver pulled the steering wheel to the right before over-compensating to the left and then back to the right. Harry timed his turn-in to perfection. The

Audi was now out of control facing right, towards on-coming traffic, then left towards parked cars, and back to the right.

Harry pulled up and became an interested spectator.

'Let go!' he shouted.

The crash was inevitable: the wildly fish-tailing Audi lifted up onto its two left-hand wheels, came down with a bang and speared itself across the road and into a wall. The impact was frightening. Once the car had come to a halt Harry got out of the 924 and walked at a steady pace to the scene of the crash. Cars had already stopped, and people were running over to what was left of a very nice Audi. Harry was more concerned about the car. By the time he made the scene he could see the airbag had deployed and the man was sitting, groaning, still in the front seat. It was best not to stay long.

Back in the 924 his mobile rang.

'Hello?'

It was David.

'Harry?'

'It's me!'

'You're in danger!'

Now you tell me, he felt like saying.

'Yeah?'

'Real danger!'

'How come?'

'Raquette. Willis says he's having you tailed-'

'Yeah, I've seen him and I'm looking at what's left of him and his Audi.'

There was a moments' silence as his words sunk in.

'Oh.'

'Thanks for the heads up.'

'My pleasure, I owe you. Stay safe.' David hung up.

'So that's the game.'

It was revenge for Moore – Harry was more than willing to play this game. It brought with it an intense burning pain that Raquette would not have countered for, nor ever will, and this pain was going to be the hammer to drive the final nail into that bastard's coffin. Harry gripped the steering wheel until his knuckles went white and his fingers hurt.

An ambulance arrived with the police and the man was stretchered away. The police directed traffic and Harry left for home.

The drive was sedate, but he was watchful – this was now the norm. Gone were the days when he could take out the 924 for a nice quiet drive and enjoy the day, but why should he feel bitter about it? Life was there to be enjoyed and you have to make every second count.

Baslow Drive was quiet by the time he got home. There were a few cars parked in his part of the road, as if their owners had abandoned them, knowing some imminent disaster was about to hit Manchester.

Harry parked in his drive and remembered the brunette – one corpse conveniently dumped on his property was enough for any man.

The front door was eased open and Harry stared at that section of floor where she lay.

Every floor was untouched, just the way he left them – on previous occasions he would have been angry at being timid or apprehensive, but today he was tired: the past few days began to drain his reserves. He collapsed on the bed and fell asleep.

* * *

Harry woke fully clothed, undressed and got underneath the duvet. He was asleep again in minutes.

The morning brought with it a standby duty from 8am until 2pm. The phone never rang. Gary was okay. At least Harry had been given the head's up.

The day was spent re-charging the batteries.

The following day was a Tuesday, and if it was Tuesday then that meant Tenerife. The crew-room was the usual. Harry ignored everybody and dumped his bag by an empty terminal and logged on to the company intranet. Flying was to come to his rescue once again.

He checked his watch; for once Harry arrived only 5 minutes before check-in. His normal routine was to be 20 minutes early so he could grab a cup of coffee on the way to the jet. There was no first officer – no coffee today.

Check-in time came and went. Harry studied the crew sheet to see who the first officer was: it was John O'Connor. Harry text the man: he had made a point of putting his mobile number in his phone the last time they flew. He would meet him at the jet.

The reply was instant: he was waiting for the courtesy bus and was late due to a serious road traffic accident. Harry completed the pre-flight paperwork, ordered the fuel, sent the information through for the load-sheet and was off to grab a coffee.

Security was quiet and he was through within minutes then up the stairs to departures. John sent a text that he was right behind him and would pay for the drinks. He would have the same as Harry this morning.

Harry quickened his pace: free coffee does that to you.

Exactly two minutes after Harry ordered the beverages John arrived and paid for two extra hot lattes with caramel syrup.

'I'm taking a leaf out of your book, Harry,' John said waving his contactless debit card over the machine.

An efficient member of staff rustled up the hot drinks in double-quick time and they were on their way.

The jet was parked on stand 24 in Terminal 1 and inside was all hustle and bustle. Harry liaised with the cabin manager, Adam Grayling, confirming with him how long fuelling was going to take, any aircraft defects that impacted him and the crew, and that he could start boarding passengers when the fuelling was finished.

Travers was flying the outbound leg and set about his duties.

Everything went smoothly, without a single hitch and they pushed back off stand five minutes early with a full complement of 180 passengers. The flight time down to Tenerife was four hours and ten minutes with a return flight time of a shade under four hours.

Push-back and engine start were completed, the tug and tow-bar were disconnected before they ran the After-Start Checklist and requested taxi clearance.

It was a beautiful, crisp autumn morning without a cloud in the sky, and Harry finally felt at ease for once – he had accepted that adapting to this new life was not going to happen overnight: nothing took him by surprise him anymore, instead he found it somewhat strange if there wasn't anything out of the ordinary just lurking below the surface.

On this autumn morning, Manchester Airport had single runway operations in use with the departing and arriving traffic using runway 23 Right. Taxi time would be the same as for dual runway ops.

During the taxi, flight control checks were completed by both pilots and Harry gave his R.I.S.E brief: runway in use; the instrument departure designated, as per their flight plan; the initial stop altitude or flight level; and the Engine Failure Procedure. When that was done, with both men singing from the same hymn sheet, he called for the Before Take-off Checklist. The Ground Controller handed them over to the tower.

The holding point for 23R was busy with three aircraft ahead of them waiting to depart. From the conversations between other aircraft and the Ground Controller there were at least three more behind them.

Harry brought the jet to a halt at a safe distance from the one in front and applied the park brake. He took the opportunity to make a PA to advise the passengers and crew of the slight delay: passengers, in his experience, were less likely to anger if they were informed as to the cause of any delays. It is when they are kept in the dark that problems arise.

A Boeing 737 landed and an A330 lined up. They departed as soon as the 737 had vacated the runway. This became the pattern until Harry lined up the A320. The remainder of the Before Take-off Checklist were run and a PA was made to advise the crew to prepare for departure.

Take-off clearance was received, acknowledged and Harry set take-ff thrust.

They launched into the air shortly after and Harry engaged the autopilot on this beautiful, crisp morning to enjoy the view. He was reminded of Tennessee. They were truly blessed to be able to view the world as the Almighty does.

The four-hour-ten-minute flight time seem to evaporate in an instant as Harry taxied in at Tenerife South Airport and turned right onto stand F6; this stand was connected to the terminal via an air-bridge. With a bit of luck, they could get a quick turnaround and land back into Manchester early.

Once on stand, and all the checks completed, Harry turned on his mobile phone and began to fill out the aircraft's technical log.

His phone audibly informed him of an incoming text message: it was from an unknown number requesting they call him. They signed themselves Adam Chivers.

He dialled the number when it was convenient. A hard, deep voice answered: the man, by his tone, was clearly used to getting his own way when talking to subordinates.

'Is this Mister Adam Chivers?'

'You must be Mister Harry Travers?'

'I am,' Harry replied equally as abruptly.

'I am the late Mister Cantlay's solicitor.'

A cold chill descended the length of his spine.

'I had a feeling this was not going to be good news,' Harry said rubbing his eyes.

'No, it's not,' Chivers said in a matter-of-fact tone, 'he died at home a few days ago.'

'How?'

'Peacefully in bed.'

Harry didn't believe a word of it.

'Why call me?'

Harry knew the answer before it arrived.

'You're in my client's will, and I have been given strict instructions to hand you personally what Mister Cantlay wanted you to have. When can I see you?'

'Tomorrow should be fine.'

Harry was again on standby: the winter programme was never as busy as the summer's and there were more days spent on standby as a result.

The solicitor passed on his address and the time he expected Harry to be there: eleven o'clock was fine with Harry.

The turnaround went smoothly, and Harry pushed any feelings he had regarding Cantlay's sad demise to the back of his mind. They would have to wait.

The flight home was as blissfully uneventful as the one out.

Walking to the bus stop, Harry lowered his guard for all of a second. The courtesy bus had not arrived yet to take him to the staff car park. A tear came to his eye, anger soon followed.

The bus arrived and Harry boarded, refusing to make eye contact with any of the other airport staff heading home.

Harry dropped his flight bag in the passenger foot-well and leant on the roof of the 924. An overwhelming feeling of being watched caused him to stay as he was and look relaxed and unconcerned.

A red Volvo drove past. The driver stared straight at him.

'What the fuck are you looking at?'

Harry's outburst shocked him, but when a second driver did the same, he became incensed and repeated the outburst.

The male driver of a third car made eye-contact, but he put it down to him seeing Harry talking to himself.

'What's wrong with people?'

Harry closed the passenger door and walked round to the driver's side, boarded and fired her up. He was itching to see who Raquette was sending this time.

The answer was no-one.

The house was untouched. He ate a late tea and hit the sack early. Things will seem different tomorrow.

The morning brought with it no new-found contentment; Harry still felt the same: he was tired when he went to bed and was tired when he woke up. These were among the classic symptoms of fatigue, but he still had a job to do.

Harry called Gary: Raquette may attack him to get to Harry. All was good and the lad even thanked him for removing the nuisance from his life.

If only you knew the truth, thought Harry, but most people don't want to know the truth. Harry accepted the gratitude, adding that any recommendations from a happy client would be most welcome.

A phone call from Crewing called him off the standby to operate the late Las Palmas, which would then be followed by a rest day, another standby then three days off. He'd try and get some much-needed golf practice in along with his two self-defence classes and generally keep his fitness levels high – the older one got the harder it became to maintain a high level of fitness; even the smallest break in training, or rounds of golf, eroded it.

Over the past few months Harry's lifestyle had altered considerably: he drank less; cooked more, ate less takeaway food; and the catalyst for all of this was her, but just when he thought he was getting over her, a memory re-surfaced to wreck any and all his hard work. Harry changed as much as he could in order not to place himself in a position to remember. It was a forlorn hope on some days, but the gaps between these days was steadily growing.

13

The solicitor's office was as he expected: airy, light and full of photos of the man with various dignitaries, invariably playing golf. Harry thought about asking the man if he wanted a game but abandoned the idea pretty quickly.

On the red painted wall, behind Chivers' desk, he had hung all his certificates detailing his qualifications.

'Please, take a seat,' Chivers said politely.

There were two directly facing the man. Harry took the left one.

Chivers was a dark-haired, broad shouldered individual in a silver double-breasted suit, white shirt with a cerise coloured tie. Harry put him in his late forties. His brown eyes seem to interrogate him the moment he entered the office. Must come with the job, he thought.

'I'll come straight to the point, Mister Travers.'

'Please do.'

'Mister Cantlay left instructions for you to have certain documents.'

Chivers slid a large thick brown envelope across his desk towards Travers: 'I was given explicit instructions to hand them to you personally. You will see the envelope is still sealed.'

Harry picked it up. It had not been tampered with, but that was not to say this was not the original envelope. On the front it was noted for his attention.

'The thing is Mister Travers, and I will not deny it makes me feel very uncomfortable,' Chivers said rubbing his hands with his elbows on the desk,' is that the will was only drawn up the day before his death.'

Harry said nothing. It was best.

'I don't want to know my clients business normally, but......'

Chivers paused. He was gauging Harry's reaction.

'I am as much in the dark as you are, as to the contents of that envelope.' Harry had a good idea what was in there.

Chivers' eyes searched for any sign of weakness or false testament – he found none.

'Do you need me to sign for anything?' Harry asked.

Chivers slid a sheet of neatly typed paper towards him. Harry didn't bother reading it and took a pen sitting on the desk and signed at the bottom.

'Well, if this is all,' Harry said standing, 'I'll be on my way.'

Chivers stood and put out his hand: 'Cantlay was insistent I be ready to represent you, should you so need it.'

'He did, did he?'

Harry shook his hand.

'Yes,' Chivers said smiling, as if he knew for sure there would be work coming his way. 'So, you can see my fascination with that envelope.'

'From my knowledge of the man, it will be nothing illegal.'

'If it is then I'll be getting paid for my services.'

'That you will, Mister Chivers. May I take a card?'

Chivers handed him one of his business cards from off his desk.

'Hopefully, I won't be in touch,' Harry said accepting the card.

It was Chivers' turn to say nothing.

Harry knew it was best not to prolong his departure.

* * *

Harry checked-in for the Las Palmas. John O'Connor was again his partner. John was early today.

The day was pleasant enough, but Harry's mind was elsewhere whenever it was given free rein to wander, and it always wandered to Haffenden, Raquette and now that envelope.

Harry still had not opened it; he was leaving that duty to a time when he was ready – there was no rush.

The short drive home was uneventful, bar a couple of brainless morons trying to outdrive each other and prove to themselves which one was the biggest idiot, and he softly closed his front door and ascended to the first floor. The house was cold and deathly quiet. He made coffee and drank it on the sofa after depositing his flight bag and jacket in the bedroom. The envelope sat on a small table by the sofa.

Harry tore open the envelope and removed ten pages of white A4 paper. The notes were detailed – Cantlay had been busy and thorough: Haffenden had been a regular visitor, as well as a few well-known dignitaries.

'Well, well, well,' Harry said, chuckling to himself, 'we have been busy boys!'

One client caught Harry's eye: it was Raquette. Cantlay had not mentioned anything about the man personally, but from the physical description it matched him perfectly.

Half-way through the ten pages Harry discovered a smaller A5 piece of paper containing a handwritten note to Harry from Cantlay. Harry put down the letter and finished his coffee. A terrible chill came over him and froze him to the sofa. The opening line was blunt and to the point:

"Harry, if you are reading this then I am surely dead......"

He put the letter down then picked it back up; it was proving difficult to read, but Harry forced himself: Cantlay was himself being watched, but he could not discover by whom. He always suspected Haffenden. His house had been broken into with nothing taken or disturbed, but he knew there had been an unwelcome visitor and he believed they were looking for these notes. As for his boss, there was no one single client that stood out. Harry was to keep these notes safe. His killer, he was convinced, was in these pages. Haffenden, or his boss, would not want to get their hands dirty.

Harry carefully filed the letter back among the A4 pages and made another coffee. All he could think about was cold-blooded murder. Harry had come full circle in a very short space of time: first his uncle's murder and now Cantlay's. Only this time there was a body.

With a fresh mug of coffee, Harry set to studying the new set of notes and comparing them to the original ones given to him by Cantlay. It reminded him that he still had to cross-check all missing persons against these clients, but that could wait for another time.

Later that day Harry visited Cantlay's house and found various family members squabbling over the dead man's belongings. 'Glad I'm not the lawyer dealing with you lot,' he said quietly as he navigated his way to the back garden. It was immediately obvious by the state of the garden that the old man was gone. Even in such a short space of time it was a sad sight. Harry didn't stay long. On his way back to the Porsche Harry did his usual and scoured all the parked cars in the road. There was nobody looking even remotely suspicious. He was about to board when movement off to his right caught his eye. Hiding round the back of his car was Jasper. The dog looked at him with sad, doleful eyes.

'On your own now, eh? Well, I know how that feels.'

The dog approached him, tail wagging.

Harry opened the passenger door. Jasper didn't need a second invitation and jumped in.

Travers turned his attention back to that house and had the urge to goad; he had parked right outside and almost across the driveway. He stood there for a full fifteen minutes studying the windows for any sign of life. Eventually he marched straight up to the front door and stood there in full anticipation of an attack on his person. Cantlay wasn't an idiot, and he did not die peacefully in bed: he presumably had no visible damage, so that put paid to any violence; the only way to get the old man would be to poison him, and if he had a history of ill-health would there be need of an autopsy? The only question was how? Datura Stramonium.

Over the next few days Harry did his research on that dreaded plant then late one night re-visited Cantlay's. His first port of call was the garden followed by that house; the garden was as he left it, but even on a second investigation he found nothing untoward; the house was quiet, but he was in a mind to bear this with all the calmness of a saint. For the first time he rued having to sit in the Porsche. It was not the nondescript car required this night.

A couple of clients came and went; a man walking his dog paid him no attention, almost as if he knew why Harry was there and didn't want anything to do with it. Haffenden never appeared. At three in the morning Harry went home.

The standby duty came and went before Harry was back hunting Haffenden, knowing that Raquette was hunting him.

Of all the virtues required to oppose the seven deadly sins, patience is the one that is a must for the would-be private detective. It took two whole nights before Haffenden showed his face.

The odious Mister Haffenden appeared looking smug.

'Thinking Raquette's done your dirty work for you, do you?'

Haffenden boarded a brand-new Jaguar and slipped effortlessly out of the house's drive.

Harry waited before following at a discreet distance. On the first night Harry was alone, but tonight he had Jasper for company.

Haffenden turned right at the end of the road. Harry waited at the junction watching the Jaguar's rear lights make good progress up the road.

As soon as the lights disappeared Harry smartly pulled out into the road and accelerated. It was very quiet at this time of night bar a few taxis, and they were easily identified. Harry soon found the Jaguar's lights. Haffernden kept on a steady course heading South to South-East by Harry's calculation. Travers would again utilise his satnav to find his way back to base once Haffenden's final destination was known. Harry laughed: he would send the man to his final destination. Any rising humour was tempered with the thought that Haffenden was leading him into a trap. Harry constantly checked his rear-view mirror. It was clear.

Harry held back at least five to six car lengths. He was mindful not to stay on the man's tail for too long. At one intersection they began to head North-East and Harry took a gamble that Haffenden would turn right onto the A57, so he took the right turn before that junction into Polebrook Close and disappeared for a brief moment from the man's mirrors. Haffenden did indeed turn right and Harry resumed his tail six car lengths behind after joining the A57 via Grey Street.

By Harry's reckoning they were heading South-East again. A road sign indicating directions to the airport off to their right confirmed it. Haffenden kept on going.

Harry checked the car's on-board clock with his watch: both read 01:32. His rear-view mirror was still clear.

He could finish Haffenden right here and nobody would know. Harry put his left hand inside his jacket pocket and felt for the Colt Detective Special he had acquired that night at Moore's. Right here, right now and nobody would know. He checked for street cameras and naturally fell back an extra car length. Haffenden began to slow as they approached Gorton. Harry pulled in on seeing the Jaguar's brake lights come on. Haffenden came to a stop. Harry turned left into the first convenient road and parked up.

He was out of the car within seconds and peering around a garden wall at the end of the road within a few more.

Haffenden had pulled in behind a black Audi. A beautiful, slim blonde exited the Audi and glided over to the Jaguar. Haffenden never left his car. He handed the beautiful blonde a slip of paper. She accepted it with a ready smile.

Haffenden pulled away and continued on the A57. Harry was now more interested in the beautiful blonde.

She glided back to the Audi and made her way back towards Manchester.

Harry hurried back to the 924 and followed enthusiastically; his skin began to tingle. Even Jasper took an interest in her. He knew tonight there was going to be the kind of action guaranteed to stir the blood.

The blonde lit a cigarette and blew the smoke out of the driver's window in the most seductive way imaginable. She oozed sex appeal and knew it.

Harry needed to concentrate.

The Audi stuck to the A57 until in merged with the A6, crossed the motorway and headed towards East Manchester. At Ducie Street she turned right then left onto Dale Street.

From the slickness of her driving and lack of visible indication, as to the direction she was planning to take, Harry could tell this route was one that had been followed many times in anticipation of this night. Poor soul, thought Harry, you'll be as high as a kite and dead just as quick.

They were now travelling North towards the A62 Newton Street but took a left then a right to follow the one-way system and ended up on Lever Street. A further left turn put Harry onto Stevenson Square. Harry contemplated pulling in for a second or two, but the blonde never paid him any mind, so he carried on. When the road became Thomas Street, they took the next right onto Oak Street and after that the second left, first right and straight towards the A665. Harry let the Audi pull ahead once on the major road. It was easy to keep tabs on her: she was so intent on listening to the music and chain-smoking cigarettes that she was oblivious to Harry and his Porsche.

The A665 passed by the Manchester Arena and the Audi indicated for the first time and turned left onto the A6042 before indicating again to enter the car park adjacent to it. Harry kept on going. From his side mirror he watched the Audi pull up beside another car.

He had to wait before he could head back and managed that at the next junction. When he did make the car park the two cars were still side by side. Harry pulled in on the left by the entrance to Dutton Street. He turned his lights off and shut down the Porsche. The roads were quiet.

'Well Jasper, what do you think we got here?'

The blonde appeared from the other vehicle and boarded the Audi. She wasted no time being on her way. Harry fired up the Porsche and continued on the A6042 Eastbound then swung the 924 through one-eighty degrees at the junction with the A665 and made a beeline for the other car. The Audi appeared ahead of him exiting the car park and heading Westbound.

The other car was a Ford; Harry did not take the time to see the model. He parked up and ran over to it. The male driver sat with his head in that position all victims do when they have had their throats cut. The blonde was clearly not bothered about CCTV, that's if she is a blonde.

Harry was back on the A6042 Westbound within seconds with that image of the driver burning itself into his memory. It did not take long to spot the Audi: the blonde was driving at a sedate pace not wanting to draw any attention from the Law.

The A6042, also known as Trinity Way, curved South-West to join the A34 to head South, South-East. She was heading towards Harry's side of town.

The blonde began to speed up once the A57(M) motorway was behind them. The two passed through Rusholme, Ladybarn, Burnage, across the M60 and on to Heald Green.

Harry rubbed his right hand across his throat.

'Doing a double shift tonight are you?'

He knew a quicker route home and took it without thinking.

Baslow Drive was made in good time, and with the 924 parked in the drive, Harry entered the house with Jasper leading. He left all the lights off.

Ten minutes later the blonde stood outside his front door and rang the bell. Harry quickly changed into his night clothes and answered the door. Jasper never barked.

The blonde smiled sweetly and took a step towards Harry when he answered the door. She was wearing a tight-fitting white dress with matching high heels.

'Good morning,' Harry said, trying to look as though he'd just got out of bed.

'Good Morning,' the blonde replied, stroking the side of Harry's left cheek.

'And to what do I owe this pleasure?'

The blonde kept on stroking Harry's cheek. He did nothing to stop her.

The blonde leant forward and kissed him on the cheek: 'You are a valued customer of the casino, Mister Travers.'

'I need to renew my membership.'

'What better way is there to convince you,' she cooed.

'What better,' Harry repeated.

A quick glance up and down the road revealed no nosey neighbours. The blonde breezed past him into the house.

'Do come in,' he said over his shoulder after her.

Harry quietly closed the door.

The blonde was up the first flight of stairs before Harry could say another word. He walked slowly, but deliberately, up the stairs taking one step at a time. He found her sprawled on the sofa in a seductive pose. She rested her head on her left hand. Jasper knew it was best to stay out of sight and disappeared.

'And I don't even know your name.'

'Sasha,' she said softly.

'Well, high Sasha. I didn't realise my presence, or lack of presence, was missed at Nero's.'

'You are a valued customer, Harry.'

You are way too confident, Blondie, Harry thought staying on his feet. He could keep a better eye on her from the vertical stance.

'I'll make a note to myself to spend more of my hard-earned cash at the place. Drink?'

'Gin and tonic would be lovely.'

Harry backed into the kitchen to rustle up two large gin and tonics. It would be his first drink since Tennessee, and it will go straight to his head. The second glass he filled with just tonic.

The blonde was where he left her, with the exception of her right hand which she rested on her right thigh. Harry put her drink within easy reach on a table. Again, he backed towards the kitchen by two medium sized steps. He sipped his drink. The blonde reached over and took a large hit of gin and tonic. In a flash she was off the sofa, the drink was back on the table, and facing Harry. He continued to sip his tonic.

Where did she hide it? The sofa was clear. The white dress was tight with no obvious hiding places. Harry put down his tonic and wrapped his hands around her waist. She was fit and the dress clung to her every curve. She placed her hands on his hips and kissed him fully on the lips. Harry could taste the gin and tonic. She pulled back almost in slow motion and let out a sigh as their lips parted.

'You taste good,' the blonde whispered. Her eyes never left his.

'Why rush,' Harry replied. He locked his gaze on her beautiful blue eyes. His mind was working overtime. Any slip up and he was dead.

Her hands cupped his cheeks and she kissed him again softly on the lips. He was safe if he kept kissing. Harry placed his hands on hers and kissed her back passionately. She did not close her eyes when they kissed a second time. In that second before their lips parted, he figured it out.

Her right hand moved in one swift, slick movement and whipped a hairpin blade from her soft blonde hair.

Harry grabbed her right wrist with his left land and the tip of the blade stopped millimetres from his left eye. His right hand cupped her waist and he twisted as best he could; she had placed her left foot between his legs preventing him from stepping across her. He threw her back against the wall. She pushed hard with the hairpin. Harry tipped his head back and the blade impacted his left cheek. Blood ran down his cheek onto his chin. He held the blade in his cheek with his left hand and rammed home a hard, right uppercut into her solar plexus.

The blonde stepped back winded, but she prevented herself from doubling over. She threw a sharp left hook that smashed into the side of Harry's face. He was stunned but kept his senses intact. She went to throw a second, but it was a doomed move: the blonde concentrated on the left hook and not the blade. Harry took the punch with a turn of the head and pulled the blade out of his cheek.

Her determination for the kill never faltered now that the game was up. She went for the blade with her left hand, released it from the grasp her right hand held on it and went for Harry's throat.

Harry's feet were now free to position him for this second onslaught and he threw her over his left hip with his right hand gripping her left wrist in a vice-like grip. She hit the ground with a bang.

The blonde was a pro, and this was not the first time she had found herself in this position: the split second she impacted the floor her legs were up above her waist and wrapped around Harry's neck in a choke hold.

Harry tried manfully to release her legs with his left hand. His right hand was still preventing the blonde from stabbing him. He remembered the brunette and swung the blonde towards the door frame, but she lifted herself up until her head was level with his and went to bury her teeth into Harry's neck.

Harry fell back, tipping his head as far rearward as the neck muscles would allow. The blonde failed to get a bite and pulled her head away. Harry knew what her next course of action was and beat her to the punch: he head-butted the girl hard, twice on the bridge of the nose. The blonde screamed and swore she'd cut his balls off. She tightened her grip around his neck and spat blood into Harry's face.

He was struggling to breathe and could feel his cheeks flush red. The blonde was stronger than the brunette. Raquette and Haffenden were both dead if he managed to extricate himself out of this mess and he'd dump the blonde's body right on their fucking doorstep.

A vicious left hook smashed into the blonde's jaw, but she took the punch well: again, that was clearly not a first for her. She dug the fingernails of her right hand into his face and went for the eyes. Harry hit her repeatedly while shaking his head from side to side. His jiu-jitsu training to date was not adequate enough to deal with her, and tang soo do was not a grappling form of self-defence. He needed to be resourceful while he could still breathe.

Harry grabbed her right hand even tighter and pulled it off his face. While he was still conscious, he carried her into the kitchen and sat her on the gas stove. His head was starting to spin, he didn't have much time left; he was desperate for a breath and to release his right hand. At the stove he leaned forward, turned on all the hobs and hit the ignite button.

'Good luck!' he rasped.

The blonde let out a scream, released her grip on Harry's neck and rolled off the stove, but not before kicking him in the chest with a stiletto heel. Harry released his grip on her hands.

Travers desperately filled his lungs with air to prevent his head spinning wildly out of control.

The blonde was back on her feet instantly still holding the hairpin blade. She swiped violently at Harry to make him back up but lost her balance in the heels. Harry lunged for a drawer containing the cutlery and knives and pulled it hard. The drawer came out of the unit and spilt its contents over the floor.

The assassin smiled a beautiful smile and flashed her blue eyes at him: he was dead. She kicked the cutlery across the floor as she closed the gap on the gasping Harry.

'You'll pay for that. This dress is French.' She flicked the hairpin blade casually towards his face.

Harry didn't flinch.

She flicked the blade a second time while holding a devilish smile that spelt death. The smell of gas filled the room from the hobs that didn't ignite. Harry swung the drawer at the hand holding the hairpin and threw all his weight at her chest. The two of them fell backwards onto the floor. Instantly he was on top of her, preventing her from getting in the closed guard position. She instinctively pushed at his chest with her right arm and tried to stab him with her left. It was what he wanted. In a flash he framed the arm with both hands, rocked forward allowing him to move freely, kicked out his legs and spun though 90 degrees. With her arm now clamped between his thighs, he squeezed his knees together, raised his hips and got her in an arm-bar. She cried out but didn't tap out. She tried and tried to stab his legs.

'Give it up!' he shouted.

'Never!'

Harry held onto the arm-bar.

'You can't win!'

'I'll die first before I give in to you!' And she went to try and slice his femoral artery. She cut the inside of his right leg, close to the artery then went to stab the thigh. She was taking the pain to get in the killing blow. Harry released the hold, swung his legs to the right, clear of her strike, picked up a large kitchen knife off the floor and stabbed her through the heart, killing her instantly.

14

Harry left her in the kitchen, after clearing up the knives, and went and had a shower and clean the wounds to his leg and face. He was leaving the knife used to kill her where he plunged it: the last thing he needed was blood all over his kitchen floor.

The shower refreshed him, cleared his mind, showing him the course of action required.

Harry returned to the kitchen after putting on jeans, a black jumper, a pair of tan coloured loafers and dressing the wound to his leg. He carefully removed the knife from the blonde's chest and soaked it in bleach. He washed his hands thoroughly and put on a pair of black nitrile gloves. Next, he put all his dirty clothes and shoes in the washing machine and put it on. None of them had her blood on them. He would wash the clothes and shoes twice then donate them to a charity shop.

He needed to be patient, but at the same time act quickly: if the blonde didn't show, the police would be round his house a second time and they would be more thorough after receiving another tip-off.

Harry wrapped the blonde in a large plastic sheet that was left over from some DIY. He cleaned the sheet first then checked on the blonde's car; she had not locked it and her handbag was on the front passenger's seat. He would move it later.

It was still dark when Harry slowly pulled out of Baslow Drive and he drove at a sensible pace. The drive calmed his nerves: they weren't frayed, far from it, but his heartbeat began to slow, and he was Harry Travers once more.

He paused outside Cantlay's house, said a quiet prayer for the man, and then dumped the blonde, still in the plastic sheeting, outside the front door of that house.

The 924 was left running and Harry softly closed the passenger door and pulled away keeping the revs low. Dawn was beginning to break, and it wouldn't take long for them to discover their dead comrade. She was there problem now: her DNA was all over the crime scene in the car park and Haffenden was smart enough to avoid any police interference. He was home studying his front-room and kitchen in no time and spent the next three hours cleaning that floor of his house thoroughly and moving the car.

The next two days were quiet. Harry deliberately kept his head below the parapet and stayed off everybody's radar; if Haffenden or Raquette want to pay him a visit then he'd accommodate them, but until then he was keeping himself to himself.

Harry studied the national and local news for any information on the dead blonde, or the guy in the car. There was nothing: they had a clean-up squad, people to take out the trash once the job was done.

* * *

His leg caused him no bother, and he strode confidently into the crew-room for a flight to Malaga in Spain, brimming with confidence. The marks to his face had healed quickly.

He was early and the crew-room for once was quiet. The Malaga check-in time was 5am local and barring any unforeseen delays he should be back by 13:00 and home by 14:30 at the latest.

The first officer was a Rebecca Brightstone, a slim, pretty, brown- eyed brunette in her late twenties who always wanted to be a pilot since she was young. She arrived right behind Harry and cracked on with the paperwork. Harry left her to it and went to talk to the crew to pass on flight times: a recent innovation by the company was to email all the paperwork to the pilots three hours before the flight was due to depart so they could study and familiarise themselves with both sectors before leaving the house. It was all done with the aim of improving on-time performance and customer satisfaction: in a recent survey, passengers were asked what would make them more likely to book their next holiday with the same airline and the overwhelming response was to depart on time. The drive now was for the crews to save a few minutes here and there and push back on schedule. Harry passed on the flight times; they had all flown with him before, so introductions were not necessary. Harry noticed that two of the female crew were good friends of Tony Belisse and from their friendly smiles they clearly knew.

He returned to Rebecca. The two confirmed the fuel figure for the outbound sector and they departed soon after for an extra hot decaf latte.

Harry chose to fly the outbound sector: he had not flown into Malaga for a few years and was relishing the opportunity to fly somewhere other than the Canaries and Turkey.

The day became one obstacle after another preventing them from maintaining their on-time performance: first the inbound flight came in with a technical fault which needed rectification; fuelling was slow; boarding was equally slow due to missing passengers enjoying themselves too much in duty free; and they needed to renegotiate an air traffic slot after failing to make the first one. Between the two of them they managed to push back only twenty minutes behind schedule, but with a few short cuts en-route and a quick turnaround in Malaga they should still be able to land back in Manchester on time.

The obstacles petered out and they did indeed get a good turnaround in Malaga and landed back into Manchester five minute ahead of schedule.

The day mirrored Harry's recent cases and those he still needed to resolve. The drive home presented its own obstacles in the shape of two hard-looking gentlemen driving a blue Volkswagen

Golf GTI. This was it: revenge for the blonde. Harry didn't care. He was tired of this: tired of Haffenden; tired of Raquette and he'd only met the man the once, but once was enough for some people. The Golf kept on his tail and was not afraid to let Travers know they were there. It was not immediately obvious where they would make their strike, but if he was going to fight today then where better than on his own patch. Travers headed for home.

He had become so used to being followed, threatened, that it was nothing but an annoyance to him on those days where he hadn't the patience and was simply a mister angry, but on the others he relished it: these were the days that invigorated him, enabled him to appreciate life. To quote one of his favourite actors, Oliver Reed: "Life is for living – that's all there is to it". Harry Travers would live life today, and he had the patience of a saint.

The Golf was goading him with its bumper only just behind the 924's. They knew Harry wouldn't brake hard and risk damaging the classic Porsche. Harry had the Colt in the glove compartment. Bad idea and he dismissed it. He also had a nine-iron in the boot. Now there was an idea.

Harry pulled into Baslow Drive and stopped short of his house. He put on a pair of black driving gloves, got out leaving the engine running and went to open the boot with a spare key he carried with his house keys. The Golf continued on, but Harry knew what they were about: Baslow Drive went in a complete circle and they would reappear in a matter of minutes behind him.

The nine-iron was extracted from the boot of the Porsche. Harry ran over to where he calculated the Golf would appear. Sure enough, it arrived just in time to collect a hard blow to the windscreen. The glass fractured and the driver slammed on the brakes. Harry smashed in the driver's side window. The driver ducked before a third blow clipped him behind the ear. The passenger froze to his seat. The driver never said a word.

'Tell your boss to fuck off!' Harry snarled.

Neither man spoke.

'You want to join the blonde, just show your faces round here again!'

'Which blonde?' The driver finally said.

'Tell Raquette, if wants a piece of me then make it personal and don't send monkeys.'

The driver's head snapped right, his eyes aflame with indignation.

'Get out of the car, and I'll kill you!' Harry did not care which of his neighbours were enjoying the free show.

Neither man moved a muscle. They sat frozen in time like a couple of waxwork models. Harry backed off. He watched their hands for any sign of movement: it would be a cinch to shoot Harry through the door, wound him, then finish him off in quick-fire fashion. The driver moved his left hand down and to the right. Harry smashed the golf club into his face. The man never made a sound: he was unconscious before his head hit the steering wheel. Harry leaned in and removed a snub-nosed Magnum from the man's inside jacket pocket. He aimed it straight at the passenger: 'Suggest you fuck off! Tell Raquette it's my turn to come for him.'

Harry walked back to his 924 with his head permanently cocked to the left. He carried the Magnum in his left pocket out of sight of the nosey neighbours. No curtains flickered and no vehicles passed him on the road. Once out of sight he heard the opening and closing of car doors and the Golf drive off.

Back in the house he checked his pulse: it didn't break 80. He smiled. He was getting good at this: half the battle was won when you could control your own nerves; much like the game of golf, 70 percent of that was mental. Harry made coffee and waited for the police to arrive. He considered cleaning the weapon, but that would point the finger of guilt firmly at him. No, keeping it 'dirty' protected him and incriminated them, especially Raquette. Harry sunk into his sofa and thought of Moore and the two other men who met their maker that night. He was there again with hate in his heart, and again he was ready, ready to send more deserving souls to meet the Lord.

Was he an atheist for thinking this way? He didn't think so. It had occurred to him in the past that murderers would have to be atheists when you considered the Decalogue: also known as the Ten commandments, a set of biblical principles which help form the very foundation on which most societies are based, and the implications inherent for ignoring them, so to commit a murder one would have to forsake the Lord and disregard the Almighty's warning therefore qualifying you as an atheist. Harry always considered convicted murderers becoming born again Christians while in prison as fucking hypocrites. This then begged the question, where did he stand? Was he a fucking hypocrite for killing those three men? But they killed the woman he loved and tried to get away with it. If they had stayed, admitted their guilt to the police, and accepted their punishment then Harry could not and would not have been there that night seeking revenge. An old friend, a far more intelligent man than him, once told him, one night over a few beers, that in the Commandment "thou shalt not kill", the Hebrew word for kill and murder were the same and it was the context that changed its meaning. Where did Harry stand now? Had Harry disregarded that Commandment? Was he not protecting his family, everybody's family, from murderers, or was he just another would-be fucking hypocrite trying to convince himself through a lame-ass excuse that his revenge was justifiable? Either way Harry did not care: Raquette and Haffenden were better off out of the way. Harry knew their guilt, knew they would kill again, or try and kill again and that was enough, that was sufficient to force him to keep going; he would sacrifice his soul to damnation in order to protect those souls from the odious, insidious Misters Haffenden and Raquette.

Harry made a coffee. Coffee had replaced alcohol in his life: he did not want alcohol to be the trigger, to be the necessity when the time came to deal with undesirables. He wanted to be sober, to be in full control of his faculties and coffee fitted the bill exactly. The brew was enhanced with caramel syrup acquired during the latest shopping spree. The hate warmed his heart as much as the coffee warmed his innards.

* * *

Nero's was busy for a Wednesday. Harry confidently strolled around the blackjack tables dressed in casual, comfortable clothes: he wore dark blue chinos, a white long-sleeved shirt and tan coloured loafers. Clothes guaranteed not to restrict him in a fight. He left his coat in the cloakroom. Harry flaunted his presence; he knew that Raquette would be informed if he was not already monitoring his every move via CCTV. Harry played some blackjack. A male player sat next to him on his left. He blanked him. Harry was back in 'gambling' mode, but it was a mode with an underlying couldn't give a damn attitude, an attitude coupled with a desire, a need for a scrap. He quelled the combative side to his nature long enough to go on a winning streak. The player on his left came out with some comment they knew would get a reaction. Harry turned to face him. It was the driver of the Golf. He had the same build as Harry, but by his dark eyes, hair and complexion there was Latin blood in his make-up.

'I'm so glad it's you,' Harry said.

The man never replied but looked to his right.

Harry followed his line of sight.

Raquette stood with his hands in his pockets flanked by two men. On his right was the passenger from the Golf. He was fair when compared to the driver with mousey coloured hair, light brown eyes, slightly smaller in build, but Harry noticed the man walked on the balls of his feet; a fast mover and one to watch. Harry got out of his seat, leaving the chips on the table.

'You took your time!' Harry said to Raquette.

The man on Raquette's left was a tall, skinny gentlemen who seemed by his body movements itching to prove a point. He spoke. His voice was high pitched, and it fitted his long thin, blue-eyed face perfectly. He took a step forward. Raquette held out his left arm and halted him. Harry noticed his blonde hair was thinning. Funny how you notice tiny little details with heightened senses.

Macho, far too macho, thought Harry.

The tall thin man waited patiently to make his move on Harry. Harry smiled at him; it was a goading kind of smile, a smile guaranteed to rile the blood. Harry knew the next move before the man consciously made that decision to disobey his boss' orders.

The passenger from the Golf got the nod from Raquette and advanced. Harry took a step back; this allowed him to see all before him and the driver from the Golf. He made no conscious move of the head towards the blackjack table. The driver was now standing.

When the passenger was three strides from being within striking distance, Harry swivelled to his right and shot out his left foot in a hard front-kick to the driver's solar plexus. The man was not expecting such a swift offensive move and doubled over immediately. With his left still off the floor, and the passenger still advancing, Harry fired out a side kick in quick succession. The passenger didn't have time to react and took the blow on his ribs. It winded him badly and he fell to the floor. The driver recovered just in time to collect a two-punch combination to the face and nose.

Harry was on a roll and the tall skinny man was on the move, but clearly anticipating, by his fighting stance, where the next attack was coming from. He threw a sharp right roundhouse kick to Harry's head. Harry blocked the first, but the man was good and caught him with two more quick-fire roundhouse kicks. Because the kicks were aimed with the dorsum part of the foot, and not the harder ball section, they did not achieve their goal. Harry was stunned, but that was all and was ready for the follow up sidekick.

He blocked it with a hard block with his left hand, took a step forward and to his right and delivered a two-punch combination to the bridge of the man's nose and his solar plexus. To finish the move Harry stepped behind the man with his left leg and swung a hard, left hook at the same time. The tall skinny man hit the ground with a bang.

Raquette had not moved a muscle.

Harry faced him knowing within seconds reinforcements would arrive.

Raquette started clapping: 'Bravo, Mister Travers, bravo.'

From his right came three more men. Raquette kept on clapping, slowly.

'See how you get on in round two, Mister Travers.'

Travers had two choices: try and make a run for it, not a good idea; or take a beating to give a beating, which was probably the better of the two less than ideal choices.

The three men could have been triplets: each was six-foot, broad, dark-haired, and quick on their feet. They came initially in single file, but Harry anticipated them fanning out. Which one to attack first, it was folly to wait for their onslaught.

Harry chose the rear most man from the single file. Once they had fanned out, he was on the right.

During Harry's latest Tang Soo Do lesson a student, higher ranked than him, taught him the jumping turning-back kick. Harry practiced it, but he was ropey at best. The last man made his position on the right flank to be met by Harry's ropey attempt at a jumping turning-back kick. The kick with his right leg caught the man on the left shoulder sending him flying over a blackjack table. Female customers screamed as the man crashed to the floor. Before Harry could set himself to attack the other two, he received a blow to the top of the head and then a punch to the bridge of the nose. His eyes instantly filled with water and blood oozed onto his chin. Harry threw a left hook to get some breathing space. It missed, but it did allow him a valuable second or two to position himself for the next attack. The previous blow and punch came from the lead guy and he naturally stepped to one side to allow his other colleague some game time. Big mistake: Harry's eyes cleared, and it allowed him to aim a right-foot roundhouse kick at the other colleague before side-kicking the lead guy. Now all three men were momentarily stunned. It was time to leave.

Raquette made his move, but it was predictable at best; the man may look like a complete thug, but he sure as hell couldn't fight like one, and Harry had been in too many scraps of late to be caught out with the old fake kick to the knee cap trick. He kept his eyes on Raquette, blocked the straight right and countered with a fierce left uppercut, which found its target and nigh on ripped the man's head clean off his shoulders.

The Frenchman stumbled back but did not fall and these few valuable wasted seconds allowed the five men behind him to regroup and attack with a renewed ferocity. Harry by now had accepted he was not going to escape without injury and threw out a mule kick. The lead attacker, the driver, took the full force of the kick and he was done for. That left four, for Raquette was not for continuing his fight.

The second guy jumped on Harry's back and started wailing into his ribs. Harry swung through one hundred and eighty degrees and backed up violently into a blackjack table sending the chips flying. The man groaned as the edge of the table impacted his kidneys. Harry now had the other three in front of him, but it didn't prevent him from taking a thundering blow to the stomach from the passenger. The other two men were right behind him and Harry blocked numerous blows to his head and ribs, but still some got through.

He knew he had to take a blow to give one and concentrated his mind in order to deliver his retribution. Harry elbowed the guy on his back and threw him over his shoulder onto the passenger. Both men ended up on the floor. Harry stamped on the passenger's groin. Three down, two to go.

Out of the corner of his eye he made out Raquette retreating to his office. Willis was noticeable by his absence. He clearly didn't want to know.

Harry took a punch to the left side of his face because of his loss of concentration, for all of a second. Harry looked at one of the two men standing in front of him just in time to receive a second to his right eye. This punch sent him sprawling onto a table. An elderly lady was not pleased to see her winnings scattered over the floor by Travers' body landing squarely in the middle of the table.

The two men made their move on him, seeing Harry prostate on the table. Harry kicked out hitting one of them in the chest. The other rained down a series of short, sharp hurtful blows to Harry's head. He could not block them all and did a backward roll off the table. Their colleague managed to get clear of the passenger and jumped at Harry with a sidekick. Harry blocked it as best he could, but still got knocked backwards. He was slowly but surely making his way towards the exit.

All three men closed in on him as he tried to maintain his balance. Another flying sidekick came his way. It was predictable and Harry sidestepped it, picked up a chair and knocked the guy clean out with it. Definitely only two to go now plus he had the exit within his reach.

Harry smashed the chair against a railing, which separated an elevated table from the floor below, leaving him with two of the chair legs. He now had two sharp implements to ward off his attackers. The two advanced on him.

'That's enough!'

Harry recognised the voice.

'I said that's enough!' Willis was more forceful the second time and the men did indeed back off.

'Harry you need to leave.'

'Sure thing,' he replied, backing towards the exit. 'If you don't mind, I'll keep these for now.'

Harry took sizeable steps until he felt the swing doors that signalled his entry into the foyer.

The foyer was cool when compared to the casino and he turned and hurried outside after collecting his coat. The evening was mild for this time of year and after throwing the remains of the chair in the gutter made his way briskly to the 924.

15

Harry was pushing his luck, and he knew it, but he didn't care, he didn't give a damn. It would only be a matter of time before the two of them pooled resources and then he'd be in serious trouble. With such resources at their disposal the end result was inevitable. He needed to come to a decision as to which one to take out first and scare off the other for sufficient time for him to conjure up a worthwhile plan for their removal. They had been amiss in not dealing with him.

Raquette would give him a wide margin for a short time, but only a short time, so Haffenden became the obvious choice.

Travers' roster was quiet: it was a week on standby. He was reluctant to call in sick, but would have to have yet another accident falling out of the shower if called off standby: his lower back was sore; his right eye was swollen, but not shut; there were numerous marks over his face, but thankfully no cuts; as for his nose, it was painful, but any bleeding had stopped. His face looked a mess.

* * *

His mobile vibrated in his rear pocket and Travers woke sprawled over his sofa. The TV was off, and his face was sore. Worryingly his teeth hurt; he was going to get an abscess behind one of them eventually: any hard impact to the teeth invariably caused one. It was List.

'Afternoon,' Harry said half asleep. The clock off his mobile read 15:30.

'Afternoon, Harry. I must apologise to you-'

'What for?'

'I haven't settled my bill. How much do I owe you?'

'Nothing.'

'What? Come on I owe you something.'

Harry thought for a second then it came to him.

'I need a car for an indefinite period. No questions asked.'

There was a moments' silence.

'Sure. No questions asked.'

'I'll come and see you tomorrow.'

'Make it after eleven.'

'See you after eleven.'

Harry hung up. His beloved 924 was too conspicuous.

* * *

The following morning at a little past eleven Harry arrived at List's car dealership via a taxi to collect a smart looking Mini Cooper.

'I thought you'd like something a bit nippy, to cut through the traffic,' List added while handing over the keys.

'It's perfect,' Harry replied. It was just that: perfect for the job.

Harry jumped in and fired her up. List leaned in through the open driver's door, as Harry familiarised himself with the car.

'I've written her off,' he said earnestly.

'You sure?'

'I've covered the insurance for you. Whatever this is, and I can tell it's important to you, it's best I don't know. You take the car and do whatever you need to do.'

Harry studied the man for a second. He was sincere.

'Thank you.'

List wished him happy hunting and went inside to deal with a new customer. Harry headed to Cantlay's old house after a quick visit to Baslow drive for essentials.

* * *

The road was quiet, as he suspected and hoped it would be. Harry parked down the street from Cantlay's and walked briskly past a for sale sign to the rear of the old man's house. Within seconds the locks were picked, and he was inside. He would wait here until dark.

Harry slept well, better than he'd slept in many a night. He checked the time by his watch: it was 23:30 exactly.

He unbuckled his belt and fed onto it a small black pouch with a Velcro cover which contained a handyman that doubled up as an axe: in its handle, among other things, was a knife, a saw and a screwdriver plus the axe could be turned around and used as a hammer. Hidden by his dark coloured jacket was a shoulder strap containing the Smith and Wesson 1911. Around his ankle he'd strapped the Colt using duct tape.

Harry put on a pair of black gloves to complement the jacket, black jeans, shoes, woolly hat, and a hoodie. He pulled the hoodie over his head and left the house by the backdoor.

He walked up the street, past that house, to gauge the movement outside and within. All was quiet. Never at any time did he question his actions or motives.

Harry did an about-turn and marched back to the house neighbouring his objective. There was no car in the drive, and it didn't take but a second to reach the back garden and vault the fence. The rear of the house now faced him: the lights were on with the curtains open allowing him a full view of proceedings. They were busy tonight. He crouched down behind a small shed and made himself comfortable.

Haffenden never appeared. Harry didn't care: if it was tonight then so be it, if not he'd come back. For an organisation that surely must pride itself on its privacy, he was finding it awfully easy to get close to them. Harry reminded himself off some of their clientele.

An hour passed and Harry needed to stand up to stop from stiffening up, due to the temperature plummeting to near freezing on this night. Even though he'd budgeted for that, twenty minutes later Harry was losing feeling in his hands and feet and wrote the night off. He returned to his car via the way he came, but not before he covered his tracks removing any sign that he had been anywhere near that house.

One advantage of the Mini was it warmed up pretty quick and he was grateful to get feeling back in bones. Oh, well, he thought, it's all a learning curve.

Harry hit the sack around 04:30. He didn't sleep well and woke every 45 minutes. Banking on not being called from another standby duty, he decided to play golf and booked a tee-time online. The day would drag until it was time to search for Haffenden again; the beauty of it all was he knew where he'd be eventually, whether or not it happened on one of his standby days worried him not a jot. Harry looked upon himself as virtuous, as righteous: he was patient and for the time being not mister angry, but his vengefulness was threatening to be the undoing of him. How long could he keep pushing his luck like this?

What was the greatest worry? What would harm him the most? Be the root cause of endless sleepless nights? If Haffenden and Raquette were left to go free to continue to wreak havoc and create misery without fear of retribution, for eventually there would invariably be another Bennett or Cantlay, and Harry was not willing to placate the little angel perched on his shoulder urging for forgiveness and the exercising of the proper laws. No, he was for the demon sitting opposite on the other shoulder advocating bloodlust and the survival of the meanest. If Harry was anything on these nights, he was mean.

Golf was good: Harry shot five over par for the front nine and six over for the back; his best round ever and in the eighties and not just scraping into the eighties, but comfortably in. It all boded well for his second night in the garden.

The second night was only slightly warmer than the previous one, but Harry wore thermals this time and more comfortable shoes, albeit still in black. The same women were on duty and it was again busy for a weekday. There was definitely enough custom to go around.

Harry had to wait an hour before his longing for bloodlust could be satiated: Haffenden arrived around 01:00. He was animated. Harry had never seen him this worried, but then again, he'd never properly studied the man. He was worried and Harry flattered himself that it was because of him.

'You need another blonde,' he said quietly, 'and a brunette.'

Haffenden began to point in an accusing kind of way, making a point of aiming a digit at each girl in turn. None of the girls nodded or acknowledged having the finger aimed firmly at them.

Harry watched the scene play out. Not being a lipreader he could only guess at its meaning. Suddenly Haffenden pointed outside directly at Harry. He instinctively ducked out of the way, but Haffenden never looked his way.

His prey wiped his forehead on his sleeve.

'My, my, Mister Haffenden, you are under pressure.'

Haffenden continued to stress whatever message he was delivering to the girls.

A cold chill came over him: he could make out the name "Travers". On this word two of the girls took a step forward and began to exchange words with Haffenden; they didn't seem to be arguing more like stressing their point. One of the girls pointed at herself then her colleague. The second girl nodded then did the same.

'Want the job, do you?' Harry whispered.

Haffenden seemed pleased.

Harry concentrated on the two girls: their hair colour; body shape; how they carried themselves; any idiosyncrasies they had; how they interacted with the others. He wanted to remember them the next time they should meet, for this mission was all about Haffenden.

Haffenden looked at his watch; this was Harry's cue to leave. He was over the wall, back in the street and in the Mini within minutes. And there he sat with a good view of that house.

At first, he thought he'd made a mistake and contemplated returning to the rear garden, and even had the driver's door open, but he stood firm and stayed put. Ten minutes later Haffenden appeared in a Jaguar. Harry was determined that this was it: he'd have one less headache after tonight.

Harry kept the Jaguar in sight. Haffenden would not recognise the Mini and he was banking on him not realising who he was until it was too late.

Haffenden drove at a sensible pace. Harry was calm for he now had his man. Haffenden was calm for recruiting two harpies to deal with Travers.

The Jaguar led him onto the A6, and there they stayed five car lengths apart. South of Stockport the Jaguar passed through Heaviley then turned left onto the B6171. The B6171 connected with the A626 before continuing South-East towards Marple. Harry dropped further back, but not too far so he could not see the Jaguar's rear lights.

Harry was not familiar with Marple; didn't know anybody who lived there, hadn't even driven through it. At least this job was showing him the sights around Manchester that he would not normally see. Harry laughed and closed the gap on Haffenden.

The Jaguar began to slow and indicated left into Bowden Lane. Harry kept on going and took the next left; Manor Hill Road led onto Norbury Drive. Harry turned left again into Norbury Drive and doubled back towards Bowden Lane. He didn't need to wait long to see the Jaguar parked outside a smart looking semi-detached house set back from the road. The BMW was parked in the drive. No lights were on in the house. Harry parked up opposite, checked the time: it was 02:45. He set his alarm for 04:00, reclined his seat and took a power nap.

His mobile started to vibrate, bringing him back into the here and now. The Jaguar was still outside. The BMW in the drive. Harry stretched while contemplating approaching the house. No, now was not the time: he had this address and it would enable him to get the jump on the man. Harry would be ready, not only for Haffenden, but the two eager Harpies dispatched to bring him to book. Harry fired up the Mini and gleefully went home.

* * *

Harry was never used on his standby week, and every night he waited patiently for Haffenden to turn up at Norbury Drive again and each night he was bitterly disappointed. It got to be that he began to think that Haffenden knew he was coming. Harry left it alone for a few days and recharged his batteries with golf and martial arts.

Three days after his short sabbatical, Harry was once again outside the semi-detached house waiting on the man. Boredom began to raise its ugly head: should he bother wasting any more time? But he killed Cantlay. Harry was convinced he was behind it, he knew he was behind it, Cantlay as good as told him from the grave, but he had to be sure: you can't go killing a man on the correspondence of a dead man. Harry had to be sure. He fired up the Mini and went home. Harry had to find the evidence to justify removing Haffenden.

Once home Harry went straight to bed; he wanted to be fresh to begin his search: he could easily find him and follow from there. The blonde sprung to mind; he had witnessed Haffenden converse with the girl, but did he instruct her to kill the man in the car and Harry? Was Harry being soft? He had to be sure and could feel himself getting angry.

* * *

Harry crouched down in the rear garden and once again spied on the comings and goings in that house. Haffenden never materialised. One of the girls though captured his attention: it was one of the two who had spoken to Haffenden the last time he was here. She left the room for the front of the house. Harry's sixth sense cried out for him to follow her. He was over the wall and racing back to the Mini in seconds.

The dark-haired Harpy casually sauntered over to a dark-green Audi, opened it via a remote control and climbed aboard. And there she sat for a good ten minutes.

'Where are you off to?' Harry said, not taking his eyes off the target. 'You're not carrying a bag, so that was pre-loaded; Baslow Drive is too obvious a target, your colleagues put paid to that. So where are you going?'

The target was studying something in her lap.

'Well, you drive nice cars!'

Then he got it.

Harry reversed into a neighbour's drive and slowly left via the far end of the street.

Harry was caught in two minds as whether to drive fast or not. It didn't really make any difference he decided: if he was wrong then there would be one more casualty, and there was nothing he could do about that: he couldn't protect everybody. Harry stuck to the speed limit. On his way to his chosen destination Harry passed two police patrol cars. He had made a smart choice.

Harry passed the house and looked for signs of life. All the lights were off, and it was deathly quiet.

'Quiet as a graveyard,' he said with a smile.

The Mini was parked well out of sight and with each step back to the house, Harry expected to witness the green Audi turn into the road.

He stopped opposite the house on the other side of the road. His hood was up and Harry new the look was doing him no favours.

The road was quiet. Harry took a gamble and was across the road and up and over the gate in no time. He landed softly on the drive and was up the left-hand side of the house, towards the double garage in seconds. Harry crouched out of sight behind some bushes bordering the far left of the drive and waited.

'Made your choice now, Harry,' he muttered. 'Just got to wait and see.'

He leant back against a wall and shut his eyes.

The bushes did their job admirably. The sound of feet on the drive woke Harry out of a light sleep. The figure was crouching in exactly the same position as Harry had done. He positioned himself for the strike: if the figure was also thinking along the same lines as he was then these bushes were in for a treat.

The dark, lithe figure moved quickly over the ground, keeping low at all times. It made the front of the house near the double garage. Harry could see they were all in black, including a black balaclava. They turned to their right to try and peek through a front window. The figure was female. He'd been proved right.

The woman was around thirty yards away by his calculation, and to be too hasty in closing the gap would leave him open to attack if this assassin was anywhere near the standard of the blonde.

This victim was not a client: clients got the personal touch. This one was getting the ninja treatment.

The woman kept close to the side of the house, after her failed attempt to see into the victim's front window and disappeared out of sight in the walkway between the garage and the house.

Harry waited and listened. He heard nothing. Several minutes later Harry moved out from behind the bushes, hugged the front of the garage and slowly made his way for the walkway.

The walkway, when he finally geared himself up to check it out, was empty. The door at the far end was closed. Harry swiftly made the door opened it, slipped inside and softly closed it behind him.

It was so quiet you could have heard someone move about from next door. Harry checked the hallway both ways. He chose to head to the right, as this led towards the main body of the house. The first two doors, one on each side were closed and no sound emanated from behind the doors; this reminded Harry of the house where he finished off Moore.

Harry moved effortlessly towards the downstairs: the kitchen was open plan and tastefully decorated, expensively designed. Just how he imagined it would be.

The kitchen led into the dining area: six high back chairs circled a glass table with a large bowl of fruit situated in the middle.

Harry examined the room in fine detail. Nothing had been moved or looked out of place: studying a room, studying a person carefully gave him a good feeling about them. The room looked as though it was in the condition the owners had left it.

All the ground floor looked untouched and Harry took the stairs two at a time. At the top of the stairs Harry stopped. There was still no sound. To his left he figured was the bathroom, ahead was a bedroom with three more doors behind him, half hidden by the banister. Harry crouched down and scanned the first floor. Five doors, he had five doors to choose from. He stood up and was hit hard from behind.

Harry fell forward and impacted the bedroom door ahead of him. His head, he needed to protect his head. Harry put his left hand over the back of his head with took a sharp blow over his fingers. He rolled right and kicked out. The feet of his attacker were forced back by the blow and they fell towards him, only keeping their balance by pushing against the bedroom door. Harry punched them in the stomach, and they lurched forward, exhaling as they did so.

Harry looked up and focused as his head tried to clear. He hit out again and pushed them away.

The overwhelming feeling of déjà vu was shattered by the female figure spinning round and planting a turning-back kick firmly into Harry's chest.

Harry smashed into the bedroom door and disappeared inside. He landed on the bed and bounced off onto the floor. The room belonged to a girl. Harry didn't know that List had a daughter, and the dark female figure didn't know Harry was carrying the Colt Detective Special and the axe this night. They were both tucked in his belt: for emergencies only.

He only just managed to get to his feet before the female figure came down on top of him with an axe kick. Harry rolled out of the way and narrowly avoided having his collarbone broken. He tried in vain to sweep her standing leg, but he was inept at such a skill: his proficiency at Tang Soo Do didn't extend that far, yet. The woman stayed upright and stamped on Harry's groin. He let out a cry and rolled out of the way of a second attack on his manhood.

It was a good job Harry had a high pain threshold; years of playing rugby built that up and this assassin would not be the last person to try and cripple him in such a way. Harry took a deep breath and forced himself to his feet. The woman was not for giving up and attempted a third strike down below. It was pure folly: Harry sidestepped the kick, blocked it with a right hand and hit her hard in the face with a sharp, straight left punch. His attack was not folly and he achieved his goal: her nose exploded over the left side of her face. She let out a scream and side-kicked Harry on the chest. Again, it was anticipated, and he blocked it sufficiently to stay upright.

Harry jumped over the bed to put some space between him and the girl. Only now did he get a good look at her. She was blonde. Where was the dark-haired girl?

The blonde read his look: 'Not who you were expecting?'

'No matter!'

'It does to me. She was my friend!'

'You should choose them more carefully.'

The dark-haired girl appeared in the doorway.

Harry knew he'd been set up.

'List's on holiday,' said the dark-haired girl.

'I know,' Harry replied. It was a lie.

'We've got all the time in the world,' the blonde added.

Harry began to sing the Louis Armstrong version of the song with the same name.

It was time to use the Colt, but he decided against it, for now. He wanted to win this fair and square.

The blonde sprang at him. Harry shot out a four-punch combination, as he stepped back. The girl was good, but not good enough to block them all and the last punch to her face hit home, stunning her momentarily.

The dark-haired girl made her move.

The blonde was nearly on top of him, but in that second it took her to compose herself and strike, Harry head-butted her on the damaged nose. She cried out, grabbed her nose and fell back on the bed with blood flowing freely from between her fingers.

'Cantlay was my friend,' he shouted.

The dark-haired girl now got his full attention: Harry stepped sharply to his left and fired out a left front-kick. The girl fell for the bluff and went to block it. As quick as you like Harry turned the front-kick into a roundhouse kick and struck her on the jawbone. She was rocked but did not fall. Harry now attacked her with a front-kick to the solar plexus followed by a three-punch combination. She blocked the kick, and all but the last punch then retaliated with a left roundhouse kick of her own. The kick hit its target and Harry fell to his left.

With the bed cutting the floor space in half, and there being two of them, taking the fight to the ground was not an option. Harry positioned himself with his back to the bedroom door.

The dark-haired girl helped her colleague to her feet. The blonde produced a zipped pouch, which had been tucked in behind her back. She unzipped it and removed a syringe.

'My turn to be "as high as a kite"?'

'Not for long,' the blonde spat. Blood still oozed down her face.

'This how you dealt with the old man?'

Neither girl answered.

'You might find me a different proposition.'

'The end will be the same!'

The blonde lunged at Harry with the needle.

Quick as a flash Harry grabbed one of List's daughter's blouses that she'd left hanging over a chair and swung it at the hand carrying the needle. Thank heaven for messy kids, he thought, as the blouse covered the hand carrying the needle. Harry followed up by punching her again in the face. It failed to stop her: she kept on trying to inject him with the deadly poison. With Harry having his hands full, the dark-haired girl went for the kill. Similar to her partner she revealed a loaded syringe from behind her back. She wasted no time attempting to stab Harry in the arm. His only defence was the blonde and he swung her round to block the attack. The poor girl took the needle between the shoulder blades. She let out a sickly scream and fell to the floor.

'The car,' the blonde cried, 'the car!'

The dark-haired girl froze with her right hand still raised up in an attacking pose.

'Get to the fucking car,' the blonde pleaded. 'It's in the glove compartment.'

The dark-haired girl was gone before the blonde finished her sentence.

Harry leaned over the blonde: 'I'll be taking my leave then.'

'Don't leave me. I need water.'

'Okay, but you tell me why Haffenden set me up.'

The blonde failed to answer.

'Bye!' Harry headed for the door.

'I'll tell you, but get me a drink of water first, please.'

'Why?'

'My throat dries up, I can't swallow; if you want me to talk you better get me a drink of water.'

Harry contemplated the idea of his being set up a second time, but the colour was beginning to wash out of the blonde's face. He went to get a cup of water from the bathroom. When he returned, he was mindful to make sure all was as he had left it.

The blonde gratefully accepted the water and drank the lot in one go.

'Thank you.'

'I'm listening,' Harry said, trying to sound impatient. In truth he was willing to wait. He wanted to hear what the dark-haired girl could add.

'Haffenden had your friend rubbed out.'

'He got too close to the truth, didn't he?'

'Not quite, but close,' the blonde rasped.

'Who did it?'

'He did: Haffenden paid the old man a visit under the guise of friendship, to help build bridges, etcetera etcetera!'

Harry didn't need to ask any further questions: he now had the proof he sought, heard it first-hand. The dark-haired girl returned and injected the blonde with something to help relieve her symptoms.

'You told him?' she asked of the blonde.

'Only what he needs to know,' she replied.

Both looked at Harry anticipating another question.

'How?'

'Teabags,' the dark-haired girl said with pride.

'He was my friend,' Harry said as a reminder.

The dark-haired girl looked away. It was best.

Harry pulled out the Colt with his left hand and aimed it straight at the dark-haired girl's forehead then the blonde's. It was time: 'There will be no confab next time and no words will be exchanged.'

Both girls nodded.

Harry lowered the Colt. 'If I find he's been tipped off-'

'Not from us,' the blonde interjected.

'He was a frail old man,' the dark-haired girl added.

'That he was!' Harry said angrily before adding: 'Don't interfere!'

He left before they could answer.

The coolness of the night helped calm him down. He made the Mini after checking the coast was clear then drove home. Tomorrow Haffenden would be gone.

* * *

The following day was quiet, quiet enough for Harry to get all his housekeeping done: it was amazing how calming ironing could be. Harry always did his while watching a film or a sporting event on the TV. In the afternoon he got his hair cut short: there must be no hair fibres linking them to him.

He packed his essentials into the pockets of the black jacket he was going to wear: one pair of nitrile gloves; a pair of black driving gloves; a small bottle of bleach, to kill any DNA; his small

Swiss army knife; a Bowie Knife in its sheath, which he attached to his belt; and the Colt for back-up. The axe got the night off.

To say he was dispassionate would be an understatement: there would be no feelings or emotions to influence this night; Haffenden had organised, planned and executed the murder of a man Harry regarded as a friend and colleague, and he would not be the last thorn that Haffenden would remove if he saw fit. As for the two girls he left at List's, he was not kidding himself as to where their loyalties lay, plus they would be counting down the hours to see if Harry was true to his word, or just full of shit. Whatever transpired this night Harry was well prepared to have to look over his shoulder, and if need be remove any souls wanting to make a name for themselves at his expense.

* * *

His usual spot in the garden was just how he left it. It was a good start. Where was his conscience? It should be kicking in about now, not that it would stand much chance of success given Harry's current state of mind, but still there was part of him hoping that Haffenden was smart enough not to show his face here again.

Day one proved to be fruitless and Harry drove the Mini home tired and frustrated. This was going to take time. Time Harry did not want to waste.

16

The loss of time, Harry remembered in a quote, brings us on the greatest loss of all. The only complete loss was not going to be his. Harry comforted any vexation that Cantlay's loss, courtesy of Haffenden, was not of the Lord's doing.

Days two and three were also fruitless. He was back on standby for three days and would have to wait. Harry convinced himself that the delay would help the cause: Haffenden would indeed think he was full of shit and drop his guard. Harry played golf during the three standby days and struggled due to lack of playing time prior to these three rounds.

* * *

Harry sat down on the icy ground and let out a huge sigh: he was tired this night and his whole body ached. He was coming down with something and gave serious thought to going home. A noise behind him snapped him back to the job at hand. He looked over his shoulder and took a blow across the side of the head. He went like a light.

If there was ever a time to question the propriety of his actions, then taped to a chair in a darkened room was it. His head hurt like hell. Those bloody girls had grassed him up; next time he was not going to be so charitable. Harry pulled at his hands: they were bound together behind him; his legs were taped to each chair leg with his chest strapped to the back of the chair.

Harry had no idea how long he had been in this position when a door off to his left opened, allowing a huge shaft of light to enter the room and blind him momentarily.

'Good evening,' said a man's voice.

'Fuck you!'

'Good to see you haven't lost your sense of humour.'

Harry's eyes adjusted to the light levels and a tall man stood hands on hips in front of him.

They don't know me, Harry thought, if it was Haffenden then they would have referred to me by my name. Then the smell hit him: perfume.

The tall man moved closer and bent down. Harry tested the strength of the tape securing his hands to the chair. The pins and needles in his hands told him all he needed to know.

By now the man's face came into view. Harry leant back and the chair moved. They haven't secured the chair. Play it cool, Harry said silently and look for anything in the room that can be used to break the tape.

The man had a long face covered with short, thick brown hair, his nose was crooked from being broken at some point, his jaw was too small for his teeth for they were all crooked and he smelt of garlic. The eyes were a dark brown and interrogated Harry. Harry tried hard not to look away and give the game away: over to his right clamped to the wall were two brackets for supporting a radiator. Just get through this and you'll be free.

'Why were you in my garden?' said the man

'Your garden?'

'Yes, my garden!'

'I like looking at the girls.'

'Do you now!'

'Yes, I like watching them.'

'A voyeur, are we?'

Harry nodded. Just get through this.

The man took a step back and hit Harry hard across the face. He tasted blood. He pretended to cry. To his amazement he was good at it and tears streamed down his cheeks. The man hit him again and Harry cried some more.

'What is your name?' asked the man calmly.

'Further, Neil Further,' replied Harry.

'Well, Mister Further, we will talk again very soon after I've discussed you with the girls.'

The man backed out of the room, then locked the door. Harry was once more plunged into darkness.

Quick as he could, Harry shuffled over to the right-hand wall, found a bracket and began to rub his hands as fast as he could against the sharp edges. He didn't have long, maybe minutes, until they figured out who Neil Further really was.

The tape stayed firm and Harry cussed. He rubbed harder. His wrists became damp; he accepted the pain and kept going. Voices outside did not halt his progress. A key in the door forced him to try and pull his hands apart. The tape began to split but stayed firm. The door opened then shut just as quick. The voices got louder: they began to argue over his proper disposal.

Harry pulled hard a second time on the tape and his hands come free, but the effort to free his hands toppled the chair and he crashed to the floor bruising his right side. The voices stopped.

Harry tried desperately to free his legs. The pain in his head was only matched by the pain in his right hip, but Harry welcomed the pain: it was the Swiss army knife digging into him.

The knife sliced through the tape binding his legs and he stood up the split second the door swung open to reveal the tall man silhouetted against the light. Harry cut the tape holding his chest and stepped clear of the chair. The tall man fatally paused and failed to take advantage of his position. Harry lunged at him, slashing the knife's blade at the man's face.

The man let out a scream and fell backwards towards the door. Harry continued to go for the man's cheeks and throat. The tall man hit the doorframe and collapsed against it.

Harry stood over him ready for the kill. It also allowed him to keep tabs on the door. Nobody else appeared.

'We do not have an issue with you, Mister Travers.'

'Really,' Harry said with real menace.

'It was not my idea to strap to you to the chair,' the tall man pleaded.

'Who ordered the hit on the old man?'

'Haffenden!'

'I will cut your throat without compunction.'

'Haffenden ordered it, on the grounds that the old man was now a liability; he was a renowned gardener by reputation and had been ill for a while, so it was easy to make it look like a heart attack and if anybody delved a little deeper then they will find that he had traces of jimsonweed in his system.'

Harry felt like killing the man there and then.

'Where is he?'

'He's not here!'

One of the girls came to the door. For a second or two Harry believed she was about to defend the tall man, but she simply looked at him and shook her head.

'This hasn't worked out quite how you wanted it to,' she said to the tall man.

The tall man shrugged his shoulders.

The girl stepped into the light. It was the blonde he had seen injected earlier.

'We said nothing,' she said before Harry could speak.

Harry nodded.

'He was doing his rounds and spotted you crouching in the garden spying on us.'

The tall man was shocked to hear that the blonde knew Harry: 'I didn't know you knew him.'

'It's been a short acquaintance,' she replied before gesturing to Harry to follow her.

Harry left the tall man on the floor.

'Don't worry about him Mister Travers, or Further, either one is fine with us. He likes to act tough!'

'What do you want?' Harry asked, as she led him towards the front of the house.

The blonde guided Harry into one of the larger downstairs rooms. Business must be quiet, he thought, for tonight all the girls were in the room and there was not a single client in sight.

'Nice to see the Executive Committee is here to greet us,' Harry said sarcastically.

'Mister Travers,' a redheaded woman said, taking a stride forward, 'we would like to have a polite and civil, if that is at all possible, conversation with you.'

'Sure,' Harry replied, 'but I don't want a cup of tea.'

Then he remembered the other redhead.

That redhead noticed the look in Harry's eyes: 'Yes, no tea.'

'That was sneaky!'

'You were perceived as a threat, Mister Travers.'

'Apparently, so was Cantlay.'

'That's why your here, Mister Travers.'

At least he could drop the Neil Further masquerade.

'I'll take a coffee then.'

Harry took a seat in one of three empty chairs to his right. The redhead sat opposite on a sofa. She motioned to someone behind Harry to make coffee.

'What do you want?'

'Straight to the point, Mister Travers, I like that.'

'Call me Harry.'

'Okay. Harry, we need you to remove a thorn in our sides, a thorn whose removal is beneficial to all of us.'

'You're kidding?'

'No Harry, I'm deadly serious.'

'And what do I get?'

'You get to live,' the blonde said butting in.

'That's awfully kind of you!'

A dark-haired girl, who was standing directly behind the redhead, nodded in agreement.

'I get to live,' Harry repeated.

'You took two friends of ours-'

'Occupational hazard, for them that is,' Harry said sharply.

'Still, you did take them,' the redhead said equally as sharp.

'It was them or me!'

A girl arrived with Harry's coffee. He took it without looking at her.

'Agreed; another reason why you get to live.'

Harry sipped his coffee. It tasted like coffee, but he still only took small sips to gauge any reaction.

'Who is the threat?' he asked, visibly relaxing with the hot drink.

'Haffenden!' answered the redhead.

Harry burst out laughing: 'Seriously?'

'Deadly!'

'Become a liability, has he?'

'That's not your problem, but ours!'

'But you want me to remove him and now made him mine, so why me?'

'You want him dead, that's......obvious.' The redhead deliberately paused for effect.

It was Harry's turn to pause.

'What do you want?' the blonde asked, breaking the short silence.

'You gone, and proof he killed Cantlay,' Harry said slowly.

The redhead was obviously expecting the answer for she nodded in agreement almost instantly: 'Agreed, and he did: it was the last straw for us, the old man was harmless. We knew he kept notes, but he couldn't prove anything. Killing the old man was not the done-thing.'

'I need to know the man's itinerary, and it's done at my pace, not yours!'

'Agreed.'

'Where will you go?'

Harry sipped more coffee.

'Not your concern, Mister Travers.'

'Agreed,' Harry said smiling and drank more coffee.

The redhead stood and offered her hand. Harry did the same and the two shook hands on the deal.

'You'll be wanting these back,' she added handing him the Colt and the Bowie Knife.

'Tell me,' Harry said smiling: he needed to know the answer to the question that was bugging him to the point of distraction. 'What's your modus operandi? And why?'

The redhead didn't answer straight away, and Harry was on the verge of asking again when she did: 'It's done to order,' she said before pausing, 'and don't drink the tea!'

'I'll stick to coffee then,' Harry said with all seriousness.

'We'll send you the details.' The redhead left without saying another word.

Harry felt like a spare prick at a wedding as he watched all the girls file out of the room one by one. 'What a way to go though,' he whispered.

Being left to his own devices, he left soon after.

The Mini was nice, but it wasn't the 924. Tomorrow he would return it.

* * *

List was still away on holiday. Harry feigned surprise and left the Mini and keys with one of the salespeople.

Today was a day to hit the little white ball: he was confident of a quiet day on the driving range followed by nine holes. This was

Travers' new strategy to improving his game: practice, practice, play. It's what's on the card that counts, not how it gets there, or to coin a well-used phrase: "it's not how, but how many".

* * *

She had a long, loose swing, which was the complete opposite to his short, compact swing with a wide stance and very reminiscent of the legendary Doug Sanders' swing. She was two bays up from him and Harry was hooked: he couldn't take his eyes of her slim, tight body with her long brown hair tied back in a ponytail. She was a member: he knew that by the club jumper she was wearing. A gym monster came up and spoke to her during mid-swing. You don't do that, ever. He clearly wasn't a golfer and missed all the tell-tale signals that she was severely pissed off. Harry hit a couple of balls down the range with his nine-iron. She took at least three swings to get her timing back after the rude interruption. The gym monster moved in to the next bay up from her and after three attempts to hit the ball, all of which sent it whistling along the floor at daisy-cutter height, began to try and open another conversation with the object of Harry's desire.

Harry found to his delight with Sheila that he was the jealous type, but not to the extent of overstepping the bounds of decency: the unwritten laws of never dating a mate's girlfriend, or even a recent ex, or anyone married, were adhered to religiously. Outside of that she was fair game. If she told him to "jog on" then so be it, but you've got to be there to hear it.

The brown-haired girl turned to her left, so Harry got her in profile; she was beautiful, no, stunning. She put the club she was practicing with, Harry guessed a seven-iron, back in her bag and removed a metal wood. From the shaft length it looked like a nine-wood. The gym monster kept on talking. The girl was polite and answered whatever question he'd asked. Harry lost interest and hit more balls.

Half a bucket of balls later, Harry looked up and the brown-haired girl was gone. The gym monster, though, was manfully still trying to hit the ball straight. Give him his due he was sticking to the task, and occasionally, achieving just that. The brown-haired girl returned with another, smaller, bucket of balls and looked Harry's way. He smiled. She smiled back. His mind was made up: she was that beautiful he had to make a fool of himself and hear those two words or not. The brown hair was matched by equally captivating brown eyes and by the way she moved her five-feet-four-inch frame, she was fit. The club jumper looked fantastic on her.

Should he go now, or let the gym monster fuck it up? But then again, he might come out with that one line that breaks the ice and he'd be fighting an uphill battle. Harry hit three more balls and gave it some thought. He was beginning to get his timing just right and striped all three.

The sound and feel the ball makes as it leaves the club-head, when everything comes together, is a thing of beauty and immensely satisfying. The bonus for Harry was all three went where he intended.

Harry had hit those last three using his seven-iron and returned the club back to his bag and removed his driver. It was all for vanity: the fact that he'd hit them so well, was behind his decision to make some noise. It was a gamble. His driving was improving but was inconsistent.

The gym monster watched Harry pull the "big dog" from the bag and pretended to line up his next shot while keeping an eye on a rival.

Harry carefully placed the range ball on the rubber tee, thankfully for him it was the right height for his driving wood, lined himself up, relaxed and swung hard at the ball. It exploded off the club face and flew straight as an arrow out to 250 yards. 'Not bad, Harry my boy,' he said quietly, 'not bad at all for a range ball.'

He went through the same procedure again and the result was exactly the same, bar the flight of the ball being slightly more to the right.

Could he do it a third time? The answer was yes. The ball flight mirrored the first swing. Harry looked up to see the brown-haired girl looking his way. Harry smiled and placed a fourth ball on the rubber tee peg. The pressure was on.

Harry took a step back and lined up the shot he wished to hit, following the line he hoped the ball would take through the air with his eyes. Happy he now had the shot clearly defined in his head, Harry approached the ball and wasted no time standing over it before beginning the backswing; Harry wasn't one to waggle the club. Certain professionals he studied on the TV seemed to waggle the club a set number of times, clearly in an attempt to get mind and body in perfect harmony before taking the club back to begin the swing. Harry waggled twice, an act he had never before given any conscious thought to, and pulled the club back to begin his short, compact swing. The downswing was aggressive, probably too aggressive for the contact was not good, Harry instantly felt this, and he looked up expecting to see the golf ball careering hopelessly off target. To his surprise, and immense delight, the ball was bang on target, flying on the perfect flight path, albeit shorter than the previous three. He'd accept that any day, especially knowing he had an audience. Harry looked over to the bay containing the brown-haired girl. The gym monster was making yet another concerted effort to make an impression. Harry hit four more drives before practicing with a fairway wood.

His practice sessions took on a familiar pattern all of their own: Harry always began the session hitting with the sand-wedge, the club having the shortest shaft, this helped loosen up the muscles and get in much needed practice on the short game; then came the pitching-wedge followed by the rest of the irons depending on club shaft length. Once the irons were finished Harry hit with the woods, but the order was reversed slightly: Harry began with the driver before turning attention to the fairway-woods and rescue clubs. He finished the session with ten practice chips with the sand-wedge. The brown-haired girl and gym monster had already departed, and he was one of only three players left practicing. Oh well, he thought, there's always tomorrow.

Harry put the clubs in the back of the 924 and contemplated grabbing a coffee at the clubhouse. Coffee won out.

It was at the perfect temperature to be shared with a double chocolate-chip muffin. Harry sat back and turned his attention to Haffenden; the girls would not play like amateurs and send a text or an email that could be traced back to them, the information he required would arrive in a small white sealed envelope with no name on it and definitely no fingerprints. The only incriminating evidence would be that it fell on Harry's doormat. This along with the police visit would be enough to have him out of their hair long enough to disappear.

Harry took a bite out of his muffin.

'Can I join you?'

Harry looked up to see the brown-haired girl holding a cup of coffee.

'Sure.'

'You were hitting the ball well today,' she said taking the seat opposite.

'You weren't doing too bad yourself.'

'I'm okay.'

'You're more than okay: you have a lovely swing, unlike my thrash at the ball.'

She laughed. It was a great laugh.

'You thrash at the ball, do you?' she said smiling.

'I can't think of a better description.' Harry was beginning to relax. A good sign for him.

'You hit the ball a long way for "a thrash"', she added, sipping her coffee.

Harry looked around the clubhouse. The gym monster was conspicuous by his absence.

'He's gone,' she said between sips.

'Sorry.' Harry didn't want it to make too obvious he was looking.

'The annoyance, he's gone,' she added.

'This annoyance, you know him?'

'What makes you say that? Are you a policeman?'

'Not quite!'

'Not quite?'

The brown-haired girl's eyes searched Harry's: she was interrogating him, looking for a sign of weakness that he knew with confidence was not there. Was she police?

'What are you then?' she asked, resigned to the fact he was not going to offer anything up.

'And we haven't even been properly introduced.'

'Sorry,' she replied laughing, 'my name is Sally.'

'Hello, Sally, my name is Harry. Just like the film.'

Sally laughed.

'So, Harry, what do you do?'

'I find people!'

It was not what she was expecting, and it took a few minutes for those three simple words to sink in before she could form a reply: 'For who?'

'Whoever has need of my services,' Harry uttered in a level just above a whisper.

Sally was fascinated by this man. This man who hit the ball hard with a short, compact swing which no self-respecting pro would teach.

'What do you do, Sally?'

'I'm a primary school teacher.'

'That must be a rewarding job?'

'It is, but it's not as exciting as yours.'

'It has its moments.' Harry knew it was coming, he was asked the same question regularly when strangers discovered what he really did for a living.

'Had any scary moments?'

The answer would normally be a resounding no, but this was different: the urge to dramatize events, even more than they actually were, was overwhelming, but how can you over-dramatize nearly being killed? He'd give it a go.

17

Harry folded the small white piece of paper into a square and tucked it in his left back pocket.

The house was warm and comforting and it was later than he planned to be on his return. The day after tomorrow he was on a day flight to Tenerife. It being a Wednesday meant the new rosters being released covering a two-week period six weeks in advance. Harry read his with one thought overriding all others. He was disappointed: the new two-week period covered the first two weeks of December, and he was back in the simulator. It was that time again? And then off to Cap Verde for a week. A week in the sun would be ideal after the completion of his task: Cap Verde was a new destination for the airline, but one that was popular with British tourists: the Cap Verde archipelago is a series of volcanic islands that sit off the West coasts of Senegal and Mauritania, they are known for their Creole Portuguese-African culture, traditional morna music and beaches that are popular during the winter season for tourists, especially for kite and windsurfing. It was a new destination for Harry.

Harry saved the roster to his phone but was interrupted from giving it a further detailed examination by the sound of post hitting the floor. He maintained station: there was no need to run down to the front door and appear too eager. He heard a car drive away. Why had he not heard it arrive?

The envelope was indeed plain, small and white which self-sealed. He ascended the stairs and carefully opened it. There was one sheet inside with all the information printed. Any forensic investigation would reveal a printer that sold in the millions and be utterly untraceable.

Harry placed the sheet of paper on the kitchen table and made coffee. He set fire to the envelope using the gas hob. The remains were put in the trash. Tomorrow was bin collection day and it would soon be out of his life forever, much like Haffenden. He paused making the coffee why the kettle boiled; had he really meant to get to this point: a contract killer. But he was now of the mindset to remove guilty parties from the public domain, putting them out of harm's way if the proof was there to their guilt. He had to stay strong and follow this through. Here was another acid test.

Harry made coffee and drank it watching a Tom Hanks movie. Tom Hanks never made a bad movie in his opinion: he was always watchable, and it allowed him some peace before he studied the A4 piece of paper in greater detail.

* * *

The standby day Harry spent planning his interception of Haffenden: the man's agenda, if he could trust it, was there for the next seven days. It must be done in the next seven days.

* * *

Harry entered the crew-room in a detached frame of mind; it was if he was experiencing all the comings and goings through a camera lens and not actually a valuable cog in the airline's machine and there to add his weight and expertise to the day's business.

He again printed off the flight paperwork all the while keeping one eye on the door for Curtis Traherne. He had not seen his friend for a while and was eager to catch up with all the latest gossip. Curtis arrived exactly three minutes later.

'Hello stranger,' Curtis said, slapping Harry on the back, 'how's tricks?'

'Fair to middling,' he replied without looking at Curtis, 'and you?'

'I'm still here!'

Harry laughed and returned the slap on the back.

'You and me both!'

Curtis asked to fly the outbound leg, and Harry not really having any preference, said he didn't really have a preference. Curtis studied the paperwork and chose a fuel figure, which both men agreed on. Harry rang it through.

Harry asked his usual question at this time: 'Coffee?'

The two friends began the long walk out to the jet. For once Harry had not sourced out the crew and sauntered casually over to the large white door in-between Terminal One and Terminal Three that led to the temporary airport security channel used by airport staff. Curtis talked away constantly, but he only managed to catch every other word: Haffenden invaded his thoughts.

With security behind him Harry ascended the stairs to the terminal and coffee. Still Curtis chatted away. Harry just agreed; he had no idea what the conversation was about, he just agreed.

Harry ordered his usual and a large extra hot Americano for Curtis. The queue for the drinks evaporated like morning mist on a warm September day and they both continued their walk to gate 26. Harry only found that out by surreptitiously studying one of the many screens displaying the gates for departing traffic. Still Curtis talked away and still Harry agreed. He could have been agreeing to jump in front of a London bus for all he knew. Haffenden and his face refused to go away.

The agent met them at the gate and immediately asked could he start boarding, to which Harry replied he would let him know as soon as. They entered the air-bridge sipping coffee.

'So, what do you think, Harry?'

He was utterly lost on this current thread of their conversation: 'Go for it!'

'You sure?'

'Yeah, what have you got to lose?'

'She's ten years older than me!' Curtis added.

Harry turned and faced Curtis on the air-bridge two paces short of the A320 at one door left: 'Do you love her?'

'It's a bit too soon for that, Harry.'

'Do you fancy her?'

'Fuck yeah!'

'Then go for it!'

Harry turned sharply and boarded the A320. Some of the crew were supervising catering of the forward galley. Harry silently entered the flight-deck and pushed the square button on the overhead panel with 'Avail' illuminated in green to signify that electrical ground power is plugged in and all external power parameters are normal. The flight-deck burst into life.

Curtis, still in the forward galley, was heard talking to one of the crew. From the tone of the conversation it was clearly the cabin manager.

Brian Hart put his hand on Harry's right shoulder: 'Good morning big guy.'

Harry recognised the voice of an old friend and it put a smile instantly on his face. 'Morning, Mister Hart, didn't hear your dulcet tones in the crew-room.'

'This is my third straight Tenerife, and like you I needed a coffee.'

'Ouch,' Harry said looking sideways at his long-standing friend.

'I've clearly upset somebody.'

'You have!'

'Can we board, Captain Travers?'

Fuelling had yet to start, and company procedure had changed recently to help speed up boarding: this now required somebody to be on fuel watch while refuelling to allow boarding to take place at the same time: 'We'll get the agent to organise the fuel watch then we'll get them on.'

'Aye, aye captain,' Hart said gleefully. 'I see you have coffee and that gives me one less job to do, thankfully.'

Harry was about to let fly with his witty riposte, but Curtis interrupted the conversation and the moment was lost.

Both men completed their Preliminary Cockpit Inspections.

Harry left for the Exterior Walk-around, but not before he'd discussed with Curtis and Brian the defects the A320 was carrying, which didn't amount to much, and tasted his coffee: one of the disadvantages of not flying the outbound sector was you had to do the external inspection, and by the time you got back to the flight-deck the extra hot coffee was, on occasions, no longer hot.

Curtis set to work programming the FMGC (Flight Management Guidance Computer).

The first of the passengers began to board when Harry returned carrying the fuel receipt. All was going well.

He then completed the technical log while finishing off his coffee.

The agent appeared carrying a load-sheet; he had that look on his face, that look that spelt grief for Harry: 'What?'

'We're four passengers down: they're a family of four. And now you have a 10:12 ATC slot.'

Harry checked the time: it read 09:42. They had fifteen minutes to push-back.

'Have they got bags?'

'We're looking for them now.'

'Good. If you find the bags first, we'll have to offload them, if not-'

'They are putting out a PA as we speak.'

There wasn't much else they could do bar signing the tech log, calculating the take-off performance using the load-sheet they had; even if they offloaded the four passengers and their bags the actual take-off weight would be less than that used for the calculation. Once both men had completed their respective take-off calculations, and crossed-checked them, Curtis gave Harry his take-off brief. All this was completed before the agent returned still carrying that look.

'We found them,' the agent said before adding the inevitable: 'The father looks like he's been drinking. What do you want to do? Would you like to talk to him?'

Harry felt that he needed to see for himself how bad the father was: if he offloaded him the whole family would inevitably miss out on their holiday, so it was best to be sure. He went back to talk to Brian.

Brian just stared back at him why he explained his thought processes. He didn't add anything once Harry had finished, just a caveat that on a previous flight he'd been on where a similar situation transpired, the passenger kicked off half-way through the outbound sector.

'Do you want to talk to him or shall I?' Harry asked.

'You can take this one, I've got some seating issues to sort out,' Brian replied.

'If we take him, he gets no alcohol and we search the bag for anything hidden,' Harry added before disappearing up the air-bridge with the agent.

The father had consumed some alcohol but wasn't drunk and Harry could see the mother was concerned for her husband's welfare. Their two daughters were crying. Harry made a polite enquiry after the father.

The father lowered his head and stared at his feet. Harry could see the man was embarrassed.

Harry looked at the daughters, the mother, then the husband: 'I thought I'd come and talk to you myself.'

The husband lifted his head. He'd been crying.

'He's not normally like this,' the mother said in a pleading tone, 'he's a nervous flyer and we had some bad news today.'

Harry felt sorry for the guy.

'Sorry,' the mother added, 'but it's been hard recently.'

The father nodded. The daughters stopped crying and hugged him.

I'm going to look a right prick here, Harry thought. 'Just wanted to talk to you myself-'

'We'll be no bother!' the mother interposed.

'Right then,' Harry replied, grateful that this was going to be resolved peacefully, 'let's get you on board and be on our way.'

The daughters smiled.

Well, I'm not a prick today, he mused, as he re-entered the air-bridge with the agent escorting the family close behind him. Harry explained the situation to Brian before entering the flight-deck.

Harry took a second to settle back into his seat. Curtis was informed of his decision and that he was confident they would not be hearing from the father. Curtis requested the Before Start Checklist. The checks were completed before the agent appeared and was presented with his copy of the load-sheet after the passenger figure was confirmed. Finally, Brian asked could they close and arm the doors before confirming the passenger figure and how many wheelchair passengers required assistance in Tenerife. Harry gave him the thumbs up.

Harry requested permission to pushback and start engines and then waited for the inevitable negative response, as they were closing in on their ATC departure slot, but he was to be pleasantly surprised to hear permission was granted. Curtis liaised with the ground-crew before calling for the remainder of the Before Start Checklist. Pushback began seconds later once the air-bridge was off.

Events of the previous few days were not permitted to invade his thoughts and the motion of the jet soothed his constitution and calmed his soul. Harry was happy that the mother and daughters would keep watch over the father for the four-hour flight to Tenerife. Whatever the hard time the father was living through it was not his position to ask; some things are private and must remain that way: he would never discuss Sheila with anyone, not even a priest. Those memories were for him and the Almighty, but what would the Almighty think of him now? He was doing mankind a favour by sending one more odious, pernicious, homicidal sinner their way with a happy smile and another entry in his book. Today though, he was happy. Today he had a job to do.

The flight down to Tenerife was blissfully uneventful with not a word coming from the father: Brian informed him at top of climb that the gentlemen was asleep and stayed that way until top of descent.

* * *

Harry stood at the top of the steps positioned at one-door-left, once all the passengers had disembarked at Tenerife, and took a lungful of air and soaked up the sun. The heat reinvigorated him and fortified him against any thoughts of Haffenden and Raquette.

The turnaround took 50 minutes and they pushed back early off stand after being given instructions to face East, in order to taxi off the apron via the Eastern exit to depart off runway 07.

The sun had done its job admirably on Harry's constitution: he was positively itching to begin the hunt.

The flight home was so quiet that he struggled to remember even the simplest part of it the moment he heard the crew-room door close behind him.

Harry sauntered over to the bus stop. It began to rain. Harry liked the rain: it had the same effect on him as the sun; these opposite ends of the weather spectrum had the same effect on his constitution.

The bus arrived shortly after he placed his flight-bag on the ground. Harry boarded alone, sat at the back and closed his eyes. The bus waited a few minutes. Three more crew boarded, chatting away constantly to themselves. Harry opened one eye. He didn't recognise any of them, closed it then folded his arms and grabbed a few minutes rest. The bus pulled away. A metallic blue Ford Focus tailed the bus keeping three car lengths back.

Harry was the first to get off and continued his leisurely walk to the Porsche. Not once did he check to see if there were eyes on him. Why bother to attack him here?

18

Harry scoured the road ahead. All seemed quiet. The barrier to the car park lifted and he slowly pulled forward.

Harry wasn't in a position to say whether any car in or out of the staff car park had the right, or not, to be there. His only hope was to monitor the driver's general driving style and take a few risks to lose them. Risk for Harry fell into two categories: acceptable; and the obvious unacceptable. This fell into the former.

The roads appeared safe by the time he reached the traffic lights marking one of the entrances to the airport. Harry took the exit leading to Heald Green. It was pointless trying to fox anybody. They knew where he lived and could find him whenever they felt the need.

The traffic was slow at this time of day and seriously hampered any effort to spot a tail. Harry gave up shortly after; they weren't going to or couldn't make an attack on his person in broad daylight with traffic this heavy. The approach to Baslow Drive was a different proposition.

Harry crawled home. He was getting frustrated: he wanted some action; he had worked himself up though the entire day for this very moment and now it was letting him down. It was worse than being the only sober guest at a wedding.

Finally, he was on Finney Lane, then onto Queensway, which led onto Haddon Road then Baslow Drive. Still there was no tail. He slowed to ten miles-an-hour and went anti-clockwise around the road to get to his house. Why had he not thought of doing this before? It was so obvious it was brilliant.

The metallic blue Ford was parked on the left-hand side of the road three houses before his but would have been obscured by a white van if Harry had taken the more logical clockwise, and shorter, route to his front-door. Harry clocked it straight away and pulled in, putting three cars between him and the Ford. Now what to do? The Ford held two passengers. From the rear he could not make out their sex.

Five minutes went by and still he could not decide on the next course of action. Harry needed to make a decision: the neighbours would soon be peering through curtains wondering what on earth was going on.

By minute six Harry had selected reverse and parked the Porsche out of sight. And there he was going to wait, all night if necessary. He reclined the driver's seat, set the alarm on his mobile phone for an hour's time and grabbed some much-needed zeds.

That alarm woke him from a deep sleep. Harry reset the back of the driver's seat, got out, stretched his legs, locked his car and went for a walk. The metallic blue Ford was gone. Harry kept walking until he had covered every inch of Baslow Drive. The metallic blue Ford was indeed gone. He left the Porsche where it was, after removing his flight bag and jacket, and went home.

His home was untouched.

* * *

The following morning Harry wasted no time getting dressed once he was awake. He was out of the house in less than thirty minutes and on the road in thirty-five with a bag of essentials as a companion.

The garden was out of the question. Harry couldn't afford to be reckless: not all the girls he figured would be for him.

He parked down the road from that house, thought of Cantlay, and decided he would wait one hour only before making a beeline for Bowden Lane.

The hour came and went. Harry headed for Marple, and never gave the house another thought.

He wasn't in the Mini now. He would park the Porsche safely out of harm's way. It began to rain. The rain coupled with the cold would make for an uncomfortable day. Again, he thought of Cantlay; the old man was the trigger for the animosity required for a day like today.

Harry started this journey with the desire to help and protect the weak and vulnerable from those who believed they were above the law, but for the umpteenth time he questioned his motives and where he stood. He could not stand by and do nothing knowing that innocent people were going to get hurt; if he contacted the police what was he going to tell them? He argued, there was no proof, nothing concrete to link Haffenden with Cantlay's death.

Harry made a detour. He needed inspiration, guidance.

It was still raining when Harry first stepped over the threshold of the cemetery: Harry gave attending Cantlay's funeral serious thought, but instead opted to witness proceedings from a respectable distance. When suitable time had passed, he paid his respects.

The tombstone still had that new look about it and the flowers were still fresh. He was pleased.

Harry squatted by the side of the gravestone.

'What to do?' he finally said.

Nobody answered. Nobody would.

'What to do?' he said again, standing.

Harry looked over his shoulder on hearing someone pull up opposite: a sad looking, well dressed lady in her sixties vacated a silver Nissan Micra. She had been crying. Harry felt sorry for her, but it didn't last long, he needed to concentrate on feeding his hatred and animosity for that man. He struggled.

The old lady came and stopped right next to him; her moist eyes fixed on the grave to the right of Cantlay's. Harry read the wording on the gravestone: Mister Felix Cattermole was 68 years old when he died less than a month ago.

'Your father?' asked the old lady. She'd been reading, too.

Harry lied: 'Yes.' She would be more inclined to talk if Harry needed to know who else visited his friend's grave.

'Your husband?'

'Of forty years,' she said softly.

Harry noticed she was carrying flowers and a bag. Her trembling hands made the tops of the flowers quiver.

'This is the first time I've managed to visit the old man.' Harry squatted again and adjusted some of the flowers at the base of the gravestone.

'I come every day.'

The old lady produced a towel from her bag and with no small amount of effort placed it carefully by the side of the grave and knelt on it. 'It's getting harder and harder,' she added putting the bag down by her right hand.

Harry felt the need to say something: 'Whenever I'm here I'll keep it tidy.'

'That's very kind, but there's no need.'

The old lady began to replace the flowers. 'Anyway, you have your brother to help you.'

'Oh, he's not that reliable.'

'Your father must have travelled extensively as a young man?'

'He was a Merchant seaman.' It was all Harry could think of at such short notice.

'He must be your half-brother then?'

Travers knew where she was coming from: 'French.' Harry didn't know what Raquette's exact nationality was, or whether it was his henchman sent to source him out. 'We don't see eye to eye, I'm afraid.'

'Yes,' the old lady started, 'he was a most disagreeable man.'

'I must apologise for him. What did he say or do?'

She stopped arranging the flowers. 'It was his manner, and the tone of his voice, rather than what he said. He knew little or nothing about your father that was obvious, for when I politely offered my condolences, he cut me off in an instant.'

'They never saw eye to eye.'

Harry stood: his legs were beginning to stiffen up.

The old lady looked up at him. 'Is your name Harry?'

'It is,' Harry said not at all surprised that Raquette had mentioned him.

'When was the last time either of you spoke?'

Harry paused.

'You can tell me to mind my own business if you want.'

'I wouldn't do that. It has been a long time. My half-brother has issues that he has failed, or didn't want, to address and it didn't matter what either my father or I did to help him, it was always our fault and never his.'

'I could see that in him: he didn't have anything nice to say about you.'

Once again Harry paused before replying.

'I'll let you know when he comes,' the old lady said reading his mind perfectly.

'Thank you.'

'Is there just the two of you?'

'No. There's more.'

Harry could see from the old lady's face what she was thinking. He knew it was time to go: 'I'll leave you in peace. And thank you.'

The old lady smiled, nodded and continued to prepare the new flowers.

Harry fired up the 924 and ran over the conversation in his head. He had a way to get the jump on Raquette, to put himself one step ahead of him. The old lady could possibly have saved his life. It sounded melodramatic, but it was probably true. He pulled slowly away from the kerb. Next stop Marple.

* * *

Bowden Lane was how he left it: he felt like he was visiting an old friend. Harry parked the Porsche in Norbury Drive and strode at a leisurely pace carrying his bag of essentials in a small shoulder bag. It would be getting dark in a couple of hours and then it would be time to have a closer look into the world of Mister Haffenden.

None of the lights at the front of the house of the semi-detached were on. The house looked lonely and forgotten. He opened his small bag of necessities and furtively removed a Bowie knife in its sheath and fed it onto his belt. The bag also contained the pouch with the lock picks and the Snub-Nosed Magnum. He tucked the Magnum into his belt and covered it with his hoodie.

Harry made his way down the right-hand side of the house. There was no car in the driveway and Harry could access the front of the garage at the far end of the driveway beyond the end of the house. The garage and house were connected by a wooden fence with a gate. The gate was bolted from the garden side but had a metal circular handle facing Harry. He tried it more out of wishful thinking. It was locked.

Halfway down the driveway next to the house were green and blue plastic wheelie bins. Harry pulled over the blue bin, placed it in front of the wooden gate, climbed on top and manoeuvred himself with great care over the gate and down to the garden on the other side. It was only now that Harry considered the possibility of a guard dog. He was quite safe on that front.

He wasted no time attempting to unlock the backdoor. It was not easy, and he hands began to hurt. The lock was proving troublesome. Harry took a break from the backdoor and took a few minutes to study all the windows. All were locked. This was not going to plan. Harry tried the side door to the garage. He had it open in minutes. It made him feel a little better, but only a little. The garage was full of bric-a-brac and general household rubbish: an old bicycle; a second-hand washing machine; an assortment of tools and spanners; a hydraulic car jack; two axle stands; and two plastic black sacks full of clothes. Everything else was covered in a thick layer of dust.

Harry took a closer look at the assortment of tools and spanners. What he wanted was a hammer and centre-punch: it would give him the option of taking out a window; his only worry was the noise. So far luck was on his side. No police had come-a - knocking.

He was becoming frustrated; to take out a window and potentially alert the entire neighbourhood to his presence, not to mention anybody in the house, was not ideal, but was his only option. Harry shook his head: he had to remain patient and keep trying the lock or come back another night.

Buoyed by his success with the garage door, Harry attacked the backdoor to the house with renewed vigour. His hands began to hurt, but he kept on prying pressing and twisting with the picks. Suddenly the locked moved and he rotated it until he felt the door fully unlock. He was in and put the lock-picks back in the bag.

The backdoor opened into a small utility room with a door to his right leading into the kitchen and another straight ahead. Harry guessed a downstairs toilet. He was right.

The kitchen was spacious, of the modern design with granite worktops, a large fridge-freezer incorporated into the oak coloured kitchen cupboards and the open plan layout connected to the dining area. It was well designed, but the bonus was it used gas and not electric. Excellent, he thought, he could destroy evidence with an unfortunate gas leak if required. He soon abandoned that idea: the house was a semi-detached and innocent people would suffer as a consequence, but he could burn evidence.

The door to the front of the house was closed. Harry softly made his way over the cream coloured tiled floor and put his left ear to the door. All was quiet. He had to wait and listen. Any rash move could spell disaster.

Three minutes, Harry waited all of three minutes before opening the door and taking his chances with whoever was waiting on the other side. The hallway was clear and so were the downstairs rooms.

Harry took a deep breath and exhaled slowly and as quietly as humanly possible. From the bottom stair he could make out two doors of the upstairs rooms. Both were shut. One he figured was the bathroom from its position on the landing.

He took the first step cautiously, the second even slower then stopped on the third and listened for any sign of movement. All was quiet.

Harry took the decision to expedite the ascent to the landing and keep low to the ground as much as possible. He took the stairs two at a time followed by a forward roll, so his back was to the wall separating two of the bedroom doors. It was now he could see that all the doors were closed. He was breathing heavily, and it took most of his powers of concentration to maintain a listening watch.

After a minute of controlled breathing there was not a sound emanating from any of the rooms.

Harry stood and composed himself before choosing which of the rooms to explore first.

The landing was in the familiar 'L' shape with the stairway connected to the landing on the longer vertical part of the 'L'. Harry decided to work his way methodically through all the rooms starting with the door on his far right and then working in a clockwise direction from there.

He softly approached the door, tried the handle, it moved silently, and the door opened with a small amount of effort: the room had been recently carpeted, and the bottom of the door was rubbing against it.

Harry stood rooted to the spot, partly through astonishment, partly to take in all that was ahead of him.

He knew about drugs, but wasn't what you'd call an expert, especially on its manufacture, but you didn't need to be to figure out exactly what was going on here. Harry opened the blind a little on the one window in the room to get a better look and take a few photos on his phone. He took eight.

They were mixing, or cutting, cocaine. Harry had read they used baking powder on occasions, but this wasn't baking powder, it was something far worse.

Fentanyl,' he muttered, 'the bastard's cutting cocaine with fentanyl.'

Fentanyl, or fentanil, is an opioid that was developed as a painkiller; it is hugely addictive and normally used by injection. Harry had seen a documentary on the TV about the effects of this drug: how it is easy and cheap to manufacture; is mixed with cocaine and heroin; is 100 times more powerful than morphine; and an analogue called carfentanil is thousands of times stronger. It is lethal, causing tens of thousands of deaths every year in America, not counting the hundreds of thousands of lives it ruins.

'Motherfuckers,' he said slowly.

Harry was careful not to disturb anything and put the blind back how he found it.

Back on the landing he prepared himself to enter the next room now immediately to his left. He was halted from pulling down on the door handle by the sound of a car's engine. Seconds later he heard two doors shut and the engine noise died. Three people, he conjectured.

The door handle reached the bottom of its travel and he eased the door open. A sharp, straight fist impacted his nose with such a force that his head snapped back, and he fell back against the banister, slid to his right and hit the floor.

Harry's eyes instantly began to water, and the tell-tale trickle of blood oozed down over his lips and onto his chin. He sensed the figure bear down on him and from past experiences kicked out with his left foot and rolled to his right. The foot impacted something solid. He had a few valuable seconds. Harry sprung to his feet and threw a wild left-hand haymaker. He missed, but guessed they ducked. A right uppercut landed flush on the button. The attacker fell back against the door at the far end of the landing. Harry rubbed his eyes quickly to try and clear the water and focus. It didn't work as much as he'd hoped: all he could see was a watery blurred figure straighten up before him in readiness for another attack. They would see how disadvantaged he was, and that coupled with the three individuals outside, made Harry's predicament dire.

He fell back against a wall and slid to his left until he hit the doorframe of what he figured was the bathroom. The figure closed the gap between them, and Harry aimed a straight front-kick at them with his right leg. They easily blocked it. He kept on sliding and fumbled behind him for the door-handle. Harry found it, pushed down and the door fell inward with all his weight acting against it. Harry hit the floor and kicked out. The kick caught his attacker in the kneecaps, and they swore at him. The attacker was a woman. Some had stayed loyal to Haffenden; potentially three women and him. Harry rubbed his eyes; they began to clear to reveal a redhead armed with a syringe and a smile guaranteed to send a shiver down all but the most hardened of spines.

'I wanted you to see this before I gave it to you!'

'More fool you,' Harry said swinging his bag at her in an attempt to dislodge the syringe. It failed. He threw the bag at her. She ducked. He got to his feet and grabbed a towel and wrapped it around his right hand.

'Good luck with that!' The redhead stepped to her left in a very calculating, premeditated way.

She had opened an avenue for him to try and make a getaway. To pull the Magnum or Bowie knife at such an early stage, and show his hand, was not his way. All avenues needed to be explored before that.

'Fentanyl,' Harry said, smiling, 'nice touch.'

'Glad you approve.'

The front door opened and closed. Harry was waiting for the redhead to warn them of his presence.

What little he knew of the synthetic man-made drug was its effect on the human body: it had a rapid onset and lasted between one and two hours. Addicts have been known to overdose while the needle is still in their arm; the biggest at risk seemed to be those who had kicked a heroin habit then relapsed with fentanyl. Harry stood no chance if the redhead managed to get that needle inside him. She said nothing.

Harry put his right hand behind his back and felt for the double-action short-barrelled revolver. It would only take a second to pull the Magnum and release a round into her abdomen, kick the needle out of her hand and unload the remaining 5 rounds into the other three, as they advanced up the stairs.

He pulled his hand back and scratched his right leg. The redhead's eyes flicked between him and the door leading onto the landing.

'In the bathroom,' she finally shouted.

Harry's left hand was behind his back in one smooth, flowing motion and returned in an even slicker move with the Bowie knife showing blade first. Before the redhead could let out another syllable the knife was in her abdomen just below the ribcage. The shock of being outwitted took her breath away. Harry stepped forward grabbed the syringe and injected her before she could speak, emptying its entire contents in one movement.

Harry took her weight and gently lowered her to the floor, removing the knife as he did so. From the gap in the doorway Harry made out Haffenden bringing up the rear. He drew the Magnum from behind his back with his right hand.

Harry readied himself for the strike. Was this really happening? He looked at both his hands in turn. The girl was dying, bleeding out on the floor in front of him, and there were three more victims waiting to be dispatched. His present predicament was now beyond surreal.

The bathroom door flew open accompanied by the hideous screams of yet another loyal Harpy. She had short blonde hair, which made Harry think of the other blonde: her hair was longer; he liked it that way, not the short style. This one had the obligatory blue eyes and the whitest teeth Harry could remember seeing.

An axe came in a wide arc beginning over her right shoulder.

He had not expected that: an axe.

Harry ducked just in the nick of time; the axe blade whistled by his right ear. That was close, too close for comfort. And to add insult to injury, a brunette followed the blonde into the bathroom carrying another syringe. Axe, or syringe, take your pick. The brunette and the blonde must have the same personal trainer, for there wasn't an ounce of fat on either and both were dressed as if they'd just come from the gym.

Harry needed to stop the flippancy and get with the programme. He slammed the grip of the Magnum straight into the face of the brunette then slashed the Bowie knife at the blonde. She didn't seem to care; the axe came back in a lower arc aimed straight at his midriff. Harry was done for.

He jumped back and brought the knife down to block the axe blade. The two blades impacted. The axe slid over the top of the Bowie knife and Harry needed to bring down the Magnum sharply to save an impact into his right side.

The redhead was still bleeding out over the floor, but the fentanyl had kicked in and she felt nothing: a nice way to go.

The brunette held the syringe in her right hand and a small amount of blood oozed out between her left fingers, as she held her nose. She mumbled something, but Harry struggled to make head or tale of it. He body-checked her into the shower cubicle and pushed past her and onto the first-floor landing before the blonde could retaliate. A thunderous kick struck him in the centre of the chest, and he flew back against a door that belonged to one of the smaller bedrooms. The door gave way under his weight and he crashed through it and onto the single bed positioned parallel to the far wall.

Harry aimed the Magnum directly at Heffenden's chest, but a second kick sent the gun flying out of his hand. He was left with the Bowie knife to defend himself against an axe, a syringe full of a drug guaranteed to cause an overdose and now the man he really wanted dead carrying a knife of his own.

A quick scan of the smaller bedroom failed to reveal the final resting place of the Magnum. Harry removed the towel off his right hand.

Haffenden went to plunge a large kitchen knife into Harry's chest. Harry attempted to grab hold of the man's wrist, but only managed to deflect the knife. It sliced through the arm of his dark jacket and hoodie but didn't reach skin. Harry kicked Haffenden back into the doorway, jumped to his feet and slashed at the man's face.

'Get him,' Haffenden snarled.

The blonde once again screamed the most awful obscenities at Harry and swung wildly with the axe at his head. Harry kicked out at her kneecaps while stepping to his left to avoid the attack. He struck the left one, slowing her advance and putting a temporary stop to the assault. Harry thumped her with a violent right hook, knocking her clean out.

His victory was short-lived though: the brunette re-appeared and attacked him with a flying sidekick. Harry was impressed given the restricted space available. The left-footed kick was accurate and once again Harry found himself on the bed, only this time badly winded. The brunette followed up the sidekick with a right leg axe kick onto Harry's left shoulder. He dropped the knife under the sheer force of the blow, grabbed the right foot and twisted as hard as he could. The brunette fell to her left and tried desperately to inject Harry. Harry stood, pulled back as far as he could, bearing in mind Haffenden was behind him, and the needle missed him.

He was now off balance and at the mercy of the man; he could sense him waiting to pounce the next time the brunette attempted to inject the fentanyl. Harry mule-kicked him back along the first-floor landing and heard him trip over. A quick glance to his left confirmed it. He needed room to manoeuvre and expeditiously moved out onto the landing after letting go of the foot. Haffenden was now on his feet and closing the gap between them.

Harry took one full stride over the prostrate blonde, who was making the usual sounds, as she begun to regain consciousness, placed his left hand on the banister, and hurdled it in one smooth motion. His landing was anything but smooth and he immediately lost his balance on the stairs and tumbled to the bottom. The fall hurt him, but he ignored any discomfort and got to his feet as quickly as possible.

The pain down his right side was bearable and he took three steps towards the rear of the house to check out his hip and leg. Any movement was not hindered in any way, and it was just as well for the brunette followed him down the stairs in a more conventional way and wasted no time on her assault.

Here was a classic case of attack being the best form of defence. Harry sprang at the brunette the split second her feet reached the ground floor; she blocked the front, side and roundhouse kicks, but Harry was learning fast and spun round to deliver a turning-back kick to her ribcage. The brunette was knocked off her feet and hit the ground hard, but no sooner had he repelled one attacker than another went for the kill: the blonde had recovered her senses sufficiently enough to make the bottom of the stairs and swung the axe with even more venom. Harry had no weapons to help defend himself and was left with no option but to retreat to the safety of the kitchen. There would be weapons-a-plenty in the kitchen.

The blonde was never more than two paces behind him and by the time he even reached the kitchen and searched for something, anything, to defend his person the axe would be embedded in his skull.

Harry slowed one step before the kitchen door and mule kicked the blonde back along the short hallway towards the front of the house. She put her foot down to steady herself, caught the door mat, and ended up hitting the tiled floor headfirst. Having been concussed once, her recovery time was long enough for Harry to arm himself with, of all things, a rolling pin. It did bring a smile to his face, which evaporated the split second he re-entered the hallway to be met with Haffenden with his gun.

Harry took a step back and launched himself to his right, narrowly avoiding the round of .38 Special, which embedded itself into one of the smart looking kitchen cabinets. The tiled kitchen floor did little to help his already bruised right side. He was back on his feet before Haffenden could get him in his sights and let off another round.

Once on his feet he made out Haffenden enter the kitchen through the gap between the door and the doorframe. Harry kicked the door shut with all the might he could muster.

Haffenden was knocked back as the door closed. He let off a second round, wasting it into the solid wooden door.

Harry ducked instinctively as he passed the kitchen door on his way out of the rear of the house. He could hear Haffenden swearing violently, but any further profanity was missed as he climbed the rear gate and headed for the front of the house.

He was foolish, but only reached that conclusion when he burst through the front door and the brunette clocked him with the hardest right hook he'd ever felt. If it wasn't for all the self-defence training, and his history of playing rugby, that would have been that, but Harry clattered into a small table to the left of the door, on which the house phone was kept, sat on it, rocked back against the wall, and maintained the hostilities by kicking the brunette with both feet. The table rocked again and gave up staying upright. Harry ended up on his arse, as did the brunette. Haffenden appeared in the doorway of the kitchen a split second later followed by the rather unsteady blonde.

Harry rolled to his right, jumped to his feet and threw the rolling pin. It was a perfect throw and hit Haffenden square in the forehead putting his aim all to shit. He didn't pull the trigger and waste another shot.

It was time, that time in any fight where it was all or nothing, and damn the consequences.

Harry kicked the brunette hard in the stomach, twisted the hand that held the syringe, released it and injected her with the fentanyl. He didn't wait to see the effects of his actions.

The blonde had still not dropped the axe and staggered towards him with it in her right hand but dangling down by her side. She made no attempt to strike him with it. One swift hard left put her down and that was it for her.

Haffenden attempted to hide behind the kitchen door. Harry had spotted him move to his left and out of sight. He picked up the axe. The rolling pin was lying on the kitchen floor, but too far away to be any good to him.

'What's keeping you?' Haffenden snarled from behind the door.

'Your troops are of no help to you now,' Harry said trying to buy some time and think of a way of not getting shot.

'They were expendable.'

It was now that the incomprehensible mumblings of the brunette hit home. Harry, for all his shortcomings, could not stand there and let her die: he felt guilt over the redhead, but his hand had been forced; here he had a way out if he chose to take it. He went to her aid. She was sitting up but slumped over. He picked her up to walk her around.

'Naloxone,' he just about heard her say.

'Where?'

'Upstairs.'

Harry picked her up and ran up the stairs and into the front, smaller bedroom. There was a box marked Narcan, which he knew was a brand-name for Naloxone, sitting on the desk. Harry opened the box and removed a small syringe with a white cone on the end. It had been preloaded with the drug. He inserted the white cone into the brunette's nostril and gave a short vigorous push to spray the drug into her nasal passage. It took a few minutes, but she started to come around. He laid her down on the floor in the recovery position and mentally prepared himself to run the gauntlet of getting down the stairs alive.

Harry vacated the smaller bedroom to be met by the blonde. She was unarmed and crying.

'Not again?' he snapped.

'How is she?' she said wiping a tear from her eye.

'Alive!'

'Thank you,' she said, before adding: 'He's gone.'

'Great, that's just great!'

'If you want him, I know where he'll go.'

'You're suddenly going to help me? What is it with you lot?'

'She's my sister!'

'Blood thicker than water, eh?'

'He's abandoned us: probably hoping we'd get you and save him the trouble.'

'Where?'

19

Harry had an address, how reliable or safe was this info he had no idea, but he had an address plus Haffenden had the jump on him with time to either make good his escape or set the perfect trap. Harry spent time removing what evidence there could be linking him to the house in Marple. What was left was down to them to clear up: it was their operation and their necks on the line. Now here he was ready to finally remove Haffenden, with the bleached Bowie knife safely in a plastic bag in the back of the Porsche, wearing a fresh pair of gloves and a clean hoodie. Haffenden had the Magnum. That was not his problem: there was none of his DNA on it and he'd never fired it. No gunshot residue. He kept the axe.

* * *

The semi-detached house was just like any other in East Stockport. It was on a quiet street with a smart looking car in the drive: another Audi, red this time and four-door. Obviously takes passengers, maybe he's a family man. Harry had never considered that.

Harry made a note of the registration. He sat there for nearly an hour before making the decision to return home.

Baslow Drive was quiet. Harry put a wash on after soaking his clothes, shoes and gloves in bleached water. The knife and axe were soaked in a sink of bleach and scrubbed clean. Next, he valeted the Porsche.

He made a mug of coffee and went to watch some football on the TV. Harry ran a hand through his crew-cut hair. He liked the style: it removed any worry of hair being left at the scene. The coffee was good and the football on the TV was entertaining. He was asleep within minutes of finishing the coffee.

The time off his mobile phone read 23:32. Harry staggered up the stairs and fell into bed. When he woke the time was 10:17. The sleep had been heavy and not refreshing. A power nap would be needed later in the afternoon.

* * *

The red Audi was still parked in the driveway of the semi. It had been moved: Harry could tell by the angle of the front wheels. He would leave it half-an-hour then go hunting.

Thirty minutes later Harry left the 924 parked out of sight of the house and went hunting armed with the axe tucked inside his trousers and hidden from prying eyes by his jacket, plus the knife in its sheath attached to his belt. He had thought about bringing a gun but dismissed the idea: the axe and the knife would make this feel more personal. Harry needed this to be done with the minimum amount of noise.

He felt strange as he approached the house, almost as if he couldn't be bothered any more, as if it was all too much trouble, but his reputation and own survival now depended upon it: the ladies of that house will come hunting him if he failed to deliver.

The gate to the drive never made a sound as he slowly swung it open then closed it softly behind him. It was dark and nobody was going to pay him any attention at this time of the evening.

The house looked quiet. The driveway, like the previous house ran down the right-hand side of the building. Even the wooden gate was in the same position.

The red Audi on closer inspection had indeed been moved, but more disconcerting was the child's seat in the rear immediately behind the front seat passenger. This was not going to be easy. Harry needed to dig deep and block out any thoughts daring to weaken his resolve. He strode up to the wooden gate, took a deep breath, composed himself and peered through the gap in the wooden slats. He could make out the conservatory. From its design it was an addition to the house. There was no sign of life in the rear of the house, and Harry knew he needed to take advantage while it was quiet. He adjusted the dark hoodie, tightened the gloves over and his hands and attacked the gate. Thankfully it didn't tax him too much and he was over the gate and safely down on the other side without sustaining any injury. A quick scan of the conservatory and the kitchen through the kitchen window calmed any nerves.

Behind him on the garden side of the wooden gate were two bins, one green and one blue. Harry looked inside. Both bins were half-full. Voices behind him caused him to duck down below the level of the window. He made out Haffenden's. Harry hid behind a large plant standing to the left of a set of French windows off the side of the conservatory. He could make out two other voices, that of a man and a woman.

The woman was pleading with Haffenden: 'Why can't you ask another of your sources?'

'Because I'm asking you,' Haffenden said menacingly.

'Suppose the police are there!' The man was not comfortable with what he had been asked to do.

'Better pray they're not.' Haffenden's voice kept the menacing tone.

The woman began to cry, or so Harry thought, but her voice stayed firm. She was made of sterner stuff.

'You wanted that better life,' Haffenden started, 'and this is your way of proving to us that you can be a valuable addition to the organisation.'

'That's not fair: we have been more than valuable.'

The woman interrupted the man: 'We have done everything you have asked of us.'

'Then do this!'

'I can't carry it all,' the man said trying to find Haffenden's sympathetic side. He failed.

'Then make more than one trip. It's not rocket science.'

A child's voice broke up the conversation. She was asking for mummy. Mummy went to her child's aid. The man Harry presumed was the father came into view walking towards the rear of the conservatory. He was in his thirties, slim, brown-haired, wearing jeans and a dark blue t-shirt. Harry instantly checked the man's fourth finger of his left hand. He wore a ring. The father picked up a small teddy bear.

Harry moved as far back as he could until the whole plant obscured him from the father's line of sight. The daughter came into view. She couldn't have been more than five years old.

'What are you doing?' Harry whispered angrily. 'What are you doing getting mixed up with this man?'

The daughter appeared and moved behind her father. It spoke volumes.

The father put up his hands and spoke, but Harry couldn't make out what was being said. The body language spoke of threats.

The daughter ran off to the left and out of the scene being played out before him; from the look in the girl's eyes it was at the behest of her mother.

Harry strained to hear the conversation. Haffenden was laying down the law; the father had one last chance, or his family would suffer. Harry contemplated barging through the French windows and getting the jump on the man. It was a stupid idea: he had no idea if the windows were locked or not and Haffenden had the Magnum.

Suddenly Haffenden produced the gun and waved it at the father. The mother appeared from the left, waved to their daughter to stay put. She was attractive, roughly the same age as the father, slim with long straight brown hair in a pair of tight jeans and a white t-shirt. Harry could hear the daughter crying. He'd seen enough and slipped back towards the backdoor. He kept to the shadows as best he could, but the three adults were so wrapped up in their conversation that Harry needn't have worried.

The door was unlocked and once in the house the voices were clear and the gist of the conversation was immediately obvious: the father was to collect the fentanyl, cocaine and all the equipment left in the house. Not if the girls haven't taken it first, thought Harry.

The father was reluctant to go in case he was walking into a police trap. It was a fair argument. The mother sided with her husband. The daughter had stopped crying but was still asking for her mum. Haffenden's voice was beginning to get that hard edge. He heard the gun cock. He didn't need to do that, as it was a double-action revolver, so this was for dramatic effect.

'You'll go today!'

Haffenden was losing patience, but this was an argument that Harry wanted no part of, not now: the father would go to collect the drugs; Harry would tip off the police, who would catch the man red-handed; and then shop Haffenden. When the man was in police custody, evidence would surface to his involvement in Cantlay's murder. Harry would see to that.

It was time to leave.

The daughter made the first move. Why? Harry delayed his move for the backdoor and the coolness of the rear garden.

Haffenden shouted: 'I want it today!'

'It's too risky,' the father replied. There was a mixture of anger and frustration in his voice.

'You will get it today.'

The mother tried to placate him. Harry moved to his left but could only see the rear of the mother and the top of the daughter's head. The daughter let out a short, high pitched cry followed by the sound of a slap. The mother flew rearwards over the kitchen table and onto the floor. The daughter started to cry and went to her mother's aid. The father screamed oath after oath. Haffenden took three or four large strides towards the prostrate mother. He aimed the Magnum straight at the father threatening to shoot him where he stood before pointing the gun at the mother and threatening to shoot her and his daughter. The father didn't reply. He suddenly appeared charging from right to left and rugby tackled Haffenden. The two men began to fight it out on the floor. The mother got to her feet and went to pull Haffenden off her husband. The two men continued to swear they were going to kill each other. A clap of thunder ended the fight. Silence descended on the scene.

'What the fuck have you done,' the wife said with real fear.

The father slowly got to his feet. There was no gun in his hand. The daughter screamed.

'It is okay baby: mummy and daddy and daddy's friend were just playing. He'll be up in a minute and then it'll be daddy's turn.'

The daughter stopped crying and the mother led her out of the room.

Harry kept out of sight and the mother returned a few minutes later.

'She's watching one of her favourite programmes on TV,' she said putting a protective arm around her husband.

The father had not moved and could not bring himself to pull his eyes off the body lying on his kitchen floor.

'It was not your fault,' the wife added, in an attempt to snap him back to the here and now. 'He threatened to kill our daughter.'

He snapped back.

Harry moved away from the backdoor and positioned himself in such a way as to see the gun and the body on the floor. There was a large pool of blood immediately behind his head. On closer inspection the bullet hole could be seen just below the chin. A quick scan of the magnolia coloured wall behind them, and a best guess of the bullet's flight, showed the point of impact with the wall.

The couple only realised his presence when Harry was less than ten feet way. 'That's going to take some explaining,' Harry said sarcastically.

'And who the fuck are you?' The wife said, startled to see a stranger in her house.

'Your salvation,' replied Harry, cocking his head to the left to get another look at Haffenden.

The father stepped forward, bent down, and picked up the Magnum.

'That's my gun!'

Harry's claim to owning the firearm prevented the father from aiming the revolver straight at him.

The wife saw the axe. The look did not bode well for peaceful negotiations. Harry needed to act fast: 'Figured out how you're going to get rid of the body, have you?'

Neither of them replied.

'What about your daughter?'

'What about her?' the mother snarled.

'You can't keep her out of the kitchen forever, and sooner or later, preferably sooner for you two, you're going to have to move the body.'

'Can you help?' the father asked.

'I want my gun.'

The father looked at the revolver in his right hand then handed it to Harry grip first. Harry took it and tucked it away neatly into his right jacket pocket.

'I know that took a whole lot of trust to hand me that gun, but believe me it was the best move,' Harry said looking the man straight in the eye. 'Right, first things first, once we've tidied up this mess, wash your hands, remove your clothes and burn them. The same goes to you.'

The mother nodded.

Harry spoke to the father again: 'Got any plastic sheet?'

'I have some dust sheets in the garage I used when I painted one of the ceilings.'

'No, it has to be plastic: forensics will have a field day with that dust sheet. Okay, leave it with me.'

Harry could tell from the body language they were both beginning to relax a little.

'Find some gloves, preferably disposable ones, then take a plastic bag, wipe it clean, then put the head in the bag, so we don't spread any more blood, then clean up the mess with water and bleach, and plenty of it. I'll get some plastic sheet.'

'I have disposable gloves in my garage,' the father replied, stepping over the body and heading for the garage.

'I'll check on Sara.' The mother was gone before Harry could say a word.

And there he was, alone with the dead Haffenden. They had saved him the bother, and in some twisted honourable kind of way he felt duty bound to help them. The father returned.

'Do not pick up a plastic bag until those gloves are on: they will get prints and partial prints off everything. When they find the body, they'll know it's been moved, but that's my problem.'

'Why are you doing this?'

'Why were you so agreeable to let me help?'

'I'm not a murderer, but he threatened my family, and do you know what he's like?'

'It's why I'm here. You beat me to it!'

The father froze.

'You and your wife and daughter are quite safe.'

The father nodded.

'Now, I'm going to get some plastic sheet.'

The father nodded again.

'I will leave and enter via the backdoor. Do not answer the front door, not to anybody, you understand?'

The father nodded a third time.

'Plenty of bleach, use paper towels, and flush them down the toilet after. I won't be long.'

Harry was out of the house and heading back to the Porsche before the father could think of anything else to say. He scoured the street for any sign of the police or any nosey neighbours. All was quiet.

Back at the 924 Harry opened the rear of the Porsche, lifted up the carpet interior and extracted some large plastic sheet from the right-hand storage area. This plastic sheet was now about to earn its keep, and Harry was grateful for his own sagacity in carrying it in the first place.

By the time he'd returned to the house the father and mother were in full flow. The smell of bleach filled the air. Harry immediately checked to see if they were both wearing gloves. They were. Keeping them both out of prison meant keeping himself out.

He walked over to Haffenden's body. The head was not in a bag yet, but a plastic bag was sitting on the floor beside the body.

The father read his mind: 'We couldn't bring ourselves to do it.'

Harry now saw that the mother was crying.

'I'll do it.'

You have to detach yourself from the job at hand, that's how Harry saw it. It must be the same for pathologists, he reasoned, when it comes to cutting up a human body; the soul, good or bad, has left the body and the vehicle for that soul is all that remains. Harry wiped the plastic bag clean then placed the head inside.

'How's Sara?' he said to the mother.

'Oblivious. She's still watching TV, thankfully.'

Then right on cue, Sara called to her mother saying that she was hungry.

'Best you see to her,' Harry said softly, 'we don't want her in the kitchen raiding the fridge.'

'What do you want?' the mother called out.

The reply was crisps and a drink.

The mother removed her gloves, carefully placing them on the floor, washed her hands and went to get her daughter's order.

'Why were you after him?' the father asked.

'He killed a friend of mine!'

'How did you know he'd be here?'

'Tip-off,' Harry replied, smiling at the thought of Haffenden's girls betraying him.

'He wanted me to go to a house that had been compromised, and retrieve some drugs for him.'

'It was compromised by me!'

'Oh!'

'Best we get this cleaned up, and then I can remove the late Mister Haffenden from your premises.'

The father returned to his cleaning duties with renewed vigour.

An hour later Harry backed the Porsche up the drive, once the father had parked the Audi in the street, and the two men carefully placed the package on the back seat then covered it with an old blanket, supplied by the mother, to keep out of view from any prying eyes.

'Give me your clothes, shoes and gloves,' Harry demanded of the couple. The two failed to move. 'Do I have to explain why?'

Twenty minutes after that Harry was on the road. He knew their best chance of avoiding capture was to dump the body as far away from Manchester as possible. He headed North up the M6 motorway towards Scotland. Harry had spent some good times in Scotland and there were plenty of quiet country roads ideal for dumping a body. The clothes would be burnt later in an incinerator. He knew a couple of disused garages where some discreet burning could take place.

Harry gave the couple one other instruction: do not use their mobile phones, not until the following morning, things had to look normal. He took their numbers but didn't give out his. He'd buy a burner phone, call them then dump it.

The round trip took a little over ten hours. Harry was back home by 08:00.

Haffenden was laid to rest on a quiet road off the A75 near Blackerne, East of Castle Douglas. Harry had never visited the place before and arrived there a little after 02:00. A perfect time to offload a body. He had driven along the A75 when taking the ferry from Stranraer to Belfast and guessed there would be some quiet country roads in this part of the world at his disposal. He was careful not to park on the grass verge and leave any tyre tracks and stuck to the speed limit throughout the journey. He was exhausted when he arrived home.

20

Harry was patient, even if his whole being was crying out to call the couple and find out if they had followed his instructions. Names were not swapped. It was best not to know in case of any future investigations surrounding the late Mister Haffenden.

It was 10:25 when Harry called the husband from a recently acquired burner phone. It was a short conversation: they had stayed calm, cleaned the kitchen a second time and properly disposed of all the cleaning materials.

Once the conversation was over Harry packed up the bleached clothes, gloves and shoes, smashed the burner phone to bits and packed them in a black plastic sack with a load of other rubbish piled on top and, along with other clothes that needed to be disposed of, went down the local municipal tip. In a separate black sack were all the cleaning materials from when he was in the house.

He prayed it would be busy. It was. And to improve his situation at least three other people deposited black sacks in the skip marked out for household waste. Nobody gave him a second look for wearing gloves throughout.

Burning the evidence was deemed too risky.

Back home Harry made coffee and ate lunch. Breakfast was bypassed. He hadn't been hungry, but with a 12:00 standby about to start he was ravenous.

* * *

The phone rang at precisely 13:05. He was wanted for a Tenerife tomorrow with a 08:40 check-in.

Today was a Tuesday and now that he had the rest of the day to himself, he was going to play a quick nine holes of golf while the light was good. Twenty minutes later he was out of the house with the broadest of grins on his face and a spring in his step. The weather was set to be dry and now that one thorn was out of his side, he was confident of an enjoyable couple of hours' golf.

The course for a Tuesday was quiet and Harry managed to get twelve holes in before the light made it too difficult to continue. He was content with his performance: the first three holes were best forgotten about, but the next nine he played in three over par and that brought a smile to his face. Golf was proving to be the perfect stress buster.

* * *

The crew-room on this bright sunny Wednesday morning was a hive of activity and it allowed Harry to enter and slide up to the nearest terminal and print off the paperwork. Simon Weston appeared ten minutes later when all the paperwork had been printed with Harry standing nonchalantly sipping on a hot vending machine coffee.

'You're not drinking that shite now?' Simon said, putting down his flight bag.

'Bored!'

'You're so bored you got the uncontrollable desire to drink vending machine coffee!'

'It's not that bad.'

Simon collected the flight paperwork, sorted it into its relevant sections then stapled those sections together.

'That's the hardest I've ever seen you work!' Harry said, mockingly.

'Nearly broke into a sweat there!'

Harry gulped down the last of the coffee.

'You take it out, I fancy bringing it back today.'

'Sure,' Simon replied, and rattled off a fuel figure.

Harry concurred and it was ordered along with all the figures being sent to load control for the load-sheet.

'I hear on the grapevine we're going all electronic soon, in a bid to save money on paper and admin,' Weston said, leading the way to the exit. 'I take it you'll want another coffee?'

'Stupid question, that. Are you going to continue like this all day?'

The two men swapped the hustle and bustle of the crew-room for the cool morning air. After a short walk to airport security, and even shorter one negotiating it, they made their way up the flight of stairs leading into Terminal One and coffee.

Harry was calmer this morning than on previous mornings; he couldn't put his finger on it, he was just in a good place this morning and looking forward to flying down to the Canaries: it was such a regular destination for JaguAir, and many of the other charter airlines in the U.K, that one could easily become bored, or worse complacent, but today Harry was positively relishing the thought of a day trip to Tenerife. Maybe it was the fact that flying was now breaking up his day to day duties as an Investigator. Harry laughed at that one: he still struggled to see himself in that light and even more so after his failed attempt to remove Haffenden. Any guilt soon evaporated with the thought of Cantlay's demise.

Simon led the way to the first coffee shop, which was unusually quiet today; it was best to take advantage of an unexpected lull in custom. Simon has been chatting away constantly. Harry had not been listening to a word. Thankfully, the coffee order was put in, Harry paid, and the topic changed to Simon's new girlfriend. Simon stopped mid-sentence.

'What's up?' Harry asked, sliding his contactless debit card back in his wallet.

'I think it could be love,' Weston replied.

'Wow,' Harry said, placing his wallet in his back pocket. 'What's her name?'

'Brenda.'

'Brenda! Don't hear that name much these days.'

'She's a gal, Harry, she's a gal.'

'She sounds it.'

The coffees arrived and they made their way to the gate. No cabin manager came up to him while in the crew-room, so they were already on the jet, and Harry needed to check their gate off one of the many screens.

'Gate 23 for us,' Simon uttered between sips of hot coffee.

Gate 23 came into view and Harry felt his pace quicken. It surprised and pleased him in equal measure: the joy of flying was back. Mixing with people from a different world put his into a whole new perspective, and the joy was back.

The familiar face of Ricky the cockney cabin manager met him as they boarded. This day was getting better by the minute.

Their gate sat on the South side of the Western Pier, Pier Charlie, of Terminal One at Manchester Airport and their pushback off stand, when it came, pushed them momentarily down taxiway Lima, which runs parallel to the left-hand side of the Southern Pier, Pier Bravo, of Terminal One, and then forward until they faced West-North-West looking at the Cargo Area. From there it was a simple taxi straight ahead followed by a left turn to join taxiway Delta.

This morning, Manchester Airport was in dual runway operations with Runway 23 Left as the departure runway.

Taxiway Delta linked with Taxiway Papa and crossed Runway 23 Right via Papa One (P1) taking them eventually onto the Victor taxiway and holding point Victor Bravo Two (VB2) for Runway 23 Left. Both pilots need to be on guard at all times when crossing an active runway, and when instructed to do so by Air Traffic the crossing must be expeditious with no delay: modern international airports with dual runways will have a take-off and landing every minute during rush-hour periods.

Harry and Simon were number four for departure and thankfully they had no Air Traffic slot this morning. Simon taxied the A320 to the holding point, set the parking brake and gave his R.I.S.E brief once the first part of the Before Take-off Checks were completed.

They only needed to wait a few minutes before being instructed to line up on the runway. The remainder of the Before Take-off Checks were completed, Harry gave a PA to the cabin crew to warn them that departure was imminent and Simon lined up the A320, brought the jet to a stop and set the parking brake.

Harry, as was his want, ran through his mental checklist; it was his way of guaranteeing all the checks were complete and confirming what his actions would be in the event of a rejected take-off, bearing in mind that Simon was the handling pilot and only the captain can call "stop". The closer you got to Vee One speed, or the stop-go speed, and depending on the failure, it was better to be go-minded. The V1 call by the pilot monitoring is made three knots before the actual V1 speed because at that speed the decision has already been made. You must go. It is now safer to get the aircraft into the air, deal with the failure and come back for an approach to land at your departure aerodrome, if weather and go-around performance permits: there is at least one aerodrome that JaguAir flies into where the go-around climb performance is too restrictive to make an approach single-engine at heavy weights with the weather on limits.

The tower controller cleared them for take-off. It was blissfully uneventful, as was the Standard Instrument Departure they were required to follow.

Harry sat back on passing ten thousand feet, once the seat belts sign was switched off, all the departure information had been cleared from the secondary flight plan and radio navigation pages in the Flight Management Guidance Computers, done on request by the pilot flying because it was no longer needed, and the

Optimum/Max flight levels had been checked. He was going to enjoy this trip down to the Canaries: he didn't care what today was going to throw at them, it was a day Harry was determined to cherish.

In the cruise Harry entered what information he could into the aircraft's technical log and began that sector's paperwork.

It was a pleasant flight with a very professional, competent first officer. Even the passengers were all well behaved. Ricky was extremely complimentary of them; they had one hundred and eighty perfect passengers on a perfect flight down to Tenerife, but Harry couldn't expunge the thought that something was going to try and upset the applecart.

Harry was relaxed and ran through the list of scenarios that would and could ruin the day. Running them over and over in his head with those inevitable questions: what would I do now? Where would I go? Along with the classic enquiry by air traffic: what are your intentions? These all allowed him to narrow down those options that best fitted the bill for that phase of flight. Harry carried out his usual thirty-minute fuel check; they had burnt 500 kilos more fuel than planned due to not getting their optimum flight level. Harry and Simon, when first perusing through the flight paperwork, made an allowance for this so that by the time Harry made his fuel check they were 600 kilos over the Company Minimum Reserve: Company Minimum Reserve, or CMR, is the minimum fuel that the airline expected them to have on arrival: it is made up of Final Reserve Fuel, which unless they are in an emergency situation is the absolute minimum fuel they could land with and is usually around 1300kg for the A320, based on thirty minutes flying time at holding speed at 1500 feet above aerodrome elevation; and the fuel required to divert to their alternate aerodrome and called logically Alternate Fuel. The alternate today was Las Palmas in Gran Canaria.

Top of descent was approaching and Harry gave Simon the radios to monitor while he got the latest weather for Tenerife South: it was a typical Tenerife day with the wind from the East-South-East at 15-20 knots, clear skies, a temperature of 23 degrees centigrade and landing on runway 07. Harry took control of the radios on his return, read back the weather, which Simon entered into the FMGC. Harry had received the arrival brief earlier and politely checked with Simon if he was happy to start the descent. The reply was in the positive and Harry requested decent clearance from Canaries Radar.

The controller cleared them to descend to flight level 250.

So far so good, Harry thought, as he waited for the call from Air Traffic to instruct them that Tenerife could not accept them, and a diversion was necessary. It was the only scenario that could possibly ruin the perfect outbound sector, but no he was to be disappointed, if disappointed is the right word, for they were cleared to further descend to flight level 110.

The island of Tenerife was now clearly in view with Mount Teide dominating the skyline: the mountain is an active volcano reaching a peak of 3,718 meters (12,198 feet) and the highest point in the Canary Islands; if measured from the sea floor it reaches 7,500 meters (24,600 feet) and is the tallest volcano base-to-peak after the Islands of Hawaii. Before the 1496 Spanish colonization of Tenerife the islands native people, the Guanches, believed a powerful being lived in the volcano, and the mountain was sacred to them. Its modern Spanish name is El Pico del Teide. Mount Teide is still monitored regularly for seismic activity; the volcano itself has not erupted since 1909, but there still exists the very real possibility of future eruptions.

The radar controller cleared them to turn South-East onto a heading of 160 degrees and descend to 7,000 feet. Harry read back the instruction and Simon obeyed it. From here they would track down the western side of the island and eventually be given a further turn East to intercept the ILS (Instrument Landing System) approach onto runway 07. Canaries radar handed them over to the approach controller, who cleared them down to 3,000 feet on their present heading. Due to the loss of track miles with their heading, Harry informed the cabin crew early that they were nearing ten minutes to land and put the seat belts sign on. They were also above their descent profile and Simon increased their rate of descent with the help of the speed-brakes: the speed-brakes are like barn doors, called spoilers, on top of the wings. When the pilot flying moves the speed-brake lever rearwards these spoilers lift up, disturb the airflow over the wings, effectively reducing lift and increasing downforce, causing the jet to have an increase in its rate of descent. On the A320 there are 5 spoilers on each wing, but 1 and 5 are for ground operations, therefore only spoilers 2, 3 and 4 are used as speed-brakes in the air. If the spoilers were used on the ground to help with speed retardation they are referred to as ground-spoilers. Then all 5 on each wing will be deployed.

Simon kept the speed-brakes extended, even past 10,000 feet where there is a maximum speed restriction of 250 knots: the jet will naturally pitch up to reduce the speed, but this will have a negative effect on the rate of descent culminating with being even further above the descent profile, so maintaining speed-brake deployment will help with speed reduction while maintaining a relatively good rate of descent.

The jet was back on profile when they passed 6,000 feet and the speed-brakes were stowed. The A320 was kept at 250 knots until it reached 3,000 feet. The jet levelled off and Simon manually selected 250 knots. On the speed tape running down the left side of his PFD (Primary Flight Display), the speed target index, now being manually controlled via the FCU (Flight Control Unit), turned to cyan from magenta to inform both pilots that manually selected speed was now being used. Simon brought the speed back to 220 knots in preparation for extending the first stage of flaps. They were now number 2 for arrival, with a Boeing 737 ahead of them.

Simon requested Harry activate the approach phase through the FMGC: this can only be done on the performance page corresponding to the active phase of flight and now enables the jet to automatically manage speed reduction with the associated flap position. Pushing the speed knob reduced the speed to Green Dot Speed: the speed that corresponds to the best list-to-drag ratio in the clean configuration. Pushing the speed knob in all other phases of flight turns the speed target index to magenta: the speed is now automatically controlled by the FMGC in managed speed mode.

Simon requested flap one. Harry cross-checked the speed to make sure it was below the maximum speed for that flap position then selected flap one.

The radar controller gave them a heading of 115 degrees and cleared them for the ILS approach onto runway 07 before passing them over to the tower frequency: an ILS is a precision approach in that guidance is provided both laterally via a localizer beam and vertically via a glide-slope beam down to a Minimum Descent Height.

Simon turned the jet onto the heading and armed the approach, so the A320 would capture the localizer beam before capturing the glide-slope beam from below. Harry checked in on the tower frequency. They were told to continue the approach, as the B737 was on short final. He could see a jet waiting at the holding point; he mentally prepared himself for a late landing clearance.

Capture conditions were met and the A320 automatically captured the localizer. Simon as pilot flying confirmed this, Harry cross-checked it.

Simon requested flap 2 and Harry obliged.

Seconds later the glide-scope was captured and again this was confirmed and cross-checked.

The gear was lowered followed by the landing flap selection of flap 3: Tenerife South has a 3,200 meter runway, which is plenty long enough to land with a flap selection of flap 3 rather than flap full; the advantages of landing today with flap 3, with a wind blowing 15-20 knots, is that it rides through the turbulence better and there is less chance of a sudden gust pushing them close to the flap limiting speed for flap full.

Harry could see the B737 land deep, roll forward and stop.

Even before there was any call from Air Traffic, Harry knew all was not well. The B737 was still on the runway.

'Get ready to go-around,' Harry said, to allow his friend and colleague to mentally prepare.

'I think we've blown a tyre,' the pilot of the B737 said.

A split-second later Tenerife South tower ordered Harry and Simon to go-around.

Simon advanced the thrust levers into the TOGA (Take-off Go-around) gate. The autopilot had not been disengaged: it is recommended to keep the autopilot engaged until the landing traffic ahead of you has vacated the runway for this very reason. The jet pitched up to 15 degrees and went into go-around mode.

Simon called out: 'Go-around flaps.'

Harry moved the flap lever forward one position to flap 2 and called it out.

Simon read the annunciation off the FMA, to confirm the jet was indeed in go-around mode and tracking the published missed approach procedure in the FMGC.

'Positive rate,' Harry called out when the A320 was climbing away.

Simon called for the landing gear to be retracted and it was.

Both men monitored the situation. Harry was looking at the remaining fuel: they didn't have much over CMR and he would rather have that fuel in hand at the alternate.

Simon reduced the thrust on schedule at the thrust reduction height and the remaining flaps were brought in until the wings were clean, and the speed settled down at green-dot speed: the speed was 218 knots.

The controller gave them a heading of South and a climb to flight level 70, due to following the published missed approach procedure taking them back towards other arriving traffic that would now be going-around.

Harry asked the tower the obvious question, even though he already knew the answer, but it needed to be asked: 'How long will the 737 be on the runway?'

The tower could not give him a definitive answer and then asked what his intentions were.

Harry requested an immediate diversion to Gran Canaria.

The tower handed them over to the approach controller who gave them a heading of 120 degrees. For the first few minutes following their go-around, air traffic went into overdrive telling the jet immediately behind them to go-around and informing all the traffic in the final stages of their descent for the approach onto runway 07 that the runway was closed and what were their intentions. Most requested the diversion to Gran Canaria, others to Tenerife North: Las Palmas, for JaguAir, was the nominated alternate for Tenerife South, rather than the nearer Tenerife North because of its close proximity to Tenerife and its two runways running North-East to South-West providing a greater chance of landing safely.

Tenerife Approach passed them over to Gran Canaria Approach. Harry could see from TCAS (Traffic Collision Avoidance System): the system that enables aircraft to see and identify each other and therefore monitor each other's heading and height, that there was an aircraft in their ten o'clock descending through their level. It was far enough ahead not to be a worry.

Gran Canaria approach gave them a heading of East and a climb to flight level 90.

Simon turned the jet due East and continued the climb to flight level 90 before giving Harry control and re-checking the FMGC for an approach for runway 03 Left at Gran Canaria: the route to the alternate aerodrome, in case of a diversion, was entered on the way down to Tenerife, but it was always prudent to re-check.

Harry put the second radio on low volume and listened to the ATIS (Automated Terminal Information Service): the frequency for receiving the up to date weather, the active runway and available approaches for that aerodrome.

The runway in use was indeed 03 Left, and the weather was fine with the surface wind 360 degrees at 20 knots and veering between 330 degrees and 030 degrees.

The easterly heading would take them to the North of the island, behind the aircraft they had on TCAS and in front of any aircraft descending into Gran Canaria. In short, they were being slotted in for an expeditious arrival. The distance between Tenerife South and Gran Canaria is roughly 60 nautical miles as the crow flies, probably around 90 with an approach onto runway 03 Left, and at 218 knots would take around 25 minutes.

The Auto Flight System calculated green dot speed using the jet's weight based on the Zero Fuel Weight (weight of the jet minus fuel) entered into the FMGC during initialisation. The computed green dot speed can then be used in selected phases of flight to aid fuel consumption. Today, time was of the essence with them being fed into the pattern, so Harry sped up sufficiently to maintain good separation from the traffic behind and in front, but at the same time not to burn off too much fuel.

Harry monitored the traffic behind diverting from Tenerife South: most were diverting to Las Palmas. Simon finished re-checking of the FMGC. He gave control back to Simon along with the radios.

Now that the decision was made to divert to Gran Canaria, the cabin crew and passengers needed to be informed. Harry called back to the forward cabin and spoke to Ricky. Ricky would relay the information to the rest of the crew. A few minutes after that Harry made a PA to inform the passengers as to what was happening. He could hear the groans from inside the flight deck, but their hands were tied, this was something outside their control. Harry took control of the radios on his return. Simon briefed him for the ILS approach and selected the appropriate auto-brake level for the runway and landing conditions. Auto-brake Low was selected.

The split second later the approach controller turned them onto a heading of 160 degrees: from this heading they would be turned downwind before heading West and North-West and the approach onto runway 03 Left.

The number of diversions grew steadily. Harry was grateful that they had been the aircraft immediately behind the B737 and the first to divert.

They were turned downwind just as two aircraft inbound to Las Palmas from the U.K came on frequency.

It would only be a matter of minutes before they would be on the ground and parked on a remote stand: being a diversion they would not be allocated an air-bridge and probably wouldn't get the use of a ground power unit.

The jet ahead of them was on a four-mile final when they were turned due West and then North-West onto a heading of 350 degrees, cleared for the ILS for runway 03 Left and handed over to the tower frequency.

The advantages of Las Palmas were clear for them to see: the traffic ahead would land and if the worst should happen, and they had trouble on the runway, a quick sidestep to the right and they could land on 03 Right. The traffic landed and vacated. A jet waiting at the holding point was cleared to cross 03 Left for 03 Right. The tower advised them what was transpiring.

Harry was confident nothing was going to prevent them from landing.

The aircraft was slowed down, and the flaps extended on schedule. The landing gear was lowered as the glide-slope beam was captured. To guarantee a stable approach the landing flap was again flap 3, due to the length of the runway and weather conditions and was extended at around 1500 feet. The A320 was stable shortly after and landed without incident.

Simon vacated the runway using the high-speed turnoff. The tower handed them over to the ground controller to receive their taxi instructions and stand number.

The A320 vacated the runway on the high-speed exit Sierra Three (S3). Harry checked in. The ground controller instructed them that their stand was the remote stand Papa Twenty (P20), which was accessed by turning immediately left after the exit and following taxiway Romeo.

It took less than five minutes to taxi onto stand with the help of a 'follow me' truck.

21

Harry had his company mobile fired up the split second the engines were shut down and the Parking Checklist was complete.

If operations didn't already know, they soon would. He wasn't surprised to learn that their handling agent in Tenerife had been in touch. Operations brought Harry up to speed of developments in Tenerife: the Boeing 737 had damaged its undercarriage on landing and blown a couple of tyres during braking.

'Wonderful,' was all he could say.

Harry fired up his personal mobile phone and noticed a missed call and voicemail from an unknown number.

Operations promised to call him when they had an update and hung up.

Their handling agent in Las Palmas arrived in swift time with a set of steps for one door left. Harry opened the flight deck door to inform Ricky.

The ground handler was an attractive slim, twenty-something lady with dark hair, brown eyes and a beautiful smile. Simon was the first to speak when she arrived in the flight deck, even though she was looking at Harry.

Oh, yeah, thought Harry, giving his colleague a wink. Simon, never broke stride, paused or stuttered in any way. He was impressive in his application and clearly smitten.

'Captain,' the agent began, 'we have no spare ground power units.'

'We have a perfectly serviceable APU,' Harry said. He could see out of the corner of his eye that Simon had not taken his eyes off the young lady.

'We are waiting to hear from our operations department,' Simon interposed.

'We think Tenerife may be shut for a while,' the agent added. 'I will have to go and then come back when you are ready. Do you require fuel?'

'Yes, we do; when we talk to our Operations Department, we'll be able to give you an accurate fuel figure for the return to Tenerife, but if you need us to refuel now, we'll take seven tonnes,' Harry replied. It would allow them enough fuel to keep the Auxiliary power Unit (APU) running and to leave as soon as the runway became clear. Simon promised to give the dispatcher all the figures for their load-sheet as soon as he could.

Harry liaised with Ricky and kept him in the loop before making a PA to the passengers and doing the same with them.

Next on the agenda was this unknown number on his personal phone.

Harry left the flight deck and went and stood on top of the stairs by one door left. Passengers were moving around the cabin to stretch their legs and paid him no attention. He played the voicemail when he was finally alone. It was David requesting he call him urgently. Those people came back, he thought, and smiled; they were just what he needed right now to let off some steam: he was missing his other life even after such a short time, he was missing it more than he gave it credit and without another job to do he was getting withdrawal symptoms. The adrenaline rush hit him, and his hands began to tingle.

He listened intently to the message: those people had not come back, and the disappointment was threatening to ruin his day. This diversion was part and parcel of his normal job. Harry called David.

David answered after the first ring: 'Harry.'

'David, what can I do for you?' If David was not in trouble, then maybe one of his friends was.

'It's Willis,' David replied.

'What's happened?' Harry could tell from the way David mentioned his partner's name that this was going to supply him with all the adrenaline he needed. His hands began to tingle again.

'Raquette is making a move on him; Willis hasn't said anything to me, but I believe he wants to take over the business.'

'And Willis naturally said no to any outside involvement.'

'More than that: he told Raquette he'd have him removed instead.'

'Willis has played into his hands, David. He wants Willis to make the next move: it will justify everything he'll do. How much support does Willis have?'

'Enough, I think.'

'Raquette will set him up. I know I'm probably stating the obvious, and your partner already knows this and is making plans, but you need to be watchful too. He will come for you to get to him.'

'I'm fine and well out of his reach.'

'What do you want me to do?'

There was a pause, but Harry could hear David's breathing. He was searching for the right words. Harry took a deep breath and tried to calm himself. Ricky came to the top of the steps and made the 'T' sign with his fingers. Harry gave him the thumbs up.

'Take care of Raquette,' David finally said.

'That could be taken a number of ways: there is the obvious one, and there is the less obvious one.'

Again, David paused.

'That'll be the obvious one then?'

'Could you do it?' David finally added.

'Yeah, but you haven't asked me whether I want to or not.'

'Okay, I'm asking.'

'No!'

David became angry: 'Why not? He aims to kill you, too.'

'When that time comes, I'll deal with him.'

'You're weak!'

'No, I'm just not a murderer.'

'It's not murder, it's self-preservation.'

Ricky appeared on top of the steps and handed him his tea. He was respectful enough to leave Harry to his conversation.

'Then I'll deal with my self-preservation when the time comes. Does Willis know you've called me?'

It was evident he didn't.

'Get him to call me,' Harry said and hung up.

He needed a minute on the steps alone. Harry kept his back to the jet, so the passengers seated in the forward rows on the left-hand side of the aircraft could not see the anger and disappointment etched across his face.

He would call Willis tomorrow.

Simon came to the door. The company had been on the phone: Tenerife was now open. He had informed the ground handlers via their dedicated frequency and passed them all the figures for the load-sheet. The jet was now fuelled up to seven tonnes and the tanker driver came to the bottom of the steps to have the fuel receipt signed.

'Call them back to get the flight plan and load that, I'll do a walk-around and we'll get the hell out of here,' Harry said while descending the steps to the apron.

The exact second Harry signed the fuel receipt the agent appeared in a Peugeot 206 company car with two copies of the flight plan and three of the load-sheet. She was off up the steps in double-quick time; these diversions were extra work she could well do without and the sooner they were out of her hair the better. Harry was all for getting out of her hair in double-quick time.

The exterior check of the jet took less than fifteen minutes.

Once back in the flight-deck with Ricky up to speed on the current state of affairs, Harry made a PA to the passengers before finishing the technical log, signing the load-sheet, so the dispatcher could be on her way, running his take-off performance calculation, which was cross-checked with Simon's, and completing all the Before Start Checks.

Ricky appeared to see if it was okay to close and arm the doors. It was.

Thankfully, they had no departure slot and they were on their way in another fifteen minutes.

It was only a short hop back to Tenerife, but due to the volume of traffic making their way back it took an extra ten minutes more than planned before they successfully landed on runway 07. The whole episode had added an extra 90 minutes to their working day, but all were just grateful to be making preparations to return home.

The return sector was blissfully uneventful, and Harry loved every minute of it. Even when the job had those moments, he still loved what he did. He loved his other job just as much.

* * *

Harry called the casino first thing to talk to Willis. The man was out of his office. He would call every thirty minutes.

Three more attempts to make contact failed. Harry called the number that David used yesterday.

David failed to answer the first time and Harry knew something was up. David answered the second time. He'd been crying. Harry hated to ask, but it was part and parcel of the job.

'He's dead,' David said in a voice that gave away nothing.

'When?'

'Last night,' David's voice cracked just a little.

'How?'

'Not over the phone.'

'What's your address?'

David gave him an address in Manchester.

Harry was being presumptuous in thinking David still wanted his services: 'I'll be right over.'

His standby duty wouldn't start until 12 noon, but the chances of being called today were minimal.

The house was upmarket, detached, with five bedrooms and a detached double garage, but if you have the money you might as well spend it. Shame Willis wasn't in a position to enjoy his wealth. He found out for sure five minutes later.

David met him at the front door. Harry didn't need to knock. The door was open and there was David.

'I followed your progress from the Porsche.' David said, completely filling the doorway.

'I figured,' Harry replied, trying to resist the urge to steal a peek inside the house. He needed to be patient.

'Come in.' David turned, leaving Harry to close the front door behind him.

By the time he'd made sure the door was closed, David was almost out of sight in the kitchen.

The kitchen was of the modern design with an electric hob and state of the art appliances. He liked it. The worktops were grey stone, which got his vote, and the cupboards looked like they were made of oak. To the left of the kitchen the open plan design flowed naturally into a dining area. The floor was covered in Italian ceramic tiles. Harry knew they were Italian because he'd looked at similar tiles for his kitchen.

These tiles had one flaw: they were partly covered with the corpse of Willis.

There was not much blood. That was Harry's immediate reaction. He took a step towards the corpse, stopped and waited for David to speak. He didn't. It was okay to proceed.

Wills had hit the ground headfirst. Harry examined Willis' head: there was extensive damage to the area around the eye-sockets and nasal passage consistent with hitting the ground headfirst.

'Have you moved the body?' Harry asked.

'No!'

'He was dead or unconscious before he hit the floor.'

'You sure?'

'He hasn't made any attempt to protect himself by raising his hands. They are, as you see, by his side.'

'I never noticed that.'

Harry checked the back of Willis' head. There were no signs of head trauma.

'He wasn't attacked from behind,' Harry said, looking up at David. 'Was there any sign of a break-in?'

'No, and I would have noticed.'

Harry studied Willis' corpse again. How could someone get the jump on him? Harry considered David as the culprit and kept one eye on the man, but he was too upset to be the killer.

The right arm was the giveaway. Harry didn't know straight off what alerted him to the arm, but something didn't sit right: a private detective must follow his gut instinct. Harry put on a pair of rubber gloves and lifted the right arm carefully and respectfully. It wasn't the arm that raised doubt, but the sleeve of Willis' jacket. It was crumpled more in the elbow area than the left arm.

He pulled up the right sleeve. The tell-tale signs were there, visible for anyone to see: two small red pinpricks with bruises beginning to form around them.

'We're looking for three!' Harry stated, pointing to the bruising on Willis' arm.

'Three?'

'Willis was not into drugs in any way?'

David didn't answer.

'Two to hold him down, one to administer,' Harry added. 'And I'll hazard a guess and say fentanyl.'

'Fentanyl! He would never get into that!'

'Does he, did he, or do you, know anybody who does?

'No!'

'Well Raquette surely does.'

Again, David didn't answer.

'Can you get close to him?'

'Maybe,' David answered, not looking Harry in the eyes.

'What is it?'

'I can't stand being in the same room as him.'

Harry stood up.

'Do you want to get him or not?'

'No, I want you to get him!'

'Prove he did this, and I promise you I will.'

'Then I'll get in a room with him.'

Harry rubbed his chin. It was done for effect.

'What is it?' It was David's turn to ask the question.

'Make him admit to it. He'll check your phone to see if your trying to catch him out, so we need to get you wired.'

'I don't know anybody in that line of work.'

'Neither do I, but I know a man who might.'

'What about Willis?' David's voice began to crack.

'You'll need to call the police, there's no way round that one.'

For a third time David didn't answer.

'He overdosed, David. He may not have administered it, but he overdosed. That's the story and stick to it.'

David nodded.

'I'll be in touch.'

22

The house was how he remembered it and he approached the front door in exactly the same way: carrying a plastic bag containing two bottles of whiskey. He rang the bell twice. The familiar voice cussed all the way to the door. It swung open.

'Your finger stuck to my bell, or what?'

'Hello Patterson.'

'Travers! I might have known it would be you smacking the crap out of my fucking doorbell.'

'I hate to disappoint, you know that.'

Patterson caught sight of the plastic bag. Harry handed it to him.

'You remembered, again.'

Patterson took the bag and peered inside: 'Jameson's!'

'I thought it would make a change.'

'That's what I like about you Harry: you won't be second-guessed.'

Harry laughed.

'Come in, come in; don't stand there like an unwanted relative.'

Harry stepped inside the house, looked at the door where Patterson kept all his goodies and wondered if he had what he was looking for.

Patterson closed his door and strode purposefully towards his kitchen.

'How are the neighbours?' Harry asked.

'Unwanted....as always,' Patterson answered without looking back.

'They're keeping you on your toes then?'

'They're all bloody unwanted, just like my relatives,' Patterson said putting the bag down on the kitchen counter. 'All they want is for me to drop dead and get the house.'

Harry forgot that Patterson was an only child. His parents had died a few years ago.

'Leave it to charity.'

'Maybe,' Patterson added producing two glasses from a cupboard and he poured two large whiskies. 'You are staying, aren't you?'

Harry checked his watch: he had timed his arrival to coincide with his standby duty finishing. He now had three days off.

'If it's acceptable?'

'It most certainly is.'

Harry picked up the glass and downed the whiskey in one go: he hadn't had a drink in a while and was due a session, and a session with an old friend was most agreeable. His request could wait until tomorrow.

Harry and Patterson spent the night reminiscing about old times, the adventures each had, people they'd flown with, trying to remember where they were flying now and the current state of affairs within the airline and the industry as a whole. Both bottles disappeared along with a Chinese takeaway.

* * *

Harry woke first and made coffee. There was no sign of life from Patterson's room. Harry made a second coffee. Patterson finally appeared. He looked like shit.

'You look like shit!'

'Cheers,' Patterson said, staggering over to the kitchen sink.

'Coffee?'

'Please.' Patterson took some medication off the worktop and swallowed two pills without water.

Harry made him a coffee.

'Got any plans?' Patterson said, leaning over the kitchen sink and trying to decide whether to be sick or not.

'No, have you?'

'Not now.'

Harry was waiting for the ideal time to make his request: he didn't want his friend to think he was just using him to get what he wanted; Harry liked Patterson a lot, and his last visit only highlighted how much he missed him, and would, terribly, when he was gone, which by the look of him was not going to be long. But it was not his place to lecture his friend; if this was the way he wanted, intended, to live his life then so be it: for some pilots, life without flying becomes unbearable.

Patterson started to come around when the coffee began to take effect.

'You know a lot of people, Patterson,' Harry began. 'Do you know anybody who would have access to a hidden microphone and recording equipment? I need to record a conversation.'

'Why not use your phone?'

'Far too obvious,' Harry said, looking at Patterson with the most serious expression he could find.

Patterson pointed his right index finger at Harry: 'You haven't told me about the last time, yet!'

'Maybe later,' Harry replied keeping the serious expression.

'Come on Travers, spill the beans.' Patterson lowered the finger.

'My girlfriend died.'

There was an uncomfortable silence.

'Yeah, maybe later,' Patterson said breaking the silence. 'What do you want again?'

'I need to record a conversation.'

'I'll do it.'

'What?'

'I'll do it,' Patterson said again.

'No!'

'Yes!'

'Why?'

'I'm fucking bored, and you're clearly having a great time, apart from the girlfriend........if you know what I mean?'

'Yeah, I know what you mean. Can you do it?'

'Can I do it?' Patterson resumed pointing the finger. 'You bet I fucking can!'

'Then I take it you can get hold of all the gear we'll need?'

'Obviously,' Patterson said, pretending to be insulted, and again lowering the finger.

'When can you get it?'

'It's urgent, right?'

'Real urgent,' Harry said.

'Tomorrow, I can get it tomorrow.'

'Excellent.'

'Better get sober.' Patterson could see that Harry had finished his coffee and made them both a fresh one.

'Why?'

'Good point, Mister Travers, good point, but as I can't drive, you'll have to.'

'Like I am going to get behind the wheel of the Porsche in my state,' Harry stated, taking his wallet out of his back pocket.

'You want to walk?'

'You must have money to burn Patterson?'

Patterson handed Harry a fresh mug of coffee: 'I have an account with the local taxi firm.'

'Wow, money to burn.'

'There's a supermarket down the road, we can go there after breakfast and top up on essential provisions.'

* * *

The supermarket was busy. Harry didn't like busy supermarkets: it was difficult to keep tabs on all those people around him. Patterson stormed on ahead and pulled out a trolley from one of the trolley stations, once they'd vacated the taxi. Harry studied the car park; it was an impossible task trying to identify anybody of interest. He went inside.

Patterson, for one hell-bent of giving his liver a good workout, was filling the trolley with vegetables and fruit. A tall, well-built man, clearly a bit of a gym monster, brushed past his friend and knocked him into the bananas. Harry held station and studied the stranger: he was bald, around six-foot two inches, in jeans, a jumper and a black leather jacket. Patterson and the man exchanged words, but nothing else. The man strode off. Harry went after him.

'Fucking amateur,' Harry whispered to himself.

The stranger looked back at Patterson, as he exited the supermarket into the car park. Harry stayed three paces behind him to his left, but never looked straight at him.

The man approached a metallic blue Ford. There was a second man behind the steering wheel. The stranger went for the front passenger door. He didn't make it.

Harry closed the gap between them in seconds and smashed a right into the man's kidneys. It stunned him. A right sidekick to the kneecap of the man's left leg brought down his head. As he buckled down towards him, Harry grabbed the back of his head and drove his left elbow up into the man's nose. It broke instantly. The man crumpled to the floor. Harry took Patterson's wallet from the inside pocket of the black leather jacket.

'I see any of you two fuckers around here again......'

Harry left the words hanging in the air and returned to the superstore. He kept one eye on the Ford and its two occupants. That was his first mistake: he allowed these two miscreants to fully occupy his attention. If he had not, he'd have clocked the silver Skoda and its four occupants parked three rows further over to his left.

Patterson was in the bread aisle by the time Harry caught up with him.

'Where have you been?'

'Getting your wallet back!' Harry tossed it over to him.

'Mothefucker!'

'Oldest trick in the book,' Harry added while studying the healthy options filling Patterson's trolley.

'Some people have no moral code,' Patterson added, before carefully placing three thick sliced loaves in his trolley.

'Damn right,' Harry whispered.

Patterson was slick when it came to food shopping: he knew what he liked and didn't procrastinate when it came to filling the trolley with his favourites. Harry remarked that he always filled his with the bare essentials plus whatever took his fancy on the day. It probably explained why he threw a lot of food out when clearing out his cupboards.

Thirty minutes later the two men filled the boot of the taxi taking them back to Patterson's with six bags full of favourites and essentials.

The Skoda started its engine. Harry was still oblivious to the danger.

The taxi pulled away. Harry and Patterson chatted away in the back about microphones. Patterson made a call. A man answered and Patterson said he was just checking to see if he was in and would call him again in roughly twenty minutes.

Twenty minutes later Patterson and Harry placed the six bags on the kitchen counter. Patterson removed a bottle of the supermarket's own brand whiskey, cracked the seal and poured out two large glasses into tumblers conveniently positioned on the counter for that very purpose.

Harry took a sip of the whiskey and braced himself against the sharp taste of cheap whiskey. To his surprise it was most agreeable.

'Nice, isn't it?'

'Yeah, most agreeable,' Harry said taking a larger second sip.

'When you're on a budget, like yours truly, you got to shop around and re-educate the taste buds.'

Harry instantly felt guilty for not helping his friend sooner: 'You know if you need anything, just ask.'

'I know I can,' Patterson said smiling, 'which is why I don't, but it's nice to know I can.'

The shopping was soon dispatched to its respective storage space followed by another large measure of whiskey.

Patterson lived in the kitchen and conservatory when occupying the space downstairs and the two men retired to the conservatory and sat down in two large armchairs. They were new additions; Harry did not remember these from the time when he was picking locks. Patterson brought the whiskey with him and the house phone. He dialled out between large shots of whiskey.

Whoever this man was he was more than willing to lend Patterson the gear required and there was no mention of money. Harry deduced that this was a favour returned.

'We can collect it tomorrow,' Patterson said once he'd hung up. He was pleased with himself and it showed: 'He doesn't normally lend his gear out.'

'Unless of course it's you,' Harry said before finishing his whiskey.

Patterson topped his glass up.

'Aren't you worried?' Harry's concerned tone caught Patterson by surprise.

'No,' he replied. 'I'm fucked Harry: I can't fly, I can't do the one thing I've always wanted to do, I've had it taken away from me and it hurts, some days more than others. I've got to take medication to prevent migraine type headaches that otherwise blur my vision. I can't drive and if I've got to live this way then I'll live it on my terms.'

'Okay,' was all Harry could muster as a reply; he'd never heard Patterson talk so openly about anything, let alone his love of flying.

'That's put a downer on proceedings,' Patterson added, composing himself after his admission.

'I didn't know it was that bad. Certain individuals, and you can take an educated guess who they are, always seem to be complaining about something or other,' Harry said, slowly shaking his head.

'It's not until something, or someone has been taken away from you Harry, that you realise how much you needed it, or them.'

'Yeah,' Harry said, trying to suppress the pain.

'Sorry dude,' Patterson said with genuine remorse. 'You must have really loved her?'

'It was intense, but I loved every inch of her.'

'I'll always be here, dude.'

'Ditto.'

'Let's get drunk.'

Patterson's suggestion was the only way open to Harry to kill the pain, and his friend knew it.

Outside the Skoda parked opposite the house and waited. If this was a test to gauge the four occupants' skill in remaining inconspicuous then they failed miserably. All four men looked like real bruisers: the two occupying the rear seats had been boxers, which was obvious by the damage to their noses; the man in the front passenger seat was covered in tattoos, right up his neck and over the entire bottom half of his face. The tattoos stopped short of a scar that ran the length of his right cheek; and the driver, who could not take his eyes of Patterson's front door, had his hair shaved short, which was done for effect to show off the scar that ran over the rear left half of his head.

'How long does he want us to wait?' the boxer immediately behind the driver asked.

'He didn't say,' replied the driver.

The second boxer took a zipped-up pouch out of his jacket pocket: 'Let's get this over and done with.'

'One's a cripple, the other's a fucking amateur playing with the big boys,' the first boxer added.

The front seat passenger said nothing, but simply nodded in agreement.

The driver took a deep breath: he knew he could not hold back the other three for too much longer, so it was better if he initiated their exit from the Skoda: 'Let's go!'

The four men were out of the car and up the short pathway to Patterson's front door within seconds. All four adjusted their coats with a small shrug of the shoulders or flicking up the collar. If they were armed, then neither man made it obvious.

The driver rang the doorbell. Nothing happened for a few minutes. He rang the bell again.

From inside the house Harry was instantly on full alert: 'Expecting visitors?'

Patterson shook his head.

'Wait to see if they ring again,' Harry said slowly getting to his feet. He led the way down the hallway towards the front door.

'Harry?'

'What?'

'If it's trouble, you can come again.'

Harry laughed: 'Thanks.'

'What's your gut telling you?'

'Trouble,' Harry replied, stopping short of the door and entering Patterson's Aladdin's cave.

Patterson eased past him and navigated his way over some dust filled boxes to the window that looked out onto his front porch. He was careful not to disturb the curtains. Through a small gap he viewed his porch. It was now he realised he was still holding a glass half full of whiskey. He finished it and placed the glass on one of the boxes. Harry had a quarter glass left over. It was similarly dispatched, and the empty put next to his friend's.

'You can definitely come again, Harry,' Patterson whispered.

'How many?'

'Four of the meanest bruisers you ever did see.'

'Is there a back way out?'

'What?'

'When was the last time you had a tear up?'

Patterson pondered the question.

'I'll take that as you can't fucking remember,' Harry whispered.

'You never lose it,' Patterson boasted, taking up a boxing stance and throwing a few jabs.

This is going to go horribly wrong, thought Harry, and made his way back out into the hallway.

'You have first crack at them, Harry, and show us how's it's done these days.'

Harry had to laugh, but the laughter didn't last long when he heard the front door lock being picked.

'Bastards!' Patterson growled and ran back to the kitchen.

A split second later the front door burst open followed by the four bruisers, a second after that Patterson returned wielding a baseball bat.

Harry fell back against the weight of the four men pushing their way in. He hit the floor with the driver on top of him. Patterson stepped over him and smashed the baseball bat down on the shoulder of the front seat passenger. The two former boxers brought up the rear and the second one hit Patterson with a hard, straight right. Harry watched his friend fall back. He head-butted the driver from his prostrate position and drove a left into the man's ribs. He kicked him off and took a stamp on the chest from boxer number one. Harry managed to cushion the blow somewhat, but it still winded him. Patterson re-appeared with the bat screaming blue murder and delivered a devastating blow to the boxer one's head rendering him unconscious. The former boxer collapsed back out of the open door and onto the narrow pathway.

Harry tried to get to his feet but was pulled back by the driver. A sharp left elbow to the man's temple stunned him sufficiently to allow Harry to get free. The second boxer attacked Patterson. His friend was tiring. Harry got to his feet and took a right -hander from the front seat passenger. He ignored the hit and threw the man over his shoulder when he tried it a second time. Once the man was on the floor, and he was in the classic "ground and pound" position, Harry retaliated with such ferocity that it took all his self-control to back off and not kill the guy.

Harry looked up towards the kitchen and saw Patterson taking a beating. He was off after the man and up the hallway in an instant. He got all of two paces before being rugby tackled by the driver. Harry hit the floor hard, but the driver needed to release his grip to close the gap for the kill. Harry lifted his right leg and kicked him hard in the face. The man let out a cry. Harry was on his feet quickly before the driver could re-group and kicked him hard in the ribs. He broke at least three by his reckoning.

From over his shoulder he could hear the blows Patterson was taking and spun round to charge the former boxer.

The fight had moved to the conservatory and Harry arrived just in time to witness Patterson, with blood streaming down his face and on the wrong side of a kicking, fall to one knee, pick-up one of the empty Whiskey bottles and smash it over the boxer's head. The former boxer was stopped in his tracks. Patterson rose to his full height and knocked him clean out with a vicious left hook.

Patterson turned to face Harry and smiled a bloody smile: 'That was fun!'

'Where's the bat?'

'Dropped it,' Patterson replied between spitting blood.

'You okay, 'cos you look like shit!'

'Never felt better.'

'We gonna have fun cleaning this shit up; your nosey neighbours will have a field day.'

'Fuck 'em!'

Patterson was unsteady on his feet but remained upright.

Harry heard noises coming from the hallway, but the noises were becoming distant.

'Here, give me a hand,' he said to Patterson. And the two of them lifted the former boxer and deposited him outside the front door.

The Skoda was still parked over the road, but only two had boarded. The driver leaned against the driver's side front wing and rubbed his side. Harry looked him in the eye and then shut the door.

'What will you tell the police?' Harry asked when they had made the kitchen.

'I fell down the stairs. Everything else will be flatly denied.'

Harry could sense the first signs of anger in his voice.

'You want me to leave?'

'Hell no!'

Patterson produced a half-empty bottle of whiskey and poured two extra-large measures into two clean glasses.

'It's time for the poor man's painkiller.' And he took a large gulp of whiskey.

Harry picked up his and took a sip: he could do without drinking further, but his friend was hurting, and he'd brought this down on him. He finished his glass and recharged both his and Patterson's.

'I get the impression you need to make a call,' Patterson remarked between mouthfuls of whiskey.

'Can I borrow your phone?'

'Help yourself.'

Harry heard a car pull away at high revs. He'd save them the bother of reporting back.

Harry dialled the number for the casino.

23

Harry was forced to wait nearly a minute, but finally he was put through to the man.

'What do you want?' Raquette sneered.

'I'm coming for you,' Harry said calmly.

'And that's supposed to what? Scare me.'

'I don't care, I know you removed Willis. And that's all the information I need.'

'I did you a favour.'

Harry hung up: there was nothing more left to say.

* * *

He left it three days, to see if Raquette would come to him, but all had been quiet. He was disappointed. The three days had though given him ample time to collect another car from List. He never asked why. Next it was a quick visit to see the couple and acquire three syringes, in case one should break, and enough fentanyl to overdose an elephant.

His new roster contained changes: his next block of standby duties following another flight to Tenerife preceded his six-monthly simulator detail, but for now there were four days off.

* * *

It was déjà vu for Harry: he was outside the casino again. List's car was a dark blue Ford Focus. His beloved Porsche would stand out, it was one of the reasons why he bought it, but that would work against him here.

People came and went. He recognised none of them. Should he go in and force their hand? That surely had to be his last resort and any element of surprise needed to be protected. The whole idea of the threat was to force Raquette's hand, so what was the purpose of storming into the casino, Raquette's back yard, and get himself cornered.

Harry got out of the Ford and went for a walk. If there was a tail on him that tail required removing. Sheila's beautiful face appeared to him fuelling the hatred building inside for the man. All was clear. A slow walk back towards the casino proved uneventful. He knew tonight was going to prove fruitless. He checked his watch: it read 01:45. Even though the time of day was early he was not tired. From experience, and knowing how his own constitution behaved under pressure, it would hit him around 8am, not the low of 4am, which affects most people: years of charter flying, simulator details in the middle of the night and sleeping odd hours had accustomed him to working under extreme pressure at all hours of the day. It concentrates the mind landing the jet in tricky weather conditions after a deep night flight. Harry was used to being alert at 01:45 in the morning. He walked back to the car and settled down for a long wait. 06:30 was the time Harry had chosen to head home: he would reach home before 08:00 and guarantee still being alert. In the glove box were notes from previous simulators and study material for the next one. Wasted time brings us on the greatest loss of all, he thought, and began his revision. He thought of Sheila and the hate returned. Best to study and keep the mind focused and he pulled a thermos flask of coffee from a bag in the passenger foot-well. Along with the bag were three rounds of sandwiches. Not good for the diet to be eating at this time of day, but it was only a small price to pay.

The mobile phone on the passenger seat began to vibrate and sounded the alarm. It was 06:30. Funny how time flies when you are having fun. The coffee and sandwiches were all gone and nobody of any interest had arrived or left. At least he'd managed to get some quality uninterrupted study time in.

Harry fired up the Ford and headed home at a sensible pace before the rush hour traffic got really bad.

The Ford was parked round the far side of Baslow Drive and not outside the house. One major schoolboy error he was not going to succumb to.

Harry was to be disappointed and frustrated for the next two nights outside the casino. He did though receive a letter informing him of his Uncle's court date in December; the court case had slipped his mind with everything else going on. Then his luck changed. A familiar face vacated the casino: it was the driver from Patterson's. Harry fully appreciated the similarities with before.

He slipped down further in the seat until he could just about see over the dashboard. Raquette exited the casino shortly after. He looked nervous, checking first left then right and then left again. Harry looked at his watch; if he used the mobile phone it would illuminate him and give away his position. The time was 02:47. The two men boarded a Silver Mercedes Benz. Harry made a note of the registration. He was about to pull away when David appeared and boarded a taxi.

'Well, well, well,' Harry said, firing up the Ford. There was no need to follow him.

David must know that he would be tailing Raquette, Harry thought, as he drove to the man's house. Why make it so obvious? The answer was even more obvious.

Harry got there first and parked out of sight. David arrived exactly three minutes later, paid the taxi driver and entered his house.

Harry sat there shaking his head: 'Was I that stupid? I have been that stupid?'

Harry filled one syringe with fentanyl and put it in his left jacket pocket. The remaining two and the bottle went in his right for backup.

He was out of the car and outside David's front door in seconds. There were no CCTV cameras on this road, but Harry was wearing a dark, loose jacket with baggy pockets, so no one could see what he was carrying, dark trainers, jeans, leather gloves and a woolly hat. He rang the bell. The curtains of a room Harry took to be an upstairs bedroom moved. David would answer, he would feel obliged to, but not before he'd warned Raquette that he was here. Time was of the essence for Harry. Less than a minute later Harry was standing in David's hallway following him, inevitably into the kitchen. Harry fingered the syringes in his jacket pockets.

'Did you find him?' David asked while putting the kettle on: 'Tea or coffee?'

He was calm and assured and behaving like someone who had a conscience as clear as a coral sea.

'Coffee, please, white no sugar,' Harry said, leaning with his back to an oak coloured kitchen worktop that ran the full length of the kitchen. The kitchen was in the old-fashioned cottage style. Not to his taste, but it still looked expensive.

'I found him.'

'What did he have to say?'

'I'm saving that conversation for later.'

David paused while making the coffee, it was only a slight pause, but it was there, that fatal delay in executing a simple motor programme like making coffee, an act most people have done a thousand times, but here it signalled worry, transmitted guilt. David finished making the coffee and handed him his drink.

'Not having one?'

'Caffeine keeps me awake.'

Harry took a sip. 'What did the police have to say?'

There was that pause again. 'Nothing much; like you said they're treating it as a simple overdose.'

Like fuck they are, he thought, a fentanyl overdose being treated as a simple overdose. The police will want to know how he came by it and he'd not seen one patrol car, or anybody remotely looking like a plain clothes policeman outside the casino the entire time he was there, so that was another lie.

'Why did you do it?'

Another pause.

'Do what?'

'Kill Willis!'

'I...I didn't!'

'Nobody could have got that close, not even Raquette or any of his men. I didn't see it, even though it was staring me in the face: the angle the needle would have gone in; no signs of a struggle; the only one who he trusted enough to get that close to him was you.'

David leaned back against the kitchen worktop, mirroring Harry's posture. Harry could see the man's left hand beginning to move. Behind him in a wooden block was a collection of knives.

'Why did you do it?'

David didn't answer.

'What did he offer you? Nero's?'

There was a slight flicker in David's eyes.

'The casino,' Harry said shaking his head. 'I can see how that would be tempting.'

'Willis was going to dump me for a younger model. Raquette offered me half the casino if I removed him. It was an easy decision, but good luck trying to prove it.'

'Good job for you I'm not taping this conversation.'

'I'll pay you to remove Raquette.'

'And give you the casino.'

'You like to be the righteous one, the man fighting for the downtrodden like some guardian angel righting the wrongs of the world!'

'And?'

'Raquette likes his little pleasures, if you get my drift, usually aged between 5 and 8, and of the male variety!'

'And you can prove it!'

'I can, but you can also if you really wanted to.'

David's left hand had not stopped moving and now it was resting on top of the kitchen counter.

'That still leaves you!'

The word "you" was the trigger, the catalyst for the violence to erupt, as Harry knew it would: David grabbed the largest knife without a backward glance. He'd done that before. Harry threw the still hot coffee straight into his face. David let out a scream and held his hands to his face, the blade of the knife now facing the ceiling.

As swiftly as he could Harry dropped the mug and pulled the syringe and closed the gap between the two of them, but David saw him coming and slashed at him with the knife. Harry kicked him in the chest with his left foot, sending him crashing against the wall separating the kitchen from a utility room. David slashed wildly again.

'I'll fucking kill you for that!' he screamed.

David threw out a kick towards the hand carrying the syringe, but it was a poor effort from someone not practiced in those arts. Harry aimed a left kick hard and low on his standing leg: David couldn't kick and slash at the same time. David's leg buckled and he lost his balance. Harry followed it up with a straight right to his jaw. David hit the floor hard. Harry kicked the knife out of his hand and was on top of David in an instant, pinning him to the floor. Harry stuck the needle into the right arm, emptied it and then waited.

This was 100% pure fentanyl, and it's lethal. Harry reckoned the man was dead even before the syringe was empty. He was out of the house in under a minute after washing the coffee mug. Harry waited half-an-hour to see if Raquette would dare show his face. He didn't. Nobody did.

Harry should have felt some kind of satisfaction, but it just wasn't there: he had been set up and would have walked right into their trap like a patsy. It infuriated him to think they thought he was that easy to remove. Everyone has their weakness and Raquette saw his and exploited it.

He re-entered the house and stood over the prostrate David, his eyes wide open, staring coldly into space. Harry needed to stay focused and suppress any emotion long enough to eradicate this last thorn and thanks to David he now had a reason.

THE END

Printed in Great Britain
by Amazon

72141935R00210